# M-Trait

## By

## Brandon Franklin Hurst

*Moose Hill Books*, Inc.
Anchorage, Alaska

Copyright ©2006 Brandon Franklin Hurst
All Rights Reserved

M-Trait. Copyright © 2006 by Brandon Franklin Hurst. All rights reserved.

Published by Moose Hill Books, Inc.

No part of this book may be reproduced, stored in a retrieval system, or transmitted by any means, electronic, mechanical, photocopying, recording, or otherwise whatsoever without the written permission of Moose Hill Books, Inc., except in the case of brief quotations embodied in critical articles and reviews. For more information, please address the publisher at Moose Hill Books, Inc. PO Box 22271, Anchorage, AK 99522 or write to: publisher@moosehillbooks.com.

This book is a work of fiction. Names, characters, places, and incidents are products of the author's imagination or are used fictitiously. Any resemblance of actual events or locales or persons, living or dead, is entirely coincidental.

**Printed and Manufactured in the United States of America.**

This edition is printed on acid-free paper that meets the ANSI/NISO Z39.48 Standard.

| | |
|---|---|
| Editor: | R. P. Davis |
| Logic Editor: | Peter Masson |
| Copy Editor: | Marthy Johnson |
| Proofreader: | Jean Ayers |
| Cover Design: | R. P. Davis |
| Author's Photo: | David Rose |
| Cover Photo: | ©2006 Getty Images |

A special thanks to the members of the Anchorage focus group, whose critical feedback was instrumental in making *M-Trait* the best story possible.

Library of Congress Control Number: 2006934568

ISBN-13:     978-0-9728627-1-4
ISBN-10:     0-9728627-1-4

First Trade Paperback Edition: November 2006

Moose Hill Books, Inc. is always seeking great works of fiction from new and unpublished authors. If you have written such a work or need help building your work into something great, visit www.moosehillbooks.com for information about submitting your manuscript.

Forever thanks to my beloved Faye...

# Acknowledgements

A number of people have helped bring *The M-Trait* to print. Alexia Casale first suggested turning my short story into a book, and her insights have been welcome from the beginning. Ron Davis of Moose Hill Books then offered just the right mixture of warm encouragement and brutal criticism to make the most of the editing process. The focus group in Alaska, who gave such helpful feedback, also deserves a mention. Jerry Katzman provided some useful thoughts when it came to signing a contract. Expert biologists Paul Mazumdar and Jessica Prett corrected many of my mistakes about DNA sequencing; any remaining errors are all mine. Last but not least, special thanks go to my wife Jennie, who had to wait so long before I let her read a draft.

*To the other Brandons...*

# M-Trait

# Prologue

Another midnight passed, but Dr. Edward Sherman didn't notice. The computer scrolled out letter after letter in front of him, endless combinations of the four DNA characters: G, C, A, T. Though he had not slept for almost three days, all thought of rest was abandoned until he obtained his final result.

The DNA sequencing analysis ran on and on, GCGTACGTTGAGCAT..., filling screen after screen with letters that were meaningless to almost every other human on the planet. Transfixed, he sat motionless for hours, waiting for the answer that had taken him years to detect.

The software program was inexorable and uncaring of the implications it displayed. Each new gene combination released his burden, and the cumulative years of torment melted away. GCGTTACAAGT...despair, frustration, loneliness—they all slowly evaporated from his being.

Finally the letters stopped coming. The cursor silently blinked as if seeking praise for the answer it provided. Edward quickly scanned the results—*I was right!*

Unwilling to take his eyes off the wondrous gene trait on the screen, Edward let his head rest against the back of the chair, his light brown hair lying unkempt against its polished hide. Even in the simplified, encoded format, the patterned letters somehow looked beautiful to him. What would he call this new trait? There would be plenty of time to decide.

Outside, the rain began to fall, drumming the windows of his London office. Edward barely registered the sound, caring only for what he saw in front of him. It was early in the morning, Sunday—the last day of his old life, a life he had lived so long that it was hard to imagine anything different. On Monday, he would be back at the

University, teaching his students and going through the motions with his contracted research at the lab. But it would be mere lip-service, a show for the rest of the world's benefit, as he prepared for the most significant work of his life.

Sometime in the hours that followed, a growing desire to sleep stole over Dr. Edward Sherman, gradually replacing the sense of exhilaration. Truly relaxed for the first time in years, the thought came to him as he drifted into a long, peaceful sleep. *Life could be new again—even for me.*

# 1

The only risky part of breaking into the house was gaining entrance to the back garden. The stone wall was old but well built, almost ten feet high, with a sturdy metal door that opened to the rear alley. The door's double lock could be picked, but it would take time, and the danger of being seen by others would be too high. Though the aging mortar afforded only a little purchase for his fingertips, he negotiated the wall in seconds, nimbly moving up and over the stone cap with the ease of an acrobat. Once inside the perimeter of the property, he was effectively shielded from the neighbors' eyes.

The intruder sat with his back to the locked garden door, knees drawn up against his chest, appraising his new environment. He waited silently in the shade, the cool fresh breeze in his nostrils bringing a scent of damp soil, moss, and leaves. The garden was well cared for, if not immaculate, the lawn recently mown and the flowerbeds carefully tended. The neat little summerhouse occupied one corner near where he had hidden, and a larger greenhouse stood in another corner, tomato plants and sweet peas in evidence inside. On the patio near the back door, a prim-looking tabby cat sat sunning herself, eyeing his trespassing with skepticism. After a full ten minute wait, with no signs of being noticed—footsteps, voices, or sirens—he rose to his feet and moved silently across the yard towards the back door.

Dr. Edward Sherman's house was much like the others in this upscale London suburb: gray stone, comfortable, well kept and easily worth half a million pounds or more. He had watched the house for two weeks before he made his move, sitting low in his car a little way up the street. On Wednesday mornings a cleaner stopped by for a couple of hours. On two other occasions, a younger woman had come back in the evening with Dr. Sherman. She had not stayed the night, and it seemed clear from the silhouettes he observed that there was no romance, only friendship there. Perhaps a relative? It would no doubt become apparent in time.

Dr. Sherman was otherwise a very private person, and did not deign to share his space. The intruder was confident that he would not run into anyone else inside. If he did, he resolved to try talking his way out of any immediate difficulties by posing as a visiting friend. If it came to it, he knew how to take care of himself, and always had the reassurance of the blade concealed along the back of his waistband. Grey-blue hardened steel; he had sharpened it to a vicious edge.

Today was Tuesday; the cleaner had not been for six days and the house would be at its least clean. He doubted that it was ever even remotely close to dirty inside, but the difference might be enough to cover his tracks—every little bit helped.

The next obstacle was the heavy wrought-iron gate that shielded the rear door from a meter or so out. The gate seemed to be Sherman's own addition—none of the neighbors' houses had one. Finished in smooth black gloss paint, its bars were wide enough to admit the sleek frame of the cat, but not much more. The chunky brass lock set into the gate was solid, shiny, and almost as secure as the sturdy five-pin door locks he had spent time practicing on back in his flat. With a last glance around in case of unwanted company, he knelt on the swept patio, pulled on a pair of latex gloves, and under the watchful eyes of the tabby, began to pick the lock. A thin flathead screwdriver, bent ninety degrees at the very end, served as a torsion wrench to turn the cylinder of the lock. A large paper clip, opened out so that it resembled a flattened, lower case *"e"* made an effective pick, though a little more flexible than was ideal. It had been hammered down and filed with a tooth at the end. As a result, his homemade tool was just as effective as a "professional" set sold for around fifty pounds over the Internet.

The pins on the tumbler lock would need to be picked sequentially, and in the right order. Theoretically, that gave 120 combinations for a five-pin lock, not counting the extra variable of the height to which the pins must be raised. In practice, the back pin was almost always the first to go, and it was usually possible to work straight from back to front. This lock was new, clean, and moved easily, and it took only ninety seconds for him to finish, the cylinder rotating a tantalizing fraction clockwise as every pin was raised to the right height. The resistance abruptly eased as the sequence was completed and the mechanism sprung open. The gate opened smoothly and noiselessly as he walked through and considered the next problem.

The house was dark inside, and his still youthful face reflected off the glass of the patio-style back door. He saw his short, blond hair, darker at the roots, spiked up with a bit of mousse, his high cheekbones accenting eyes as black as coal, limpid pools of molten onyx sucking in the morning light. The blond hair was new for him—his choice for this project. While rubbing his head in amusement, he thought of his new name—Tom. He hadn't chosen it, but it was simple and easy for people to use, unlike the hideous ethnic name given to him at birth.

Tom squatted in the narrow alcove behind the gate. Peering into the lock, so close that his nose almost touched it, he smelled its sharp metallic tang. The device was a cylinder lock, which worked on a principle different from that of a pin tumbler, and was a little trickier to pick for the reputable locksmith and housebreaker alike. Often the solution was simply to file a key on the spot from a blank. Inked, placed in the lock, and twisted, the pattern of the lock appeared on the template and had only to be cut away to make a working replica. It took a quarter of an hour to file the aluminum blank to the right shape, sitting in the cool of the alcove and catching the dust-fine filings in a sheet of newspaper he had brought expressly for the purpose. Finally, after trying the filed key a few times and making final adjustments, the mechanism gave way with a satisfying click.

Would an alarm sound? Would there be a bolt or a chain on the inside, too? If either happened, he would have to leave and come back another day with a better plan.

Tom turned the handle and pushed. The door opened easily—no alarm sounded and no chain impeded him further. *I'm in.*

# 2

Dr. Emily Preston stood in the lab, hands on her hips, waiting impatiently for Dr. Sherman to notice her. Sherman sat at his desk in his office, engrossed with something displayed on the 21-inch flat-screen monitor in front of him. The office adjoined the larger lab, and Emily could see inside through the open door and the two large windows on either side.

When he finally looked up, she again motioned at Edward through the window—his next appointment was ready. Emily bent back into a stretch, while simultaneously pushing a strand of her long blond hair behind her ear. She was five months pregnant, and beginning to feel the strain in her lower spine.

On the raised hospital-style couch behind her lay a student named Khan who had volunteered to donate a few centiliters of blood to further Dr. Sherman's research. Turning to him, she applied the blood pressure cuff to his arm, her pale skin in sharp contrast to the student's dark forearm. She handled all the patients for this part of the procedure—Edward wasn't much good at it. He sometimes missed the target and she just felt that the patient appreciated her gentler touch with the use of a syringe. Khan winced anyway as the needle found the vein in the crook of his elbow, though it seemed more of an emotional reaction than one of actual pain.

From his application, Emily had read that Khan's great-grandfather recently died after celebrated his 106th birthday. His great-great-aunt had already outlived that by two years. Longevity ran in his family. That was why Khan himself was here—to see if his family's genetics had indeed rubbed off on him.

Longevity ran in Emily's family too; she appeared closer to her early twenties than the thirtieth birthday she would reach later in the year. She finished filling a series of labeled vacuum tubes, dressed the puncture with absorbent lint and a strip of surgical tape, and smiled with the knowledge of another job well done. She was good at what she did.

"Just press here and hold." She smiled to Khan. "The doctor will be with you in a second."

Dr. Sherman, who had tutored Khan during his preclinical medical exams the previous year, came in and addressed his former student as Emily turned to one of the nearby lab worktables to catalogue and process the blood sample. With her back to the conversation, she could unobtrusively listen in. She often enjoyed Edward's banter with his students, though it could get a little repetitive, too.

"Hello, Khan—thanks for coming in. Can I update you on our little lab research project?"

The captive student nodded while sipping some orange juice.

Emily stole a quick glance as Dr. Sherman sat in a rolling chair behind her to converse with his subject. His face was healthy, tanned, and creased with innumerable fine lines that showed when he smiled. People generally guessed his age to be around forty-five at first glance, and were often surprised to learn that he had already taught a couple of decades of students at the university. Physically too, he was in great shape. Strong, deft and quick, rumor had it that the doctor could still play a mean game of squash—despite the angina condition he kept under careful control with medication. Emily had never known him to have a bad angina attack, though she knew exactly where he kept the pills in case of emergency. Emily wondered whether Khan would look that good in a few decades.

"How old are you now, Khan?"

Emily knew Edward had filled in the database entry for the student only minutes before—she realized he was gearing up for one of his standard discourses.

"Twenty-two," the student answered. There was a short pause, during which Sherman conspicuously failed to volunteer his own age.

"I'm a little older than that," he finally offered, with a smile. From the safety of her vantage point, Emily smiled too, anticipating what was coming next.

Khan nodded, thinking he knew roughly where this was going. He was wrong.

"What do you think will kill you, Khan?" Dr. Sherman asked.

Startled a bit, Khan gave a rather standard answer. "Old age, hopefully."

The doctor tilted his head and shrugged as he briefly considered the possibility. "Unlikely," he concluded, "Old age doesn't get much of a chance to kill people."

Possibly Sherman's many years working with genetic faults and diseases had led him to personify the phenomena he knew so well. To Emily, it was if he gave a personality and character trait to the mischievous "Old Age," a goblin or imp that ran around in the shadows, stalking us, but never getting the chance to take our lives.

She listened as Sherman explained further.

"Old age has an awful lot of competition. If a fatal accident or a contagious illness doesn't get you, chances are heart disease or cancer will. If not, there are still a thousand and one other contenders to do the job first."

Dr. Sherman paused to regard his volunteer with his pale blue, sparkling eyes. Eyes could say a lot about a person, and Sherman's said he was an exceptionally intelligent man, though that was common knowledge among the staff.

"One of the things we do here is to test for genetic predispositions towards certain disorders," he continued. "A lot of them have a tendency to run in the family, although you wouldn't necessarily know it. Sometimes it's obvious—every male for the last four generations of the family dropping dead of heart disease in his fifties, for example. Others aren't so easy to spot. They skip generations, hiding on the X chromosome so they're carried on the mother's side, finally striking a male child in a later generation. Some lie dormant, waiting for an unknown trigger to set them off—and there's a lot we're still not sure about."

"But every once in a while, someone with no genetic predispositions, or only a few insignificant ones, is born. Perhaps it's one in a hundred thousand, maybe more, maybe less. If you beat the odds and reach old age, you might live to celebrate your hundred and tenth, possibly even hundred and twentieth birthday. That's the highest recorded age, even with all the advances in medical science we've had over the last century or so. Our very own Dr. Preston should be such a person—her DNA slate is very clean. Yet even so, one day we will lose her, too."

Emily rolled her eyes as she pulled up a stool to take the weight off her feet. She was used to Edward's odd sense of humor; it was one of the things that had first attracted her to him—though she still cringed at some of his odd scientific ideas. Even after working together for a few years, she couldn't understand where he came up with some of his theories.

Dr. Sherman paused, apparently lost in thought. Khan felt that maybe something was being asked of him at this point, so he volunteered, "So, if you can screen for those diseases and eradicate them..."

Sherman shook his head, breaking in on his former student's poor conclusion. "I'm afraid it doesn't work like that. Even if you don't die of something like cancer, you still age. Your body's cells try to renew themselves on a regular basis, but the process becomes less and less efficient. More and more mistakes occur in the new cells, and the body gradually degenerates until it's unable to support itself anymore."

Dr. Sherman fixed his eyes on Khan. "Old age, my friend, is merely the slowest possible rate at which one can expire. Your body won't live forever because it was specifically designed *not* to. Think about it this way—as an organism, you've been specifically programmed to die."

Khan blinked.

# 3

Tom received the phone call only a month ago, and had never thought that in such a short time he could be standing in this house, breathing Dr. Sherman's air and sharing his personal world. He was thrilled with the privilege of searching him out for his employer. A flat in the suburbs of London would serve as a base while he found out all there was to know about the good doctor. A passport and new papers had been arranged for him before he even arrived. Now it was time to seek this man's secrets.

He first noticed a set of spare keys hanging on a hook just inside the back door. They would be copied before the doctor returned that night and the key he had filed himself would afford him easy access to Sherman's house whenever it suited him. *This was too easy*, he thought.

The house, as he had fully expected, was clean and as well kept as the garden. It was lived in, but orderly. Tom made sure that he noted the position of everything before he touched it, did not leave any doors open that had been closed—disturbed nothing that would make his subject suspicious. He checked that his shoes were clean and free from mud, and kept the latex gloves on as he stole from one room to the next. The very first thing he did was put the chain on the front door to slow down any unexpected visitors. The chain was added to his mental checklist—he must remember to take it off before leaving.

The house was a little on the large side for a single man, with separate living and dining rooms, a downstairs bathroom, and a big kitchen. He spent a few minutes looking around the kitchen to get a better idea of the person he was dealing with. Kitchens said a lot about a person, perhaps more than any other room—what they ate, how they looked after themselves, how clean and organized they were, and what they valued. Often it was the most lived-in room of the house.

Dr. Edward Sherman's kitchen was immaculately clean, but did not have a surgical or sterile feel to it. There was nothing out of place, nothing to suggest a regular intrusion by someone else into this comfortable order. The impression was that this space was very important to Sherman, and that he did not share it willingly very often. He had two coffee machines, which Tom regarded carefully. The first was a filter machine, with a mesh rather than paper filter, and a hotplate for the jug. The second was an espresso maker, an Italian-made manual pump-handle model that must have cost several hundred pounds. Clearly, this was a man of wealth and taste. Tom ran the very tips of his fingers over it, the smooth chrome surface inviting him to deeper acquaintance through the latex gloves … perhaps another day.

A glance inside the refrigerator revealed shelves of fresh juice, semi-skimmed milk, vegetables, free-range eggs, and organic chicken cuts. There wasn't anything exciting until he noticed a vial on the door—it looked like a spare, unopened prescription. The contents of the pill bottle read "Nitro-Z." Tom filed this information away for later study.

Upstairs were three bedrooms, one of which had been converted into a study, and another bathroom. A number of quality reproduction paintings hung on the walls: Monet, Turner, and, coming down the stairs, Dali's Christ of Saint John on the Cross, Jesus' head hanging and his feet pointing down to Golgotha, far below. There were originals too, expressive pieces in bright acrylics, and several melancholy dark seascapes, none of them by anyone Tom had heard of before. On the landing, the only pieces to be displayed were very old Orthodox religious icons; the Virgin Mary holding the baby Jesus, three saints, and a crucifix hung in their small, ornate frames on the walls. Tom could not guess how much money was represented by the pictures he saw in this house. It did not surprise him when he later learned that Dr. Sherman had several other properties, both in England and abroad. Money was not an issue for Dr. Sherman.

Tom spent most of an hour in the study, looking but touching little for now, merely standing motionless and absorbing the atmosphere of the room where the doctor clearly spent a significant part of his time. He closed his eyes and inhaled—he was an unbidden stranger in a private world. It smelt faintly of polish and leather. At first he thought the smell came from the swivel chair by the desk, but on inspection its material turned out to be man-made. Three shelves of books set on the wall at eye height provided the answer: the doctor's collection of leather-bound antiquarian volumes. They were primarily religious and historical texts and treatises, written in a variety of languages and in remarkably good condition for their age. There were vellum Bibles in English and Spanish, an early copy of *Paradise Lost*, and a couple of unbelievably rare Latin incunabula for which he must have paid an enormous amount. That one shelf alone represented an absolute fortune, and Tom wondered whether the doctor prized them for their cost, their content, or their age.

The locked filing cabinet in the corner he would address another day—he was in no hurry. The computer, an impressively powerful and expensive PC, its fan gently whirring and the shifting colored images of the screensaver flowing smoothly across the broad face of its 21-inch monitor, could also wait. To the left of the computer was a framed photograph of a pretty, blond woman probably in her mid to late twenties. He stared at it, wondering what part she played in Edward Sherman's life.

It was late in the afternoon by the time Tom returned to replace the key he had copied, still a few hours before Sherman would return, even on his earliest expected arrival. He carefully retraced his steps through the garden and house, checking one last time for anything that would draw attention to his entry. Back in the study, he happened to gaze at the photograph again. It was now lit only by the computer screen, the shapes and colors shifting in reflection in the glass. Focusing on the coppery eyes of the woman, he wondered how much she knew about her friend, Dr. Sherman, and more importantly, what she meant to him.

He let himself out, leaving the spare keys swinging on their hook by the back door and locking both door and gate behind him. The copies were safe in his pocket, allowing him access to the house whenever he wanted. It was now dusk and no one saw him slip out of the garden in the surreal half-light that accompanied that time of day, at the back of the house and away from the harsh lights of the street.

The Russian proverb came to mind naturally. *Preeshlah byelah, Eduard, otvoryahy vorotah. Open the door, Edward, disaster is coming.*

Tom knew many languages, and he spoke Russian fluently, as did Dr. Sherman—though "Sherman" was probably not his real name. That was one of the many things Tom needed to find out about his quarry: where he had come from, what else he had done since leaving Russia, and how many lives had he lived since.

# 4

Sherman's next question caught the science student off balance. "Have you read Genesis from the Bible, Khan?"

*Here we go.* Emily listened to the growing silence, stealing another glance over to the couch. Khan was at a loss, halfway to forming an answer but unsure of where to begin. Presumably he wasn't the creationist type, but wasn't confident enough to say so. She also knew from painful experience that it wasn't worth her while trying to bail him out. She had no intention of being drawn into an argument about the relative truths of science and religion, especially when she knew Edward would give nothing away about his own beliefs. Fortunately, he let the student off the hook before it became too embarrassing.

"In Genesis it reads, 'And it came to pass, when men began to multiply on the face of the earth, and daughters were born unto them, that the sons of God saw the daughters of men that they were fair; and they took them wives of all which they chose. And the Lord said, My Spirit shall not always strive with man, for that he also is flesh: yet his days shall be a hundred and twenty years.'"

Edward began to expound. "Before the great flood, the 'Sons of God' lived for several hundred years. Unfortunately, these semi-divine beings took it into their heads to sleep with human women. God saw the risk that all humans might live forever, and decided not to allow it. About the time of the great flood, God somehow sets a limit on the age that humans can reach—one hundred and twenty years. Not so smart on the part of these 'Sons of God'—I'm sure they weren't the last to have their lives foreshortened by an injudicious marriage."

Emily could at least agree with that bit; her own experience of marriage had not been a happy one.

## M-Trait

The doctor smiled at his student's look of complete bewilderment. "Noah lived for 950 years. Methuselah, Noah's grandfather, lived for 969—the oldest recorded age in the Bible or anywhere in modern history. How was that possible?"

There was no answer from Khan. Emily saw him swivel his head and give her an uncertain look: a cry for help? Instead, she turned her eyes towards her work, waiting for the first volley of Edward's pet theory.

"It comes back to genes again; our bodies are genetically programmed to age. The theory is that certain genes—two genes, possibly—prevent us from reaching the kind of ages you read about in the Bible."

Now back on familiar, more comfortable ground, Khan realized where he had been going with this. "So people are born without these genes?"

"No. It doesn't work like that. *Everyone* has the genes that actually promote aging. However, random mutations occur all the time so, on rare occasions, maybe a person could be born with these genes not working or turned off. We call this unknown gene combination the 'M-Trait'—the 'Methuselah Trait'—for obvious reasons. It wouldn't quite be immortality; aging would still occur—I think that would be unavoidable. But aging would be vastly slowed down into a life of 'Ultra-Mortality' perhaps, if I can coin a word."

Emily sighed; she heard this line too much. They had argued continually about the possible existence of "Ultras" as Edward liked to call them privately. Emily could never figure out why he was so adamant about this far-fetched possibility.

"We think that the M-Trait must have two specific genes turned off. Some people may have one gene off—they might even pass that characteristic on to their children. But the design seems to be failsafe because there are two entirely separate switches that have to be changed. If one is inactivated, the other is there to ensure the job of death is completed. So, aging happens—you get old, you die."

Khan, now more curious, asked the obvious question. "What are the odds of having both of the genes turned off?"

"The odds of a person being born with both genes inactive are astronomical."

"How astronomical?"

"It's so hard to say for sure. There is so much background noise, so many other factors to take into account. There are so many things working against us."

Emily thought the doctor sounded almost wistful.

"Roughly, though?" Khan was impatient for a number.

Finally Sherman gave up, with a sigh and a wave of the hand. "Ah, perhaps it's one in ten billion—a hundred billion—who knows?"

Emily had talked with Edward about this before—it was unlikely, very unlikely. The calculation was too absurd on any mathematical or scientific level. Take the one-in-a-million human who has the blessed mutation that turns off one of the death genes, multiply that by the odds of meeting and mating with another person of the opposite sex who has miraculously mutated the other death gene, while living in the same time period and same geographical area out of all the persons who have ever lived on this earth—don't forget to factor in the possibility of being cruelly weeded out by accidents, war, and plague—and maybe, just maybe, some lucky human has walked this earth for as long as Methuselah did.

Though it was seemingly impossible, Emily couldn't help but think: *Now that's a slightly scary thought.*

Khan was tentative in his next question.

"How many…?"

Sherman knew what Khan was asking. "We have found no one so far who even has one gene turned off." His voice was tinged with disappointment. "Probably because there is no one to find—the odds are just too great."

That was probably just as well, Emily thought. What kind of state would a person's sanity be in after a thousand years of watching history go by? Outliving everyone they ever knew—seeing parents, friends, and loved ones die. Every relationship, long or short by conventional measures, would become transient. Emily knew she had a long life to look forward to—accidents aside—but she would not wish this on anyone. There would be no lifetime companion, no partner, no one to grow old with. It would be a lonely life, its end determined only by fate or suicidal impulse. The soul of a mortal trapped in the body of a god; maybe the odds were too great for a good reason. No one had been found, possibly because there was no one to be found

"Presumably you could maybe, at least in theory, genetically engineer such a being?"

Sherman shook his head at Khan, dismissing the idea instantly with a half laugh, as if he could not even entertain the possibility. "We don't know the combination—we can't even pick the lock yet. Besides, the legalities, not to mention ethics of such an action, are unthinkable. We just map genes here. It's a case of 'look, but don't touch.'"

Dr. Sherman stared at Khan before ending the conversation, "I think that's best, don't you?"

# 5

No one thought the child would live long. Born in the aftermath of a local epidemic of the Black Death, into a remote Polish village that was starving from repeated crop failure, his father was dead within days of seeing him into the world. His mother lasted only long enough to wean him before succumbing to the disease that had already claimed half of the village. Before he died, his father chose for him the name Michal, after himself and his own father. Michal, Mikhail, Michael, a name Hebrew in origin. *Mi-kha-'el: who is like God?*

The young Michal was left without parents and with precious little hope. He was raised by his uncle, who somehow managed to create subsistence out of what little the fields produced during the famine. By the time he reached adolescence, the once thriving village was a quarter of the size it had been. Michal was often forced to steal in order to feed himself, and more often went hungry. Death was no stranger in those early years, and before long he had buried everyone he had ever been close to.

Finally, the long years of famine ended. For the first time in living memory, there was enough food. In that period of relative prosperity, Michal took a wife and settled down to raise crops and a family. This brief time of happiness for him was not to last as his bride, Elzbieta, died in childbirth less than a year after their marriage. Her death also claimed the life of their unborn daughter, and once again, Michal was alone in the world.

By the time he reached fifty, long past the average life span for a man, Michal lived in comparative isolation on the edge of the forest that grew up the mountainside behind his thatched hut. He had not married again, and had had no close family for over twenty years. In that interval, his face remained young and healthy, and his body as wiry and strong as it had been when he married. The villagers at first had respected his age and health. Then, as the generation around him withered and died, they came to fear him, and the rumors began. When the plague returned to decimate their community once again, the villagers, in their superstition, found a focus for their anguish in Michal.

For some days beforehand, he had known that he was a marked man and that his time in the village was coming to an end. Those few square miles were all he had ever known in his life, and the injustice of having to leave was almost more than he could bear. He did not yet understand and could not yet embrace what he was, or grasp the ostracism and fear that would always accompany him. When the moment finally came, it was not his rational mind but some animal instinct deep within that found the ability to act.

His persecutors, twenty or thirty men and women bearing their makeshift weapons of sticks and farming tools, descended upon the little hut at dusk. Their shouting warned him minutes in advance, but he found himself unable to do anything until the last moment. Turning this way and that in his hut, scared and confused like a trapped animal, he stalled until it was too late to flee. As he heard the first feet against the door, Michal's hand found the handle of a knife and closed upon it. Knuckles white and breath catching in his choking throat, he remained petrified in the shadows for what must have been only seconds, but seemed to stretch for hours as the blood thundered in his ears and his heart pounded audibly in his chest above the shouting outside.

The first man broke through the door and triumphantly stepped across the threshold to seize him, only to stop dead in his tracks as the knife Michal wielded pierced his stomach and tore up through his trunk until it ran against his sternum. Grasping his head and holding it back by the hair, the snarling Michal hurled him backwards into the doorway. In that instant, the victim's face, stupid in the grip of mob mentality, registered only dumb surprise.

The villagers had intended only to beat their victim and hound him out of the village. Their reaction to this violent retaliation was one of astonishment.

There was a heartbeat's silent pause as Michal raised his bowed head to survey his tormentors, and finally managed to draw breath in the moment before their stunned minds could react. Then screaming filled his ears and mind. Without turning his back, now certain in his victory, he retreated into the hut, knowing what he had to do. As the hysterical noise crescendoed and the crowd moved forward to exact their revenge, Michal swept the lamp off the table with one hand to smash it over the doorway and the corpse that now obstructed it. The clay lamp smashed on the wooden doorframe and burst over the body, engulfing it and the nearest villagers in flames and sending them running in blind panic and pain. He overturned the table behind him to block the door, while breaking through the thin back wall of the hut, thus escaping into the darkness with only the clothes on his back and the knife still frozen in his hand.

It was a windy night and fire from his hut spread quickly. By the time the rain came at midnight, his thatched hut lay in ashes, the village was all but burned out, and part of the forest that grew on the slopes of the mountain was ravaged.

It was no coincidence that Michal's departure from them also marked the end of the plague. The fire had swept through the tight clusters of filthy dwellings, killing and driving out the rats and cleansing the village of the disease that they carried.

Michal never turned back. On that night was born a new self-knowledge, an overriding survival instinct, and a precedent for the decisive action that would characterize his long, long life.

# 6

"Is it *ethical* to let a woman have a child without a father, or any kind of family?" a female student asked.

Emily usually left the last ten minutes of her undergraduate lectures for question and answer. The advantages of this were twofold. First, it gave her students the chance to check back on anything they weren't sure about—which, after all, was the point of giving a lecture in the first place. Second, it allowed the students to explore their initial thoughts on the subject. On the downside, you often received emotionally charged questions that were frequently ill conceived. This wasn't her lucky day; it turned out that the subject of cloning brought out the worst in some people. Teaching could really be a pain.

Lucy, a plump blond student in a halter top, which revealed considerably more than was necessary, felt it her duty to implicitly question Emily's decision to have a baby.

"I mean, why should a woman have a carbon copy of herself, just to satisfy a maternal urge? Surely nature requires biodiversity—not a gene pool we've reduced through cloning."

Emily chewed her inside lip for a moment and considered how best to answer this without lashing out. She had crossed swords with Lucy before—mostly on ethical issues that would have been suited for a philosophy or sociology class, not in her biology lecture.

"First—and, like you, I'm not a moral philosopher—your argument concerns human behavior, which is best left to others outside the field of genetics. I do, however, believe it is quite ethical for any normal woman to conceive a child in our society—whether a man is involved or not. What I do find completely unethical is when parents unthinkingly have a child, and don't love and nurture it with all their might." Emily spoke to the whole class now.

"Second, cloning doesn't necessarily decrease the gene pool. If—for example—my child were a clone of me, by definition it would be genetically identical: no net increase or decrease. But that's not happening here. The father will have his genetic stamp on my child—as much as I will."

"But surely some of the stuff we can do now is just morally wrong? And certainly what we will be able to do soon. Cloning, making people smarter, prettier, tampering with nature—"

Emily cut off Lucy without making eye contact, continuing to address the class at large. "Genetic science is not, and will hopefully never be, a fashion panacea. At this moment, we can't choose our offspring's eye color or breast size or temperament. That's science *fiction*."

"The fact is," she continued, "we can barely even clone a sheep. It was an incredibly difficult task, and believe me, there were a lot of casualties along the way. And some people here are already talking as if cloning humans was an everyday occurrence."

"Surely it will happen soon?" Another student called out from somewhere in the middle rows.

"One day, but not necessarily soon." she argued. "It will be your generation, or maybe your children's generation, that decides if the process is safe and reliable."

In fact, Emily thought, the more genetic scientists learned the more complex the mechanical issues of cloning became. But then there were scientists like Edward Sherman. He showed unbounded enthusiasm, had every confidence in his science—it was almost a religion, to him. But the kind of theories he spoke of to his students were still outside science's grasp. He didn't want to restrict that vision; his hope was that one day, miracles might truly be possible. And she was the one who had to redress the balance—dragging their young minds back into reality.

Emily was aware of her brusqueness with Lucy, but it rankled her that anyone would question her own ethics. Her child-to-be, Zoe, wasn't a clone or anything else close to it, though she *was* a product of genetic science—a detail Emily wasn't going to discuss with an arrogant science student in any kind of depth. What did Lucy understand about motherhood and a twenty-nine-year-old woman's desire to have a healthy baby and her own family?

Ignoring several hands that were still raised, Emily noticed the time and happily ended all further discussion. "That's all. You can go."

# 7

So who was the real Edward Sherman? Tom couldn't wait to find out. He unlocked the door to the garden and stepped through, closing it behind him. It was only a week since his initial entrance to Dr. Sherman's house and already it felt a little less strange, a little more routine. The grass was damp and he slipped his shoes off before stepping through the back door in his socks.

Last time his goal had been to gain entrance to the house—which, he reminded himself, he had done with accomplished ease. Today, he had something more specific in mind. He needed to find out where Sherman had come from, whether this was the right man.

Tom knew where he wanted to look first, and made his way straight up to Edward's study, skating across the smooth floor of the hall before climbing the stairs. The room was semi-dark again, the computer humming away quietly on the desk. He was not interested in that for now, though Sherman's work and personal files would no doubt be of interest at a later stage. No, what he wanted to find out, Edward wouldn't have discussed with anyone. If it was anywhere, it would be hidden.

Last time he had been here, he was impressed by the ancient books Edward kept in his study. Looking up at the shelves now, he wondered whether there might be more to them than he had first thought. If they were a window to the past for Sherman, perhaps they could be for him too. There was one that had caught his eye last time.

Taking the enormous Russian Bible in his gloved hands, he gently eased it from its place. It was heavier than he had expected, its padded leather covers each a full half inch thick and the spine cracked and worn by the passage of time and its years of use protecting the mass of stiff pages inside. Resting it on the floor to open it, he knelt with his nose an inch away from the pages, breathing in the musty smell from its ancient leaves. Reading the first page, he found that it had been printed in the middle of the nineteenth century. It was a family Bible of a style that was rarely made anymore, with a family tree at the front that had been filled in meticulously. Sherman had written, in Russian letters, the initials of who Tom assumed were his wife and child in two of the spaces on the opening pages, with a set of dates after them.

He smiled to himself. The circumstantial evidence was building, but he still needed proof. Placing the book back on the shelf, Tom turned to the filing cabinet. A monstrosity from some office clearance sale, its enormous bulky form of angular gunmetal-gray steel stood in sharp contrast to the old books on the other side of the room. When Tom tried the drawers, he found them locked, but that did not worry him. After the gate and back door, this one would be child's play. He was about to start tinkering with his paperclip and screwdriver when he realized that Sherman probably kept a key somewhere in the room. Sure enough, after a few minutes of checking every unseen surface of the cabinet, he found a spare key taped underneath the bottom drawer of the desk.

Tom unlocked the three drawers of the filing cabinet. Starting at the top, he worked downwards. The top one was empty. The middle one held Sherman's financial records—bank statements, share certificates, and property deeds. There were some very impressive numbers there: Sherman was richer than he had guessed. But he was not interested in that for now.

The bottom drawer was in some disarray, and held papers concerning his work. There were piles of magazines and articles that Sherman had contributed towards or found fit to keep, sheets of results and lists of data from tests he had run. And that, it seemed, was all.

Tom felt utterly cheated. There must be some records here, close by where Sherman could always reach them in a hurry. He slowed down and examined each drawer separately, searching the contents carefully. He also used his hands to touch each drawer and sense its composition. Back down at the bottom drawer again, while tapping the back of the drawer, Tom realized that the sound emitted didn't resonate as did the other drawer backs. Looking more closely, he noticed the rods that held the hanging folders failed to reach as deeply into the drawer because a metal box, the same metallic gray color as the cabinet, blocked the drawer end.

He should have noticed it the first time and chided himself for not seeing something so obvious. Slowly he pulled the box out, watching for any mechanism attached to it that might later inform its owner that the box had been temporarily extracted. Sitting back in the desk chair Tom waited a moment before lifting the lid. Opening it was like finding buried treasure, and he was overcome by an almost childlike excitement when he saw the old and crackled documents folded within.

Moving down to the living area where there was more space, Tom spread out the contents over the dining room table. There were numerous birth certificates, one marriage license, a birth certificate for a son and, later on, driver's licenses and degree certificates, mostly in the name of Edward Sherman or variations thereof. Before the twentieth century, the documents were in Russian, and there were longer gaps between them. At the very back of the pile, in a plastic pocket, was the oldest birth certificate. Reading the spidery, handwritten Russian in the sunlight, Tom found what he was looking for. Sherman had been born as Eduard Chermen, in a village near St. Petersburg, in 1831.

Tom spent an hour carefully reading the mementoes and memorabilia of nearly two centuries that Sherman had not been able to bring himself to destroy, one by one in the bright light of the sun that streamed through the south-facing window. He turned the pages over with his gloved hands and placed them in a neat pile next to him, ready to be replaced in the box without disturbing their order. The older and more fragile of the papers, yellowing with years, were already encased in polythene pockets to preserve them against further damage. Later, he carefully made photographs of every sheet before returning it to its hiding place at the back of the filing cabinet.

It was insanely expensive to call America at peak rate from a mobile phone in England, but money was no object for Tom in this case. The phone rang only twice before being picked up.

"What?"

Tom was used to the characteristic terseness, but it really didn't impress him this time. "I found it. I know who he is, and I've got all the proof you need." It was hard to keep the excitement from his voice.

"Send me the proof."

Under the circumstances, a word of congratulation might have been in order, but Tom wasn't going to hold his breath. Long experience had taught him to know better. "I'll express-mail it—you'll have it in a couple of days."

"Now find out what he's doing."

"No problem, I'll check out the—" Tom halted abruptly as the line went dead. *Damn you, old man!* he fumed silently. Just this once, would a little appreciation have hurt?

He'd had enough for today. Sherman's work at the lab and his computer could wait for another time. He had unearthed Dr. Sherman's past; now it was time for something more interesting—as a reward. Who *was* that woman in the photograph on the desk?

Tom decided to learn more about her—in his spare time. Not every detail of an assignment needed to be entered into a report.

# 8

Emily was relieved to take the weight off her feet. It had been a long day at the lab.

She was glad of the work during the pregnancy; it kept her mind active, and she spent time with people rather than sitting at home on her own and trying to find excuses not to do the decorating. Lab research was infinitely more interesting, though Edward gave her the flexibility to work or not during Zoe's gestation.

Emily slipped her shoes off and pushed herself onto the couch which, for the last few hours, had been occupied by a string of blood donors. Four months left—she was starting to feel the extra weight of the baby, and it took some effort to get her feet off the ground. Once she was on the couch, she swung her feet around and lay back. Edward was finishing off a few things in his office, and would be another twenty minutes or so. As usual, he had offered to drop her home, and she was grateful for the help. She did not mind waiting. It was good head space, a chance to put her thoughts in order after the day. She closed her eyes, listening to the faint sound of Edward's computer keyboard through the open door of his office.

Occasionally, just occasionally, she felt a little stab of regret when she looked at Edward in the lab. In some ways they had been so good together; it had been so right. They had gone from a strong friendship to what had felt like love over the course of a few months. It had not felt forced or pressured in any way. She trusted and admired him, and he was the one man she felt safe with after the turmoil of her failed marriage.

But the relationship with Edward just did not work out, and Emily had known it within a few months. The initial closeness that she felt with him disappeared as quickly as it had arrived. It was if he'd made a mistake in letting her get so close. And he wouldn't talk about it. It was just easier for him to have the relationship end.

It felt okay going back to being friends, and the change had not been nearly as painful as she had expected. Nevertheless, the heart sometimes takes a while to catch up with the head, and she still felt that occasional hurt inside.

She had toyed, of course, with the idea that things might work out between them after all—with the conception of Zoe, Edward showed more interest again. Zoe was going to be someone very special, thanks to Edward, and he would make such a good father to her. And he could be a good partner too, if only he could work things out. But how long should she wait? Maybe some things just weren't meant to be. The past was the past, and she wasn't about to get hung up on what might have been at the expense of the life she had to lead now.

Emily sighed, pushing her feet out to stretch her back some more. The plastic of the couch surface squeaked underneath her. She still didn't know exactly what Edward thought about his relationship with the baby and how he was going to deal with Zoe in reality. Maybe he wanted to be more like an uncle. If that was his decision, it would be best to stick by it.

She heard the shutting of Edward's office door. Emily opened her eyes and sat up, looking around for her shoes. Edward moved over to her and put a hand on her shoulder.

"Ready to go, sleepyhead?"

It *was* time to move on—she was ready now.

## 9

Edward liked to contemplate a popular legend, probably medieval in origin, of a character known as the Wandering Jew. This man, who lived in Jerusalem at the time of the Crucifixion, was cursed with immortality for angering Jesus on his way to the cross and condemned to walk the earth until Judgment Day. Tradition is divided on how he came to earn this penalty. Some say that the Wandering Jew was in fact a Roman soldier, a gatekeeper who struck Jesus on the back on his way to Golgotha and forced him to walk faster. Jesus turned to him and replied, "I am going, and you shall wait till I return."

In a later version, the offender is said to be a shoemaker in Jerusalem. When Jesus paused by his house to rest under the weight of the cross, the shoemaker, who believed him to be a heretic and a deceiver of the Jewish people, drove him away. He hoped that by doing so he would improve his standing among his peers. Jesus answered, "I shall stand and rest, but you shall go on till the last day."

In either case, the punishment appears to be a terribly harsh one. Even Judas Iscariot, who committed the unforgivable crime of betraying Jesus, is treated more leniently and allowed a quick, if gruesome suicide—although the precise details of his death are again uncertain. Hanging, disembowelment, or both are suggested, a far cry from the torment of restlessly roaming the earth until the end of time. No retribution at all is recorded for Pilate, whose weakness and cowardice allowed Jesus to be handed over and crucified, though he knew him to be innocent. Judas' sin was greed; Pilate's simply his weakness.

Perhaps because these two were instrumental in history—pawns in God's great plan for creation, Edward Sherman had often mused—they had been let off so lightly. The Wandering Jew's interference was outside of God's plan, so He brought a terrible wrath down on his head.

*Outside of God's plan*—he sometimes wondered if that was where he stood. He was uncertain when and where the first near-immortal being had been born, had himself only known the village community in which he was brought up and, later, the inner circle of those like himself who did not age. He had seen generation after generation of ordinary men and women come and go like the grass of the field—alive today, only to be cut and left to die tomorrow. Even for Ultra-mortals like him, it seemed that nothing could last forever. After so long, the doctor still did not know whether or not he believed in God and whatever plan He might have.

Edward recognized that the Wandering Jew was only one view of everlasting life found in biblical legend. Elsewhere in the Bible, immortality was seen as a blessing—as in the story of the Sons of God that he had told Khan, who had been denied their natural immortality as a punishment for taking mortal wives. Another legend also arose in which Jesus promised John, his "Beloved Disciple" of the fourth gospel, that he would not die until the Second Coming. Who could say, perhaps he would some day pass some of the long years of his life with this wanderer, swapping stories about the ironies of their condition.

It was strange that the legend of the Wandering Jew had captured popular imagination so well when there were biblical examples of men alternately blessed or cursed with immortality. How could the same attribute be viewed in such polar extremes? Perhaps they were really two sides of the same coin, dependent only on the perspective of the beholder. After all, the Hebrew word for "bless" came to contain both meanings, as it was sometimes used euphemistically for "curse." Even in modern English there was an antithetical meaning for "blessed," in an ironic or intensive sense. Somewhere along the line in the development of the language, it had links with the proto-Germanic word for "blood," from a time when a blessing entailed being sprinkled with the blood of a sacrificed animal. In today's world, "blessed" was a term from religious language, and "bloody" was a piece of mildly offensive British slang. Yet Edward understood that both words were literally the same. Such wordplay and etymological games appealed keenly to his slightly offbeat sense of humor.

Dr. Sherman sometimes identified himself with both Wandering Jew and Beloved Disciple, seeing himself as alternately cursed and blessed. He knew he did not want to die—he had lived so long by being very careful when it mattered most. Although his body had barely aged and he was in general fit and healthy, he knew that he was not indestructible. He also knew that one of his biggest dangers was exposure, and he protected his true identity from even his closest friends. It was the flip side of the gift he had been born with: the loneliness of being set apart from the rest of humanity, unable to confide in another mortal, no matter how close. The necessary emotional distance had sabotaged his relationship with Emily—and she had not been the first—but it was the only way.

Edward would not be the first of his kind to die at the hands of those who feared the unknown. Neither would he shy away from killing to protect his secret if it came to it. Edward disliked violence and thought murder distasteful, but taking life was a right, his prerogative as a being whose life was worth many times more than that of an ordinary human. Mortals had so little time; they were already dead without knowing it, only the briefest of intervals separating the ephemeral present from that irreducible reality. The potential for his own life, by contrast, was almost limitless, and he was prepared to make the necessary sacrifices for it along the way. It was sad that one of the necessary corollaries to the blessing of longevity was that it required a certain amount of bloodying of the hands.

Eventually, he knew, nature would catch up with him, but he was in no hurry for that day. A large part of his work was aimed, either directly or indirectly, at postponing it as long as possible, and perhaps indefinitely. Increasingly, he was becoming able to look forward to the long future he would enjoy, and less to the pain of the past and the mysteries of his origins. One day soon, he would again be able to share his life with a special someone—a woman—without fear of recriminations or natural aging.

The blessed thought intoxicated him.

# 10

Michal ran and ran, through a driving rain that soaked his clothes and branches that lashed at his face, leaving him scratched and bleeding. He did not stop until he ran out of strength, though no one followed him, either then or at any time afterwards.

As far as the villagers were concerned, the devil had left them and they were in no hurry to meet him again. They were kept busy salvaging their homes from the devastation of the fire and working to rebuild them from the ashes that his climactic departure had left behind. Michal never returned to the village in which he had been born.

The rain did not cease until dawn, when he finally fell to the ground to huddle in the lee of an oak tree, shivering uncontrollably as the sun came up behind grey clouds that stripped it of any warmth. Exhausted, hungry, and confused, he drifted into a fitful sleep that left him tired and disoriented when he reawakened, as the rain started to fall again.

Those first few days after Michal left the village blurred into one incoherent memory—drinking rainwater from muddy puddles and the drips from the coniferous trees, eating only unfamiliar berries and bark that his stomach brought up again as often as not, shivering in clothes that would not dry, and sleeping only when sheer exhaustion dictated.

Ever fearful of retribution, he moved whenever he found the energy, until his chaotic wanderings finally brought him to the edge of the forest, utterly spent. He would have died there, delirious in the grip of his fever, had a traveler not found him on the way back from Krakow, then the capital of Poland. Michal never questioned the providence that saved his life, bringing the stranger to the place where he had fallen, half-hidden by the undergrowth and unable to move.

*M-Trait*

The Good Samaritan did what he could, and carted him back to his house to tend him. Michal awoke—a day, a week later?—when the fever broke, leaving half-remembered nightmares of terrified voices and faces.

The first sensation he felt was the scratchy woolen blanket pulled up around his neck. The room in which he lay was quiet and dark, and for a time he could hear or see nothing. He was no longer wearing the clothes he had fled in, only sodden and tattered rags by the time he had passed out on the edge of the forest, but was dressed instead in something clean and warm. For a while, he drifted in and out of sleep—healthy, natural sleep, rather than the fevered unconsciousness he had suffered before. Presently there were voices outside, and light at the door. A man came in—he could tell little else about him in the dark—laid a hand on his forehead and spoke in a language that Michal did not understand. He later learned that it was Yiddish.

It is unknown when the first Jews arrived on Polish soil, but it is likely that many families had already settled there by the end of the first millennium AD. In later years, persecuted and chased from many other countries as the victims and scapegoats of religious and social upheavals, Jews looked for a safe haven, and found it in Poland. Michal, too, found his safety among these people.

Although a predominantly Catholic country, the Polish prided themselves on their religious tolerance and welcomed the merchants and craftsmen who crossed their borders looking for protection. The largest influx came towards the end of the medieval period, as the effects of the Crusades and the Holy Inquisition emptied western European countries of their Jewish communities. By the seventeenth century, Polish Jews numbered 750,000 and composed half the urban population. The millennium that they spent there before the Holocaust would prove to be vital to the future of Judaism, as without that period of recovery, there could have been no Jewish nation or modern state of Israel.

They spoke Yiddish, the mishmash of languages that had arisen in the ghettos of Central Europe: numerous medieval German dialects, Hebrew, and loan words from several other European languages.

Michal recognized only a few words since he had, until that point, spoken only his native Polish. But this was a new chapter in his life and during the long period of his recovery, he discovered a latent talent for languages, and grew to love the soft, guttural, and emotionally expressive tongue that his new host and his daughter spoke. He learned new words and expressions and, as his body grew stronger, he began to spend more time out of doors, helping the daughter in the fields that adjoined the house, and talking to her father in his workshop. Piece by piece, as he was able think it out, his made-up account of events came out.

"We were attacked," he improvised one day, when he knew the language and his story well enough to try and convince his rescuer.

"What happened?" asked Barak slowly, not knowing that Michal's Yiddish was already good enough to understand the conversations he overheard between father and daughter. In fact, for weeks he had listened to their speculation about who he was, and where he had come from. Was he a homeless beggar, the victim of robbers, or a criminal himself? Ever careful, Michal had picked up the story and vocabulary of his plight from the very people he would tell it to.

"My family. Other families—escaping the plague. We traveled through the forest."

Barak nodded, absorbed in Michal's first account of his troubles. "Bandits?" he suggested. "Robbers?" he offered again when Michal feigned ignorance.

"Yes, robbers. They took ... everything. Killed many of us."

"But you escaped!" Barak was intrigued.

"I ran away, but I became lost. I had nothing. I was tired, cold, hungry ... for many days. I did not want to stop running. If they found me, they would kill me." Barak placed a hand on Michal's shoulder in deep sympathy. "And I knew if I stopped ... when I fell, I would never get up." He looked Barak in the eye. "Thank you, friend."

At that moment, he knew that it was all the story he would ever need. Barak believed him entirely. As he saw the tears come to his new friend's eyes, Michal decided to press his advantage.

"What about your family?" Michal asked. The more he could find out about Barak and Leba, the better his chances of survival. He was learning fast that knowledge was power, particularly knowledge held without another's appreciation.

"I have only Leba. Her mother died of a fever some years ago. Now I am becoming old, and I have no son—no one to take over from me when I am gone." He gestured around the workshop. Michal nodded in sympathy.

The short conversation had indeed been fruitful. Here was a family without a son. And Michal was a son without a family. He said nothing, but allowed the juxtaposition of ideas to hang in the air as he and Barak stood in silence.

He did not know whether it was out of sympathy, or because they did not yet share the words, but neither Barak nor his daughter, Leba, pressed him for details. Michal himself remembered little after the fire, though scenes from the events immediately before were stamped on his memory with an indelible clarity and vividness. He pushed that knowledge to the back of his mind and locked it away from conscious thought, coming to believe his own story as much as the truth he left unspoken. He grabbed his second chance and began his second life.

There was soon an unspoken agreement between the three of them that Michal would be staying indefinitely. He had nowhere else to go, and another man and pair of hands would be useful around the house and farm. Michal recognized that they were good people, and genuinely appreciated the opportunity to start again.

That period of Poland's history saw the rise of the Jewish Enlightenment movement, which encouraged assimilation into the country's social and cultural life without rejecting the Jewish religion or traditions and, although Michal was not Jewish himself, he soon came to be accepted as one of the family. Barak was pleased to find that he and Michal quickly became good friends, despite the apparent difference in their ages. In fact, Michal was far older than Barak. In addition, as time went by and Michal settled into a life of farming and learning Barak's craft of working in textiles and trading, he found himself drawn to Leba, and she to him. Denial is a powerful force, and he was able to push away the knowledge that this marriage would end the only way every relationship with every mortal could ever end for him. The present was the present, and it was good. The future could wait for another day.

# 11

The DNA molecule is enormous; a twisting double-coil wrapped over and over on itself like a torturous train track, spiraled and tangled in three dimensions. Inside every microscopic cell in the human body is a blueprint for life measuring almost a meter long, if it were unraveled.

Edward Sherman never failed to marvel at its beauty, even the pale imitation of reality the computer simulations and models provided, or the banded patterns produced by the gel electrophoresis procedure used to read DNA results. Whatever the superficial differences across the countries and continents of the world, through all the cultural and linguistic barriers, under the skin every human is almost identical. Only 1 percent of DNA varies from person to person: 1 percent to determine every way that a person physically differs from their neighbor. It governs skin color, blood type, the shape of the face and the shade of the hair and eyes. Combined with environmental factors, it controls height, weight, and intelligence. More subtly, it charts out life itself, a snaking meter-long roadmap consisting of thousands of signs, warning of potential twists and pitfalls. Some signs can point to dangers ahead that require careful attention, while others indicate the end of the road, which no amount of cautious driving will be able to prevent.

It was Sherman's work to compile a list of these road signs, and provide their translation and interpretation to volunteer subjects, like Khan. Sometimes a solitary indication is enough: some diseases are caused by just one mutation in a single gene. They are the easiest to spot, like a red traffic light: do not go past "go." More common, but also more complex and difficult to see, are the groups of genes that display different characteristics and make up other illnesses, or the susceptibility to certain conditions.

This is rarely a precise science. The presence of a particular gene combination does not guarantee a certain disease. Rather, it points to a tendency, the danger looming if precautions are not taken: a "WARNING" sign painted on the road of life. One half of the dilemma is determined by nature, the circumstances beyond our control. The other part of the responsibility rests squarely with the human driver. Now that the warning signs can be foreseen with scientific tools, many conditions that might have been fatal to an earlier generation can be avoided if appropriate steps are taken. A change in diet, giving up drinking, exercising more—such changes can perhaps offset the genetic disadvantage and return the odds to normal.

In some cases, the odds were stacked unfairly, with greater disadvantage than a patient could ever work to counterbalance. Such as the fitness fanatic who ran several miles a day, avoided smoking and alcohol religiously and rigorously stuck to a diet that seemed to eliminate all the best food—only to drop dead of a heart attack prior to middle age. Or, at the other end of the scale, the genetic profile that revealed a constitution so resilient that even gross abuse had trouble denting the body's defenses—like the pensioner who reminisced for hours about fighting in the First World War, while working through a two-pack-a-day smoking habit. Sherman, who possessed a genetic constitution that would put the chain-smoking pensioner's to shame, thought the irony beautiful.

Besides those subjects with chronic illnesses, or family histories that drove them in a panic to his lab, Sherman also had to deal with the hypochondriacs and the morbidly curious. They were the ones who were perfectly healthy, but through irrational fear or overly inquiring minds sought to reassure themselves of their genetic well-being. These parasites wasted his time with their self-obsessed insecurities that rarely turned up anything of significance. Of more interest had been the volunteers who had come forward in response to his search for a longevity gene. He was now certain that he had pinpointed the combination of factors that led to the closest approximation to immortality that could exist outside of mythology.

Analysis of his own DNA and carefully selected others had given him a clear model to work with. Two genes each independently governed aging, and both needed to be in the abnormal state to "switch off" the process and effectively stop the subject from growing old. That, in itself, was of little use if there was an accompanying disposition towards an eventually fatal condition. Only if the roadmap was free of danger signs could the patient expect life to continue indefinitely, unchecked by the ravages of time and programmed illness.

In addition to these factors, Sherman had found that his immune system was particularly strong. There was a combination of genes that he had managed to link to detoxification, the body's ability to cleanse itself of harmful chemicals. In his case, the combination was unusually good, efficiently defending him against toxins such as heavy metals, alcohol, and nicotine.

Needless to say, he had never taken this knowledge as a carte blanche to indulge himself, but instead respected the head start it gave him. It had been a bad scare when he found out about the angina, and now he did not tempt fate by throwing caution to the winds—whether or not his body could deal with it. A small but significant focus of his research was the study of his own heart problem. For the moment he was in no immediate danger. It was a stable, predictable condition that could be controlled by drugs, and the white Nitroglycerin pills were never far away, whether he was at work or home. The angina was only really a symptom of the underlying problem, a narrowing of the blood vessels to the heart. It was not serious enough to require further treatment in the form of surgery, usually required only in advanced cases. Eventually, he hoped that his work in gene therapy might discover a more permanent or long-term solution. Then, perhaps, he could seek to rebuild his family and his life.

Emily was the closest thing he had to family now—Emily and Zoe, her unborn baby. Zoe was his child as much as Emily's, in some ways. He would be there to protect her, raise her, to treat her like a queen. And one day, he hoped that was exactly what she would be to him.

# 12

Usually Tom fell asleep within minutes of lying down, but tonight was different. He returned from a nearby gym, where he had worked out on weights, running machine, and a punch bag. Left stimulated, awake, and alert, he had walked the long way home, pacing the dark streets like a cat out on the prowl, aware of everything, seeing anything that moved. It was 11 p.m. when he returned to his flat, and he relaxed with a beer while playing his classical guitar. Usually he did not go to bed until late. He did not require much sleep, often rising early.

The flat he had leased for an initial six months was comfortable and spacious, decorated in light colors that made it feel even more expansive. The only issue he had with the residence was its lack of sound proofing. Next door, his neighbor was arguing with her boyfriend again, as she had done twice already this week, their raised voices audible through the dividing wall. This time it sounded worse than usual. The noise stopped when she screamed a final *Get out!*—the one message to which the boyfriend apparently listened. The door slammed loudly shortly afterwards and Tom was finally left in peace.

By one in the morning, Tom still wasn't sleepy, so he decided to watch *Gattaca*, a DVD he had picked up some time ago but had not found time to see yet. He slipped it into the machine and let the trailers play while he retrieved another bottle from the fridge.

Tom thought that Ethan Hawke did a superb job of playing Vincent, a man whose imperfection in a perfect society makes him the object of discrimination: one of a genetic sub-class whose lives are limited by others' prejudice. Prejudice was a knife that cut both ways, and Tom had seen the two edges of it. He had purchased the film shortly after coming to London, when he heard about Dr. Sherman's work; he had wondered whether it would give him an insight into the way the doctor's mind worked. Perhaps Sherman thought of all mortals that way, lesser beings only fit to do menial tasks, like Vincent. But Vincent had surprised them all in the end, and Tom hoped to do the same.

By two-thirty, the film ended and he finally felt like turning in. It was a warm night, and he stretched out on top of the duvet cover, lying on his back with his hands behind his head, staring up at the ceiling in the semi-dark, the room half-lit by the electric glow that permeated the curtains from the city below.

Through the wall, Tom could still hear his neighbor, a twenty-something bank worker named Sarah, crying over the last row. He had met her a few times, in the corridor and in the lift on the way up to their floor. When he moved in, she had called round to see if he needed anything.

He was drifting off to her muted sobs, in that strange, semi-conscious state halfway between sleep and wakefulness, when he was alerted by another sound. Out in the corridor, he heard someone noisily unlocking the door to Sarah's flat. Instantly Tom was awake again, lying still but listening carefully to assess the situation. He heard Sarah scream and run to the door, but it was too late. The boyfriend had returned. The arguing started again, mainly his raised voice this time, protesting that he wasn't going to hurt her; then Tom heard her pleading for him to go, and the sounds of a struggle.

Sobs he could sleep through, but not this. Tom swung his legs onto the floor and pulled on a pair of trousers, grabbing a shirt and making his way to the front door of his dark flat. He left his door on the catch and stepped out into the corridor, blinking once in the light and rubbing his eyes.

Sarah's door was open, and he paused just inside it as he waited for the two of them to notice him. The boyfriend—presumably ex-boyfriend by now—was shouting at her, jabbing his forefinger at the air in front of her to make his point. She had a fervid red mark by her left eye, presumably where she had been hit in the face. He could tell even from the other side of the room that the boyfriend had been drinking. Tom wondered which way this would go. Either way was the same as far as he was concerned, though he hoped for something exciting. He cleared his throat.

The man—Tom would later learn that his name was Steve—looked around sharply, with the slightly birdlike, too-quick movement of the drunk. He stepped towards Tom and pointed his finger at him instead.

"Who are you?"

He was a big man beneath his rumpled gray suit, and it was clear from just that movement that his coordination and judgment were both badly impaired by alcohol. Tom did not move from the doorway and his voice was level and calm as he answered.

"I think you should leave now."

He was rewarded by a torrent of swearing as Steve turned his anger against his new antagonist. Tom took a step into the room to allow him the space to move for what he knew would come next. Steve was clearly past the point where reasoning would work, and his body language was growing more aggressive by the second. Tom did not go out of his way looking to fight, but when it came down to it, fighting was something he was very good at. He tried one last time for a peaceful resolution, hoping just a little bit that Steve would give him an opportunity by refusing.

"I think you should leave now."

His answer was fast and nonverbal. Steve stepped forward and swung his fist at him, but it was a clumsy, untrained punch that Tom easily saw coming and sidestepped. The first shot was for free, to give his attacker the chance to reconsider—but to no avail. Steve stepped towards him again, with the same slow, awkward punch that he had already tried. This time, Tom moved forwards, inside the circle described by the fist, and dealt a light, fast strike to his stomach, moving away before there was time to retaliate. Nonplussed, Steve was still not ready to give in. He was sobering up fast and came in again, swinging both fists this time. Something switched on inside Tom, too. *That's more like it.*

Tom knew that little, in our time and culture, truly threatens our personal safety. Rarely anything we deal with on a daily basis highlights how fragile life is. In the regulated comfort of the twenty-first century western civilization, few people really *live* their lives. Tom had been to a lot of places, seen a lot of things in his life, and there was nothing that surprised him anymore. As he moved, circling this man in the confined space of Sarah's flat, he realized that he had not felt this alive for a long time. He was good at this. When he fought, it felt like he was dancing—no, more like *flying*.

Steve was frustrated and furious that he could not hit his target. Somewhere on the edges, outside their instinctive world, Sarah was pleading with him to stop. Finally, when Steve was off balance from his last wild swing, Tom grasped the opening and took his leg out from under him with a sweep to the ankle. Steve stumbled forwards, and Tom pulled the man in towards himself, bringing his knee up hard into his stomach, driving the breath out of him and leaving him winded on the floor. He ignored Sarah for the moment and dragged Steve out to the lift, pulling him in and dropping his dead weight on the floor. After retrieving the key to Sarah's flat, he pushed the button for the ground floor and stepped out.

"If you come back here again I'll press charges. I'll make sure Sarah does too."

Steve had no time to reply before the doors closed, and was in no condition to speak anyway.

Back in Sarah's flat, he found some ice for her face and sat her down on one of the kitchen chairs. Her place was an exact mirror of his, presumably to simplify the plumbing and electricity in the apartment building. She thanked him, and would not stop apologizing for the trouble. She finally started to relax after drinking the stiff vodka he poured from a bottle on the sideboard.

Tom stayed for a while to make sure she was okay. When he rose to leave, she thanked him again and hugged him. There was maybe the suggestion of something else, but there were too many reasons he could never reciprocate in that. He had a job to do and a different life to lead. He returned the hug, told her to sleep well, and retreated to his flat next door.

# 13

The first years that Michal spent living with Barak and Leba were among the happiest of his life. It was a time of comparative peace and prosperity, and the three of them wanted for little. It was a far cry from his childhood. The Jewish Enlightenment movement brought with it a reform of Jewish customs and their greater integration into the wider Polish society, although many of the poorer craftsmen and farmers continued to speak Yiddish alone and could not mix so freely. Michal's own Yiddish progressed to the point where few people realized that it was not his first language, and he became increasingly important to Barak as they expanded their trading of goods into the cities where many people spoke only Polish.

Two years after he had been brought to the house, he married Leba. Aided again by Barak, he had begun to learn Hebrew and study the Talmud, the rabbinic interpretation of the biblical Law, and soon surpassed his teacher in both his understanding of the language and of the texts. Barak's pride and love for his pupil and son-in-law were evident. He was accepted unquestioningly as a member of the family, and even of the larger community. His wisdom beyond his apparent years earned him widespread respect.

Michal thought little about his previous life in the years he spent in the little town near Krakow. Consciously, he had left it entirely behind, although a part of him, buried somewhere very deep, always knew that his present happiness could not last forever. Occasionally, his memories surfaced in the form of nightmares, less specific images than undefined blurs of emotion and confusion that awakened him, upset and disoriented in the darkness, until he found the warm presence of the sleeping Leba beside him. As the years passed though, even these grew less and less frequent.

In the course of time, Leba bore him four children, two girls and then two boys. The aging Barak was overjoyed by his grandchildren and applied himself to their education as he had with Michal's. Their joy was tempered by the death of one of the girls in her early childhood from an unknown disease that racked her with fits of coughing and wasted her body. But the young were always vulnerable to death, and Michal did not yet realize the significance of her early demise.

By this stage, Michal himself was taking care of most of the arrangements for their livelihood, trading textiles and other goods in Krakow and the surrounding towns. Barak had entrusted everything to him, knowing he was capable and that they would prosper. He was not disappointed.

A decade went by, and then another. Michal's surviving daughter married and moved into another house in the town with her husband. His oldest son, Mordke, also married, bringing his wife into Michal's house. Barak became blind, unable to see the faces of his grandchildren. Now obscured by the traditional heavy beard, and often a hooded cloak as well, it was less obvious to the townspeople that time did not have the same relationship with Michal as it did with them. Without the beard, he and Mordke could have been brothers. Soon after Mordke married, Barak died.

Michal would always remember the conversation he had with his father-in-law, only weeks before his death. It was their custom to sit together after their evening meal and talk before Barak fell asleep. He knew he was nearing death, but the idea seemed to hold little fear for him.

"I have lived a long life," he told Michal as they sat by the fire, "so many years—longer than most. I have much to be grateful for. I have you and Leba, and now my grandchildren. Thank you for that blessing."

"That's no way to talk," Michal had answered. "You will live many more years."

"No," Barak had replied. "I am blind, but some things are clear to me. Death is inevitable: it is part of life." He turned to him and, for a moment, it seemed to Michal that his eyes were unclouded. "For some of us, old age is a gift we can enjoy."

Michal felt the hairs on the back of his neck rise. "I will remember that for my old age."

"Some things are clear to me," Barak repeated. "You are different."

Michal was silent, knowing that Barak would not believe him if he said otherwise.

"Who are you, Michal?" asked Barak. "I have often wondered in the years you have stayed here, helping me, caring for my daughter. You are like a son to me, but perhaps I don't know you at all."

"I don't even know who I am," replied Michal. "But you have been a father to me, and I cannot repay your kindness."

"You already have, friend. I will die soon, content with my children and grandchildren around me." He reached out and found Michal's hands, grasping them with love.

That was the only time they spoke of it, but Michal sensed that Barak felt at peace with him when he died shortly afterwards.

It was not until Leba became sick that Michal acknowledged that he could not stay there forever. She had been young when they married, and for some time he had been unaware of the gradual effect of the years on her. Though she recovered from her fever before long, it was still a bad shock to him: a reminder of the mortality that applied to everyone but him. Sometime during those days, whilst he tended her and nursed her back to health, as she and her father had done for him in their turn so long ago, the nightmares came. Night after night, in his attempt to escape from the hut, he was captured by the mob of villagers who brutally tortured him amid his agonizing screams. Often he awoke, nauseated and disoriented, searching for some cue for his senses to ground him in reality. He slept less and less, preferring to sit in an upright chair by the fire rather than lie in bed and keep Leba awake. In the long nights of her illness, he learned to be patient, biding his time while he waited for the inevitable to happen.

The week after his wife had recovered from her fever, Michal began to make preparations for the time he would have to go. Whether it would be in two years or twenty he did not know, but when Leba died there would be little to keep him in the town, and it would be safer for everyone if he left. He had no intention of allowing his children to suffer from the fear with which he would inevitably come to be regarded.

During the years in which Michal had gradually taken over from Barak in trading, the family had prospered and grown comparatively wealthy. Now, from every trip he made to sell their cloth and textiles, Michal put one fifth of the profits aside, just as Joseph had advised Pharaoh to put aside a fifth of every good harvest for seven years before the seven years of famine struck Egypt. He discussed this with no one, hiding the money in three separate places in case of accidental discovery or theft. Whenever he was able, when a month provided good earnings, Michal would add to these hoards, knowing that it would always be better to save for the coming years than spend in the present. Unlike the rest of his family, he could look to the distant future, knowing that what he put into motion now might have significant consequences decades or even centuries later.

In those last years before he finally closed that second chapter of his life, almost exactly thirty years since he had closed the first, Michal never felt truly at ease. Once he had decided on his course of action, he spent the time in a state of perpetual alertness, ready to drop everything and leave if he had to. When his wife fell ill again during a particularly harsh winter, his overwhelming emotion was one of relief that the time of waiting was almost over and that he could now go when he wished, without regret and on his own terms.

She, too, had realized that something was different about him, though she had never spoken about it. Perhaps now, like her father, she knew that she was near death. As he sat with her, her body in the grip of the fever, she reached out and touched his arm. He felt her pale, fragile hand against his own young skin, as healthy as it had been when he first arrived.

"So young," she murmured, "still so young." She reached up and ran her fingers obsessively over his face. As she began to repeat the phrase over and over again, he realized that she was delirious.

"Leba," he said, holding her wrists in his hands, "quiet now." She lapsed back into sleep, leaving Michal to contemplate this new development. If anyone else heard her—a doctor, or neighbor, or even one of the family—his secret might become known. Michal agonized about how to deal with this. Leba was dying, he thought, but what might happen if she were allowed to continue her feverish raving? He knew he could not afford that.

As it turned out, Michal was spared a decision that he would have found near impossible. Leba grew worse, and though she was occasionally conscious after that, she rarely spoke again. As he waited for her life to play out its natural course, circumstances arose that he had not foreseen, a complication that was a mixed blessing to his resolution to once again leave behind everything and everyone he had ever known, and begin again in another place.

He had watched as time took its toll on those around him, and those he knew and loved decayed and died. First Barak had aged, then Leba. His daughter had married and had children of her own, and he looked on with a mixture of pain and a necessary detachment, as they in their turn had grown up. His youngest son, Jakob, now in his twenties, had already begun to show the signs of normal aging.

His oldest son, Mordke, on the other hand, was just like his father.

# 14

"Death is a relatively recent idea, as far as the earth is concerned. After all, what is not alive cannot die, and the earliest life forms did not appear on our world until around 3.8 billion years ago, already a billion years after the earth was formed in the fires of the first supernovae and gravitational collapse."

Unlike Emily, Edward Sherman enjoyed passing on his expertise in the classroom. On this occasion, he was giving a tutorial with a small group of students—his favorite method for teaching. The six of them sat around his desk, listening to what he had to say and occasionally asking questions.

"These early proto-cells lacked a nucleus and the more complex features of later single-celled organisms, surviving without oxygen in the most extreme conditions of the planet's childhood. Even then, when life first took hold of the planet's surface, death did not affect single-celled creatures in the same way as their multi-cellular descendants. They grew, dividing and becoming two, four, eight, sixteen. Short of being crushed or burned, these organisms were about the closest thing to immortal that the world has ever seen. Primitive though they were, their simplicity itself was the key to escaping death."

"So why did death develop?" asked one of the students—a bright, freckled girl named Kate. "Wouldn't immortality be a desirable trait in evolution?"

Sherman smiled. "You would think so. But in the terms of evolutionary development, death is actually a more successful strategy. It holds an advantage for the more complicated life form, at least as far as the *species* is concerned. In the broad strokes of time, the individual does not figure at all and the species is all that is important. *Individuals* cannot evolve, cannot improve their DNA to pass on a better chance of survival to their offspring."

"So, immortal organisms continually produce offspring too much like itself?" Kate summarized.

"Nicely put. It would be unable to adapt to the changing environment, and its ever more efficient predators. Not only that, but it would be in direct competition with its own offspring for the limited food sources. Without change and diversity, a species could be wiped out quickly."

"You mean that because of death, there is continual life for a species?"

"Exactly. The introduction of the limited life cycle in a complex organism and its need to procreate before death ensures that redundancies within the species are removed. By producing ever diverse versions of ourselves, we create the best possible chance of survival for our species. It is the sacrifice we all make for our children."

That was the general rule, at least—*but not for me*. Edward knew he was an evolutionary oddity, a member of a subspecies so rare that it did not make a difference to the rest of the race. His existence constituted an uneasy truce with the rest of the natural order. Therein lay the paradox: as long as Ultra-mortals were unknown to the general human species, they could survive. The earth could not stand a large number of Sherman's breed. Their strength lay in that fact, and in their ability to hide within the larger population.

With the sense of the individual's importance came a self-image that measured everything that could be of use to long-term survival: the ultimate selfishness, combined with a ruthless streak—merciless self-preservation taken to the extreme.

As an Ultra, Edward understood implicitly, species meant nothing. *The individual is everything.*

# 15

Visiting Dr. Sherman's house had become a regular routine by now for Tom. He enjoyed a leisurely walk of almost an hour to the house, breathing in deep lungfuls of air that was still crisp and fresh in the morning breeze, away from the car fumes, the sun not yet high enough in the sky to bring on a sweat.

Closer to his destination, he stopped at a café that was becoming a favorite haunt to pick up a bacon sandwich and a cup of coffee. Often he ordered espresso here, savoring the intensity of the experience and flavors of the shot during the short walk over to the house. It is said that there are four equal factors that govern the taste of a cup of coffee: the roast of the bean, the grind, the machine used, and the barista who makes it. Here the beans were fresh every day, and ground to just the right fineness immediately before they were used. The machine was the best that money could buy, and the baristas knew how to work it. The result was a cup of coffee as close to perfect as he had ever tasted. Today, in keeping with his unhurried mood, he decided against espresso and went for a tall latté and a bottle of fresh orange juice.

Ten minutes later, arriving relaxed and supremely at ease with the world, he pocketed the paper cup and walked past Edward's house to perform his customary check, ensuring that the car was gone and there were no signs of life inside. Tom then turned the corner into the service alley and entered through the door in the stone wall. Within the cover of the back garden, he stopped to pay the tabby some attention. She purred and rolled over in her sunspot when he tickled behind her ears and under her chin, evidently appreciating the thought. Tom had not figured Sherman as being someone who had any time for pets, but it seemed to him, as he let himself in, that he was not entirely unwelcome here. The cat's pleasure at seeing him somehow legitimized his crime.

He wandered through the cool of the utility room, up the stairs to the study, where he gazed at the photo on Sherman's desk as he paused to collect his thoughts. A very fine layer of dust had collected on the frame since the last time he had been there, and he had to resist the impulse to wipe it clean. The motes in the still air sparkled in the shaft of sunlight that had successfully negotiated the curtains, lazily drifting up and down with weightless ease.

Before he continued to his day's work, he stopped to use the bathroom. As he washed his hands, he stared at the mirror on the front of the bathroom cabinet. *Not looking bad...* On a whim, he opened the cabinet to look through the contents: an electric toothbrush with several spare heads, safety razors, shaving foam—an unmarked bottle caught his interest, and he took it out to examine it further. Unscrewing the cap, he sniffed the contents speculatively. *Definitely nothing to be ingested.* Pouring a little into the palm of one hand, he rubbed the silvery liquid between his forefinger and thumb. He still hadn't figured it out until he brushed the substance on the hairs of his forearm. It was an artificial graying agent, the kind used in theatres and on film sets. This was beautiful, he realized: Sherman obviously used the dye to look older than he actually appeared. Tom wondered if he had any other tricks to put people off the scent. It must get hard trying to stay in one place more than a few years, and he'd been at the university for almost two decades.

Tom's task for today was simple: search Sherman's computer in order to find out as much as possible about the doctor's work and personal life. That was all. No concern for the actual practicalities of the task, which would be far from easy; Sherman would most certainly have protected his work with passwords and other security measures. Tom was perfectly computer literate, but he was no hacker or security expert, and knew that if he tinkered with the computer too much, he would very likely only risk drawing attention to himself.

The computer sat whirring quietly away, as it did the last time he was in the house, discovering the contents of the filing cabinet. Tom eased himself into the chair and touched the mouse. The screensaver disappeared, to be replaced by an email program. Another window displayed some kind of genetic database program. A list of the most recent files that Sherman had used was displayed under the File menu.

At the top of the list was the filename *EPRESTON12-02-76*. Emily Preston, Dr. Sherman's employee? That was strange. Why would she be a subject to study? When Tom tried to open it, he found that it was password protected. So were the other files. That level of data protection was presumably standard practice in these circumstances. Very well—he had expected nothing less, and had come prepared.

Tom brought a gadget he'd found at a computer store earlier that week. It was a keystroke logger—a small, neat cylinder of hardware that plugged in like a short extension cable to the keyboard. Hidden at the back of the computer, out of sight, it would sit there unobtrusively, using no system resources and recording every single key press that Sherman made. He would leave it for a few days, and when he came back it would provide answers: web addresses, passwords, and user identities for remote access to the lab files—everything that Sherman used on a regular basis. He could take it away, download the contents to his own computer at home, and do his spying from the comfort of his own flat.

Tom took the little device out of his pocket. It was no larger than a lipstick case, but could hold a phenomenal amount of data. He smiled; amused that it had been advertised as a backup tool. *Essential for routine file maintenance*—how about domestic espionage? He plugged it in and the process was complete.

There was little more he could do until Dr. Sherman had the chance to use the computer. He amused himself for a while going through some of the doctor's old emails, but there was nothing of any great interest there. He sat back in the swivel chair, putting his feet up on the desk as he pondered what to do next. In her photo frame, Emily stared back at him.

Emily was an enigma to him. He had discovered that she and Sherman were coworkers and seemed to be close friends. She must know a lot about him and his work, although he would hardly have told her his secret. Something told Tom that she would be valuable in finding out more about him.

Tom stared at the file name again—*EPRESTON12-02-76*. What was Sherman's interest in Emily's DNA? With the keystroke logger, he would not need to wait long to find out. Until then, perhaps he could broaden his original research brief. After all, a little extracurricular study couldn't hurt—she could be his *special* project.

He decided right then to meet Emily as soon as possible.

# 16

It did not take long for Michal to suspect that something was different about Mordke. In those days, life was short. Men married earlier, aged faster and died younger. Mordke and Jakob both grew up quickly like any other boys and became men. But his oldest son's face still showed the health and vigor of genuine youth. When the time came for Mordke to find a wife, Michal had misgivings, knowing that he might have the pain of watching his loved ones age and die around him, as he himself had.

Michal did not want to take the opportunity of a normal life from him, but neither did he wish to reveal his own secret without good reason. He kept quiet, preferring silence to the risk of exposing himself and having to run again. Though it was inevitable, he would delay that moment as long as possible.

It was not until his oldest son was thirty years old, with a young son of his own, that Michal accepted what he had long suspected. By then, Jakob already looked older than his brother, as time began to take its toll on him. Michal and his sons left their family on a two-week-long trip to trade their textiles in a neighboring town some distance away. Michal spoke little on the journey, trying to decide what he should do, and the journey passed in a strained silence.

On the first evening, they stopped at an inn for the night. While his sons ate downstairs, Michal looked at his face in the mirror. Staring at himself, it seemed that only his eyes belonged to him. Dark brown, as dark as to be almost black, they were the only feature that he felt belonged to him. For decades now, his face had been obscured by the heavy beard that hid his true form from the world. Not even knowing himself what he would find, he took a razor and carefully shaved away the barrier that disguised him.

# M-Trait

The sense he had when he looked back in the mirror after washing his face was one of déjà vu. He did not immediately recognize that face that looked back, although a part of him knew it was familiar. The eyes, ancient eyes, seemed misplaced among the other features. It was a moment before he understood. The face he remembered was his own, but from decades earlier, before he had even left his first home. In the interval, he had aged only a handful of years. He had barely changed in the course of a normal lifetime.

When Mordke returned to the room, he was confronted by a person who could have been his brother. Uncomprehending, it was only when he heard Michal's voice that he understood. Michal put his hands on his son's shoulders and spoke to him quickly and quietly. The two of them were alike, he told Mordke. Something was different about them, something he did not understand but that they must never allow anyone else to know. It was not safe. This long life was a gift from God, but they must never tell another soul or they risked the reprisals of their jealous and angry neighbors. He took a step back, lifting his hands from his son's shoulders and holding them up before him, a gesture of trust.

Mordke nodded and stood in thought for a long moment. His face then flashed a look of uncertainty. "But what about Jakob?"

Michal shook his head. "He is not like us. He doesn't share this blessing. Look at him—already he seems older than you are. I don't know why it happened like this, but we can never tell him. You understand? He must never know about this. Can you do that for me, Mordke?"

Mordke nodded, but as he looked up his face changed. Michal turned to the doorway and saw his younger son there. Jakob's dark eyes were full of hatred as he stared at his father and brother.

"How long have you been standing there, Jakob?"

"Long enough." He spoke little, but his face showed the pain of betrayal.

Mordke hastened to calm him. "Jakob, we did not mean for this to happen. We did not ask for it. You are the normal one." He placed a hand on his brother's shoulder, as his father had done to him only moments ago, but Jakob shrugged it off angrily. Mordke tried again. "This doesn't mean anything, Jakob. Who can tell what life will bring? An accident, an illness—any one of us could die tomorrow."

"Don't lie to me!" Jakob's fist shot out from by his side and hit Morke squarely on the jaw, knocking him from his feet. Then he turned on his heel and strode from the room.

Michal watched Jakob leave, and then bent to help his son from the floor. Their eyes met, and Michal knew that Mordke already realized why they could tell no one.

"What will we do about him?"

Michal shook his head. "I don't know." But he knew that was not true.

That night, for the first and only time, Michal told Mordke his story. There was much he left out, and some he had forgotten. In the decades and centuries that followed, the story would be repeated over and again among their group, gradually exaggerated in each telling until it took on the character of a legend. Mordke had more questions than Michal could answer, but grew increasingly animated as he realized what it meant for him. His excitement was tempered when Michal reminded him that his wife did not share their peculiarity, and they could not be sure that his son would either. Still, Mordke pressed his father for details. How long had he lived?

Michal did not know. He had fled through the forest nearly forty years ago, falling exhausted by the road on the other side. That was how he had come to be with Leba and Barak, Mordke's grandfather. Before that, he had outlived almost two generations of villagers, before they finally hounded him out. Scratching his head in thought, he realized his age could not be much less than a hundred years. A century old, and he barely looked thirty.

"How long will we live?" Mordke was in awe.

Michal sat in quiet thought for some time. He had lived nearly two lifetimes already. Finally, he shook his head, unwilling to guess. Impatient, Mordke did the math.

"An extra lifetime, and it seems there only a few years between us." He looked at his father for confirmation.

Michal confirmed his son's calculation. "A decade for every year; a century for every decade..." His voice was more somber than that of his son.

Mordke inhaled slowly, speechless at the thought. At the time, their peers were considered fortunate to reach fifty years; sixty was considered truly old. And yet, through some freak of nature or will of God that neither of them had sought, it seemed possible they might live for six, seven, eight hundred... "A century for every decade," he smiled broadly, "we will fill every hour with days, and every day with weeks."

The rest of their time away passed quickly, a blur of activity in which they had little time to think. Mordke seemed preoccupied for much of the time, withdrawn after his excitement and animation of the first night. Jakob, too, was surly and uncommunicative, spurning their company and spending as much time as he could on his own.

Two weeks later, when Michal's face was once again covered with thick stubble, they began the journey home to their families. Jakob walked some distance behind them, unwilling to keep their company. For long periods of time he would stay out of sight, only joining them when they stopped to sleep.

On the third day of the journey, when Michal and Mordke were ready to leave, Jakob refused to come with them. "Go on, then. Maybe I'll catch up with you later."

For all his father's insisting, he would not get up.

"Mordke, go ahead to the next village and buy some food for the day's journey. I'll meet you there later." Michal waited until Mordke had left, sitting outside until his son had disappeared over the horizon.

When he went back inside, Jakob was asleep. Standing there silently, Michal's eye fell on the heavy feather pillow on which he had slept. He took hold of it and moved over to Jakob's bed.

Mordke never asked what happened to his brother. Over the next few months, Michal observed his son's attitude towards his wife changing, as he began to distance himself emotionally from her and everyone else he was close to. Gradually, Mordke withdrew from wider society, spending more time on his own, as his father did. Only to Michal and his own son, Alexander, did he remain close. At this stage, Alex was still far too young for them to know whether or not he would share their long life, and they told him nothing. And yet, Mordke carefully watched the boy, seeing how he grew up, eager to know if he had passed on his secret.

# 17

Tom swam in long, even strokes up and down the pool, his mind focused only on the exact present: the deep shades of blue from the tiles when he opened his eyes, the splashing sound in his ears as his hands and arms ploughed forwards in a front crawl, the smell and taste of the chlorinated water, the cool of it on his skin and the air in his nostrils as he breathed.

Swimming is a total sensory experience, and one in which Tom loved to immerse himself to the absolute exclusion of all else. It was a shame that it could not be the sea, the taste of salt water instead of chlorine, and the feel of the wind and the warmth of the sun on his face. He loved the sea. Every year he took long holidays on a secluded part of the coast, spending hours walking up and down the beach, swimming, and just sitting on the sand at night gazing out at the waves, unable to see where the horizon blurred sky into sea in the darkness, away from any artificial lights.

Tom was a strong swimmer, and it was only after forty lengths of the Olympic-sized pool that he stopped at the shallow end, spent by the exercise and starting to shiver, but feeling oddly peaceful and cleansed by his exhaustion. He took a long, hot shower to warm up and wash the chlorine from his skin. His thoughts focused on the details of his newest project—Emily. It wasn't part of the master plan, but the heck with his "orders."

When Tom had finished his shower, he dressed and strolled outside to wait. It was now 7:50 p.m., ten minutes before Emily's yoga class finished. It had been almost disappointingly easy to find out where she went on Tuesday and Thursday evenings, after Tom realized that he had rarely seen her at Sherman's house either of those days.

Tom called to the lab, pretending to be one of her friends. A young receptionist of quite unexceptional intelligence answered.

"I'm sorry; Dr. Preston is away at the moment. Can I take a message?"

"She said she would be around this afternoon—will she be back any time soon? I promised I'd make an appointment with her today."

"Well, she's left for the day. She leaves early for her evening yoga class."

"Oh yes, of course—her yoga class at the Atrium."

"No, it's at the Willows, I think."

Tom thanked the receptionist and promised to call back the next day. *With more friends like that—*, he thought.

So it was that he found himself at the Willows, a sports club located only a short distance from the university where Sherman worked, convenient for Emily to go to after she finished her day. Tom had driven his car round the adjoining multistory car park for ten minutes before finding what he was looking for—Emily's auto, a light blue Japanese compact. He had spotted the car in her parking space at the university a few days earlier, and had watched her drive away in it after she finished work at 6:30 p.m. He parked on the other side of the level.

Emily's yoga class had only just started, so he estimated he had about an hour and a half before he needed to worry about her coming back out. That was plenty of time to do what he needed, and to enjoy the sports facilities too. The task took less than a minute, with the rest of the time open for some proper exercise. Now that he was settling down in London for a few months he looked forward to building some physical training into his routine again.

After the swim, he dressed and strolled out to the lobby—he was now standing by the entrance, enjoying the warmth of the foyer and drinking a can of ice-cold diet cola purchased from the drink machine there. She appeared, dressed in black tracksuit bottoms and a loose gray tee shirt, her face still slightly pink from the mild exertion of her class. Tom stepped back from the sliding door to let her pass, though it was hardly necessary as there was enough room to begin with. It was an extra courtesy, though.

"Thanks," Emily said, without looking up.

He smiled and nodded, *You're welcome,* in return—one sports center user to another, that was all. She left and turned the corner, out of sight. After waiting for a minute or so, he slung the duffel bag containing his towel and trunks over his shoulder and returned to the car park, crushing the empty can of coke in his hands and dropping it in a rubbish bin by the doorway. As he reached the top of the stairs to the second level of the car park, he took out a bunch of keys from his pocket and pretended to be engrossed in sorting through them, concentrating on searching for his car key rather than what was going on around him as he walked nonchalantly across the concrete floor.

He passed Emily on the way to his car just as she was beginning to get frustrated, now trying to start her own car for the third time. There were a couple of other people around now, mainly sports club users returning to their vehicles, but no one was taking an interest in her difficulty. There was a closed circuit video camera too, though not pointing their way. Both of these were good; it meant that she would not feel so threatened by some guy she did not know coming up to her.

This was the most critical stage of proceedings, the moment on which all of his future interactions with Dr. Emily Preston might depend. He had to get it right. If he came across too boldly and she was suspicious or wary for any reason, she would never, ever want to be around him again, and there would be little he could do to repair the damage. Thus, his aim was to meet her and no more.

He stopped in front of her car and listened to the sound of it failing to start. Staring at the dash and twisting the key in the ignition ever harder, as if that was why the engine was not running, Emily did not notice him for a few seconds. When she did, it took another few moments to take in the face and sports bag, and register that it was the same man she had seen in the center.

"You okay?" The tone was just right, as was the look of friendly concern: just enough interest, not too overdone. He stood some distance back, respectful of her personal space even behind the car window. He saw her look up sharply, surprise stamped on her face as if he had disturbed her from the all-absorbing problem. There was a flicker of something. Fear? Concern? He watched as her eyes dart to the left and right to see who else was around. When she saw they were not alone in the car park, she immediately relaxed. Tom was glad she was careful. If he was going to get to know this person properly, it would help a lot if he could respect her. Emily, realizing that she was, for the minute, beaten by the obstinacy of the car, rolled down the window a bit to discuss her predicament.

"It won't start." She sighed, a classic damsel in distress—though he also recognized the beginnings of real worry in her voice. She stood there, with the open car door between the two of them—friendly, but careful with it. How could he resist?

"Want me to take a look at it?" Tom shrugged, making sure she knew that the offer was not a big deal to him; she could take it or leave it.

There followed, as there usually does in such circumstances, the infuriating dialogue that some unspoken British etiquette seemed to demand: the brief exchange of mock refusals on the grounds that it would be too much trouble, the assurances that it would not, the first tentative capitulations, further assurances—Tom cut through the formalities and went straight to the point.

"Seriously, pop the bonnet. It's probably just a loose connection."

Emily did so, grateful that she might not have to call and wait for roadside service. She was tired and looking forward to a hot bath and a meal—she did not like to eat before her yoga classes, and now it was late. Tom regarded the car's innards for a moment, and then tinkered briefly. It was indeed a loose connection, as he knew it would be, having spent a lean forty seconds arranging it that way earlier, when the car park was empty of people.

"Try that?" He took a step back from the bumper, just in case she had left it in first—broken kneecaps did not feature in his hopes for this meeting. He wondered what he would do if, by some chance, the car still would not start. Fortunately, the engine now caught the first time and Emily, full of relief but still cautious of further problems, left the car running as she got out again to thank him. Correct protocol again demanded at least small talk, but she really was grateful for his help. She introduced herself, but Tom declined her outstretched hand with a gesture of his own oily fingers.

"I'd better not," Tom smiled. He held up his hands, which showed a bit of grease he had intentionally rubbed on while under the hood. He thought it was a nice touch.

They chatted for a short while about the only thing they currently knew they had in common, their mutual use of the sports center and respective activities there. Emily was friendly and lively, a bright intelligence shining in her eyes as she talked. Tom thought himself to be a good judge of character, and he could usually tell within minutes whether he was going to find a person good company or not. This pleasantly was one of those occasions. When they came to a natural pause, their subject at least for the moment exhausted after the exchange, Tom made to leave. He did not want to overdo things at the first meeting, running the risk of frustrating her when what she wanted most was to get home.

"I need to be off. Nice to meet you though." He smiled again, to make sure she believed him.

"You too—and thanks again for fixing the car—I really appreciate it."

"Have a good evening. I'll see you again sometime." It was a tacit offer, not to be passed by without an answer—he hoped Emily would read into it the spot of acquaintanceship he offered.

"Yes. Bye!"

She got back in the car, still idling in neutral as a safeguard against its further rebellion. Tom strolled over to his own car, sports bag back on his shoulder, and did not turn around as he heard Emily pull out of the parking space, or see her wave a further goodbye as she drove by. He dropped the gym bag on the ground by his car, opened the trunk, and retrieved the hand soap and towels brought specifically for this purpose.

*She's almost mine already,* he thought happily as he hummed nothing in particular.

# 18

Edward was reminded of a recent research study he came across in a scientific journal. An experiment has been carried out using monkeys to illustrate a point about habit and reluctance to change.

A group of monkeys are placed in a cage with adequate supplies of food and water. On a high branch on one of the trees in their cage, a particularly ripe and tasty-looking bunch of bananas is hung to tempt them. Naturally the monkeys climb the tree to eat the bananas, but when they get close, a fire hose is turned on them and they are knocked from the tree by its force. Very soon, they learn that their prize is not worth the pain it incurs.

In the second phase of the experiment, one of the monkeys is removed, and replaced with a new monkey that does not know about the fire hose. When the new monkey tries to climb the tree to retrieve the banana, the others restrain the novice, saving it from the fire hose blast. The new monkey learns quickly that it is not worth going after the bananas.

It turns out, however, that when all the monkeys are replaced, one by one, the behavior is still passed on. Eventually the group will consist of new monkeys, none of whom have ever tried to climb the tree and take the bananas, and none of whom have felt the effect of the fire hose. It may be a different mechanism, but learned behavior is also passed on from generation to generation. If there once was a known reason for a behavior, there does not have to be one for it to continue.

The study's conclusion: we do things the way we do them because we have always done it that way. It explains why, decades after refrigeration technology renders it unnecessary as a preservative, salt is still used as a seasoning. Some suggest that the taste remains ingrained in our collective memory—we crave it, but don't really need to add more to our diets.

It is not that change is unnecessary and bad. The perceived benefits of change are offset by the inertia of our current behavior. We may find ways to rationalize it to ourselves, but for this reason the idea of "change" is somehow hardwired into our brains as something intrinsically worthy of mistrust.

Edward thought this was particularly true in the field of medical science. Midway through the nineteenth century, doctors began to understand the value that chloroform might have in childbirth. Their attempts to alleviate the pain of mothers in labor sparked a furious debate. On the one hand, there seemed to be every moral reason to reduce suffering. However, the argument that raged for several decades (predominantly, one suspects, among men) centered on the fact that nature intended childbirth to be a painful experience. It was, supposedly, one of the penalties that Eve, the first woman, incurred when she was thrown out of the Garden of Eden.

And the real reason for the reluctance to accept chloroform? Who can tell, through all the layers of protective reasoning in which we wrap our decisions? But Edward suspected that a large part of it was simply the fear of change.

He believed that a reluctance to tinker with our genetic makeup was reasonable, a caution only to be expected and encouraged. The field was still enough in its infancy that the ramifications of altering genes could not yet be fully predicted. One improvement might have after effects that, at this stage, could not be foreseen. An artificially created defect could spread through future generations of the population, undetected until it was too late and thousands were contaminated.

But his work was not tinkering, or trying out something new. He was returning the DNA molecule to perfection, the state it was originally in before it was corrupted: mankind as mankind was always meant to be. The first man—Adam, if that's what you want to call him—was perfect. Six days of creation, or three billion years of evolution: it did not matter. Whether he was created out of the earth in the Garden of Eden or evolved from proto-hominids descended from apes on the African savannah, the state that man began in had never since been retained.

Adam lived 930 years. Seth, Adam's third son, lived 912 years. Enosh, Seth's son, lived 905 years. Kenan, Enosh's son, lived 910 years. The best anyone had managed recently was 122 years. Jeanne Calmet, a French woman, managed to reach that age in 1997, and that was an anomaly. The average age is far less. In the UK, men live an average of only seventy-five years, and women average nearly eighty. This is a long way from the 120-year ceiling on longevity imposed by God before the Flood in Genesis 6, and a far cry from the early days of 900-year lives.

Edward knew that his work or similar genetic manipulation was the only way to achieve that primeval state of perfection once again. He grew old, imperceptibly year by year as the rest of the world aged in fast-forward, like the grass of the field withering and dying in a day, as he lived on through it all alone.

At first, his long life had been shocking, painful with the losses it brought with it. Then he found it exhilarating—the opportunity to fill life to the fullest. Now, nearly a century after the death of his family, he was weary of the continual turnover of friends and acquaintances, of never being able to invest anything in a relationship he knew could only end in death. Certainly, time passed slowly, but it still passed, and Edward could feel its wrath as it slowly ground everyone he knew back into dust.

He even saw it in Emily—so healthy yet even her face was changing in the time he had known her. Already the first lines had appeared around her mouth when she smiled, and it hurt him to know that it was only the beginning of a process of gradual decay that would last for decades.

And, until a few years ago, he could have been in danger of envying her for ability to die. That changed when he began his work searching for the M-Trait—the key to his long life. He had pinpointed the Methuselah genes and knew immediately that his condition could be replicated. With replication came the realization that he did not have to live alone with his burden; that his curse could turn out to be a blessing after all. It wouldn't be long now.

Perhaps he was "playing God" by messing around with the DNA that had become blighted by man's fall—his profession had been accused of that before. But until God gave him a clear message otherwise, he would continue in his research. "Fill the earth and subdue it"—that had been God's command to mankind in the first chapter of the Bible. In these days of green issues and environmental paranoia, *subdue* was usually interpreted to mean "look after," or "harness" at most. In Hebrew, the word had more forceful connotations: to press, squeeze, knead, attack and assault. A related Aramaic word meant to tread down or beat a path. *Subdue* did not mean to calm or pacify, it meant to beat into submission.

Man was supposed to be made in God's image. If Dr. Edward Sherman was playing God, then he knew that God wanted him to.

# 19

Tom had studied a number of martial arts in his time, both for self-defense and for aesthetic reasons. He was pleased to find out that the Willows Sports Club offered karate and aikido, the two disciplines he had invested years of effort in.

Much of karate is taught to the student as a discipline to practice alone, learning punches, kicks, and blocks, first separately and then together in patterns of movements or *katas*. Only sparring required a partner, so Tom regularly ran through a list of *katas* formed from his training years ago. Aikido, conversely, focuses on joint locks and holds, therefore requiring that almost all of it be practiced with at least one partner. He had not trained for over a year, and was keen to start again before his skills became too rusty. The choice was sealed by the convenient fact that the aikido class was held on Thursday evenings between 6 and 8 p.m., the same time that Emily attended one of her yoga classes. That would still leave Tuesday evening for swimming.

He had purchased a *gi*, the tough white suit that was worn in Japanese martial arts, from a sports shop, along with a black belt. Several years ago he had taken his *dan* grading, an affair of muted ferocity in which he and the other students with him had been pushed to their limits to demonstrate their knowledge of the skills they had learned. At that level, the wooden and rubber knives had been dispensed with for the real thing, making it as lifelike as possible.

Within the controlled environment of the *dojo*, however, safeguards in training were present that didn't exist in the real world. It was, in any case, unlikely that the partner you were training with actually *wanted* to kill you. So how a person reacted in the presence of danger was something no one really knew for sure until they encountered it firsthand. Luckily, Tom was familiar with the essence of conflict in a heightened state of authentic brutality.

As it was his first time back after a long break, Tom took it carefully to begin with. Aikido places great emphasis on movement, and he soon felt his body's flood of recognition at the techniques he had practiced so many times before. Much of the lesson was spent on variations of *shi-ho-na-ge*, "four-corner throw," a basic technique in which the attacker's balance is taken in four directions as they are brought down. It can be used in many different ways, against an armed or unarmed opponent, at its most extreme to break an assailant's arm and shoulder, causing serious and lasting damage.

By the end of the two hours he felt tired but exhilarated, and was looking forward to resuming his training properly. He left the dojo, bowing as etiquette demanded, and made his way to the drinks machine, carrying his sports bag and still dressed in his *gi*. As he leisurely sipped from a bottle of water, it was only a couple of minutes before Emily came out of her class.

"Hi!" She took in the garb that prominently displayed his black belt, nodding in appreciation.

"It's been a while since I've trained. Fortunately they went easy on me."

"Impressive. I had no idea." She smiled, moving past him to get a drink of chilled mineral water from the machine. "How long have you been doing that for?"

"A while…on and off. So how's the—is it yoga?"

"Yes. It's good—something I can still do. It keeps me fit and flexible with…" She indicated her abdominal bulge.

They chatted on for a while, first about martial arts and then about work, as they sipped their drinks in the lobby. Emily told him that she worked in genetic research, explaining the project briefly, and was pleasantly surprised when he expressed an obviously genuine interest; she had found that it could often be a real conversation stopper. In this case it was quite the opposite.

"I read somewhere recently about a guy who's doing something similar—finding ways of predicting how long you'll live and how best to deal with any problems in your DNA. Sherman, I think was his name. It sounded interesting. Do you know his work?"

Emily smiled. "Yes, I work with Edward. It is interesting. You probably read one of the adverts he's put out. We look for people with susceptibilities to particular conditions to come in and donate some blood. We get to add their DNA to our database, and in return they get a free assessment."

Tom made her promise to tell him about her work at greater length sometime. It also caught her attention when he said, in an offhand remark to one of her comments about their research, that several of his close relatives had lived until at least a hundred.

In turn, he told her he was a security consultant and was in London for a project that probably would take six months. He added that he really enjoyed England and was thinking of moving to London permanently—the change of pace away from America suited him.

They wandered out, Tom to his car and Emily to a taxi; she did not want to drive any more than she had to at the moment. On the way, he pointed out a new coffeehouse that had opened across from the sports center. It seemed like an appropriate place to continue the earlier conversation about Emily's work with Sherman. Tom suggested they go there after her yoga class on Tuesday. Tentatively, she agreed, though she carefully introduced a get-out clause in the case of tiredness.

He did not offer her a lift. She did not know him that well and would not have felt comfortable accepting; he would have put her in the awkward position of having to refuse. Tom knew that a friendship with a pregnant woman was going to be difficult. He was going to approach this slowly and carefully and make sure he never overstepped the mark. To gain her trust was going to take all the guile he could summon.

# 20

Towards the end of the eighteenth century the Russian empire underwent dramatic expansion under Catherine the Great, a German princess who married the Russian monarch and later seized the throne. It is true that she had her fair share of vices, apparently including a talent for deception and a weakness for love affairs with men far below her in social status—although it is hard to separate fact from the fiction of the French propaganda against her in these regards.

Catherine had married the heir to the Russian throne in 1745 when she was only fifteen. She joined the Russian Orthodox Church and, largely self-taught, learned the Russian language and gained a brilliant general education through her widespread reading. After seventeen unsuccessful and unhappy years of marriage, she played an active part in the coup against her own husband, Emperor Peter III, who was overthrown and later killed by one of her lovers. Catherine herself assumed the throne as sole ruler of Russia.

Her long reign saw a number of reforms, including the continuation of Peter the Great's policy of introducing Western European culture to Russia; issues of public health and education were addressed and, before long, her new economic policies had gone some distance towards repairing the extensive legacy of neglect and damage that her predecessors had left behind. Science and the arts were allowed to flourish, and St. Petersburg became a cultural center. Catherine herself is credited with writing several operas.

On the death of Augustus III of Poland in 1763, Catherine used her extensive influence to have her own candidate, former lover Stanislaus Poniatowski, elected as the new king. Some years later, a treaty to divide Polish territory between Prussia, Russia, and Austria was signed in St. Petersburg, and Poland lost a third of its land and people. The largest part, some 36,000 square miles and home to two million people, went to Russia. The Poles revolted, but were quickly defeated by the Russian army. A second treaty in 1793 was signed by Prussia and Russia alone, Russia this time gaining another 89,000 square miles and three million people. After the following revolt had been promptly and conclusively suppressed, and the third treaty signed in 1795, Russia gained yet more territory.

By Catherine the Great's death in 1796—during a reported episode of unbridled passion—Poland had disappeared from the map. So it was that, as the eighteenth century drew to a close, Michal found himself living in Russia. He decided to travel even farther east, this time with Mordke and his grandson, Alexander. They were three generations of the same family who, all things being equal, could pass for three brothers. Michal, now known by the equivalent Russian name "Mikhail," knew that their best chance of survival and acceptance was to assimilate as thoroughly as possible into Russian culture. He also realized that they could not settle for too long in any town or city, but would have to move to a new location every twenty years or so to avoid suspicion. It was a necessary precaution in their daily existence, but a lifestyle they would all grow weary of before too long.

The three of them traveled alone, Mordke's wife having recently died—leaving him, as the last surviving member of the family, her own family's estate. The younger Alexander had to leave behind his bride-to-be, along with everything that could not be carried with them. Alexander did not understand why they had to go, for unlike his father he was not yet old enough to know that he was different.

"Why? Why do we have to leave?" he demanded.

Indeed, at this stage, Mikhail did not even know whether his grandson would be like them or not, and could not yet explain their reasons for leaving. "You will understand when you are older," was the only reason he could give for now; one that Alexander could not accept. "I can't tell you now."

Alexander was furious. "Either let me stay behind or let Reina come with us," he shouted. "You can't tell me why we're leaving, but you won't let me bring her either? So I have to leave behind my woman, and I get no reason why?" Mikhail could not yet tell him that they were both sacrifices he would have to become used to.

"Reina is promised to someone else," he told his grandson, knowing that the lie hid a far more dangerous truth. "I have seen them together and I have spoken to his family. If you get in his way he will harm you, as they threatened to harm me when I tried to intervene."

"I don't believe you," Alexander began angrily, but the smallest seed of doubt had been sown.

"It is true," Mordke confirmed. "We wanted to leave you behind with Reina, but it is best that you come with us now."

"Why?" he demanded.

"Reina knows that your mother was not Jewish," began Mikhail. Mordke had married a Christian woman—something they had not considered overly significant at the time. "She wishes to marry a Jewish man. You are not."

To Mikhail, the idea of sharing his life in marriage, once so appealing to him, held less and less interest. He had decided never to spend his life with a mortal woman again, except to exploit his own personal needs. Even Mordke, who had buried only one wife, understood the heartache that was best left uncultivated.

Alexander did not know this. Inconsolable in his grief and anger he had even attacked Mikhail; half-blinded by his tears, he had hurled a series of ineffective punches at him, only to find his elbow pinned to his waist with one hand and his grandfather's other hand at his throat in an iron grip that belied an unanticipated and surprising strength. Mikhail had dropped him to the floor, purple and semiconscious, after he had felt the struggling weaken and a long-forgotten memory had flashed through his mind: another face, shocked and unable to draw breath, helpless in his grip on the night he had left another life behind.

"Get up, Alexander. We're leaving now."

For the first time, Mikhail wondered what had happened to the knife he had used against his first attacker in Poland, the memory of which had returned to him. Perhaps he had dropped it in the forest, or perhaps Barak had found it when he found Mikhail's unconscious body, but had said nothing. He did not remember, but knew he needed to replace it.

He hauled Alexander to his feet, no longer angry. There was no emotion in his voice this time, only firm resolve. "We have to leave now."

Alexander did not argue with him again. No one spoke as they gathered their possessions and Mikhail retrieved the money from its hiding places. The last thing he took, while his son and grandson were waiting in the dark for him to come outside, was one of the long wooden-handled knives that Barak had taught him to use in making textiles. He would file it down later to something he could hide in his belt.

They left that night in silence to begin a long journey east, away from anyone who might know or remember them. Passing quickly through the villages and towns where Mikhail had once traveled to trade, first with Barak and then with Mordke, they stopped only infrequently and avoided any place where Mikhail knew he might be recognized. As they traveled further they saw only isolated clusters of houses, and comparative civilization gave way to vast tracts of empty land.

Mikhail's foresight had served them well, and in the years before Leba had finally passed away he had accumulated enough money for them to begin a comfortable new life on the shore of the Black Sea. He was still different, but no longer unique or alone—this time he had a family with him. Alexander grew up and learned what he was from his father, as Mordke had in turn once learned from Mikhail. Although Mikhail was and always would be first among equals, they lived together ostensibly as brothers and no one could ever have guessed that there was a decade, let alone almost a century, between oldest and youngest.

For a long time there was only the three of them, carrying on their business quietly and avoiding drawing attention to themselves. Mikhail began to sow the seeds of their future. Knowing how long they would live, they carried out their business on the scale of decades and centuries, not weeks and months. Making money fast was not necessary, and he taught his family to avoid investments with anything but the lowest of risks. Where an imperishable commodity was cheap, they bought, knowing that it did not matter whether it was months or years before the price rose: they could wait. When they were able, they bought land and houses and rented them to tenants.

Some years later, as time passed and their business prospered, they began to feel the burden of living a nomadic existence, and sought a way to put down roots without attracting suspicion. Mikhail did not voice his misgivings about finding a permanent place to stay, wanting a home as much as the others. Once again each felt the loneliness of his existence, and each sought female companionship.

## 21

Edward Sherman first met Emily Preston Richards when she was working on her PhD in biology. Their academic interests overlapped to an extent to where they crossed paths several times over her last two years of study. Edward was often a guest lecturer at the Oxford university that she attended, and they spoke briefly a few times at conferences and academic events, mostly about their shared areas of interest.

Emily had found Dr. Sherman to be a remarkably intelligent person—more than usual for a research scientist. She quickly realized that his expertise spanned more than the areas of genetics that his work encompassed. And, as well as being interesting, he was also considerate and polite—a rarity among elite scientists.

Sherman's own first impressions of Emily were of an intelligent and capable but otherwise unexceptional scientist. She was quite friendly and bright, although there was nothing that set her apart from the other researchers he met on a daily basis. They had parted ways at the end of the last conference, a large gathering held in Germany, without either of them thinking much more about their meeting.

A year later Emily had turned up in his lab in London, looking to apply for a research post at the university. Sherman had taken the time to show her around, explaining the project and demonstrating some of the equipment they used. On this occasion they talked in a little more depth about his work cataloguing rogue genes, and his theories about specific genes for longevity. Emily had shown a real interest in the work, he remembered. She had told him that two of her great-grandparents had lived to over a hundred, and that her grandmother was well into her nineties.

"Maybe there's something in it." He remembered her words exactly, the inflections in her voice and the way she smiled when she said it. He had almost laughed when he heard that; he found her understatement dryly humorous, knowing that there was more in it than she could guess, and more about him than she would ever find out. Instead, he had taken the opportunity it offered.

"Perhaps you would like to find out?"

She was momentarily uncertain what he meant, before he explained himself. "A lot of our data come from people who believe—or have convinced themselves—that they are at particular risk from genetically related diseases. That takes care of one side of things. What we don't get enough of are people who have absolutely nothing wrong with them. We've been looking for people like you, who have close relatives who lived a long time, to see if we can pinpoint a genetic characteristic that might explain their old age."

"What would I have to do?" she asked cautiously.

"Just give us a few cc's of blood. We'll do the rest."

Emily made mild protestations, and Sherman found out later—much later, when they were good friends—that she had a phobia of needles. "What about the cost? Isn't it still extremely expensive to sequence someone's DNA just on a whim?"

"It is expensive for those who seek us out, but for those we want to study—it's covered by government and private grants." He paused, as if to give her a sense of her responsibility. "Besides, aren't you just a little curious?"

Emily smiled and agreed to the test, despite her lack of enthusiasm for syringes. She had to admit she *was* more than a little curious, and it was an opportunity she wasn't likely to see again.

She left to return to Oxford the same evening, interested in his work and convinced she would apply for the post. Sherman had decided not to hire her; he perceived Emily as too inexperienced for his leading-edge research. Anyway, he had several other candidates that had interested him more, and were better qualified. That changed a week later when the result of her test came back. He thought there had been an error at first, and sent one of the spare samples out to be reprocessed. They came back with the same result.

For two days he stared at her DNA sequence, unable to believe what the computer had told him. He did not let on to his colleagues, only asking if they had taken due care when preparing the samples. Emily Preston Richards really did have a clean slate. She was free of any of the defects and abnormalities usually found in donors.

*But there was more.* Ms. Preston Richards also had one of the two gene combinations for the M-Trait, the Methuselah characteristic he suspected of stopping him from aging—*she was halfway to being an Ultra!* The odds were enormously against it, yet there it was: Emily had found him.

At that moment, Dr. Edward Sherman knew he would hire her. She represented a chance that might never come again, and he had been alone for long enough. He was tired of that life. Emily would be the basis for his prize work.

# 22

Emily lay back in the bathtub, a CD of Bach's cantatas playing on the stereo in her kitchen through the open door of the bathroom. Her schoolgirl German was pretty rusty, but she still enjoyed picking out some of the lines she learned years ago when she sang in the choir.

She was seven months pregnant now, and it felt really good to take the weight off her feet and relax in the hot water. Stiff joints, knotted muscles, sore back—the aches and pains gradually melted away; the hot water did its work as she lay prone in the half-dark bathroom, lit only by a flickering candle.

Bath time was her time to unwind mentally, to perform emotional stocktaking and untangle the contents of her mind at the end of a long week. In another two months, she knew, these opportunities for peace and time out would become a lot rarer. Parenthood was difficult enough as it was; the demands on her as a single mother would make things harder still. It might have been good to have a child with her now ex-husband—to have been a proper family. Sadly, that was not to be.

She had met James Richards at Imperial College as an undergraduate, and they had married during the third year of her PhD at Oxford, when she was twenty-six. He had studied electrical engineering and then found a consultancy job in London, which required a 100-kilometer commute to the city each day from their rented flat in the center of Oxford. For a while everything seemed to be going well, although between the long hours at work and his three-hour round trip, they did not see as much of each other as they would have liked.

As James' job responsibilities increased—along with the pay—his hours grew longer still and he decided to rent a flat in London and return to Oxford only on the weekends. It would not be so bad, he insisted; he could come back Friday evenings and leave Monday mornings. Knowing that her postgraduate work tied them both to Oxford, Emily felt she had to make the concession. It would only be temporary after all, she told herself.

When Emily finally graduated, she lined up the research job with Dr. Sherman in London and it seemed that, at last, things would work out. The long distance had brought with it a distance in their relationship—James always seemed tense, and they argued constantly. She looked forward to moving into the flat in London, and spending quality time together.

But it was not to be. Two months after moving to London—during which time it seemed that they somehow saw even less of each other—James moved out to live with someone else. Emily never suspected anything, and she had no choice but to file for divorce. It was devastating.

Emily had seen them together only once, a few months after he left her. She had gone out after work one Friday with some of her colleagues, keen to make the effort to make some new friends. They ended up at a bar drinking cocktails, somewhere near James' office. He was there, sitting at the bar with a drink in one hand and his arm around her. Emily stared for several seconds, unable to choke back the tears as all the feelings she had been keeping back boiled to the surface. Then James glanced over—looking at her and right through her—before turning back to the bar again without so much as an acknowledgement, though she knew he surely must have seen her—she was nothing to him. That set her back months; it felt like the first day he had left her. After that, she was careful to avoid any of the places she thought he might go.

Amidst the breakup, there had been one positive thing—Edward Sherman had proven to be more than an employer. And it was largely due to his friendship that Emily had managed to trudge through those first agonizing months. Somehow, despite his busy research schedule, Edward always managed to find time for her, taking her to dinner, or forcing her out to see a movie or play.

Edward remained a good friend as she gradually dealt with the divorce and slowly returned to a normal state of emotional equilibrium. And she slowly began to develop feelings for him, and he for her in return—all the more significant for the way he had treated her as a friend first, never asking for more than that. Though they found that they were best suited to friendship in the end, the six months she had spent in that close relationship with him had given her back the self-confidence and independence that she had lost during her divorce. Edward had definitely been a silver lining around that James-shaped cloud.

Emily reached for the faucet with her toes to run some more hot water into the bath. It had been half an hour now, and her skin was starting to show wrinkles, but she wasn't ready to leave her watery sanctuary. The Bach CD ended and the stereo paused with a *whirr* for a second before the next one started to play, a collection of Beethoven sonatas.

With the heat of the new water, Emily relaxed again. From Edward, her thoughts moved to that new man in her life, the man who had seemingly appeared out of nowhere. Emily was not sure what to make of Tom. It was quite possible that his intentions were platonic, and that he had just seen something in her that interested him, but why would a single, handsome man be interested in a pregnant woman? He hadn't asked about a husband or boyfriend. Perhaps he really didn't care, and was honestly looking for a little friendship. Still, it was a bit strange.

She had talked about him with Karen, one of her friends from the university, over lunch the day after he had offered to meet up after her yoga class.

"So, what, he just asked you out of the blue?" Karen was instantly skeptical.

"No, it wasn't like that. We met before, he fixed my car last week after yoga. I could have been waiting for hours otherwise. Then we bumped into each other again after his karate class."

"Ok, fair enough, so he's the knight in shining armor. Still, what's a single man doing going after you? No offense intended, Emily, but you don't exactly look available."

This had crossed her mind, and the only answer she could think of was that he *wasn't* interested in romance—so why lose out on a friendship as a result? "Sure, it's strange, but I don't think he was hitting on me. I mean, I'm obviously not free for that."

"Does he know that, though?"

"Hmm," said Emily, leaning back on her seat to show off the extent of her bulge. She raised an eyebrow at Karen. "I'm guessing he probably noticed at one point or another."

Karen conceded the point, though not entirely happily. "If in doubt, I always go with my gut instincts. What were your first impressions of him?"

"To be honest," she began, "I was so worried and fed up about the car that I'd probably have been pleased to see Genghis Khan if he was a halfway decent mechanic. After that—he seemed nice enough. No bad vibes, not too intense—just friendly." The other side of it had also come to mind: that he was being nice to her precisely because it was obvious she was a single, expectant mother. In that case, the offer was a sympathy vote—a depressing thought. "He might just have felt sorry for me," she wondered out loud.

"He's got nothing to feel sorry about," corrected Karen immediately. "Neither do you. Just because you're pregnant doesn't make you a charity case."

This time, Emily conceded the point without arguing. "I can't figure it out," she said, simply.

"What's to figure? He met you and saw something he liked. Okay, so you don't know his motives, but don't go jumping to conclusions and feeling sorry for yourself without finding out first."

"I guess. Maybe I should just go along and see."

"You've got nothing to lose, as long as you don't do anything silly like give him your phone number. If he's a good guy, then fine. If he does turn out to be Genghis Khan after all, it's not like you have to see him again, right?"

This was what Emily had been thinking. She could meet him once, see how things went, and judge what to do on the basis of that. If he turned out to be weird, or clingy, or needy—so long, Tom. If not, it would be a nice surprise.

In the end, she met him at the coffee place he had suggested. It turned out that he was a recent divorcé, and it was obviously something he was still working through. Her overall impression was that he was just a little lonely, if anything. They had chatted over their hot drinks, and at the end of an hour and a half, she found herself glad she had gone. Tom was clearly an intelligent man, and she missed smart company outside her work. They even talked about her work at the university, and she managed to persuade him to go in and give a blood sample sometime, just in case it turned up something.

The water in the tub had turned cold. She sighed, knowing how hard it would be to extricate her pregnant body from the tub. Emily stared at her round protruding abdomen and wondered about the living being within. She had thought long and hard about having this child—not about having *a* child, she had always wanted a child—but about having a child alone.

Edward discussed it with her at length and helped her come to the conclusion that she could have one without fear. With a good job in a growth industry, money would never be an object. And, since genetic research wasn't exactly stressful, she knew she could spend the time required to ensure a loving home.

After that, the decision had been easy. Edward had checked and fine-tuned Zoe's DNA before the egg was implanted. And he was in charge of finding the right sperm donor. Emily didn't want to know anything about the father, as long as Zoe was perfectly healthy—as perfect as a human could be.

# 23

With peace and gradual, inexorable prosperity, the small band grew into a fraternity, a brotherhood of men destined to outlive their contemporaries by centuries—*A lifetime in every decade, a decade in every year.* In their unity, they found strength and learned to put everything aside for each other knowing that the world would not tolerant their kind. Although separated by generations in time, physically they were brothers and therefore lived as equals—with Mikhail as first among equals.

As has happened before in the history of the world, these sons of God intermarried with the daughters of men and had children by them. The ones who did not age were accepted in their turn as Brothers and those who proved mortal were periodically purged as the time came for them to leave the place they had sojourned in and travel to the next town. They truly were rolling stones, gathering no moss, and time *was* on their side.

With age comes experience, but after a certain point there is not enough new experience to set someone apart. For those who refuse to grow old, there is nothing new under the sun and meaning can be found only with each other. The security of the group was the key to their identity and continued survival, and they sacrificed everything for its sake—even their closest relatives. What, when all was said and done, was a mortal life worth, when compared to the infinity of a dozen potentially endless existences? Though the Brothers did not draw attention to themselves by killing indiscriminately, they had few qualms about taking life when their needs dictated it.

Arguments within their number were few, because something stronger than blood held them together. Violence was unheard of among the twelve, for the price of taking an eternity away in killing would surely be unbearable. With each other they were in accord, Brothers in more than just name and blood. There was a quiet, almost godly peace among them, as might be expected within the walls of a monastery. For the century since Mikhail came to Russia with Mordke and Alexander, it was a golden, peaceful age for them.

Though long-lived, the Brothers knew that they were not invulnerable to disease or injury. Alexander's own son, his second to join their number, had been killed by a man who robbed him as he returned home in the dark from a neighboring town. Retribution on the murderer, his family and everything they owned had been swift, merciless, and total.

It was not only death that they feared, but the accidents and illnesses common to man, that are hardly endurable over the span of a normal lifetime. The collection of genetic anomalies that had somehow come together in Mikhail's perfect body was not always repeated, for every new marriage might introduce a new element of imperfection. Who could know how a child would turn out until it was too late? There was intelligent, incisive Anton with his raven-black hair and flowing beard, but eyes clouded by glaucoma, and unseeing. Dmitriy, once tall and handsome but now crippled by arthritis, was hunched in pain and barely able to lift his own feet to walk. Sergei limped from the polio that had afflicted him so early in life. Though they might be intended by nature to live for a millennium, it did not mean that they would be healthy forever.

Only Mikhail seemed free from any complaint, and had never been sick for even a day since the fever that had brought him to Barak's house. One pristine original, a perfect man who was the father of them all: he was a new Adam for a new race, a son of God who could beget only lesser copies of himself with the daughters of men.

The community of near-immortal men reached a ceiling of twelve, midway through the nineteenth century. For a while, there was equilibrium; it seemed that every new child born and accepted would push out another man, as if the world could not bear the existence of more than a dozen of their kind. Dmitriy took his own life, knowing that he would never again be the man he used to be, with only to further suffering and physical deterioration to look forward to. His grandson, named Dmitriy after him, was brought in when it was realized what his father and grandfather had passed on to the child. Fyodor had been a young man who had been conscripted into the army, and never returned from fighting in the Crimean War. His proud, dignified presence was replaced by the quiet and unassuming Artur.

    In 1859, four years after Alexander II had become the sixteenth Romanov Tsar of Russia, the fraternity again left their home and headed north for what would turn out to be their last move. Finally, they would achieve everything they had hoped monetarily, and it would be the height of their existence. And also, in their achievement lay the beginning of the end.

# 24

This day, Tom arrived at Dr. Sherman's house in torrential rain, one of the brief but intense showers that had sporadically and quite unpredictably been interrupting the humid July days. In the five-minute walk from his car he had become absolutely soaked, his jeans and thin cotton tee shirt sticking uncomfortably to his skin as he entered the back garden while the fickle sunlight returned. The cat had not managed to escape the deluge either, and now she arched her back and shook herself, unsure whether to trust her favorite spot of path or not. The two of them stood for a while by the back door, gently steaming as they dried. Tom tried a tickle under the chin but her hair was wet and clumped together and she was disgruntled by the shower and didn't want any of it. The tabby retired to a bush and he let himself in, feeling slightly cheated.

To compensate, he treated himself to a cup of filtered coffee from Sherman's excellent coffee machine in the kitchen. It was a cheeky move—a way to thumb his nose at both Sherman and the man who had given him his orders. Tom was tired of the repeated warnings that the doctor must never know that he had been there. He was always scrupulously careful, and knew exactly what was at stake. The lack of confidence in his abilities was at times wearying. Tom searched briefly for biscuits, but there were none; obviously the doctor was not the biscuit type. That did not surprise him; you didn't get to be as old as Edward by eating junk food, M-Trait or not.

Weather notwithstanding, he was feeling good about himself. He enjoyed these visits to Sherman's house, gathering information while his enemy was absent at the university, completely unaware of Tom's intrusion. The coffee was particularly satisfying after his drenching, and he stood looking out into the garden holding the mug against his chest to warm up. He was pleased that the doctor had opted for a mesh filter. Filter papers retained some of the coffee's natural oils and robbed the drink of its essential flavor and aroma, and he never enjoyed that type quite so much.

Once he had washed and dried the cup and coffee filter and returned them to their places, Tom decided to take another look at the computer upstairs. The curtains in the study were still drawn and the lights were out, so the room was lit only by the shifting colors of the computer's screensaver. The window faced over the driveway at the front and although it was daytime, Tom did not want to draw attention to his presence there by turning on the lights. He sat in the semi-dark, in Sherman's comfortable leather swivel chair, turning left and right as he considered the screen. Behind the screensaver, which disappeared after he touched the infrared mouse on the desk, the monitor instantly presented the last thing that Sherman had been working on.

The doctor clearly did not keep all of his research here—the kind of storage space he would need to hold data gained from sequencing so many DNA molecules made that impractical—but he did keep some of his records at home. The folder that Tom was looking at had perhaps a hundred files in it, each headed with names like *KREHMAN02-07-84* and *JDAVIS05-03-22*, which he assumed represented subjects and their date of birth. He clicked one, opening a file in the database program that was sitting in a window behind the folder on top. It was a summary of the more extensive results from a DNA test:

| | |
|---|---|
| **Name:** | **Khan Rehman** |
| **Date of Birth:** | **March 7, 1984** |
| **Ancestral Derivation:** | **Indian, Punjabis, all else <5%** |
| **Genetic Disorders:** | **Protanomalous color blindness; Poor metabolization of B-vitamin complexes.** |
| **M-Trait:** | **- - Negative** |

Khan, it appeared from this brief synopsis, was unlikely to die from any inherited diseases, though he was slightly less able to see red than most people—a relatively common condition that he might not even be aware of, and which would affect his life very little. Unsurprisingly, he did lack Sherman's Methuselah Trait, which would stop his body from aging. Unless Khan ran afoul of any traffic lights, and as long as he kept taking his vitamins, it seemed that he could expect a long and healthy life.

Sherman's computer came equipped with a CD writer, but Tom had had a better idea. Two weeks ago, partly with this in mind, he had purchased an MP3 player. Sleek, lightweight and extremely portable, he had taken to wearing it around his neck when he went running, replacing his tapes and the clunky and obsolete CD player he used to listen to. It would run for twelve hours on a single AAA cell, and the plug-and-play technology of the MP3 player allowed him to copy music files quickly and easily from his computer at home. With 256 MB of memory, it could store several hours of listening time. The beauty of it was that it could be used for *any* computer data: music files or otherwise. Kneeling behind Sherman's desk, Tom plugged it into the USB port at the back of the computer. After a few moments, the computer flashed up a message and the MP3 player appeared as a new disk drive.

It was the work of a minute to copy all the summary files for perusal at his leisure on his own computer back in his flat. Tom disconnected the player and hung it around his neck again. He had to go soon, but he could not resist a quick peek at Sherman's email first. Sitting on the comfortable computer chair, he spent a few moments flipping through the open email window, seeing if there was anything new and interesting. *Nada*.

Time to leave. He swiveled on the chair and closed the program with a click. *Damn!—only meant to close that one window*. It was his first mistake to date in Sherman's house, and it shocked him out of the complacent mood he had drifted into at his easy success. *Can't re-open it—it's password protected!*

The program remotely accessed the database at the university, and without the password Tom could not bring up the right pages. The password would, ironically, be stored in the key-logger he had installed last time. Tom unplugged the keylogger and put it in his pocket. There was no way he had time to get home, search through all the material it had recorded for Sherman's password, and get back here to fix the mistake. He sat for a minute in thought, now regarding the screen without moving as he tried to think of a solution. *Such a small thing, will Sherman notice? Probably no, but maybe. Would he attribute it to absent-mindedness on his part? Perhaps. Can I afford him to be curious? No.*

Another pause and precious seconds ticked away before he made a decision. *Better to be safe.* Tom rose from the chair. *Where's the fuse box? Under the stairs?* He strolled down the stairway and around it, finding a small alcove and a panel. *Yes. Circuit breakers—shut off each switch or just the main? The main.* Click off, click on. Sherman would now come home to blinking clocks that needed to be reset, hardly a victim from such a minor power outage. And, of course, the computer would have to be powered up again.

Tom locked up the house, painfully conscious of his mistake. It was an infuriating thing to have to admit in his report after the repeated warnings from the old man. He was not worried about being discovered, but it would complicate things if Sherman realized someone had been in his house and was more careful in the future. He would not be able to go back if an alarm system was installed. Under the circumstances, perhaps it would be better not to report the incident unless it was really necessary.

It had stopped raining now, but he drove home much more slowly than he needed to. He downloaded the files he had stolen from Sherman onto the laptop, but did not look through them. He instead practiced some flamenco finger strokes on one of his guitars in an attempt to relax.

It was a while before he went back to Sherman's house, and his next visit would be even worse.

# 25

Eduard Chermen knew little of his origins. His mother had died just after his birth, and his father had raised him until he died when Eduard was thirteen. At fifteen, Eduard married a local girl, Karina, and eventually began a family of his own. Until his son was in his teens, he supposed his life had been little different from those of any of the other villagers in agrarian Russia. Life as a peasant farmer of the rich man's fields was not always easy, but he was thankful for what he had. He did not question why his face and body had remained young and healthy, while his neighbors slowly began to age around him.

Like the other villagers, Eduard also never asked many questions about the group that lived within the walled enclosure, next to the settlement. Evidently some kind of landed nobility or religious sect, they kept to themselves. They were sometimes seen in the town, moving in groups—never alone, and they all looked the same—hooded figures in long coats and long dark beards. The older villagers called them "long with age."

Sometimes villagers would be hired to work within the walls, but even then, they knew little about their employers. Who really cared? Wages were wages, and this odd lot could be as introverted as they liked if they paid well.

Occasionally, one of these men married a woman from the village. And years later a young girl, offspring of that woman, would be returned to her family to be raised in the village. They always brought enough money with them to live comfortably, and few questions were asked. But the villagers understood. Only male children were desired. And the women who bore children to the men "long with age?" Their families rarely saw them again.

One evening, Eduard had been stopped by two of these men as he returned to his house. They had been polite, courteous but firm. Eduard was to accompany them; a man in the castle wished to talk to him. Curious, and sensing no ill will, he followed them.

That was the first time he had met Mikhail, another dark, bearded man with intelligent eyes but an expression that otherwise gave nothing away.

"So, you are Rada's son."

Eduard had not heard his mother's name spoken in over twenty years; he did not know anyone still knew it. "Yes. You knew her?"

Mikhail nodded. "She was a member of my family." He allowed a while for that to sink in. "You are a member of my family. I would like you to join us here."

Eduard had not known what to say. He had so many questions—about his mother, why she had returned to the village, why he had not known earlier—but did not know where to begin. Mikhail held up his hand.

"Let me explain. The female children of my family suffer an affliction. Usually they do not survive beyond childhood. We felt it better that Rada be allowed her freedom to enjoy her short life. It seems that she survived longer than usual and bore you. We did not know she had a son until recently."

There was no emotion in his voice as he spoke of the death of his relative. "You are her son, and you belong here." He spoke with finality; his invitation was more a statement of fact.

Eduard was uneasy. "But my life is in the village. I have a wife, and a child of my own. I can't leave them."

"They will be welcome here too." Mikhail paused. "What is there for you outside, Eduard? What kind of life do you have to look forward to? Tilling the soil until you die with the others? We can give you more than that. It is your birthright. We are your family."

Family. Eduard had barely known his mother, and his father had worked himself to an early grave. He knew that Mikhail was right; here in the rich man's castle, he and his family might have a future. A week later, he took his wife, Karina, his son, Kostya, and a few possessions to his new home. He never did forgive himself for his lack of insight.

The new surroundings brought a difficult time for the family. They mixed little with the other members of this group, who called themselves "the Brotherhood." From what Eduard could gather, there had been some doubt as to whether he should be allowed to stay there or not. It seems that the matter fell to vote in the end, and enough of the twelve of them had thought he was worth looking after to bring the three of them in.

It was some weeks before Mikhail, the one who passed for their leader, took him aside and explained what he was really doing there; he had been able to get nothing from the others. Mikhail invited Eduard to talk privately again, in the same room they had spoken in the first time. He pointed behind Eduard, to a long mirror that hung on the wall.

"What do you see when you look at yourself, Eduard?"

Eduard turned to look at his reflection. He did not know what Mikhail wanted from him.

"What do you see? A man of twenty-five, or a man of fifty?"

Then Eduard began to realize what was going on. He had only recently begun to worry about his apparent age; his youthful appearance had started to attract comment from the other villagers. They were old beyond their years, aged by their hard lives and the long hours of work, and Eduard had begun to stand out.

"As I told you before, the women of my family often suffer an illness that kills them in their early years, like your mother. But the men live far, far longer than any normal man." Mikhail looked closely at him. "And like us, you have begun to attract attention because of it. Do you understand now, Eduard? That is why we live here. And you must never tell anyone. We can protect you here, living away from anyone who might harm us. But outside, people will find out, they will be jealous, and they will kill you. And your son, Kostya—perhaps he will be the same."

Eduard had nodded, trying at once to take in what this meant and to appreciate the support he was being offered. "Thank you, Mikhail."

The other Brothers were all the same—men who looked only twenty- five or thirty but were at least a century old. They were very secretive, or perhaps that was just how they were around him. They rarely spoke Russian when he was in the room. The thirteen men ate together in the big hall, alone and undisturbed by anyone else. The women and children were excluded from that room and from several others.

The dark hall was lit by candles and torches, and he sat among the twelve men in the flickering light. To begin with, they rarely spoke to him directly, although he had the impression that they spoke to each other about him as they talked in a mixture of Polish, Yiddish, and German. He also had the distinct impression that some of them did not trust him or want him around. That became more apparent after he had heard and accepted what Mikhail had to say. He was already middle-aged by modern standards when they took him in, though his body was still as healthy as his son's.

His knowledge of the Brotherhood grew very gradually, a piece here and a piece there as the years passed. Secrecy, all-important to the dozen men, prevailed within the walls as well as without. Slowly, some of them began to trust him. Eduard, like the other Brothers, came and went as he pleased, although in practice that was not frequently. The women were rarely allowed outside the walls, though he did not see many other than his own wife. When the men did leave, it was together and at night whenever possible. Hooded figures, moving in the darkness beyond the walls; he remembered their comings and goings as they went back and forth on business in which he was never allowed to take part. He knew that there was a lot going on that he was never permitted to know about, though with the benefit of hindsight he could guess some of it now. He was not born among them and was never instructed in their ways—it was too late for him. Living outside the walls for too long and his village values were ingrained. It was even worse for his wife, Karina.

Mordke stopped Eduard in a long hallway to complain about her one evening.

"Karina visits her family in the village too much. You must curtail your wife—she puts everyone at risk," he said.

Controlling his wife was not a practice that Edward found useful in his marriage. In fact, he had often depended on Karina's inner strength to help withstand the hardships of life. But because of his special gift of youthfulness, he nodded in agreement to Mordke.

Later, he tried to explain to his wife. "Karina, please, you must not anger the Brothers. Why do you visit the village so much? You have everything you need here."

"There is nothing to do in this cold palace. I miss my family—so I visit them." Karina stared back at her husband, not in defiance, but in hope that he understood her plight. Then she reached up with her hand and stroked Eduard's face. "Ah, my Edik, you are still so handsome—almost like that spring day I first laid eyes on you in the fields."

Eduard remembered that day, seeing Karina stare at him among the rows that he tilled while she sowed seed. Plump and pretty, he too had become smitten at first glance. Now she was almost fifty, her hair gray and face withered from the years they had farmed together.

"Please Karina," he pleaded, tears welling up in his eyes.

"Your secret is safe with me—and your son's secret, too." She smiled at her husband, and patted him gently. "Who cares about the wanderings of an old woman, anyway?"

Karina died peacefully but suddenly in her sleep not long after. She had been old, though not sick. Eduard just thought it was her time. None of the Brothers cared, or expressed any concern or surprise. She was nothing to them, like everyone else mortal—temporary, only there to serve and be used. When they saw him grieving, they had actually laughed and asked, "What do you expect?"

There was a Russian proverb that they kept telling him, "*Pyeryed smyert'yu nye nadyshish'sya*"—"couldn't breathe enough before death." The Brothers thought it was very funny.

After she was buried, things started to change a little. The Brothers began to accept him and his son—Kostya was one of them, too. They wanted Eduard to remarry and have more sons, but he would not. Maybe that was a part of their reason for rejecting him.

    Life went on for another ten or fifteen years, isolated from the rest of the world except when the Brothers decided otherwise. Outside, in the village, families came and went, people were born and died, whole lives lived out while the Brotherhood changed so little. It was a privileged existence. They were rich, and away from the harm of daily life, hunger and disease. It had occurred to him before to leave, but he and Kostya had nowhere to go that was as safe, and he knew that their best chance lay in unity and the protection the Brotherhood offered.

    The end, when it came, was sudden.

# 26

Sometime towards dawn, the brightening colors of sunrise leached into the monochrome plane of grays. Tom sat in a chair near the big picture window, waiting for the day to catch up with him. Over in the kitchen, the coffee machine was ending its percolation, the noises and aroma of brewing coffee filling his world. The flat was centrally heated and well insulated and so, despite the unusually chilly start to the summer day outside, it was warm enough for him to need no clothes other than the shorts he slept in.

Tom moved over to the table and fired up the laptop computer on it. From the web browser, he started a search on the term "Nitro-Z" from the prescription he'd found in Sherman's refrigerator the first day he was in the doctor's house. The question, however, only occurred to him the day before—*why would someone who can seemingly live forever, need a prescription?*

His internet connection was fast and the search engine quickly brought up page after page of results. The quick answer: Nitro-Z was a generic brand name for Nitroglycerin. How curious that a substance that is used as a high explosive should be found in a medicine bottle. What was it for? He changed his search to "Nitroglycerin" and pressed "Enter" on the keyboard.

Tom wandered back through to the kitchen and poured himself a mug of coffee, lightened with just a little low-fat milk, before sitting back down at the computer. He opened the first page the search engine had brought up and began reading.

> ***Nitroglycerin is the accepted medication for Angina Pectoris, a recurring pain in the chest, arising when the heart does not receive enough blood (myocardial ischemia). Angina is characterized by a crushing pain, often in the chest under the***

*sternum, but sometimes also in the shoulders, arms, back, neck and jaw.*

*People with stable angina (or chronic stable angina) have episodes of chest discomfort that are usually predictable. They occur on exertion, under mental stress, or emotional stress. Normally the chest discomfort is relieved with rest, Nitroglycerin, or both.*

So, Sherman wasn't perfect after all. This was all good material, and Tom clicked the "Back" arrow on his browser and selected another page at random, looking for anything new and interesting.

*Because the attack is caused by a lack of oxygen to the heart muscle, forms of atmospheric pollution, smoke inhalation, and carbon monoxide poisoning are liable to be more dangerous than to an otherwise healthy person.*

Tom was sure that Sherman did not smoke, or drink other than in the strictest moderation; he seemed to be very health conscious from the evidence in his kitchen. The idea of emotional stress amused him. Would it be possible literally to scare the doctor to death? He read on.

*Someone with angina is at higher risk of heart attack, but an angina episode is not an indication of a heart attack. When the pattern of angina attacks changes, however—becoming more frequent and irregular, more intense or longer lasting—the chance of a heart attack is significantly increased.*

Tom browsed a few more websites before quitting the search. He wondered whether the heart disease was something that Sherman had inherited from his parents, or that had arisen on its own during the course of the doctor's long life. Most likely it was a combination, from what he understood about the subject of genetics.

He rose from the computer, finishing his coffee as he did so, and walked through to the kitchen to pour a second mug. He placed a cinnamon and raisin bagel in the toaster, which he would eat dry, and poured a tall glass of fresh orange juice to go with the coffee. Tom was exceptionally careful about his own diet and health, eager to avoid the complications that old age might otherwise hold in store for him. Caffeine, he realized as he stared into the swirling patterns of milk mixing with coffee in his mug, was his one regular vice. He did not know whether his body was capable of dealing with it or not on a long term basis. Possibly his visit to Sherman's lab could answer that question.

Tom thought about the rest of the morning. Perhaps he would go for a run and sketch out, in his mind, the rudiments of Dr. Sherman's untimely death.

## 27

The epiphany had come two years ago, only a week before Emily visited London to interview with him. Dr. Sherman's research was at its lowest point. The amount of data collected had become overwhelming and even though he had discovered the M-Trait within himself, there seemed to be no one else in the world with any hint of his unique gene characteristics from which to build upon.

For longer than he had been involved in genetic research, Sherman believed that Ultra-mortality was the preserve of the male. The Brotherhood had taught this to him—they did not waste time and resources on female offspring who didn't seem to last much more than a decade in their life span. Whereas Edward had first assumed that there was a misogynistic streak in the Brotherhood, his research unlocked the secrets of the M-Trait, and he finally understood—the Brotherhood's chauvinism was based purely on the genetic aftereffects they encountered.

Half of every person's DNA comes from each parent. A male has an X and a Y chromosome, and passes on one of those to his offspring; a female has two X chromosomes, and so can pass on only one or the other X. Since only men were Ultra-mortal, Edward had reasoned that the M-Trait must rest on the Y chromosome, the definitive genetic characteristic of the male. It was the obvious place to start, and Edward devoted hours every day to the task, above and beyond the full-time work he already carried out pinpointing and cataloguing inherited diseases.

Initially optimistic, Edward became frustrated in his efforts. Analysis of his own Y chromosome produced nothing out of the ordinary. Reluctantly, he abandoned the model and looked for another explanation. Surely the trait was somehow sex-linked? If it didn't lie on the Y chromosome, then what about the X chromosome? Maybe it was carried by females, but only showed up in males—like hemophilia. Unfortunately, that did not explain how the trait was carried directly from father to son, since it was the father's Y chromosome that was passed on to the son, not the X—the Methuselah trait did not skip generations like that.

Edward finally decided that the trait was not carried on *either* sex chromosome, which meant that women were equally affected by the trait. But why were there no Ultra-mortal women? In fact, female children of Ultra-mortals tended to die much earlier than average. Mikhail had rarely tolerated the presence of a female child in the Brotherhood, knowing they would not last past puberty, let alone live to the ages the Brothers reached. So what was this trait? Exasperated, Edward started over.

Unsure of where to begin, he sequenced his whole DNA—at that stage, a task that took considerably longer than it did now, when the sequencing software was still in its early years. His database was rudimentary, and the catalogue of genetic defects he had collected was less than a third of what they now had. At a loss what else to do, he ran his DNA through the gamut of tests. On the computer system running at the time, it would take a week to return any results. When they came, Edward stared at the list of figures—pages and pages of printouts—without a clue what he was looking for. It was the proverbial "needle in the haystack." He was ready to give up.

The turning point came the next day, late in the lab when his eyes were burning and his brain was fuddled from tiredness. He was finishing for the night, locking the store cupboard before he left. On the workbench by the cupboard, someone had left out a bottle—he did not even remember the contents now, though it must have been something toxic. His eyes were drawn only to the warning label on the side: a square of orange that contained the skull-and-crossbones symbol, indicating harmful contents. Edward, his mind full of base-pairs, codons and chromosomes, saw only an XX beneath the skull.

Newton's theory of gravity was inspired when he saw an apple fall to the ground. The chemist Kekulé grasped the cyclical structure of the benzene molecule only after dreaming of a snake biting its own tail. Edward's own revelation was sparked by the juxtaposition he saw: death and the double X—the same as the female chromosome XX. And then the answer flowed through him: the Brothers' female children didn't die because of the M-Trait. *They died because of something else passed along with it—something that affected women only.*

Two days later, after he had cross-referenced his DNA to everything relevant in the database, he finally found it. There it was, on the long arm of chromosome 18: a gene related to the regulation of tissue production in the lungs, mutated so that it could no longer do its work. This genetic component was present in males as well as females, but the ultimate development of the disease was triggered by estrogen production and so almost exclusively affected women of childbearing age.

Lymphangioleiomyomatosis was the technical term for it, a mouthful Sherman couldn't even pronounce—thankfully he found it abbreviated to LAM. The disease affected females soon after the onset of puberty: the lungs were invaded by abnormal muscle tissue that grew unimpeded, thus progressively blocking the airways. At first, a little shortness of breath would be the only noticeable symptom. Later, as the disease worsened, the subject developed chest pain, irreparable lung damage, and finally, pneumonia.

The pieces of the puzzle rapidly came together for Sherman. The M-Trait could be passed to women as often as it was to men. But it brought with it a separate, corrupt gene that could not be repaired. And it explained where Edward came from. His mother, who bore him at the early age of 13, had died when he was still an infant. Now, Edward realized that she had been lucky to reach the age she did. The condition that claimed her life in his infancy would normally have taken her life before motherhood. Because of this, he had inherited his Methuselah genes from his mother.

Edward now owned all the puzzle pieces of his own biology. He just needed to be patient—it was only a matter of time before technology progressed far enough for him to manipulate DNA. His position at the university was safe for as long as he chose to stay there—he had tenure—and the only factor that would cause him to leave was his unchanging face. He thought that he could manage another ten years before people started asking too many questions, and he would have to move on. But it probably wouldn't take even that long—scientific discoveries abounded almost daily. After that, he only needed the right specimen, the right egg to fertilize with his ageless seed.

And then a second miraculous event happened—Emily walked into his life, with her pristine DNA and one of the Methuselah genes. Had he not sampled her blood when she visited, he would have hired someone else for the job, and the fertile ground for his greatest work might have never been realized.

# 28

Sources disagree exactly when and where Grigoriy Yefimovich Rasputin was born, but it seems likely that he came from a Siberian village, far away from the Imperial Russian capital of St. Petersburg, sometime in the early 1870s. Very little is known about the first twenty years of his life, since they lay outside the realm of the written word and must be disentangled from the legend and hearsay that grew around him.

At some point in his debauched, lecherous, and immoral youth, he became captivated by the mystical powers of the Orthodox Russian religion and, in particular, by a renegade sect known as the Skoptsy. Followers of the Skoptsy believed that the only way to reach God was through sinful action. Once the sin had been committed and confessed, true forgiveness could be achieved. Understanding the potential of this doctrine, Rasputin adopted monk's robes and traveled the land as a self-styled *staretz*, a holy man. He received no formal training, but his fame spread throughout the land because of his mysterious gifts of healing and prophecy, along with the infamy attached to his zealous attitude towards sex and immorality.

People journeyed from far and wide to see him, bringing with them presents of food and money in exchange for his help. Some were grateful, others shocked, but none left without forming an opinion of the man the whole country was talking about. Along with the impressed and impressionable peasantry, a large number of respected men in the Orthodox Church fell for his charms. With their approval came recommendations, and with these he traveled to St. Petersburg to meet the royal family.

Tsar Nicholas II, who had taken the throne of Russia at the age of twenty-six after his father's unexpected death in 1894, was entirely unprepared for the burdens of ruling the vast and complex Russian empirc. Against the wishes of his mother he married a German princess, Alexandra Feodorovna, who bore the Tsar four daughters, but not the son they desired so fervently to continue the royal line. Their hope for a male heir developed into an obsession, and her next pregnancy was accompanied by fanatical prayer and the exploration of mystical practices. Wandering mystics and holy men were frequently seen at the palace, and in July 1904, the couple's prayers were answered with the arrival of a baby boy. They were delighted, and called the child Alexis, after the second Romanov Tsar.

Shortly afterwards their joy was heavily colored with bad news. When little Alexis bruised or scratched himself, he did not stop bleeding and spent long hours in terrible pain. Doctors concluded that he suffered from hemophilia, a disease of the blood inherited from his great-grandmother, Queen Victoria. They told the Tsar and Tsarina that the disease was incurable and would recur periodically, perhaps one day killing him. Unable to accept the doctors' verdict, Alexandra once again turned to mysticism.

It was under these circumstances that Rasputin first came into the Imperial court. Though he had not managed to curb his debauched and womanizing ways, he still managed to gain an influential following composed of those impressed by his gift of healing. Among his admirers were several members of the royal family and the palace staff. Under their commendation he was summoned by Alexandra to help her child.

Perhaps the wandering monk really was capable of working miracles, or perhaps he merely deceived the Tsarina, as he seemed to have duped so many others. Either way, he was able to calm the boy and put a stop to his bleeding. Nicholas and Alexandra's gratitude brought Rasputin their full support and patronage.

With his growing fame in St. Petersburg, the number of Rasputin's enemies also increased. Although he tried to ingratiate himself with other members of the royal family, he was not completely successful, and many carefully avoided him. He made powerful enemies, but even they could not persuade the Tsar to send him away.

The staretz was too important to Alexandra, who believed that only he could save her son. His influence over the royal couple seemed unshakable, and he rose to political power as the Tsarina accepted his advice in matters of government. Rumors circulated wildly; it was said that Rasputin had seduced the Tsarina, as well as the Grand Duchesses and Anna Vyrubova, a close friend of Alexandra whom he had managed to raise from a coma following a near-fatal train crash. Still the Tsar did nothing, even when state officials brought him proof of Rasputin's wild excesses. Finally, the Prime Minister took matters into his own hands and ordered the monk to leave St. Petersburg.

The respite was short lived. Not long afterwards, the Prime Minister was assassinated by a revolutionary. Then in the next year little Alexis had a bad fall. The doctors could do nothing for him and the Tsarina sat at his bedside for over a week as the bleeding child screamed with the terrible pain. In desperation, Alexandra telegraphed Rasputin. Within a few hours of the monk's reply, Alexis began to recover. Rasputin returned to the royal court, where he stayed. In the course of the following years, some say his political advice steered the country towards revolution.

Miles to the north, the Brothers knew almost nothing of these developments. Their home was not so very far away from the Russian capital, but they were insular and inward-looking, concerning themselves little with the outside world. Their very identity and security lay in obscurity, in the world that lay within their walls, rather than the larger one outside, of importance only when it was directly relevant to them. This was their mistake, and if they had only given due importance to what they heard, perhaps their history would have been very different.

The irrational belief was suggested that if the Brothers did not interfere with the outside world, it would not bother them in turn. All of them were complacent and fearless in their longevity, believing that having beaten death in one respect they were invincible in every other. None had had their lives threatened in the past; few had experienced real danger. Only Mikhail understood the gravity of the situation,

*M-Trait*

knowing that keeping themselves to themselves was no defense against the assault of those who had other ideas.

So it was that gradually, without knowing exactly what it was that he expected to happen, Mikhail planned for the future. Over a year, the instinct for self-preservation settled in him without the full awareness of how it worked. Little pieces of information, digested by his subconscious in a way that appeared logical after the events but the significance of which eluded him at the time, gave rise to an intuitive sense of what lay ahead that sometimes bordered on the precognitive and could be frightening in its accuracy. Often, the awareness of his surroundings intensified and his faculties sharpened as he waited for the unknown. And he barely slept, preferring instead to sit in an upright chair by the window, listening to every sound that filtered through the walls around him, or silently walking the corridors in the dead of night with senses finely tuned, as if listening for the answers to his unknown question. In those days, he started to carry a knife again after years of quietude and security, and the blade seldom left his side, even during the few hours of the night when he lay on his bed, fully clothed, and slept a shallow and dreamless sleep.

With Rasputin fully entrenched within the royal court, his enemies hatched a plot. A group of nobles decided that the mad monk's influence had increased to the point where he had to be killed to save Russia and the monarchy. Rasputin knew that his days were numbered. A letter to the Tsarina, dated December 7, 1916, warned of the consequences of his death. He foresaw that he would be killed before the turn of the next year, and told the Tsar that he had nothing to fear if his assassination was the doing of the Russian peasantry. But if the plot was carried out by the nobility, the blood would be on their heads. The Russian people would rise up against the nobility and the royal family would all be killed within two years.

Later that month, Rasputin was invited to Yussopov palace by a group of nobles and some of the Tsar's relatives. He was taken to the cellar and fed wine and cakes that had been heavily laced with cyanide. Although he ate enough to kill several men, the poison appeared to have no effect on him, so Prince Felix Yussopov, another of the Tsar's relatives, shot him in the back. The other conspirators rushed downstairs in time to see Rasputin's death convulsion, then retired upstairs to celebrate their crime.

An hour later, when Prince Felix returned to view the results of his crime, he noticed signs of life. When he touched the body, it felt warm. As he shook it in disbelief, Rasputin leapt to his feet and seized the prince by the neck. Felix broke free and ran back upstairs, screaming in terror. When he and the others came down again, the monk had gone.

They found him as he was running across the courtyard to escape, and shot him again in the back and the head. The body was dragged back inside, beaten and kicked. Then it was bound hand and foot and wrapped in a heavy cloth. Just before dawn, the conspirators took the body to a bridge and threw it over the edge into the icy waters of the Neva River.

The next day, when the corpse was recovered from the river, police found that Rasputin had managed to untie his hands from their bindings. He had been poisoned, shot, and beaten, but the cause of his eventual death was drowning.

Rasputin's prophecy to the Tsarina would turn out to be correct. His assassins were members of the royal family. The days of Imperial Russia were over. The onslaught of the revolution would soon reach the doors of the Brotherhood's fortress. It was just a matter of time.

# 29

Should he ask about Emily's baby?

The subject had been brushed under the carpet for so long that it seemed almost rude to broach it now. The Terry Kettering poem came to Tom's mind and he smiled involuntarily at Emily:

> "There's an elephant in the room. It is large and squatting, so it is hard to get around it. Yet we squeeze by with, 'How are you?' and 'I'm fine,' and a thousand other forms of trivial chatter. We talk about the weather. We talk about work. We talk about everything else, except the elephant in the room."

He wondered how Emily might feel about being described as an elephant. Fortunately, she merely took his smile as a return of her own. Still, there was a slightly uncomfortable air between the two of them, like two teenagers on their first few dates. They had begun meeting after their weekly sports club workouts—at a coffeehouse across the street. Tom was drinking a tall, white coffee, enjoying its sensation of warming and stimulating him at the same time. Emily, ever wary of caffeine during her pregnancy, was drinking chamomile tea. Between them they had a muffin, which Emily had declined but Tom had bought, suspecting that she would help him out with it anyway. He sat across from her in one of the big, comfortable armchairs that they had managed to claim for themselves.

Emily typically planned most of her days and evenings around work at the lab, so their outings were a break from her routine. Tom was a little surprised she chose to spend so much time with Dr. Sherman, at work and after work. Perhaps that was the point—she was looking for more time away from him.

Tom thought it was a good time for an additional low-key chat—an opportunity for her to tell him more about herself. Feigning ignorance was getting to be hard work; he had to continually watch himself to avoid saying something he should not know about.

If he could, he also wanted Emily to convey what she really knew about her baby—to confirm or deny what he had discovered after sifting through the mounds of data from Dr. Sherman's computer. The little key-logger plugged into the back of the machine had been invaluable.

Sitting in his flat a week earlier, it had taken almost two hours to dig through the material—every key Edward had pressed in the last few days—until he found out the true nature of Edward's work. Much of it was gibberish, keystrokes used to launch programs or navigate menus. Everything ran on consecutively, and it was hard to refocus his eyes as he scrolled down the pages and pages of characters. There had been evidence of emails he had typed—nothing useful there—reams of seemingly random letters, which Tom assumed were connected with some program that he used and made no sense of their own, and then finally, exactly what he had been hoping for. Edward had connected remotely to his user area at the university, where the results of all the tests were kept. To do so, he had had to enter his user details and password, and the key-logger had registered exactly what they were. Tom had only to do the same and the contents of Sherman's research, general and private, lay in front of him on the screen. *Ah, finally—some results.*

Mostly the files had been useless, boring catalogues of his volunteers' genetic faults that made for dismal reading. He closed one window, then clicked on the next file to open it. The filename read: *EPRESTON12-02-76.* The information came up in front of him.

| Name: | Emily Preston |
| Date of Birth: | December 2, 1976 |
| Ancestral Derivation: | Anglo-Saxon, Anglo-Celtic, all else <5% |
| Genetic Disorders: | None |
| M-Trait: | + - Partial |
| Further Notes: | See file ZPRESTON09-06. |

*M-Trait*

Emily was M-Trait partial? Through his conversations with her and his investigation into Edward Sherman's work, Tom had been led to believe that nobody had been found with even one of the Methuselah genes turned off. But here was proof of one—and it was Emily?

Tom thought about it more. If Sherman wanted his genetic theories validated, wouldn't he trumpet the discovery of anyone found with one of the death genes turned off? Then again, Edward had to keep his own custody of the M-Trait secret. Maybe his work was not about scientific discovery.

He then considered the note about the file: *ZPRESTON09-06*. Tom assumed that it concerned Zoe who was obviously scheduled to be born in September. He searched for the file among the others, but it was not there. Where was it? Perhaps Edward didn't want this file on the university computer system. Perhaps it was only on his machine at home.

Tom sighed. After his mistake last time, he really was not ready to go to Dr. Sherman's house again so soon. If that's what it would take, he would have to, but the house was no longer the comfortable place it had once been for him.

He was about to give up and resign himself to returning there, when he had an idea. If Sherman had edited the file while the keylogger was connected, maybe some useful information could be extracted. All it took was a brief search, and the computer turned up what he was looking for. Sherman had indeed typed the characters *ZPRESTON09-06*, and what came after:

```
ZPRESTON09-06 [RTN] [RTN] [RTN] THIRD TRIMESTER:
PREGNANCY GOING WELL.[RTN] NO APPARENT COMPLICATIONS
TO THE PREGNANCY CAUSED BY POSITIVE M-TRAIT.[ALT]FS
[ALT]FX
```

Tom blinked and then read the note again. His hopes and suspicions were confirmed in the few seconds—the concrete proof on the screen literally knocked the breath out of him. *Zoe was positive for the M-Trait.* He had been right about Dr. Sherman's having other intentions. But suspicions were one thing—seeing the actual evidence was unbelievable. *Emily's child would be almost immortal!*

In the coffeehouse, Tom wondered how she would answer his questions—what cover story she and Dr. Sherman had agreed on. Or perhaps she did not even know that Sherman had given Zoe the elusive second gene. Maybe he had deceived her—betrayed her trust to get what he wanted, knowing that she might never find out. Tom thought it a risky strategy, because if she found out what he had done, he could lose everything.

Focusing back on Emily in the coffeehouse, Tom decided to bite the bullet. "So, I couldn't help but wonder…" He held up his left hand, bent the ring finger down, and shrugged expressively to her. She smiled—the wordless question was clear. *You don't wear a ring, so you're not married, but you're pregnant—and you're out with me. So what's the deal?*

"Hey mister, it's the twenty-first century, you know. A girl doesn't have to be married to have a child anymore." Despite her mock indignation, she could not keep the proud grin from showing.

Tom cocked his head and shrugged, appreciatively this time, conceding the point. He made his play. "If you believe Luke's Gospel, you don't even need a man at all. But I'm guessing, in your case, there was probably one at *some* point in the equation?" Another gesture, palms up and a shrug: *So…?* He could have added the caveat, "If you don't mind me asking," but judged their friendship to be at a point where such diplomacies were unnecessary. If it caused offense, she would not hold it against him.

"Well, if there ever was, there isn't anymore." She deliberately hedged her answer. Emily did not want to lie to him, but telling him the truth might complicate the situation. "I'm young, free, and single, and that's how I like it, for now."

The last phrase was her caveat. Presumably, she did not think that he held any romantic interest in her but, at this early stage, the boundaries of their relationship were still unclear. She would also be aware that, as a single mother-to-be, she must appear to be vulnerable and in need. She thought she knew Tom well enough not to worry about it, but life had taught her to be careful; the last thing she wanted was to be the target of some guy who was looking for a codependency trip.

Emily, at ease with herself regardless of what Tom thought of her personal decisions, turned the conversation to other matters. "Your 'Luke's gospel' comment sounded like something Edward would say."

Tom had been looking for an opportunity to talk to Emily about Sherman. He wanted to know more about how he interacted with others, and what he might expect when they finally met. Emily was the obvious place to start.

"Yeah?" He wanted to sound curious, but not overeager. She did not need to know the depths of his interest.

"He sometimes tells stories to the students who come to help with his research—myths and legends about very old people. His favorites seem to be the biblical stories about how men used to live a long time before the Flood, and what went wrong. He sometimes mixes it up a bit by talking about some of the flood myths from other cultures." She saw the quizzical look on Tom's face and stopped, almost as if embarrassed on Sherman's behalf. "I think it's just a bit of fun for him. It's actually quite interesting."

"Is he a religious man?"

Emily thought for a moment. "Edward's funny. He never lets on what he believes—about anything. I think he just doesn't like people asking about his life. He'll volunteer information when he's ready. It just has to be on his terms." She paused, and Tom stayed silent too, waiting for her to elaborate.

"He's very private, and very independent. I've never known him to ask anyone for anything. Although, thinking about it, I've never known him to actually need anything."

Tom nodded gently.

"There are some things he never talks about. I know he had a wife and child once, although I think it was quite a while ago. I get the impression that they died in an accident of some kind. There's a memorial in his garden to them, tucked away in a corner. I guess it still affects him. I don't think he ever considered remarrying."

Tom, who had often seen the granite marker on his illegal visits, said nothing about it, allowing Emily to chatter on.

"He's been a good friend to me, and I probably know him better than anyone else, but even so—I often wonder what goes on inside his head."

*You may never know.* Tom sat, resting his elbow on the table and leaning his head on his hand, just two fingers touching his temple for support. Perhaps she knew almost nothing about him after all.

"How old is he?"

"About forty-five, though don't tell him I told you that. We have a sort of game between us, where he never lets on his age. Sometimes he'll try to give me bits of misinformation, pretending it's accidental, making out like he's thirty or sixty or eighty or whatever. But he left his wallet open on his desk once, and I saw his driver's license."

There it was then. Tom did not think she would make up a lie like that if she knew the truth. Sherman really had told her nothing about himself—nothing about his age, his past, or his motives. And if she didn't know about that, chances are she didn't know about Zoe either. Emily, noticing him staring past her in thought for the first time, waved a hand in front of his face, bringing him back to the here and now.

"Hey! Still there?" She then brushed his hand, the one on the table that was still holding the coffee cup. It was, he realized, the first time that she had actually touched him. He liked it.

## 30

James Richards represented a major obstacle to the doctor's plan to acquire Emily, although in the end as a problem, he proved less than insurmountable. James was an unremarkable man in Sherman's opinion. He possessed above average intelligence, was somewhat handsome, and had a high-paying consultancy job in London. He was a success in every conventional sense of the word, but Sherman did not measure success by conventional means.

The problem with James Richards was that he prevented Edward from possessing Emily and her DNA. Therefore, James needed to exit the field of play in some manner. Killing was risky, a messy business that could go wrong too easily, whether it was at his hands or those of a professional. In any case, even with the best of hired guns—and here, for once, he did not have the slightest idea of where to start looking for such a thing—there would be the possibility of it all backfiring catastrophically. Besides, it would be hard for Emily to hate a dead man. There had to be a better way—something more suited to the circumstances and to James' deficiencies—and only a brief time spent with James produced a possible scenario.

Emily Preston had accepted the position in March, but couldn't actually start working until the school term ended in June. During a semester break, Emily visited the lab with James, so he could meet Edward and tour the lab. Sherman immediately noticed that James had a roving eye when it came to women. When Emily was not looking—even when she was still in the same room—he found James casting an appreciative eye over any other females present. It was possible—likely even—that this was all it was, window-shopping, and that James would never have acted on his interests. Edward, however, decided it might be worth his while to assess James' devotion to his wife by leading him into greater temptation.

Since his assistant-to-be and her husband lived in separate cities for only a few more months, Edward thought it best to test James immediately. London could be a lonely, anonymous city, and with this anonymity came an associated reduction in social responsibility. If a tree falls over in the woods and there is no one there to see it, does it make a noise? No one will talk if no one sees.

Sherman hired a private detective from a small but well-regarded firm to learn more about James. A high-quality private detective was not cheap, but his investment paid off handsomely. He found that James was not the stay-at-home type in the evenings, and most days had some kind of social engagement. Usually he left for Oxford on Friday evening, spending the weekend with his wife and returning to London on Sunday evening. On weekends when Emily had other commitments, he stayed at his flat, as there was no other reason for him to leave London. To all intents and purposes, his life was there. She was the only factor tying him to Oxford.

On one such weekend, his private detective found out that James would be attending a party that Saturday evening with some of his colleagues from work. Edward judged that this would be the best opportunity to make his play, and a call to the detective settled the matter. It required a sum of extra money and a personal bonus to the detective, but he was able to keep his own hands clean and sit back to wait for the results. He was not disappointed.

If James had been looking forward to this party, he did not stay long. After a few drinks, he met an attractive brunette woman who introduced herself as a friend of one of the other partygoers—he never found out quite who. He was flattered by the attention she gave him, and after a few more drinks had left with her. That, of course, had been the outcome anticipated by Sherman, and the only reason the girl had been at the party. The private detective took photographs of them leaving the party together, and her leaving James' flat the following morning. Sherman was pleased with his work and gave him a further tip.

# M-Trait

Edward never told Emily about James' mistake. Racked by guilt and fear at her reaction, he did not tell her himself, and no one from work had seen James and the girl together. For a while he felt guilty about his unfaithfulness, though he probably accepted the alcohol as a mitigating circumstance. Besides, the woman had made the advances towards him. He had never seen her again after that, and had not tried too hard to find out who she was; why draw attention to the matter?

That had been enough for Sherman. He had the photos—all the proof he needed. If nothing else, he would have been able to hold it over James if he ever needed to, but it turned out that James was capable of wrecking his own marriage. Sherman was a good judge of character, and a precedent had been set. A month later, James met another woman, this time without any help from Edward and his private detective. The rest followed like clockwork. As long as Emily was based in Oxford, James could have them both, living one life in the week with his girlfriend and another on the weekend with his wife. But he knew that it could not last that way forever. Like so many mortals, James did not think about the future as long as it was possible to live in the present. When Emily finally came to live with him in London, her husband could not keep up the deception any longer.

James did not have the decency to tell her to her face, but took the day off work to move into his girlfriend's flat when Emily was at the university, leaving a message on their answering machine for her to find when she returned that evening.

She was alone again, on her own in a strange city, with few friends close by. Where could she turn? Edward knew that answer too, and waited with open arms.

# 31

Emily was already there when he arrived, a few minutes early.

"Hi." Tom strolled up, checking his watch to make sure that she was indeed early, and he had not arrived late. "Been waiting long?"

"No, it's ok. I'm getting slower and slower these days, so I keep leaving more and more time to get places." She grinned ruefully and got to her feet from the bench, drawing her red fleece top tighter around herself as the wind gusted.

Last Thursday, as Emily had been waiting for Tom after yoga class, she had passed the time looking at the flyers pinned to the notice boards in the foyer. Occasionally there were events of interest, although she rarely found the time to go, or anyone to go with. This time, among the adverts for book fairs, car boot sales, and personal trainers, she saw a poster for a local theater company's outdoor Shakespeare performance. She was interested enough to suggest it to him when he came out of his Aikido class.

"Don't suppose you're a Shakespeare fan?" She looked so hopeful that Tom could not bring himself to admit that he was only lukewarm about the Bard. He had never found an appreciation of the so-called classics, preferring not to waste time on something he found dry and arcane.

"Sure. Anything good on?" He glanced over her shoulder at the poster.

"A few showings this month, but I'd really like to see *Midsummer Night's Dream* on Sunday. It's one of my favorites to read, but I've never seen it performed." Her enthusiasm was infectious.

"Sounds good." Tom nearly convinced himself. "Where is it playing?"

The park was only a few miles from Emily's flat, and she knew the area well. They did not exchange addresses or phone numbers, but simply agreed to meet at 1:30 p.m. for the 2 p.m. performance, which was plenty of time to get tickets and beat the crowds.

"If it rains we can always find something else to do." Tom made a mental note to check around and see what else of interest there was nearby, half-hoping the weather would be bad.

As it happened, the rain held off. The two of them bought their tickets and spread out the blanket that Tom stowed in the boot of his car. Finally the play was introduced and Theseus, Hippolyta, and Philostrate entered, to begin a performance of a comedy that had barely changed in over 400 years. After the first five minutes, Tom reached for Emily's hand, and didn't let go for the rest of the performance.

# 32

As much as Emily cared about Edward, and vice versa, it seemed that they were ultimately suited to being no more than good friends. Their romantic relationship fizzled after only six months.

The relationship with Edward had been good for her, and she regained her inner confidence, knowing that there was someone who appreciated her and actually respected her for just being Emily. It was a new feeling for her, and the security that came with it was a surprise that took a little time to get used to. As the relationship grew, Emily couldn't help but think of a family. Before her marriage with James ended, she had wanted to start one. Now, at almost thirty, she was not getting any younger, and that hope had a limited shelf life. The biological clock was ticking.

Emily knew Edward would make a good father. He was devoted, caring, and selfless—everything she could ask for. At the same time, she did not know much about his first wife and child, but sensed that the pain of their loss was still real to him. He had never talked about it, and on the occasions that she had tried to bring it up, he had been unwilling to go into it. She stopped trying as soon as she understood how painful it was for him. But even if they couldn't talk about the past, she decided to ask him about what might happen between them in the future.

"I have thought about a family," he replied. He could not look her in the face. "It is something I want, but I don't think I'm ready to do it again." It was the first time he had made a reference to his family, and it was clearly very difficult for him. The words came slowly, and it was an effort for him to speak. Perhaps it hadn't been as long ago as she assumed.

It was this loss to which she attributed the distance in him. He kept a part of himself back—he was simply unable to let her get too close to him. She did not know when he lost his family—it must have been awful. It made Emily sad—partly for him, and partly because she knew that their relationship would not last unless he found a way to move on from his past.

Finally, the frustration became too much for her. Emily decided to end it. Knowing it was coming a few weeks ahead of time, Emily had had time to prepare herself. It was a difficult subject to broach, but as it turned out, he was very understanding. Edward had dropped her back to her flat, and she had invited him in to talk.

"I don't want to keep giving what I can't get in return. I don't mind if it's temporary, and I'd understand if you just needed a bit more time." They sat facing each other at opposite ends of the settee; Emily curled up hugging her knees as she said what she felt. "But it's more than that. It's just not *you*, is it? It's something I don't think you'll ever be able to give."

Edward nodded slowly. "No. I suppose not." His voice was level and emotionless. Emily could have assumed that he didn't care, but instead sensed that he was deeply hurting about it inside.

She hugged him. "It's okay. It's not your fault. I'm just really sorry it still hurts you so much." There was no need for him to ask what she meant. "We both went into this without any expectations. We're still friends." She had started to cry then, just a few tears, and he had held her.

Uncomfortable with her grief, he tried to soothe her. "If there's anything I can do…"

Emily dried her tears. There was something she wanted, and she had thought about it carefully in the weeks before today, when she realized that the two of them would not stay together.

"There is," she told him, taking a deep breath. "There is one thing you could do for me."

"What is it?" He rested his hands on her shoulders and leaned back to look at her face.

Emily took a deep breath before answering. "I want a child. I want a family."

Edward nodded—not agreeing, but more like he understood her need.

"You wouldn't have to do anything else. I wouldn't expect anything else from you at all."

She went on to explain that it would be her child, her responsibility. She was no longer interested in waiting for the "right" man. With her thirtieth birthday arriving later that year and her position at the university well established, she didn't want to wait any longer. There would be no legal obligation; she would expect nothing from him. And he was welcome to play a part in her life—she would be honored, whatever that role would be. But she did not expect him to be a father to her child after she was pregnant.

Edward folded his arms, one hand on his chin, tilting his head to one side as he listened to her. "Let me think about it," he said.

# 33

As he always did before touching anything in Edward Sherman's house, Tom pulled on a pair of latex surgical gloves. Thin and close fitting, they allowed him to touch and feel through them without having to worry about leaving telltale fingerprints or other marks behind. It was his practice to keep them on until he left the house, discarding them in a bin back at home.

The locks clicked open easily under his keys, as they had done so many times in the past, and he made his way upstairs to Sherman's office. Emily regarded him from the frame on the desk as he sorted through the filing cabinet, checking everything carefully. The work on the computer took longer. The database files of Sherman's test subjects had already been transferred onto his laptop at home, but there were diaries and email archives to read in case they contained anything interesting—but he found nothing more. It seemed that the doctor did not organize his life with a computer, preferring pen and paper for important writings.

It was a couple of hours later that Tom wandered downstairs to leave, having exhausted the possibilities of Sherman's house, and feeling ready for a change. He was just opening the back door when a piercing tone sounded somewhere behind him, freezing him in surprise. Resisting the urge to run, he realized that the alarm couldn't be a new security system—he had been in the house all morning, after all. The tone continued on, shrill and harsh. Was it a smoke alarm? Was there a fire somewhere? Tom could not smell any smoke.

He judged that the noise would be all but inaudible from outside the house, and he was therefore safe from any passing do-gooders. *Slowly, carefully, back into the kitchen. There, above the boiler—a carbon monoxide alarm.*

Tom reached up and unhooked the alarm, removing the back to silence it. He contemplated the two AA-size batteries in the palm of his gloved hand. There was no immediate danger to him, he knew; the detector professed to be a low-level indicator that would sound before the CO had reached a dangerous concentration. Tom stopped a moment to consider the possibilities. *Hmmm, that just may work.*

The boiler was new, gas-fired and efficient. A certificate tacked above it on a corkboard told him that it had been serviced and checked only six months previously. Chances were that there were no problems there. The vent led out to a grate in the back garden, set low in the wall of the house. Tom left the back door open to air the kitchen while he studied the vent. A brief examination showed it to be blocked with the summer growth of ivy. He squatted on his haunches and rearranged it, winding it in with itself so that the vent was unobstructed but without having to tear any of the ivy out from the wall.

It is a peculiarity of the human body that the hemoglobin molecule in the bloodstream will bind more readily with carbon monoxide than with the oxygen it is supposed to carry around the body. The more hemoglobin the CO ties up, the less is left to do its proper job of providing oxygen to the vital organs. In lower concentrations it causes headaches, nausea, and fatigue; in higher concentrations a rapidly fatal coma will result. As a colorless, tasteless, and odorless gas, it is virtually unnoticeable without a proper detector. Sherman, meticulous about his personal health and safety for obvious reasons, had been prepared. Perhaps there was another reason he saw this as a particular risk. Tom remembered reading the web page about angina. It was a condition that could easily be aggravated by air pollution, including carbon monoxide poisoning.

Tom focused more on the potential plan as he finished rearranging the ivy. The old man had already decided that the doctor had to die, almost as soon as Sherman was discovered, still alive after all this time. And Tom knew that he would be entrusted with the work of carrying out the death sentence. He thought the blocked boiler vent provided another option that the old man might approve of. Such things happened all the time: carelessness and bad maintenance. Sherman would not die of carbon monoxide poisoning today, but should he wish it, Tom might arrange that quite easily now. It would be a tidy, accidental death. People would say that Sherman really should have known better.

The control he had over Dr. Sherman's life brought a smug grin to Tom's face. That grin disappeared quickly when he stepped back into the house and found someone there.

# 34

The dreams always left Edward shaking and sweating in the darkness, searching for the light switch. They were dreams that he had regularly, though less often in recent decades. He found the bedside light and switched it on, its illumination calming as he recognized the familiar surroundings of his bedroom. In the quiet of the night, the memories came unbidden, the horror of his last days with Mikhail and the others, and the fateful night he finally left the Brotherhood.

It was long ago, yet the flashback seemed so real. He woke to the sound of screaming in the dead of a Russian winter's night. The smell and taste of fear were strong in his mouth as he fought his body's urge to freeze, to rise from his bed onto the stone floor, so cold under his feet. There were the sounds of a struggle, the crashing of things being knocked over or thrown. He was in the corridor now, running towards the knot of figures clustered in the doorway. Bela, Anton's wife, struggled against the powerful arms of the men who gripped her from either side, feet kicking at anyone coming close enough. *She tried to escape with a male child*, someone said.

Bela was an intelligent woman; Anton had chosen her for it, but it turned out that she was too clever for her own good. Realizing that no older women lived in the fortress, had come to the right conclusion—she would never be allowed to live her own life. She attempted an escape by slipping out of the compound during a bad winter's storm. Unfortunately for her, she tried to take her son, too. That kind of act was forbidden.

Finally, unhurriedly, Mikhail arrived. He held a brief conversation with Mordke at the door, only some of it was audible to Eduard over Bela's screaming. Mordke's face and hands were bruised and bleeding from nail scratches and bites, evidence of his struggle with Bela as he stopped her from leaving. Mikhail stood in the doorway now, pronouncing sentence. It was the slightest of nods, an almost imperceptible movement of the head. Mikhail turned his back to leave, not even dignifying her death with his presence: Bela's life was nothing to him.

Eduard was shouting now as Alexander pressed the pillow into her face: Alexander, who had laughed at him when Karina died. He struggled to reach Bela, through hands that would not let him, as she struggled to breathe, the room full of clawing hands, Bela's, his own, and the hands that held him back. Then he felt a sharp pain at the top of his neck, dizziness and nausea. He staggered backwards through the hands and the doorway, to be thrown against the wall opposite. Bela lay dead now, her life extinguished as his wife's had been years before. Alexander smiled at him: understand now?

The clarity of the moment pierced Eduard's heart forever. He did understand. He now knew how his wife had died. His beloved Karina—not from sickness, but from the hands of these animals—just like Bela.

Confusion reigned in his dreams as a jumble of fractured memories continued. There was another room; Eduard did not yet know where in his nausea. There were Alexander and Mikhail, and two of the others; Alexander was holding a dagger, arguing with Mikhail. Eduard was unable to stand yet, still too dizzy from another blow to the head. There was blood on his hands—his own? Mikhail looked stern, resolute; Alexander just looked angry. Mikhail put his hand on Alexander's shoulder, taking the dagger from his hand and placing it aside. "No more killing, not him, not one of us."

Alexander was shaking his head, shouting, "He was never one of us!" Eduard remembered trying to stand at last, Alexander kicking him in the chest as he tried to rise, forcing him back to his knees, choking. Mikhail and the others held Alexander back.

Now he was on his feet, still doubled over, the dagger somehow in his hand. Alexander's eyes were wide, the only one who could see the danger as they held him away from Eduard. Alexander screamed, and Mikhail turned just in time to see the threat. He let go of

Alexander, pushing him away as Eduard lunged. The dagger tore into Mikhail's arm, a nasty cut but not the fatal wound that would have been inflicted on Alexander. There was a long moment as the two men looked at each other. Then Mikhail slapped the blade from his hand. Alexander, outraged at what Eduard had tried to do, moved in to strike him, but Mikhail held him away again.

"Enough!" cried Mikhail.

Alexander continued to struggle against Mikhail's iron grip as Eduard turned and ran. "Alexander, let him go."

Running now, the bravery of his rage spent, Eduard fled, terrified of retribution, slamming doors behind him. He found his son, grabbed money and their winter coats, and ran out into the night.

In the days that followed, Eduard's hot anger cooled into a frozen knot of hate that left him with only calculating thought and cold action. *The Brotherhood must pay for Karina's death.*

In the summer of 1917, four months after Tsar Nicholas II had abdicated, the new Minister of War, Alexander Kerensky, announced a new offensive against the Germans on the eastern front. Soldiers were dismayed at the news, and entire regiments refused to move to the front line. By the autumn, an estimated two million soldiers had deserted. Many of these men returned to their homes and used their weapons to seize land from the nobility. Manor houses were burned down and some of the wealthy landowners were murdered. Kerensky issued warnings, but the government was unable to stop the bloodshed.

It was with a group of deserters that Eduard and Kostya made plans to return to the compound and exact their revenge.

# 35

Mikhail must have seen the band of men that had now reached the edge of the village nearest to the castle, but he did not show it. In the dusk, they were little more than dark shapes, their military rifles visible only in silhouette. Two figures in long dark coats did not carry rifles. One pointed to the castle, turning to the raiders as he shouted his commands. The words were inaudible to Mikhail above the howling wind.

He recognized them, Eduard and Kostya, as they too watched the twenty or so men move towards the hidden door in the castle wall, their rifles ready, expecting violent resistance. As they reached the door, Mikhail could no longer see them.

The first gunshots sounded, shattering the eerie twilight calm and filling it with the sounds of running footsteps and shouts. Mikhail's mind's eye filled in the visual details that went with the sounds he heard. Soldiers were now entering the hall, where most of the Brothers sat eating. More gunshots were briefly interspersed with shouting.

They were spreading out now, moving through the rooms so that their noise was all around him, taking anything of value that they could carry and killing anyone they found, the women and children included. Over the years, Mikhail and the Brothers had grown rich. They had slowly collected wealth and possessions over the decades, storing up money for the future, although in the present there was little to spend it on. There was much to be looted.

Outside, Eduard still stood in the swirling snow, waiting and watching as the carnage began. He told the soldiers that there were thirty inhabitants—twelve men, as well as women and children. When the Brothers had all been found and killed, only then would he tell them where the real treasures were hidden. But the soldiers weren't taking any chances, firing whenever they saw movement.

Mikhail heard the footsteps as they echoed along the corridors of the castle, then harsh voices sounded directly outside the room. The door opened. He was trapped.

# 36

Emily's proposition intrigued him. *I want a child. I want a family.*

He had known she wanted children with James, but Edward assumed that her desire for offspring had died along with her marriage. Now, some time later, she obviously wanted a family even more.

At first, he thought Emily wanted him to be the father. He couldn't accept that, for a number of reasons. But most importantly, Edward could never deliver the emotional intimacy that she wanted. Allowing an attachment to someone who would age and die—it would be the same pain as Karina and Kostya, only slower and more agonizing.

Then he realized that she hadn't meant that at all. She was smarter than that: she wouldn't finish a relationship with him and then blur the boundaries of their friendship by having a child together. No, she was asking for his help—it was his technical expertise she was after.

The Department of Fertility and Embryology at the university was a tremendous resource, and Edward's own work largely overlapped with it. Why not use it? On those grounds, Edward had no compunction about her question; there was no reason why she should not have a child that way. Emily didn't want to wait any longer, and she didn't know if she'd ever meet someone she could raise a family with. Why not simply use a random, anonymous father from the Fertility Department? It was a good enough solution under the circumstances.

Then Edward realized his own opportunity. It was a tantalizing chance for him to have what he had always wanted. But it would also mean betraying the confidence of his closest friend, and that would sit uneasily with him. She would never know, of course, and it would cause her no harm. Still, something told him she would not see it the same way as he did Nevertheless, he realized that a prospect such as this might never be dropped into his lap again. How could he ever gain the peace he desired if he let this go?

Edward asked her to let him think about it, and then he went away to consider how it would be done. When his thoughts had crystallized, he returned with his answer.

"Ok. I've thought about this carefully," he told her. "I'll help you—of course I'll help you. But there's one condition."

Emily eyed him with a mixture of curiosity and suspicion. "What is it?"

Edward could see her thinking: *What will the price be?*

"We use the technology that is at our fingertips. I couldn't bear to help you have a child and not use it."

Emily looked concerned. "Why?"

"What if your baby had some kind of genetic defect? What a colossal irony, given how long and hard we've both worked as genetic scientists to label suspect DNA! How could we justify that?"

He laid it on pretty thick for her. "If you have this kind of chance to save someone, or make their life better, and you don't take it, you might as well be responsible for the fault in the first place. However the law might see the situation, that's professional negligence to me." He paused to let her take it in. "The baby should be as genetically perfect as you are, Emily." *Or better, he thought.*

"Okay—but I don't want to know about the father. I want this to be as much of a natural, random process as possible."

"Of course."

For Edward, this answer was even better than he could imagine. Without interference, he would have enough time with the embryo to work his magic before implantation. But was it really possible? How would he proceed?

Edward did not intend to inseminate her embryo with his sperm. Where was the sense in that? He could have a child with anyone. No, if he did it that way, Emily's child stood a good chance of inheriting his faulty tissue-production gene that lay on the long arm of chromosome 18. Any female children she had would run the risk of dying of LAM before their twenties.

Besides, if he was the child's father, it would immediately close the door that was finally open to him. No, he would only need a tiny fragment of his own DNA for what he had in mind: if her child was female *and* an Ultra, he could possibly have a mate again in just two short decades—a Karina that lived for centuries by his side.

The whole procedure would be carried out in-house. He had worked closely with the Department of Fertility and Embryology in a similar capacity before. Using In Vitro Fertilization, the embryos would be screened for genetic abnormalities and only the healthy ones implanted in her womb. Pre-implantation Genetic Diagnosis was a common enough procedure they had been using since the nineties. He would pay for it all—he insisted to Emily.

He did not have much time. Gene therapy was still in its infancy, and although this was a relatively basic procedure, he could not afford to get it wrong. This was a one-time shot. Edward labored like a man possessed. He spent a week in the lab, working twenty-hour days and sleeping at his desk when he had to.

The theory of it was simple. A modified virus was introduced into the embryo and instead of delivering a disease, its payload was an additional DNA sequence—a triploid—that rendered the previous sequence useless. If successful, his faulty genes would be reworked at the core genetic level within the developing embryo.

Now the issue of who to use as the father was immaterial, as long as he was healthy. He would make sure that the embryo had no faults at all. It would be close to perfect, and then he would give it another little bonus. Emily was already a partial M-Trait—against the odds, she had one of the two genes that brought longevity. Edward would introduce the second Methuselah gene into the cell's DNA. It was only one gene, into a single cell—as simple as it could get. In the future, it might be possible to do this with a grown patient, the virus replicating in the blood and delivering its patch to every cell in the body.

Only now did he carry out the genetic diagnosis scan, using the same program he used to test the blood of his volunteers. He selected a number of embryos that were healthy, and to which the Methuselah graft had successfully taken. Soon he developed a substantial number of perfect embryos—there were more Ultra-mortal lives at his fingertips than had ever existed before. All but a few were kept in the freezers of the Fertility Department. The ones that remained to be implanted into Emily were all female.

Edward felt like he had spent a century in the wilderness, living a half-life, unable to immerse himself in a world that did not share his genes or outlook. He had existed—existed comfortably, perhaps—but only existed. He had not really lived. The M-Trait had kept him alive for a century longer than he could otherwise have expected, but it had killed his relationship with Emily, and he had held out little hope of ever finding an equal to share his life with. Now, it seemed that his time in the wilderness was over.

After a successful implantation, Edward gave Emily the good news. "Congratulations Dr. Preston—it's going to be a healthy baby girl. What will you name her?"

# 37

They stared at each other warily from each side of Edward Sherman's kitchen. Neither of them had said anything yet. They were both waiting for something to happen, something to indicate how to react, both unsure of what the situation would hold. The woman stood near the counter by the stove, surprised from her wiping down of the work surface when Tom walked in from the garden.

He had grown accustomed to being in Sherman's house, knowing he would not be disturbed during his time there, and had not seen her until he heard the sharp intake of breath and looked up. He knew if he ran towards the door, it would invite a police visit. That was unacceptable. He would have to deal with the situation as best he could.

The silence lasted a little too long. Her silence was born of fear, his of uncertainty. They remained frozen, watching each other. He recognized her as the cleaning lady who came every other week. She was about forty, he guessed, though it was hard to tell. A little too much makeup along with brassy bleached hair gave altogether the wrong impression.

He hoped she would not make a run for the hallway. Then he would have to chase her and hopefully catch her before she reached the front door. His body stayed motionless, the mind racing for the split second before the shock-response motivated him to act—how should he play this out? He held his hands up and took a step towards her, palms out in reassurance, fingers spread—*no trouble, just relax, it's okay.* A small step forward, another step—

Tom noticed that the sight of his hands with the latex gloves pushed her over the edge from apprehension into real terror. Rather than make for the hall, which required her to come a little closer to him first, she was backing away from the door into the corner, one shaking hand searching for a knife from the rack on her right. Tom realized it was way too late to salvage the situation. He took a step back, keeping his hands up in a gesture of placation. If he could just buy himself a little more time, he could think of a way out of this.

Now, as he stepped away, backing down from the confrontation, she found some courage and presence of mind from somewhere. He saw her breathe in quickly, knowing how loud the scream would be if he let her—that would be too risky.

*Time to move—right now!* Tom darted towards the woman, tossing his key ring that he had swiftly extracted from his pocket. Momentarily distracted, she swiped at the keys which allowed him to close in on her from across the room in one swift movement. At the last instant, she managed to pull the knife out of the block beside her and strike in a blind panic, an awkward stab-slash movement that he had anticipated and accounted for with his sidestep. Still, there was not enough room with the sideboard in the way and the knife struck the arm that he had thrown out in a block. The serrated blade cut the sleeve of his thin cotton shirt, slicing through to the skin and flesh underneath.

Tom did not make a sound, but seized the wrist that held the blade, drawing it down and away from him and then turning it back on itself in a smooth, practiced movement. The knife clattered to the floor as he stopped the technique just prior to the point when the bones and tendons would snap. He then smoothly moved behind her and clamped his free, gloved hand over her mouth to prevent her scream.

"I'm not going to hurt you. I'M NOT GOING TO HURT YOU!"

He held her tightly, but not painfully for a few moments, and then tentatively took his hand away from her mouth, allowing her to breathe properly. His other arm dripped blood onto the linoleum through the tear in his sleeve. He released her right hand from the wristlock and gently but firmly steered her towards one of the kitchen chairs.

"Just sit down for a moment and I'll explain," he said calmly.

*M-Trait*

While she watched and her breathing gradually slowed to normal, Tom saw to his injury. He was reluctant to use anything from the first-aid kit in the kitchen in case Sherman later noticed something was missing, but there seemed to be little sensible alternative. In the end, he settled for a neat row of tapes to draw the edges of the wound together, covered with a piece of absorbent lint and a small square of transparent waterproof dressing. It was not ideal, but it would have to do until he could get home and think about something more permanent. The cut in his arm was slightly ragged from the serrated blade—a nasty little knife that Sherman used to chop vegetables. Tom knew that it would not heal as well as a clean cut; it would scar.

"Who are you?" she asked.

Tom held up his finger in motion that told her to wait a moment. She did.

He cleaned the blood off the linoleum floor with some damp paper kitchen towels, which he folded up neatly and placed in his trouser pocket; the knife he rinsed under the tap until it was clean, dried it with another sheet of kitchen towel and replaced it in the block. After a moment's thought, he selected another knife, the largest there, drew out a chair and sat at the table. He placed the knife out of her reach. It was for insurance only, and meant primarily as a deterrent. He did not think that she would make a run for it, but could not afford to take the chance.

The woman watched him quietly as he worked in a precise manner that she was unfamiliar with in all her years of cleaning houses.

Tom noticed that the woman began to sweat profusely.

# 38

Mikhail looked up at the soldier who had come to kill him. The man was large, unshaven, and still dressed in a dirty army uniform. He carried a rifle with a bayonet, raised ready to impale anyone he found. In his left hand, he carried an oil lamp, its dirty yellow light illuminating a glowing sphere around him. Little greasy twists of smoke rose from the guttering flame, invisible currents in the air carrying them this way and that as they drifted upwards.

It was a small room, containing only the chair upon which Mikhail had sat as he stared out of the window at the men who had come to destroy the Brotherhood. The soldier crossed to the window, checking outside to ensure that no one could have escaped by climbing out. A glance downward showed that to be impossible; there was nothing but a sheer drop into the courtyard, not even the narrowest of ledges to hold onto. He grunted—whether with satisfaction or disappointment Mikhail could not tell—and left to continue his business elsewhere. Under the floorboards, Mikhail stared up through the cracks into the darkened room.

The space he crouched in was cramped, a stone cell six feet square, somewhat smaller than the room above it. The only way out was the broad, loose floorboard above him that he had replaced as he climbed down into the hiding place; a priest hole, or whatever its purpose had been to the one who had put it there. Mikhail had found it early in their occupation of the place and had told no one, knowing that it could be useful to only one person, and that was going to be him. When the reports of deserting soldiers had begun filtering through to the village and the Brotherhood, he had left a container of water there, some salted meat, and a bucket. Elsewhere, spread throughout the castle, its outbuildings and the grounds, Mikhail had hidden many other things: money, clothes, weapons—though the sharp dagger in its green felt sheath was never far from him these days. Without thinking, his hand strayed to check it was still there at his waist, though he knew it was from the feel of the sheath digging into him.

The room had been his secret, one of his contingency plans for the many eventualities that *could be*. If time and experience had taught him anything, it was essential to be prepared. The fraternity was not capable, either in training or equipment, to resist an onslaught from the soldiers who were moving through the land, dispossessing the nobility of their property and status as they went. The Brothers were not fighters, had never learned how, for they could never risk the injury.

For some time, the quiet atmosphere within their community had become tense, with a soft ambient buzz when they gathered for meals or when they met in the hallways to talk. Mikhail recognized among them a muted fear. He realized that they had been static for too long, unworried in their wealth and comfort. They would not leave, he knew—they would prefer to risk losing all rather than giving it up voluntarily to run again. No, it was more than that. They refused to acknowledge the threat, because to do so would mean admitting their vulnerability. Their false security lay only in the power of their denial.

What were his choices? To leave right then, outrunning a fear that might never have existed, but for Eduard—and to abandon his own flesh and blood and never return? Or he could stay, and leave to chance his safety as the others had done. Complacent fools.

*Na miru i smert' krasna. Together with your people, even death is respectable.* The proverb raced through his mind amid the sounds of violence, muffled by the thick stone wall all around him. He judged himself safe here, unless they set fire to the castle. There had been reports that the soldiers had been burning the properties they attacked. He would not die here, not like this. *To hell with respectability.* Mikhail softly drew the dagger from its sheath and held it in front of him. In the near blackness, he could not see so much as a glint from the blade. He pressed his palm hard against the sharp tip, not so hard as to draw blood but enough that the pain gave him a focus, something to ground him in reality. In the darkness, his other senses were sharpening, broadening to fill the gap that is left when sight can no longer be of use. Without touching them, he already knew where the walls were in the confined space. Their damp smell of mold was strong in his nostrils, and sharp on the tip of his tongue as he inhaled short breaths through his mouth, trying to calm his breathing and slow his heart. The shouting had abated now, and the screams of fear and pain had stopped. Still the trampling of boots and the sound of barked orders filled the darkness.

And then, there was no more shouting. The Brothers—they were all dead.

He could not have stopped this, and he had known it was too late to do anything when he saw the men at the edge of the village. He could have hidden perhaps one other person with him, but to do that would have been to risk others trying to follow. So he had done nothing, knowing that his warnings would have fallen on deaf ears, knowing that time had already run out. Still, a part of him somewhere inside tried to tell him that he had betrayed them as much as Eduard had. Mikhail pressed his palm harder into the point of the dagger and vowed vengeance.

He now heard a new sound, one that he immediately recognized despite the muffling of the stone walls. It was a voice, low and rich— Eduard's voice. He had come back with one of the murdering looters. Mikhail was thrilled at his opportunity for vengeance.

# 39

Tom paused for a few seconds, swallowing the anger he felt after being cut on the arm. The woman before him had caused an unexpected complication in his plans at the Sherman house. This was going to take some creative action to fix. He inhaled deeply, and held his breath while he figured out what to do. When he finally exhaled, the anger left him too.

"What's your name?" His voice was calm, friendly, and sympathetic.

"Margaret." She was still scared, that was self-evident. Tom noticed that she was looking at his hands, and realized for the first time he was still wearing the gloves. Margaret eyed him suspiciously, her gaze moving over his fingers—slim, piano player's fingers, encased in their second skin—and up to his dark eyes, to see what she could tell.

In those fingers and hands she could see the wiry strength that she had felt clamped around her wrist and over her mouth. She did not like those gloves, not one bit. Whatever his voice sounded like, the gloves told her she was still in danger.

"Who are you? What are you doing here?" The housekeeper acted as if she had nothing to lose.

"My name's Tom. I'm a security consultant, doing some work for Dr. Sherman."

"Tom?" Margaret's voice sounded somewhat older than she looked, hoarse from smoking too much. That one word also told him she didn't believe a word of it.

"Yes. Listen, Margaret. I need to know what you are doing here."

"I'm Dr. Sherman's cleaning lady." His tone was confusing her; it gave a very different message to the gloves. She was struggling to keep the panic down.

"No, I know that. I mean, what are you doing here today?" Seeing she was still close to cracking up, Tom was ever patient.

Margaret, uncertain of what was being asked, obviously had not expected him to know her usual routine. "I was cleaning." The look on her face showed him she had not understood.

"No. Why Tuesday? Your normal day is Wednesday." That knowledge placed her very much at a disadvantage, as she knew nothing about him. She had not expected that, and looked up at him in alarm. Margaret was enjoying this situation less and less.

"How do you know my normal day? What is this?"

Tom drew a long, slow breath as he held his gloved hands up. A clear message: *Stop asking questions, start answering.* As a goodwill gesture, he stripped the gloves off and dropped them into his lap. Margaret seemed to relax a little. He asked again, his tone still friendly, "Edward said you normally come in on Wednesdays. So why today?"

Smart enough to realize her disadvantage and lack of options, still afraid, Margaret conceded, "I'm going on holiday tomorrow."

No pause from Tom. He continued in the same measured voice, like a well-meaning schoolteacher extracting information from an unruly pupil. It was a slow process with an inevitable end. "Where are you going?"

"France."

"How long?"

"Two weeks."

"That sounds very nice. Who with?"

"By myself, thank you." She sounded a little put out. "I'm meeting friends there."

"How are you getting there?"

"On the train."

"You don't have a car?" He already knew that she walked to the house on her cleaning days.

"No."

"Are you married?" He didn't think so—no ring, for starters, but it was a good idea to check anyway.

"Divorced, eight years ago—as if it's any of your business."

"Live with anyone?" There was a pregnant silence; she was not impressed. Tom clarified, "Partner, kids, family…?"

"No. On my own."

There was a long pause from Tom as he considered the information he had been given. Margaret decided the interrogation was over and it was time for more of her own questions. She was feeling braver now that the immediate shock was over—and angrier.

"Am I free to go?" she snapped.

Tom did not answer immediately and Margaret, becoming impatient, made to leave.

"You can't keep me here forever, you know—Tom or whoever you are."

She was gaining confidence as she worked up a sense of indignation. "The police will hear about this, just wait."

Tom rose with her and indicated the doorway. "Sure. Sorry about all this. Go that way, not through the front door." He stood in between her and the front door, not allowing her to make a break for it.

He directed her into the utility room and to the door that led into the garage. The garage itself was mostly empty, as Sherman generally kept his car on the driveway and was, in any case, away at work at the moment. There was the usual garage bric-a-brac: cobweb-covered packing cases, another large chest freezer at the back, dust and tools on the shelves, old furniture and miscellaneous bits and pieces that had not found a place in the house.

Margaret did not see him pull the gloves back on again. When she reached to press the button for garage door opener, Tom stepped up behind her, planted his feet properly, grabbed her chin and hair and pulled her head sharply back and sideways. He heard a snap.

Margaret the cleaning lady went limp and fell to his feet with a broken neck.

Tom stood for a second and looked at his handiwork. He had never performed that technique for real before. Killing really wasn't fun—particularly not when it was this easy. He took a step back and allowed himself a minute to calm down.

After a few moments of focused thought, he decided to leave the problem to the good doctor. Tom moved the body to the bottom of the chest freezer, under the frozen peas and potato croquettes, breaded scampi and hash browns. It would probably be three weeks before anyone else in this country expected to hear from her, and well over a month before the police took an interest when her friends in France insisted that something was wrong. And if Sherman discovered the body, then he would just have to find another place for it. By that time, Tom would be finished with his work here.

After finishing Margaret's chores, Tom drove straight from Sherman's house to the sports center. The pool was quiet and he swam for a long time in the cool water. Emily waited in the lobby for him for a quarter of an hour after her yoga class before she assumed that he had not come in that day, and left. He swam until the pool was about to close for the night, washing the blood from his arm and the sin from his hands—back and forth until he had no strength left and his body merged with the water.

He knew nothing except the splashing of the water in his ears and the eventual numbness in his limbs and mind.

## 40

When people meet him for the first time, their first impression is usually that he's blind. He moves with the deliberateness of a man with that condition, and invariably wears sunglasses inside and outside, even in the bleakest weather. His dark hair, peppered with a few gray streaks, reaches the collar of his long coat in thick waves, and he favors a close-cropped beard that requires little careful attention with a razor in front of a mirror. In addition, as much as his travel permits, he is invariably accompanied by his dog—a good-natured golden retriever, the kind often favored as a guide dog.

In reality, the man's stillness and careful manner mask a strength and quickness undiminished from his younger years, and the dark glasses that protect his eyes from the sun and harsh indoor light hide the fact that he can see perfectly well.

Seeing him, standing motionless amongst the crowds at the airport gate, Tom came to the cold realization that he was being watched—the old man had been waiting unhurriedly for him to walk over. Tom did so, keeping Rufus on a short lead to avoid his straying into the throng of travelers. Since the animal had been vaccinated and micro-chipped, only a brief stay in quarantine had been required while the paperwork was checked. But Rufus ignored the throngs of travelers, having eyes only for his master. The old man bent down to greet the canine before acknowledging the human holding the leash. When he straightened up, and Rufus had taken his place at his side, the elder finally turned his attention to Tom.

"Hello, son—how long's it been?" His voice was as unhurried as his movement, a slow, slightly scratchy baritone that included the edge of an American accent. The brief, firm grip on Tom's bicep was as much greeting and as much physical affection as his father ever demonstrated.

"Hello, father—sixteen, eighteen months. I was passing through New York on my way to France for a vacation." In his presence, Tom found himself emulating his father's laconic speech.

"Ah, yes—young men and their *wanderlust*. You should come back to New York more often."

It was his father's habit to drop foreign words into conversation where English had no appropriate equivalent, pronouncing the word in its native accent before switching back to a slow drawl without missing a beat.

*You're the reason I'm here now, doing your dirty work*, Tom wanted to say. Exactly the same height as his father, Tom looked into the man's face from where he stood a foot away and saw only his reflection in the glasses. Finally, he mumbled quickly, "Perhaps I'll return after this job."

"Mmmmm, perhaps." A slow pause followed this appraisal, and Tom waited for his father to speak again. "If you carry this off, there'll certainly be a place for you."

He rested a hand on the dog's head. He had not moved since Tom arrived, as if his feet were rooted to the floor. Around them, the world moved on in fast-forward, ignored with effortless precision.

"So, why are you here?" Tom asked, feeling anxious at his father's sudden decision to fly to London. This was not his usual mode of operation—he rarely became personally involved in any project. The email Tom had received from his father had been the briefest of communications: a time, a date, a flight number and instructions to pick Rufus up from quarantine. The purpose of the visit—and Tom's father was not given to impulsive trips—had been unstated.

"I'm here for Zoe—and to make sure there isn't another of your little *contretemps*."

"That *mishap* wasn't my fault." Tom was careful not to show his anger. His father had taught him that to display his emotion, particularly when provoked, was a weakness. It would not please him now. "I had no way of knowing she'd turn up. I dealt with it. It's over." The memory of the noise Margaret made when he snapped her neck in Sherman's garage caused him to grimace within.

"Mmmmm." There was another long pause, long enough to show that the subject had been set aside but not forgotten. "Now, tell me about *her*."

Tom knew that his father meant Emily. He had not told his father about his budding relationship with Emily, only that he had discovered her and Zoe's traits on Sherman's computer. Still, the old man had an uncanny way of reading between the lines.

"Not here." It was a small gesture of defiance against his father, framed as a genuine concern for privacy.

"Let's get a drink then."

Rather than leave the airport, as Tom had expected, they went to a bar in the terminal. The travelers moving briskly within the building stepped around the man led by a guide dog. Although his steps were measured, he was not at all hesitant or stiff in his movements, merely unhurried. Sitting at a table in the bar, both of them with a double Scotch on the rocks, his father finally removed the dark glasses. If the eyes were the windows to the soul, Tom could see in no better than before.

He spoke for almost an hour, answering his father's questions, providing more detail on each aspect of the job: what he had learned about Sherman, about his project in Zoe, and about Emily. His father only nodded at the new information, but Tom could tell that his excitement was growing with each added fact. When he mentioned Zoe's name again, his father couldn't contain himself any longer.

"Perfect! Zoe means *eternity* in Greek." He followed his statement with a hearty laugh before continuing. "Every time something new turns up—it just gets better and better."

"Not that it's been easy." Tom could not help but remind his father that he had been the one doing all the work, and that his father depended on him for information.

When he replaced his glass on the table, the older man moved with an alacrity that still surprised Tom. He found his arm held in a strong grip, the sleeve of his shirt pulled up over the healing scar on his arm. Their eyes met, and although no expression registered, the message was very clear, "No more mistakes, Tanek."

"I said it's going well," Tom repeated, trying to keep his anger out of his voice. He then realized it was the first time in many years that his father used his birth name—a Polish peasant's name that he despised. He wondered why his father chose to speak it now.

"But the body is still in the freezer. Its discovery jeopardizes everything." His father then let go and rose from the table. "I have reservations."

It was unclear whether he was talking about the hotel room he had booked, or his son. He then added, "Son, I know that—possibly barring myself—there is no one on this earth you consider superior to yourself. But, please remember, Sherman is a very smart man. Be very careful—don't arouse his anger. I know what he can do."

He strode off with Rufus, the dog's paws clicking on the hard floor, leaving his son to finish his drink alone. Tom did not know where his father was staying, but assumed he would be in touch when he felt like it. He ordered another double whiskey and stayed in the airport bar for another half hour as the world moved on around him chaotically.

# 41

"Hands off, please. I'm not completely helpless, you know."

Emily held on tight to the shopping cart. The four or five cubic feet of metal basket were now her only domain. She let Edward get away with the rest, going back and forth grabbing armfuls of items, but she would not let him push the cart, too. Using her pregnancy as an excuse, he had tried to take over from her twice now, but on the second time she had fixed him with a steely gaze that left him in no doubt of her resolve. This was *her* job, her token of independence, and whatever else he did she was going to hold onto at least that.

Edward had agreed to take the afternoon off to help Emily with some last-minute shopping. It was a Saturday, so she did not feel too bad about asking him to come with her. She would have preferred to be with her best friend, but Karen was out of town on a business trip. She had even thought about asking Tom, but she wasn't sure how he would react to giving up his afternoon to be dragged around various stores. Edward, she knew, wouldn't be doing anything special.

"Happy to come with you," he said, "I've been working too hard recently anyway."

"I've picked up most of the essentials," she said, "but one last trip would be smart to make absolutely sure. Besides, when will the next time be when I can shop this freely?"

As she slowly pushed the cart around the high aisles of the department store, she wondered whether it would have been better to come on her own. This was like shopping with her mother. Edward was careful with her, so protective and overzealous that she didn't know what to think. Into the eighth month of her pregnancy, Emily herself was as cautious as any first-time mother-to-be, but Edward's concern was far in excess of even her own.

"How are you?" he asked her, as she paused to look at a shelf of soft toys.

"I'm fine!" she insisted. It was five minutes since he had last made her stop and rest.

Six months ago, it might have been touching, but now she was not so amused, nor was she sure that this kind of behavior was entirely healthy. It wasn't fair to make comparisons, but the contrast with Tom was striking. Tom, if anything, had too much confidence in her. Not that he would ever miss an opportunity to help, but he was a little better at respecting her independence.

Edward insisted on paying for as much as he could get away with and, when in any doubt, erring on the side of too much rather than too little. This was the last shop they were visiting—she could take no more—and he was still loading up the cart with more than she would ever have purchased on her own.

"Where am I going to store all of this?" she asked.

"Leave some of it at my place if it's a problem," he answered. "Better to have it and not need it, than wake up one morning and realize you're out of diapers."

"That would be one morning in 2025, at this rate," she told him.

Emily paused to gaze at a range of mobiles and other toys that hang over a baby's crib. She didn't need to buy one, but it was a good pretext to take a breather for a couple of minutes, and she didn't want Edward to know that she really was tired.

The remark about leaving stuff at his house bothered her a bit, and she resolved to find a way of squeezing it all into her flat, even if it meant she could barely move. A couple of months ago, Edward had offered his own house to her and Zoe. It had only been a suggestion, one made with the observation about having too much space for just himself in his large house. She had toyed with the idea without making a commitment, and now she was happy she hadn't made that mistake. Emily had never seriously entertained the idea of getting back together with Edward in the months after she became pregnant. They were still close friends, and she sometimes regretted the idea of Zoe growing up without a proper father. But that, in itself, was not a good enough reason to restart a romance that had ended for a very good reason. Wherever her future ultimately lay, it was not with Edward.

She appreciated his attention, and was grateful beyond measure for the generosity and consideration he had shown her, but at times she could not help but ask herself why he did it. Perhaps, she thought, he saw her as a kind of substitute for the family he had once had but lost. He was not ready to move on. Consciously or otherwise, this was his way of having what he otherwise could not: a child of his own. She suspected he was experiencing the joy of parenthood vicariously, through her.

Grandparenthood might be more appropriate. If his son had been alive, she supposed that, at forty-five, he could practically be a grandfather by now. He had never mentioned his birthday, and never asked to celebrate it with her or anyone else, as far as she knew. She had never received a straight answer from him about it, and only had the quick look at his driver's license to go on. A few years ago, on the date of birth she had remembered seeing on the license—August 15th—she had left an unsigned card in an envelope on his desk. It was meant to be another good-natured joke between them. She had been looking forward to seeing the expression on his face when he realized she'd sneaked one by him. Instead, Edward had looked so sad when he opened the envelope and read the card that she thought he was going to cry. He had recovered his composure quickly when he saw her watching, but something in his eyes—a look she had seen only once before—stopped her from asking him what hurt so much. She had not left a card for him the next year, or since. She still wondered what memory about his family it had evoked, but had never had the courage, or cruelty, to bring it up.

Not living in Edward's large house would be a minus, but she liked her flat. Property wasn't cheap in the center of London, and now that she had it, she wasn't giving it up. That was the one thing James had been good for, always caring too much about money and *stuff*. He was materialistic; he liked owning unnecessary things—expensive clothes, cars, gadgets. In that respect, Tom was far more like her. She really admired how he worked hard and fashioned his own business so he could live his own life.

She smiled and turned back to her shopping cart. Edward came back from his latest sortie holding a selection of baby clothes.

"What have you got there?" she asked—he knew perfectly well that Zoe had all the clothes she would need for at least the first two years.

"I figured one or two more couldn't hurt."

Emily let him drop the four sets in the trolley, and waited until his back was turned to take them out and leave them on the nearest shelf. It was sweet of him, but a little condescending, too. She hoped he didn't see himself as responsible in some way for her baby, and that it was just misguided friendship.

They finally finished shopping when Emily put her foot down at his latest armful of goods and pushed the overflowing basket to the checkout. She even managed to get her credit card out before he had a chance to complain. Edward drove her home, and they spent a while unpacking their purchases and finding places to put everything. Emily had set a room aside as a nursery but, because she had not finished decorating, they could not yet use the cupboards and shelves for all the toys, clothes, and endless other baby equipment. Several months ago, she had begun the job of repapering and painting the walls, thinking that she would do the job gradually before Zoe arrived. As time passed, however, she became less and less able to summon the will, patience, and agility required to climb the stepladder unaccompanied. Edward had helped where he could, but finishing it would require a good couple of days' work. He had already helped so much that she felt bad asking. Besides, his efforts had been less than expert. It had taken him four attempts to hang the first strip of paper even vaguely straight, and the result still glared at her whenever she walked in. Three of the four walls remained uncovered, the rolls of vinyl paper still lying in their plastic shrink-wrap, unopened, along with the other tools.

With only weeks to go, she wondered if she could get him to have another go at it. Beggars, after all, cannot afford to be choosers, and she was in no state to do it herself. Besides, Zoe would hardly mind how crooked the wallpaper was. The perfectionist in her still shrank from asking him, knowing the mess would mock her until she next got around to redecorating, goodness only knew how many years down the line.

Perhaps she would ask Tom to help.

## 42

When Mikhail heard Eduard's voice from the hallway in the castle, he felt a sensation he had never known before. It was an overwhelming urge for revenge, to kill the man whose selfishness had taken everything away from him.

Mikhail had never found pleasure in taking life. Unlike Alexander, he always viewed murder with a cool, analytic dispassion. It was simply a tool to be used when necessary. Alexander enjoyed exercising his power, had seen it as his right over a lesser species, just animals to be mistreated and killed for sport. It had come back on him—on them all, now.

Still, there was only one person he could blame, and that was Eduard. Eduard, whom he had taken in despite the misgivings and opposition of the others; Eduard, who had never really fit, who had cared more for his own happiness than for their collective safety; Eduard, who had never truly understood his place.

Standing up, slightly hunched to accommodate his height in the cramped hiding place, Mikhail carefully lifted the board out of its place and set it to the side. With the dagger between his teeth, he pulled himself up by the fingertips, bracing his feet against the walls below for leverage. The room above was almost as dark as the one he had left, and it took a minute as he quietly replaced the floorboard by feel.

He heard Eduard tell the soldier with him to search elsewhere. By the sound of receding footsteps, Mikhail guessed that Eduard was now alone, probably searching for the possessions he'd left behind in his rush to leave the Brotherhood. Softly, Mikhail edged his body along the passage, the dagger in his left hand and the other on the wall to guide him in the darkness. Ahead, from a doorway on the left, a faint, flickering light was visible. The room used to belong to Kostya, Eduard's son.

He stole up to the door, knowing by instinct and without conscious thought which floorboards to avoid, so that the creaks would not give him away. Peering around into the room, holding his breath, he saw Eduard, his back to Mikhail, collecting his son's possessions on the bed and wrapping them in a cloth to take with him. A flickering oil lamp by the door cast distorted, animated shadows of him, creating a twisted monster with a life of its own on the opposite wall.

Mikhail slipped the dagger back into its sheath by his waist. The dagger might not kill Eduard quickly enough, leaving him time to fight back. Instead, he took one of the heavy pewter candelabras that stood in the passage, easing it out of its bracket on the wall. It took both hands to hold and raise it over his shoulder as a makeshift club. Then the anger overwhelmed him and he strode into the room and swung it with all his strength directly at Eduard's head. His own rising shadow cast on the wall gave his presence away, but it was too late. Eduard turned and, in the awful fraction of a second before the candelabra found its target, Mikhail saw his face. It was not Eduard at all—his son Kostya accepted the horrible blow that ended his life in a brief moment.

He remembered how much Kostya had looked and sounded like his father, how he had shared his mannerisms and speech patterns and even walked the same way. He realized how, impetuous in his eagerness to hunt down Eduard, he had mistaken Kostya for his father, and that muffled voice he heard so clearly from his stone hiding place now seemed to mock him for his mistake.

There was nothing he could do. Kostya lay on the floor, the single, fatal blow to his temple a terrible and completed inevitability. Lying motionless, he looked exactly as he had done in life, and somehow utterly different as well. Something was missing. This was not Kostya any longer. It was just a shell.

Mikhail did not know how long he had stood there, stunned at his crime, the candelabra hanging heavy at his side. His anger had been for Eduard: his vengeance intended for him alone. Though Kostya was—had been—Eduard's son, Mikhail would not have chosen this fate for him. Kostya's death was another stain on his already tarnished soul.

Soon Eduard would wonder where his son had gone and would come looking for him. If he found his son dead, he would realize that a member of the Brotherhood had escaped. It would be better if that did not happen. Mikhail's eyes fell on the oil lamp, and somewhere in his mind a memory resurfaced, an old door opened. For a moment, it was a night long ago in a little village in the south of Poland—another death, another fire, and screaming hellish faces coming at him out of the darkness. Then, with a struggle, the door closed again, and the present came back into sharp focus.

He took hold of Kostya's cloak, the two sides of it at the neck bunched together in his right hand, and half-carried, half-dragged him out of the room and down the passage. It took only a minute to push the lifeless form into the space under the floor that, until so recently, he had hid himself in. Mikhail replaced the board, returned the candelabra to its bracket, and picked up the bundle of possessions that Kostya had collected. Last of all, he grabbed the oil lamp, spilling its contents along the corridor as he ran.

The fire began to gut the entire structure as Mikhail slid from the shadows of the lower kitchen and found his way out through the back of the castle. Moving slowly around the grounds as the soldiers and towns people became transfixed by the growing fire, Mikhail watched as others held Eduard back from the flames, preventing him from entering the burning fortress in a wild attempt to rescue his only son.

Fearful of continued recriminations against the Brotherhood, Mikhail immediately fled the village, his home for the last century. In doing so, he temporarily left behind his chance for revenge against Eduard. He would just have to wait for another instance to locate and destroy the source of his deepening rage.

# 43

"I saw Tom Oldham again yesterday." Emily tried to say it as casually as possible—just as small talk, nothing of consequence, as if she were telling him which film she had seen last night.

"Who?" Edward did not seem to remember the name, which Emily thought strange. His memory was exceptionally good, and he was capable of recalling whole conversations they had had months ago, practically verbatim. Names he had heard only in passing usually gave him no problem, so it was odd that he did not recognize someone who might potentially be of some significance to his research.

"Tom—I met him a while back at the sports center when my car broke down, remember? He was interested in our work here."

"Yes, of course. I remember now. Have you convinced him to come in and donate his blood to medical science yet?"

"Not yet." Emily smiled.

To be honest, she didn't want to push Tom too hard about coming to the lab. He was interested at first, but now seemed a bit reluctant, and she had not pressured him. If he really wanted to, he would come in his own time.

"Oh well," Edward said without much interest.

Edward did not seem overly inclined to continue the conversation, almost as if he was not particularly interested to know if Tom could be of service to him. For a second, she felt an insane urge to make him jealous, to stick up for Tom and make Edward know he was at least worth talking about.

"You'd like him. I think you'd get on well."

"Why, what's he like?" She seemed to have succeeded in drawing him into reluctant conversation.

"He's smart—probably one of the smartest people I've ever met, present company aside, of course. But he's really sweet and easy to talk to as well." She realized that had come out slightly wrong; Edward was easy to talk to as well. "You know what I mean."

"Where did you go?" he asked.

"We went to watch Shakespeare in the park." Emily had really enjoyed the afternoon with Tom, and had suggested they go again in a fortnight's time when *Macbeth* was on.

"Ah, very nice. What does he do?"

"He's some kind of security consultant. But what he really likes to do is teach classical guitar."

"Good for him. Nice work if you can get it." He seemed genuinely interested.

"Doing both requires him to work a lot—twelve-hour days, sometimes. He always says he fills a lifetime in every decade, a decade in every year."

There was a crash from Edward's desk. Emily stopped awkwardly, realizing that she had said "always," indicating that she had seen him many times before. Looking over, she realized the commotion: Edward was busy picking up pens and pencils from a mug that had been knocked over—he didn't even notice her slip up in the conversation. Emily turned back to her own work, checking the supplies of DNA kits and deciding what was running out and needed ordering, glad of the cover it provided to hide her moment of embarrassment.

Emily was apprehensive about starting life as a single mother and, although Edward gave her all the support he could, it would be good for her to have more company; he could not be there for her all the time. Tom was the first person in some time in whose company she felt comfortable. There was no pressure on her, and she placed none on Tom, for it to be anything other than companionship. Perhaps, in the course of time, it would indeed turn out to be something else. Who knew what could happen? But right now, that was definitely not the first thing on her mind. Perhaps, in the course of time, she could introduce Edward to Tom.

She settled back into her work, packing the DNA kits back into the box where they were kept on the shelf above her desk. *Everything in my world is going so remarkably well*, she thought.

## 44

The first months after Mikhail left the Brotherhood's compound in Russia had not been kind to him. Twice during the Russian Revolution of 1917 he ventured back to the grounds during the biting darkness of winter, returning by night to its fire-blackened remains: roofless, jagged, and surreal in the mockery of what had once been. He recovered packages hidden around the grounds and left with enough money to ensure that he would not have to work until he moved to a safer area and accessed other preserves of their wealth. But, for all the financial means with him, he was still rootless, without a home or a family for the first time in a hundred years.

The sense of desolation that Mikhail felt was almost impossible to bear. Eduard had instigated the murder of his family, but it was more than that. His race, his *kind*, had been wiped off the face of the earth by one of their own. Eduard's act had been nothing short of genocide.

Mikhail did not know why he was born different, nor why he had never met another human like himself other than those in his family. He assumed, simply, that there were no others. He had been the father of a race, the ancestor of every single member of the Brotherhood. Eduard's treachery had been complete—taking away every man he could call kin in a few short hours.

After retrieving what he could from the Brotherhood's compound, he never returned. That chapter of his life was closed for good, never to be reopened, as he could never return to the little village in Poland where he had been born, or the town where he had spent his second lifetime with Leba and Barak. Another new chapter was beginning, and everything had to change. Most of all, Mikhail would change, promising himself to be ever stronger and to never make the same mistakes again. Unfortunately, Eduard's effect on his life was not yet complete, and he was forced to swallow more treachery.

Aside from the wealth that he had accumulated in their community in Russia before the Revolution, he and the Brothers had also held cash assets in Switzerland, ever wary of the precariousness of the political environment during war. The security and secrecy of the Swiss bank accounts had been common knowledge to merchants and nobles since the early 1700s. Mikhail had taken advantage of this reputation towards the end of the nineteenth century, as the banks grew and changed to accommodate the concurrent industrial advances. The lengthy trip to Geneva would prove worthwhile, as he was confident that the Brotherhood's money was hidden away safely, protected and insured in an uncertain world.

In total there had been five Swiss bank accounts; four that the Brothers all knew about and had access to, and one that Mikhail reserved for his own use and told no one about. When he came to investigate the contents of these, he found that the first account he tried had been emptied only a week earlier. Shocked at this new act of treason, he had tried a second, and a third. In all, three of the four Brotherhood accounts had been emptied; Eduard had arrived before him, taking most of the fortune that they had built up. There was no way to tell where either he or the money had gone.

Mikhail had to think fast. A large sum of money was still left in the last of the Brotherhood accounts—money which he could put to good use. But he also knew that if he emptied that account, Eduard would realize that someone had escaped the fire. He had lost almost everything, but his one advantage was that Eduard did not know he was alive. Mikhail decided to leave the money where it was—he would never let Eduard know of his continued existence.

He hated the added injustice of Eduard looting the Brotherhood's fortune, but there was nothing Mikhail could do about the situation, and no possible way of finding out where Eduard had gone. He shelved his desire for immediate revenge in order to concentrate on the present.

For the next twenty years, he barely stayed in the same place more than six months at a time. Mostly, but not exclusively, he confined his travels to Europe. He did not wish to draw attention to himself—that had been their undoing in Russia. Now under the modernized name, Michael, he assumed a role that had once been his, almost two centuries ago, when he traded textiles between Krakow and the towns around it in southern Poland. As he had done before, at that time and again in Russia, he consolidated his position and prepared for the future.

His foresight and hard work paid off. The First World War had taken its toll in Europe, but whatever the war had left standing was the basis for growth. In the course of time, the numbered and nameless bank accounts would protect his assets during the turbulent and confused period of the Second World War.

He weathered the storm of war in a series of villages in Spain, not far from the French border, giving himself the option of moving north or out to sea if circumstances required.

In a world in turmoil, this was a period of strange peace for Michael. For the first time since he had left Russia, he could afford to stop and draw breath. He was alone in the world, and had no responsibilities—no Brotherhood to oversee, no enemies to worry about. No one knew him, and he had no history here. It was an opportunity to forget about the pain and loneliness of his previous lives, to put aside who he really was and relax.

After World War II, Michael realized that there was nothing stopping him from staying in Spain, a place he suddenly found had become his home. But when he moved, it was only a few miles to a neighboring village. It was far enough that no one knew him, but close enough that it did not feel as if he was leaving everything behind again.

With the relative calm of the 1950s, Michael toured the continent, taking stock of what he owned, buying further small properties around Europe, always in villages slightly off the beaten path, but close enough to major towns to be useful—nowhere that would attract any interest in and of itself, but near the centers of attention: England,

## M-Trait

Poland, Portugal, Czechoslovakia. His life turned into a game of strategy, buying and selling, keeping his ear to the ground for political and economic developments and staying at least three steps ahead of bloodshed or ruin, moving whenever the threat of violence or financial downturn loomed too close.

When America sought the advantages of a political alliance with Spain, he grasped the opportunities that came with it. Throughout the next decade, he saw his careful investments in industrial businesses grow, and forged links with organizations in the United States that would later prove extremely shrewd. As he nurtured his own fledgling empire, he kept a watchful eye as the government technocrats honed their policies and shaped the country's future. The 1960s vindicated his cautious decisions as Spain enjoyed a dramatic increase in wealth.

Nevertheless, when he saw the signs of growing unrest at the government's economic restrictions, he began to move more and more of his assets across the Atlantic to technology companies in America. By the time that Franco's regime came under attack from Basque nationalists, most of his investments were safe, thousands of miles away. And yet, he stayed in the country he had grown to love, out of harm's way in small towns away from the centers of unrest.

Perhaps it was the loneliness that softened him, but as the years passed he even considered starting a family again. A romance with a flamenco dancer blossomed in the 1970s and, for a while, he was able to forget who he was and lose himself in the present, in the life and the color that he found in her music and dancing, and in her spirit. But for the knowledge of Eduard, whom he had not seen for almost sixty years and who, for all he knew, was now dead anyway, he had no ties to the past—nothing to remind him where he had come from, or of his previous lives.

The romance, and the brief illusion of normality, ended abruptly when she died in childbirth, in the cottage he had bought on a hillside some miles from Salamanca. The village in which it stood was tiny—little more than a church and a handful of houses. Until that time, he had been more content than he could remember being ever before, happier even than he had been with Leba and Barak. The sun would come up, bringing with it a light breeze that blew gently through the open windows in the warm summer morning. He remembered the scent of basil and of roses, their petals strewn around the room by the breeze from the bushes outside. The sunlight had fallen across her face, highlighting the fine laughter lines around her eyes with tiny shadows. It was a reminder of the mortality that he did not share with her. This time, he did not have to wait for her to age. Only hours later she had died from complications in the birth of their son, and he was able to remember her as she was then, before the ravages of time took their inevitable toll.

That was when Michael finally realized that he had been deluding himself. His long stay in Spain, his romance and hope for a family—it had been nothing but weakness, a way of trying to convince himself that things were other than they were. He could never be normal, and could never expect to raise a family like other people. Angry at his own stupidity and blindness, Michael vowed never to allow himself to become close to another mortal again. He had been a fool to think otherwise.

He had high expectations for the boy, who he hoped would be the beginning of a new line. Leaving Spain, Michael began to put down some roots elsewhere, a more permanent base in America where he could see to his son's education. He still took frequent trips abroad, but now for weeks or months rather than years at a time. In the end, his son was a bitter disappointment, a mortal child who could never share in his hopes for a new Brotherhood.

It was around this time that Michael began to seriously question his longevity, and what it was that set him apart from other men. Until then, he had always viewed his longevity as a blessing to be embraced, no matter what difficulties it also brought with it. Though he still did not shrink from it, he now began to look for the reason why, after over three hundred years, he was still alive. As travel became faster and cheaper, he began to move further afield, roaming the world as if in search of something that even he could not yet identify.

# 45

Tom ran smoothly and easily, the gentle *pad-pad* of the cushioned running shoes making almost no sound on the pavement above the ambient noise of surrounding life. It was an early summer morning, early enough to be pleasantly cool. There were also few people around. In an hour or so, the heavy commuter traffic would begin. Children would be on their way to school, and the noise and car fumes would make his exercise far less pleasurable. For now, though, both the streets and the air were relatively clear. There were a few newspaper vendors, some early risers and joggers like himself, but it was a far cry from the usual bustle and pollution.

Jogging around a street corner, he was almost stopped by a pair of early-bird tourists, struggling with a map. "Can you tell me the way to—"

"Excuse me!" Tom had simply yelled, without malice or venom, but without sympathy or concern either. He ran straight between them, leaving them staring at him in amazement. He wasn't about to interrupt his run for something so trivial—but neither would he let the irritation spoil his mood. It was a time of day Tom enjoyed most. Wherever he lived across the world, through clear mountain air, over green plains, or refracted through layers of smog in a city, he never tired of experiencing a sunrise.

He paused at the top of a slight incline to take a drink from the bottle of mineral water and to consider his route. Often he did not plan where he was running and decided on the spur of the moment where to go. It took only a minute to orient himself, and then he was off again towards Richmond Park, about a mile and a half away, the largest expanse of green for some distance. The city was just beginning to wake up properly now, and the distant noises of traffic and activity were filtering through the still fresh air.

Tom took the headphones out of his pocket and plugged them into the CD player clipped to his waistband. *Simon and Garfunkel's Greatest Hits* blocked out the sound of the outside world as he made his way through some quieter streets to the park. He picked up the pace for the final mile or so, sprinting the last few hundred meters and arriving out of breath, heart pounding. He stood for a moment, hands on knees to support his weight, cooling in the breeze as his heart slowed, and then began a series of stretches.

It was Tom's practice to go through his karate katas after running, when he was already warm and less likely to pull a muscle. After checking the grass for broken glass and anything else obnoxious, he took off his running shoes and socks and put them to one side. The shoes were expensive, light but very well padded in the soles. Tom ran often, and joint damage from the repeated impact played no part in his plans for the future.

He took the CD player, still running with the volume turned up loud, and left it by his shoes and water bottle. He began with the first kata and worked up to the more complex ones. *Rising block, stepping-punch, turn*—ingrained in his body's muscle memory, he did not even have to think about the movements any more. *Front kick, turn, downwards block, reverse punch.* Over on the other side of the park a couple were doing tai chi, their slow, almost languid movements contrasting with the sharp snap of his own.

He finished with two sets of sit-ups, taking a few moments at the end to lie on the grass and contemplate the blue sky. The sun was higher now, warm on his skin through the light breeze, winning against the early-morning chill. It would be a hot day, and he was pleased to have made the effort to get up early to run while it was not uncomfortable.

The rest of the day was his to spend as he chose, and he enjoyed the slow walk back towards his flat, stretching his legs after the run, listening to his music and appreciating the sun on his face. *Looking for fun and feeling groovy....* He was glad he did not have to work, spending a third of his life in a meaningless grind to sustain a meaningless life. The time this gave him also meant that he was afforded opportunities that would otherwise not be open to him. He still traveled a lot, mainly in Europe, but also to Asia when the whim took him. Tom enjoyed studying languages; he had a flair for it and was fluent in several. He had no job, at least none that he held because he had to, and could leave at reasonably short notice whenever he wanted. No family, no dependents, no responsibilities...*I got no deeds to do, no promises to keep.* His life was his own, to live as he chose, not sacrificed to a career that would consume a large chunk of his time and tie him to a single location.

He was the ultimate free spirit—for now. But it appeared that that could change, if he wanted it to—if he could play the hand as it needed to be played. Soon he would have to make that decision, and stick to it. So far in his life, his father had been the only family he had had, and their relationship left a lot to be desired. Now he was finally ready to move on, and there was every indication that his new family would be a whole lot better. The decision came from an unserious moment with Emily.

"What do you want to do, Tom?" Emily had asked him at their last meeting, as they sat on the grass in the park after the play had finished.

"Don't know. Grab some coffee, go for dinner maybe? There's this great—"

"No, silly. Long-term, I mean, with your life?"

"Good question. Teach guitar, keep consulting, I suppose—maybe here in London, maybe travel some." He continued to leave it vague. "A wife, if I can find one mad enough to have me—and two point four kids, a mortgage..."

Emily had sighed. "Are you ever serious about anything?"

Tom nodded. "Hmm, you're right, I am pushing thirty. Maybe I should skip the 2.4 kids and go straight to the mortgage."

Emily couldn't help but laugh. Tom knew then he was close to winning her heart. He just had to figure out how to please his father and claim her as his prize at the same time.

The streets were bustling now as he slowly made his way through, against the flow of civilization, in all their various guises—the smart businessman with his briefcase, the kid in the hood and jeans with his skateboard, the identical Japanese tourists with their cameras and phrasebooks, and the single mother with her pushchair and shopping bags. A swarm of humanity, human ants in pursuit of their own goals, living out their lives among each other, their useless buzzing filtered and masked by his headphones and music. *Thank goodness I am not one of you.*

Back in his flat, Tom changed out of his tracksuit and showered, washing the smoke of the city and the contamination of proximity off his body. He left the CD player playing on a loop, with the volume turned up, to ensure the batteries were absolutely dead.

As he ate a late breakfast, sitting in front of the wide window and staring down on the city, he decided to visit Sherman's house that morning to read Edward's emails and test his "accidental death" scenario.

# 46

From his vantage point behind the wall, it was possible to see Tom gain entrance to Edward's house without being spotted. Michael watched as his son unlocked the back gate, cast a final glance around him, and stepped into the alcove. A moment later, he disappeared into the house.

Michael had to admit that Tom had done a good job, at least to begin with. Left to his own devices, he had easily gained entrance to Edward's house, copying the keys so he could return without anyone being the wiser. That much had been competent enough.

Of course, Michael's way was much easier. Tom had followed his usual practice of leaving the door in the garden wall unlatched, and both the gate and the door to the house closed but unlocked. Michael slipped through the garden door with a quick look around him and swiftly passed to the back door. He eased the gate open and stepped into the cool shadow of the alcove, ducking down to remain unseen. Through the glass, he saw Tom going up the stairs. Once his son was out of sight, Michael stepped softly into the utility room, closing the door behind him.

After a promising beginning, things had gone badly downhill for Tom. The incident with the cleaning lady had been an unforgivable mistake, and one that could have cost them dearly. Still, Michael needed Tom on his side for a while longer. After their strained meeting in the airport, he decided it would be best to hide his displeasure. Tom was older now, and the strict, disciplinarian approach wasn't working as well.

"You were right, of course," he told his son in a later meeting, "Killing Margaret was the only sensible solution at that point.

Anything else would have risked exposure. We could have lost everything."

"That's what I've been trying to tell you. And don't think that was an easy decision to make."

Despite his resolution to nurture the troubled relationship, that kind of presumption displeased Michael. "While I appreciate your fast thinking, it was nothing more than damage limitation, Tom. It should never have happened in the first place."

"You think I wanted it to?"

Michael had not been impressed. "It happened, and you dealt with it as best you could," he said. Then, with finality, "Now get rid of the body so we can move on." But his son hadn't disposed of the cleaning lady, and that was the final error.

Tom's mistakes had been his laxity driven from arrogance. He had gone to Edward's house too many times to gather information, which raised the chances of getting caught—whether in person, as with the cleaning lady's unexpected visit, and now her body just waiting to be uncovered. And there was Emily—his son had obviously fallen for her. Love could only cloud his judgment further.

Michael had no other choice—it was the reason he was here now. He had to take control of the situation.

Standing behind the utility room door, breathing quiet, shallow breaths, Michael listened as Tom finally came down the stairs. He heard soft steps in the hallway, the closing of the back door and finally the gate. Through the window, he watched his son cross the garden and leave through the gate in the wall. Why did he even come here? Michael was alone in Sherman's house—ready to perform some real work.

Leaving his hiding place, he moved silently around upstairs, visiting each room exactly once, taking in everything he saw. Back downstairs, he stood in the kitchen. Tom claimed he had done a good job about leaving nothing behind that would give him away. He always wore the thin latex gloves that prevented grease smears and fingerprints—Michael wore a similar pair now. And he had touched nothing without memorizing its place to begin with. Tom had been careful, and had gotten away with it for weeks, which was far more than he deserved. But now was the time to leave a few clues, to create fear in the animal. Now was the time to show Edward that he was hunted.

Michael ran his hand stiffly through his long hair. Bringing his hand down, a grey hair came away, trapped between his gloved fingers. He frowned and then repeated the process. This time one of his black hairs came out. Folding it in two, he used his steel dagger to slice it. He was now left with two short hairs. One was placed on the kitchen table. He looked around the kitchen and then left the other hair on the counter, next to the espresso maker. As an afterthought, he nudged the heavy chrome base of the coffee machine, pushing it slightly off square to the work surface. He also pulled one of the wicker-seated chairs a little further out from the table, and closed the door to the hallway that had been left wide open.

Michael stood in thought for a few more moments. Tom had screwed up badly with Margaret, but maybe he could turn that around to work in his favor. If Edward knew about that, he would be under no illusions about the stakes here. Smiling to himself, Michael went through to the hallway, entered the garage, and busied himself around the freezer a little while before returning to the house.

All there was left to do was wait. Perhaps Edward would not notice anything; perhaps he would come home, cook dinner in his kitchen without a second thought and go to bed. On the other hand, it might be enough to warn him that he was no longer safe, that he was being stalked, that his past had caught up with him, and that it was time to pay for his crimes against the Brotherhood.

It did not matter which. Sherman might recognize the danger, and take Tom out first. Perhaps he would die afterwards anyway. Alternatively, Tom could finish what Michael had sent him to do. Then Michael would have to take care of his son himself. It made no difference to him who did what to whom. There wasn't room for either of them in his world.

On his way out, Michael lifted the spare keys from their hook by the back door. He needed to borrow them for a few hours.

# 47

Edward had been somewhat shaken by what Emily had said to him in the lab. That expression, so loved by the Brothers, was one he had not heard in almost a hundred years— *a lifetime in every decade, a decade in every year....* And there it was, suddenly, from the mouth of Emily, while talking about her "new friend, Tom."

He spent the rest of that afternoon thinking about it, trying to rationalize it and calculate the odds that it was just chance. What was more likely, after all? That a man was back from the dead, or that a mere combination of words had been thrown together by accident? Having almost convinced himself that it was a coincidence, Edward drove home and let himself into the house.

He could not place what was wrong. Still on edge, he just had an uneasy feeling that something was not quite right. He stood in the kitchen, looking around. The room was the same as he had left it in the morning. Nothing was missing, nothing had changed, and yet it did not feel right. He tried to shrug off the feeling of unease, turned, and left the room walking through to the sitting room. Why was one of the dining chairs away from the table? He had been the only one in the house last night, and he had not sat there at breakfast time. Edward again shook off his uneasy feeling and went upstairs for an early night.

It did him good. He slept well and woke refreshed, and by the next morning Edward had completely forgotten about the feeling. Bleary-eyed, he stood in his dressing gown and poured a glass of orange juice from the fridge. Sitting at the table, though, the feeling of unease came to his mind again. He did not move, knowing that by doing so he might lose the stimulus for the feeling, hoping to place it now that his mind was fresh.

There, on the counter—the espresso machine had moved. It was a tiny change, no more than a centimeter or two, but it was noticeable: the heavy chrome base was off square with the countertop. Edward was fairly sure he had not knocked it the day before, but could not be certain.

Nonplussed, he straightened it and was about to make some toast when he saw the hair in contrast to the beige granite countertop. It was a short, black hair, entirely different from his sandy-colored hair. Other than him, only two other people regularly came to his house: Emily, and Margaret, the maid. Emily's hair was blonde and Margaret dyed her hair some ungodly bronze color. Therefore, it belonged to a stranger—a stranger who had gained access to his house, moved his coffee machine and taken or tampered with goodness knows what else.

Edward left the hair where it was. After first checking all the external doors and windows for any sign of damage or forced entry, he scoured the house. Everything was in place, and nothing was missing. The computer, the DVD player, his two stereos—all the natural targets for a burglar were still there. It was bizarre. What was going on?

He knew instinctively that it was a waste of time to call the police. There was nothing they could do. All he had to go on was a hair. Perhaps it had been brought in on a piece of clothing, or had been transferred from outside some other way. And yet, there was the chair, and the espresso machine, too. He could not be sure—and he certainly could not prove it—but someone had broken into his home.

Nothing had been taken or damaged, and at this point, he was more puzzled than disturbed. Still, he carefully slid the hair into a plastic sandwich bag, and placed it in one of the kitchen drawers.

Before going to work, he checked the windows once again, upstairs and downstairs, ensuring he had left no easy point of entry. Just in case, he put the front door on the chain and left through the garage. Still the feeling of unease did not lift.

It was not until he got to the lab, when he was back on safe, familiar ground, that he allowed himself to consider the worst. *A lifetime in every decade, a decade in every year.*

Edward debated long and hard whether to bring up the subject of the hair with Emily. The hair, combined with his rising suspicions about Tom, meant that she might hold a key to this mystery. How could he safely ask her? He decided to say nothing about the hair to Emily and instead, took a DNA kit home with him.

Arriving home, the first thing he did after opening the back door was to pull on the latex gloves included in the kit to avoid cross-contamination. Using a pair of tweezers, he lifted the hair from the plastic bag, and transferred it into the sterile glass tube. The top went on, and he stripped the gloves off. He left the little glass tube on the kitchen table to take to work the next morning.

Before going to bed that night, he found himself again prowling the house. Every time he thought of somewhere new to search, he was assailed by doubts that something had been touched. Is that how he left his box of valuable papers? Was that really all the mail that had been delivered while he was out at work? Had he really left the newspaper open at that page? And the spare keys by the back door—had they really been on that hook, not the one beside it?

Edward couldn't sleep. How could he relax, he thought, with this danger hanging over him? He lay awake in bed, eyes wide open, staring into the darkness. Every noise—every creak, every gust of wind in the trees outside—drove him further from sleep, his ears straining for all the information they could get. The bedroom door was open, so that he could hear if anything was going on downstairs, but it also gave him a sense of vulnerability. Finally, when a cat yowled in the neighbor's garden, he gave up and switched the light on. It was nearly 2 a.m.

Edward pulled on his dressing gown and found his slippers. He took the air pistol from the bedside table and placed it in his pocket. Then he went through to the bathroom and splashed water on his face. In the mirror, he looked tired—worse than that, he looked old. He shook his head and tried to pull himself together.

Before he went down to the kitchen to make a cup of green tea, Edward couldn't stop himself checking all the rooms upstairs. One by one, he pushed the doors open, flicking the lights on while he held the air pistol ready. Of course, there was nothing. He knew full well he was being ridiculous, but at times like these it was sometimes better to humor the mind than let irrational fears nag away. There was something faintly amusing about it—he could at least appreciate that, he thought, as he closed the last door. Some gunslinger he would make, with his slippers and dressing gown. If Emily could see him now...

Downstairs felt safer, the reassuring familiarity of the kitchen soothing his jangled nerves. The bright lights helped, too: suddenly there weren't axe murderers behind every curtain, and the malign presences in the shadows were banished. Edward thought he might be able to sleep in the sitting room, on the settee. Somehow the little creaks and groans of his old house weren't quite so threatening from here. He knew that if anyone tried to break in, he would know about it immediately. All the same, he felt the need to check every room downstairs at least once more. There was no point being careless.

Tea in one hand, pistol in the other, he made the rounds again. The garage was the last room to check. Something about it was freaking him out a little, though he couldn't say exactly what. He steeled himself to open the door and stick his head in. Flipping the light switch revealed the usual garage junk: old shelves, packing cases, and a mountain bike he hadn't ridden in over a year. To one side, his spare freezer stood. Edward didn't want to go down into the garage, but he knew he wouldn't forgive himself for chickening out, either. Sighing deeply, he descended the steps, shivering slightly from the cold, damp air.

The freezer was dirtier than he remembered. A few weeks ago, he had restocked it after the power cut had ruined most of the contents, and he had sponged down the surface when he did so. Dust collected faster down here, but this wasn't right. The top was smeared with grime, and at the edge of the lid, just next to the handle, there was an unmistakable shape: a handprint. Edward felt his heart skip a beat. He set the mug on top of the freezer and bent to look closely at the marks. *He had been here, inside the house.*

He knew immediately that there was no chance of getting a fingerprint from the freezer. The marks were smeared and dirty, without any hint of a print. The intruder was smart—he had worn gloves. But what had he wanted so badly in the freezer? He pocketed the air pistol again, removed the mug and, with growing trepidation, lifted the lid.

Nothing seemed out of place inside. Edward permitted himself just the tiniest moment of hope. Perhaps he was just over-tired; perhaps he was seeing things where there was nothing. It was just possible that it was his own handprint; had he needed food from this freezer recently?

The contents steamed icily as he opened the cover. A chill went through him when suddenly realized what was wrong. It was too full. Now his hands were shaking almost uncontrollably, and he held the mug tightly to his chest for warmth and steadiness. His free hand was barely strong enough to pull the bags of frozen food to one side. The nausea rose in his throat as he scratched away at them, unable to get a firm grip. Finally, the last bag of vegetables came away, and he found what he had been so afraid of. The mug fell from his chest and smashed on the floor at his feet as he gave a loud cry of surprise. He stumbled backwards, just managing to find the sink before he threw up, his mind reeling with disbelief and despair. Breathing deep gasps of air, he leant heavily over the basin as he waited for his heart to slow down and the nausea to leave him. Finally, after several minutes had passed, he coughed and spat into the sink. Then he took a long, slow breath, and returned to the freezer.

Whoever it was must have disturbed Margaret on her last day of cleaning. She was supposed to be on holiday in France at the moment. Edward pulled more bags of frozen food aside. At the bottom of the chest freezer was his cleaning lady, with her arms crossed over her chest, like a parody of a vampire sleeping in its coffin. Beneath her arms, hugged to her icy chest, was a box of fish fingers. *Sick*, he thought. Even needless death had to be a twisted joke to whoever the killer was.

*M-Trait*

Now that he knew exactly what he was dealing with, Edward grew calmer. There was no longer the threat of danger to him; Margaret's murder had pushed things way beyond that, and he knew without doubt that someone meant to harm him. Danger was a certainty. He now understood that Margaret was an intentional message—he was supposed to find the body. And now he felt a sense of grim determination grip him.

Edward knew that calling the police would be a pointless exercise. He had no desire to come under suspicion for murder in his own house. He had not touched Margaret herself, only the bags of food. He found a pair of rubber gloves under the sink, and carefully wiped each bag down with a soft cloth before replacing them around the frozen corpse. Until he dealt with the problem, she could stay there.

# 48

"So, are you having second thoughts about taking that DNA test?"

They sat together in a coffee shop after working out, Tom with an espresso, Emily with, uncharacteristically, a strawberry milkshake. She watched Tom shift in his chair before answering.

"Sorry, I do keep meaning to get around to it. Does it mean that much to you?"

"Edward was quite interested in you—he was impressed by your family's statistics."

"I guess it would be good to meet him sometime. You talk an awful lot about him."

Emily remained silent. She wasn't sure how he meant that.

Tom had talked about going for a DNA test in her lab for weeks—talked about it with her at great length on more than one occasion—and yet he would not get on with it. After telling Edward she had found him such a promising subject, it was a little embarrassing that she couldn't actually persuade Tom to come in. She was bewildered at the way he was acting. It made her curious.

Tom did not seem to be the kind of person to let fear hold him back, but she wondered whether his reluctance was in part due to the possibility of disappointment—of disappointing her, as well as himself. She realized that, in her enthusiasm to further their work at the university, she might have placed too much emphasis on his DNA, and not enough on Tom as a person. She did not want him to feel any pressure.

When she saw a few blond hairs on his fleece sweater that sat draped on the back of the café chair, the temptation was hard to resist. With one of his hairs, she could test it in secret, get an answer and decide what to do later. If he was clear and healthy, she could strongly encourage him to go for the test, knowing he would not be disappointed. If, on the off chance, it turned out he wasn't so lucky, she could advise him to go in anyway, on the grounds that, if something *was* wrong, it would be to his advantage to know about it sooner rather than later. The plan pleased her. Either way, she was looking out for his best interests. He had been a good friend to her, and it was the least she could do in return.

Taking advantage of Tom's usual trip to the counter for a second cappuccino, Emily plucked a promising hair from his sweater that included the entire follicle, wrapped it in an unused napkin, and placed it in her coin purse. She planned to do nothing with the sample until Sunday when she could assemble a DNA kit—Edward never came to work on Sunday.

The infuriating thing about the process was the wait. Once the sample was placed into the system, there was nothing she could do to speed it up. The process would be finished in two or three days, and the results sent to her user area. She knew she would not dare to look at them in the lab when Edward was around, but would have to wait until she could download the results at home.

In the meantime, she would try not to think about it.

# 49

The new software was wonderful, Sherman had to admit. Five years ago he couldn't do this—not even a year ago. But there had been huge advances in the field in the last few months, and since the new computers were installed, it had been worth paying a little extra out of their funding to have the program, DyNAmo, installed.

The raw data that resulted from a blood test were an enormous string of characters, representing the DNA molecule. There was no way even the brightest and most patient of scientists could search by hand for the different sequences Sherman was looking for in gene combinations that could result in disease or other problems for the patient. The software read the database and cross-referenced its entries with anything it found on the subject's DNA—flagging especially those traits in which Sherman was most interested. Programming the database with all the genetic traits had been a time-consuming task, but it had been worth it. Besides, Sherman had nothing if not time.

The result was an extremely user-friendly interface that gave him easy access to everything he needed to know about a given person's profile. From the initial menu screen, he could call up any number of different scenarios with a click of the mouse: life-threatening and serious disorders, along with statistics, diagrams, and a hundred other species of arcane data interpretation. An order of magnitude more powerful than the old software, it would save him days on every DNA sample he analyzed. He decided to christen it with the hair he had found in his kitchen.

He honestly did not know what he would find at this point. Part of him hoped it would be a mistake, a stray hair from a deliveryman or someone else, brought in by chance and deposited on the worktop. Another part of him feared that there might be more in what Tom had said to Emily. He was disappointed that she had kept the knowledge of her new friend from him—stung that she had not trusted him with that information. He was also worried for her, and the child she carried.

Biologically or not, he felt as much Zoe's father as Emily was the mother, and his daughter was too precious to be endangered. Before long, he should be able to set his mind at rest. After preparing the sample and putting it to the front of the queue for processing, he settled back into his more usual work and began the waiting game that would last for two days. After that, DyNAmo would take only minutes to extricate all the DNA secrets.

When the raw DNA data returned, Edward waited until Emily had left for the evening and immediately sequestered himself in his office. He loaded the DNA data into the new software and clicked through the screens to process the information.

He waited as the program performed the search and sort routines, collating and cross-referencing megabytes of data in complicated algorithms that would take mortal human lifetimes to complete.

The end result was more than disappointing—pages and pages, but no data results. Perhaps he had not installed the software properly, or loaded a blank database entry. Perhaps, more annoyingly, it was a bug that needed fixing. This was, after all, an extremely new and complicated piece of software. He flipped through the menus, wondering what had gone wrong. *Nothing. Click. Nothing. Click. Nothing.* No prognosis, no nothing—DyNAmo didn't work. He would have to go back to using the old software.

He picked up the phone and dialed the number he found on the company's website, hoping that there would still be someone around to help. It was after regular office hours, but their helpline was in America—their support services might still be available.

Mercifully, the phone was picked up on the third ring. "Hello, DyNAmo tech support, how can I help?"

"Hi, my name is Dr. Edward Sherman. I'm having some trouble with your software."

"Ok. Can I get your organization's name and registration number?" Sherman gave him the details. "How can I help?"

"I ran a DNA test, fed the results into the program, and I'm getting nothing."

"A completely blank screen or just no interpretative data?" asked the tech guy.

"The screens are all there, the program itself seems to be fine. And the test name is there at the top of the screen," he realized for the first time. "So something is happening. But I'm not getting any summary items."

"Okay. And is it just that one menu item, or are they all blank?"

"They're all—hang on a moment." Best make sure. Sherman flipped through a series of windows. The summary page was blank, as was the detailed prognosis; he already knew that. Cross matches to other test results were also blank, but then it would be. There was apparently nothing to match, and no other sets of results yet anyway. Sighing, he clicked on one of the customizable windows he had set up when he installed the software.

Then, he saw it:

**M-Trait:**                 **+ + Positive**

"Hello? Dr. Sherman?"

Sherman couldn't tell how much time had passed. "Uh, thank you. It seems to be working after all—my mistake." He put the phone down, his hand shaking so badly it made the receiver rattle in its cradle.

Something had to be wrong. Was Emily having a joke with him—had she planted the hair and manipulated the results before he got to them? Frankly, he would be impressed if that were the case. It would be a complicated hoax to pull off—not to mention unkind. Then he opened the biometrics window and realized that not all the results fields read negative.

Subject to environmental factors, DNA governs more than tendencies towards genetic defects: eye color, hair and skin tone,

# M-Trait

height, build, and other physiological data. Therefore, DyNAmo included a basic representation of the subject. Maybe in a few years it would be possible to feed in a string of data and produce a detailed image of what a person might look like. For now, that was impossible, but an identikit-style function filled in the gaps. Sherman looked at the picture. Medium height, dark eyes, dark hair. The readout to the left of the screen gave him a vague outline:

**Ancestral Derivation:** Unknown, Slavic, all else <5%
**Genetic Disorders:** None

Sherman's heart leapt, and the implications flooded his mind. It was only the genetic *defect* windows that were blank. This person wasn't just clear. *He was perfect.* Sherman sat heavily in his chair.

Someone else had been born outside the walls, like he had been. Or, far more likely, one of them had escaped. *Please not that.*

Edward sat back and focused his memory. Who had definitely died that night almost a hundred years ago—whose bodies had he actually seen when he went back to collect his belongings? Alexander was dead; he had seen him. Sergei had not been able to run away, crippled by his polio; Dmitriy and Mordke had been shot trying to escape. Who else? He counted all the others, his mind searching for that one image: dark eyes, black hair, and black beard.

*He had not seen Mikhail.*

# 50

Tom had mixed feelings about taking Emily to her monthly visit of her grandmother at a senior care home. Emily was unwilling to drive the three-hour round trip this late in her pregnancy, and her mother had other commitments that day—so she asked him. Emily could have asked Sherman to drive her, so the choice of him over Edward was a victory of sorts. How could he say no?

Grandma Mary was more or less housebound, and Emily would not be ready to start making social calls for awhile after the birth. It was better to see Mary now and miss next month's meeting—she was firm about that with Tom.

Emily had suggested that they have a picnic in the grounds of the retirement home after visiting Grandma Mary, and Tom agreed. Now, with time to think about the trip, he was having misgivings. The thing about old people's homes, he ruminated, was that they were full of old people—that was the catch. Tom did not have much time for the old, at least not the physically old. The chronologically old were a different matter entirely.

In any case, that Saturday afternoon he found himself driving out to the suburbs with Emily, now hugely pregnant, in the passenger seat. Emily had assured him that her grandmother, who was ninety-four, would probably be too tired to spend much time with her. That was a small mercy, but it made only a quantitative rather than qualitative difference to his apprehension.

"She finds it very tiring, so I'll probably sit with her for half an hour or so and then let her have her afternoon nap."

*"I'll probably sit." Not "We'll sit." This was promising.*

Emily continued. "I don't know what you want to do. You're welcome to come in and meet her and sit with us if you like."

Tom paused.

"Or you might just want to go and sit in the garden and read or something until I've finished. I won't be long."

"I'll come in and say hello, and then leave you two to visit—that's probably the best thing."

Emily smiled a smile he was increasingly coming to appreciate.

"Okay. There's a nice garden out the back with some benches and shady spots. I'll come and find you there when I'm finished."

It was nice that she understood the compromise well enough to accept it unquestioningly.

Tom parked the car and helped Emily to the front door. The outside of the building betrayed no hint of what he could expect from the interior. They had to sign a visitors' book at reception before going in. That seemed slightly odd, though Tom did not know what the standard procedure was; he had never been into an old people's home before. Possibly this was a high-security one.

He followed Emily through to Mary's room, one hand at her elbow to support her if necessary, taking in the surroundings with cold suspicion and unease. Nothing here felt right, none of his senses gave him anything encouraging. It was quiet, too quiet to be healthy. The walls were painted in nondescript colors, and the environment smelled of disinfectant, institution food, and something else he didn't want to identify, but probably could. He was glad of the promise of the garden; he did not think he could breathe the air here for very long. It was as if it might infect him with its age if he stayed too long. He remembered the old Welsh myth—or was it Cornish?—about a man called Shon ap Shenkin. Enticed by fairies, he had stopped by a tree on the road to listen to a bird singing a particularly beautiful song. When the bird finished and he rose to leave, he saw that the tree, which had been alive and leafy, was now dead and withered. He returned to the farmhouse that he had just left, seemingly only a few minutes earlier, but this too was changed, much older and now covered in ivy. An old man stood in the doorway, and as they spoke they came to realize that he was Shon's nephew. The old man held his arms out to embrace his uncle, but before anything else could happen, time caught up with Shon ap Shenkin and he crumbled into dust.

This place felt like it might have the same effect on anyone who remained there too long. Perhaps he would step into the garden, only to find that his body had aged to become like the other residents. Or maybe Emily would come out to meet him in the garden and try to embrace him, only to crumble into dust as Shon ap Shenkin had. This was not good. He did *not* belong here.

Mary was instantly recognizable as a family member, despite being sixty years older than Emily. It helped that she looked like a woman twenty or thirty years younger. She shared Emily's long, blond hair, copper-brown eyes and good bone structure. Mary spoke a little slowly, but in the brief time that Tom was in the room, she was perfectly lucid. He introduced himself as Emily's friend, and then again a little louder when she showed no reaction and he realized how deaf she was.

After making sure Emily was settled in a chair with something to rest her feet on, Tom excused himself and wandered off to find the garden. He had to navigate through a sitting area to get there, an obstacle course of listless pensioners wrapped up in blankets and shawls, sitting in their armchairs, or hobbling with incredible slowness out to their rooms, or back and forth in a kind of agonizing parody of the randomness of Brownian motion. Speed this up fivefold—record it, and play it back in fast-forward—and it might look something like life. He paused at the tank of tropical fish, iridescent in their blues, greens, and yellows, which was evidently supposed to be an interesting distraction. The television on the other side of the room was proving unanimously more popular, some awful daytime talk show blaring away.

The French windows were open and the garden looked particularly inviting from where Tom was standing. It was sunny out there, sunny and beautiful, and yet something prevented these people from leaving their chairs and shawls and television and going out to enjoy it. He put his head down and walked out, trying not to catch anyone's eye. He was sensing some feelings of envy from those imprisoned, and if he stopped now, he might never get out.

In the garden it was cool and pleasant, almost idyllic but for the presence of the aged horror behind him. Just around the corner, and blissfully out of sight of the home itself, was a fishpond with a bench under some shady trees. Tom sat awhile to contemplate the fat goldfish that were swimming aimlessly around it, occasionally changing their direction with an unexpected flick of the tail. At any rate, they appeared aimless to the casual observer, but perhaps there was more in it than the fish let on. Watching the aimless was better than being around old folks.

He did *not* like old people. It was all wrong. By the time people were old enough to appreciate the knowledge and experience that age brought, physical deterioration had robbed them of the ability, or even the inclination, to do anything. Seeing these hordes of wizened pensioners here, hearing gone, sight gone, their will to truly *live* gone, had been a reminder of mortality that he did not want to see. These people served no purpose that he could discern. He wondered whether Sherman appreciated what he had: the best of both worlds, knowledge and experience as well as energy and ability.

And what about Emily? She was healthy, but she did not share Sherman's genes. One day, even she would get old and die. He didn't like to think about that—the idea was distasteful in itself. Right now, in the present, he enjoyed her company and wanted to spend more time with her. All things being equal, he would never give that up. But Tom knew that his future with Emily did not depend on her genes—it depended on his. If he was Methuselah positive, as he hoped, then she would have to go. There was no question about it. On the other hand, if he was not—that held serious problems of its own, not least in the form of Michael. His father would disown him, or worse, if he wasn't a chip off the old block. Michael never had had much patience with mortals. So, the only way to know what part Emily—and Michael—would play in his future was to find out about himself. It looked like he couldn't have both. The future, previously so clear, had taken on new uncertainties in the last few months.

Tom remembered the dawning realization he had had as a child—that Michael wasn't like other men. Children always think their parents are wonderful, all-powerful. The first time they realize their fathers are not infallible comes as a shock. Tom's experience was quite the opposite, and it took a quarter of a century to add it all up.

He had always felt that distance in his father, which he attributed to the death of his mother; perhaps he reminded Michael of her too much. Now he realized that the distance was a defense mechanism— Michael could not commit love to a child he might outlive by hundreds of years.

His father had spoken a little about his mother, Amata, from time to time—usually when Tom had asked. Michael was not secretive about her; he was open enough, merely laconic. It was only natural, after all, for a child to ask about his mother. Tom traveled widely, encouraged to do so by his father, and on one occasion found himself near to Salamanca, overseeing the sale of some of his father's property there. The limited information Tom had about his mother was enough to track down her family, a sister and two brothers, together with their own children. Amazed at this surprise reunion, they enthusiastically accepted their nephew into the family.

"Tell me about Amata," Tom had asked his newly discovered Aunt Celia, when she had finished crying with emotion.

Celia had launched into a fast stream of Spanish, and Tom could only just keep up. She broke off after a minute, struck by an idea. "Wait one moment," she said, and hurried off into another room. Tom was left waiting, intrigued.

"Here it is," she said a minute later, returning with a thick photo album. She turned the first page. "Here they are at Amata's wedding— that was twenty-five years ago now. She was a beautiful woman."

Tom was searching for the history of his mother, but it was Michael he learned most about as he pored over the album. He had never seen a photograph of his father before. "How old was Michael here?" he asked.

"Forty-five, I think." Celia offered. "Yes, he said that he was born just a few years before the outbreak of the Second World War."

He must be seventy now. How is he—he never did stay in touch? I guess it was just too hard for him."

"Seventy, yes," said Tom. In the photo, his father looked not a day younger than he did now, twenty-five years later. "May I make a copy of this? I have no pictures of my mother."

Celia nodded enthusiastically.

The pieces were coming together. What did he really know about his father? The physical evidence was pitifully thin at that moment, but Tom would work on it. His father had trained him emphatically on this point—there is always a paper trail.

"Anything strike you as strange about these?" Tom had asked innocently, dropping the sheaf of paperwork onto his father's desk when he returned home, a month later. The photo was there, along with property deeds stretching back another fifty years, and an immigration record from Russia, dated 1917.

"How did you get these?" Michael had asked carefully, reserving his judgment for the moment.

"You know—I just followed the paper trail."

His father gazed at him for a long, long minute. "Well done," he finally said, impressed with the result, but the expression on his face read displeasure.

Tom snickered at the remembrance of his father's attempt to hide his true feelings. While lying down on a garden bench reminiscing about his father, the sun emerged bright from behind a cloud, and Tom closed his eyes to the glare, shielding his face from the bright light with his hands. The sun on the rest of his face was a wonderful, healthy feeling, something natural and good in this aging and corrupted environment.

He felt a shadow and opened his eyes, squinting through his fingers, as the sun was still bright. It took him a moment to recognize Emily's face, dark against the sky, though her shape was otherwise unmistakable. She sat down—at least, what passed for sitting in her condition—beside him on the grass.

"Hope you've not been too bored." She spoke innocently, as if there could not be the least thing wrong with the place.

"Not bored," he lied easily and immediately changed the subject before she could laugh at his brazenness. "How was Mary?"

"Not so good. One of her friends, Jane, died a couple of days ago. She was almost as old as Mary, a year younger, I think. She was just about the last person who remembers things the way she does—a First World War nurse and as a young woman in the Roaring Twenties. That's one of her favorite expressions; she always likes to talk about the twenties, and how she met my grandfather. She'll be very isolated now, with no one else to talk to about fashion and the postwar rationing and everything. Jane was her last real link with the past."

It was clear that Emily felt some kind of burden about this and needed to talk, and Tom lay back again to contemplate the sky, keeping half an ear out for the occasions he was required to make an encouraging noise to facilitate her monologue, or just in case she asked a direct question. He wondered again about Sherman, and whether he felt the same way as Mary did, after he had lost everyone he knew and had been alone for decades. He hoped so.

Finally the conversation turned to lighter things, and Tom collected the picnic that he had packed up that morning from the car. He sat on the grass with his back to the home and ate the ham sandwiches and boiled eggs with Emily. Sherman would have been an old man by the time Mary was born, but now he could easily pass for her son or even grandson. Somehow, he had stayed sane.

# 51

*Sukin syn!* Under extreme stress, Sherman often reverted to thinking in Russian. *Son of a bitch!*

He stared at the featureless picture produced by the DNA profiling software on the computer screen in his office, trying to fill in the details from memory. Mikhail—if it was Mikhail—had long dark hair and a thick beard obscuring most of his face, along with strong cheekbones and piercing dark eyes that seemed almost black in their intensity. The short, dark hair in his kitchen told Sherman that memory might not be enough for him to recognize his stalker. Only a few of the Brotherhood had kept their hair short. Most had favored longer hair and heavy beards, hiding their young faces from the world. A shave, a haircut and a change of clothes—take them out of the context his century-old memory remembered them in and put them in the present day—and he would be hard put to recognize any of them.

Edward immediately looked at the most obvious clue. Who was Tom—what did he really know about Emily's friend? The DNA profile suggested it might be Mikhail, but Mikhail was older than Edward, and by enough years that it would show in his face. Emily had said nothing specific about Tom's age, but Sherman assumed the man was roughly her own age—and certainly not his. He was confused. He didn't know Tom's age or even the color of his hair. If he wasn't Mikhail, who was he? What did he want?

The question of what Mikhail might want was easier: revenge. He blamed Edward for the death of the Brotherhood clan. Surely that was it. Almost immediately, he realized how easy it must have been to be tracked down. His work was well-known, cutting-edge research into gene sequencing and screening. He had not felt the need to conceal his identity; he had not thought there was anyone who would care. Now he realized how mistaken he had been—his naiveté in accepting that everyone had died in the fire, just because he had managed to accept Kostya's death. He wondered why he was not dead already. What did Mikhail have to gain in delaying? Surely, the longer he waited, the longer he risked detection.

More questions slowly began to unfold in Edward's mind. There had been no sign of Mikhail in his life yet, but what about the entry of Tom into Emily's life? His interest in Emily was clearly more than passing. Or was it? Sherman still felt a stab of betrayal when he thought of Emily's closeness to Tom. Why would a man become interested in a pregnant woman? Emily wasn't *that* special, was she? Perhaps Tom was just using her as a way to get to him—for information, blackmail, or who knew what else? Of course, there might be something more. What if Tom worked for Mikhail? *What if he had somehow found out about Zoe?*

Edward Sherman buried his head in his hands. He was not prepared for this type of problem. He had thought he was alone. Now he knew otherwise.

Zoe, who now owned a genetic profile as flawless as the one currently displayed on the screen, with a robust immune system and both Methuselah genes—this fact could only interest another Ultra. Was Tom one, too? Was Mikhail nearby?

If Tom and Mikhail were after Zoe, Emily was safe at least until she was born, and probably a while longer. After that, she might be considered superfluous—a liability, even. Sherman had to admit that he had considered her in the same terms in his most cynical moments. What, after all, was the remaining sixty or eighty years of her life compared to Zoe's centuries? He cared about Emily, and had promised to look after her, but he knew the day might come when he would have to make a painful choice. How much sooner, then, would Mikhail decide she was only a hindrance to him?

All the grim possibilities that came to his mind spurred Edward into action. He left the lab early that evening, picking up the air pistol and a tin of darts in an army and navy surplus store on the way home. Gun control in England was very strict, and he did not want to carry or use a real firearm anyway. This would do fine for what he had in mind. He spent an hour or so that evening learning how to use it, practicing his aim by firing the darts across the garden into a board propped against the door of the summerhouse. The next day he took it to the lab, reassuringly heavy in the pocket of his jacket, which he would hang over the back of his swivel chair. His status afforded him access to the drugs he needed, and he tipped a number of the darts, one of which was always in the pistol.

As a second line of defense, he left makeshift weapons where he could get to them quickly: a scalpel here, taped under a desk, the metal bar of a clamp stand there, slipped behind a bookshelf. Emily never noticed the concealed instruments in the lab.

He did not know whether the hair in his kitchen had come off Emily's clothes, or whether Tom or Mikhail had been there in person—that thought left him cold. He took to doing the same at home too, leaving carving knives, a fire poker, and whatever else of suitability around the place. He began double-locking and bolting the doors when he was at home, although an assault on his home territory did not seem likely. Stealth, not confrontation was the way the Brothers worked. His biggest fear was being caught out in the open.

For all his caution, he had one hope. Tom had promised Emily he would come into the lab for a DNA test, and Sherman hoped he would honor his commitment—as long as he did nothing to warn him off in the meantime. If it happened, the meeting would be a moment of truth, and he designed a special patch with that in mind. Very similar to the kind already widely used for long-term pain relief, he had upped the concentration of the narcotic, hoping it would either knock Tom out altogether or at least slow him down enough for Edward to restrain him. What he would do with him afterwards he did not yet know, but he would need to find out more information from him first.

Edward Sherman had spent a long time believing that the members of the Brotherhood were dead, and that each one of them had paid as much as they ever could. Now, it transpired that this was not so. Alongside the added fear, he realized with some surprise that he also felt a thrill of excitement: he had been forewarned, and now there was the possibility that he could take action against Mikhail or Tom, or whoever was in his way.

## 52

Tom could not think of a reason why Emily should not come to his flat. They had finished their picnic lunch at the rest home around midafternoon and had been enjoying the drive back into the city, the windows rolled down to make the most of the sunny weather. Their route back to Emily's would take them close to his place, and she suggested they drop in on the way. After all, she said, he would get to see her flat, so it was only fair that he returned the favor. He had agreed; they could drop in at his for a break before he took her home. That way, he could also pick up some things to cook for them both at her place later that evening. She seemed to like that idea.

Although appearing enthusiastic, Tom was apprehensive about showing her his living space. It was nothing he could put his finger on, but more of a diffuse, unfocused uneasiness about having her in his space. Was there something that might give him away; something that he was used to seeing that would stick out like a sore thumb to her? Almost everything that he had collected on Sherman he held in his head, and the information he needed some extra help with was kept on the laptop computer in the living room. What about his personal effects, arranged throughout the flat? Was there anything out of place that might arouse suspicion? Something out of character, at least for the character he had crafted for himself? He scoured his mental schematic of the flat as he drove, recalling the contents of shelves, tables and surfaces. He could not afford that kind of mistake now.

They had to park a little way from the flat and, in the short walk, he remained silent, his mind racing through the possibilities. Emily touched his arm as they finally reached the top of the stairs, tilting her head to one side with a look of concern as he turned to her, asking him without words if he was okay. Tom nodded and managed a smile.

"Sure. Just wondering what I actually have to cook with." Unlocking the door, he went in first, casting a swift eye around the living room.

People act differently when they enter someone else's comfort zone. Some like to nose around, picking things up and putting them back in the wrong place, pulling books from shelves to flick through and leave out, and treating the place with either a lack of respect or an overfamiliarity that might not be appropriate. Others are generally more considerate, looking with eyes and not hands, waiting until mutual trust is established before acting as they might in their own home. Such behavior could say a lot about a person. Tom hoped that Emily would be one of the considerate kind. From what he had seen, he did not think she would be a problem; so far she had shown him every nicety, and he trusted her to continue to do the same here.

Emily was ready for a break, as she leaned back trying to gracefully hold her enlarged abdomen. Still, she insisted on the guided tour first. Tom exhaled slowly and then showed her his flat, room by room.

She turned out to be a very respectful first-time guest, but Tom still felt the need to look wherever she was looking, checking that she would see nothing that would raise awkward questions.

Emily, for her part, seemed pleasantly surprised at what she saw. The flat was not just a place to eat and crash; Tom had made it his own, and she could see that his personal space was important to him—especially where he showcased his classical guitars. She doubted whether he invited many other people round and realized, to her gratification, that she was a special case.

Tom found her the glass of water she had asked for and sat her on the settee with her feet up, while he gathered the things he needed from the kitchen. He had intended to make pasta for himself tonight, and could just as easily cook for two as for one. Not knowing the contents of her kitchen, he packed everything he needed into two plastic carrying bags.

When he took them through, he found her reading a magazine that he had left on the coffee table; one of the popular scientific periodicals he had picked up after seeing an article on the cover that had caught his attention. It was about the growing market for DNA testing, and the possibilities of future medical treatments that were tailor-made to the genetic makeup of the individual. A recent purchase, the magazine had somehow escaped his frenzied mental examination of the flat. The article included an extract from an interview with Sherman.

"Been doing some background research, then?"

Her question took him by surprise, until he realized that she had not meant it as an accusation. He had talked with Emily about her work, and expressed his interest in going in to the lab to be tested himself. She did not know about his trips to Sherman's house.

"Just want to know what I'd be getting myself into." He smiled, more to calm his own nerves than for her benefit. "I want to make sure that Dracula isn't going to take any more than he needs." Then he added, to gently change direction, "It says there that some celebrities are patenting their DNA so that people can't get samples from glasses or cigarette ends and clone them."

Tom was very rarely flustered; when he was, he often made a joke of some kind. Emily raised an eyebrow, toying with him good-naturedly.

"Do you think there might be a market for your DNA?"

"Last thing I need is to find that some mad scientist has copied me and flooded the market with cheap imitations. Did you ever worry about that?"

"It's the risk you take, I suppose." She smiled, then paused, confused. "How did you know I've had my DNA tested?"

She looked at him slightly suspiciously, but he couldn't tell whether there was anger, mistrust, mischief, or just surprise behind her eyes. She had not known he knew that, of course, like she did not know he'd been spending his spare time snooping round Sherman's house for the past few months. Again, her reaction at his throwaway comment spoke volumes about her intuitive intelligence.

"I just figured—you know—the perks of the job? I would, in your position." He feigned a suitably remorseful look, hoping that she would be embarrassed into forgiving him the accidental discovery. It worked; a bashful look crossed her face, and she smiled again.

"You can't blame a mum for making sure her baby's going to have the best start in life. I just wanted to make sure there wasn't anything I was going to pass on to her."

From her answer, Tom determined that Emily didn't know about Zoe. When she said "the best," she meant something different to "the best" that he imagined Sherman desired.

It was still early, and they were in no hurry to leave. Tom played some slow, languid songs on guitar while Emily reclined on the settee and closed her eyes, listening with obvious pleasure.

# 53

Dr. Sherman unfailingly took Sundays off from his work at the university. It was his day for rest and recovery, and a chance to reset his mind before the next week.

He usually spent Sunday mornings in church, a sacrosanct habit that he could never break. Today he was at the Russian service at an Orthodox church he had discovered in a quaint out-of-the-way section of London. Edward paused at the doorway to sign himself three times with the cross, in very proper Orthodox fashion from right to left, and with the fingers of the hand held in the prescribed way. He took his place with the other men to the right of the building, the division of the sexes at worship being a tradition to which this church still held.

Organized chaos reigned within the building, as one service merged into another with no discernible break between them; worshippers continued to arrive and begin their own private prayers, although the priest had apparently already started the service. Some prostrated themselves; others knelt on the stone floor or merely stood with their heads bowed. The smoke and aroma of incense filled the building, spilling generously from the swinging censers like the prayers of the faithful ascending to heaven, which it represented. The greater part of the long service was spent in sung worship, led only by the small choir. There were no instruments, not even an organ.

Standing there amongst the noise and hubbub with the other worshippers, he was anonymous, alone in a crowd. There were not many places he could go in England to hear Russian spoken, and this was one of them. Edward had not returned to his home country since that day in 1917 when his son had died in the fire and he had fled, uncomprehending, into the night. The memory had not lost its pain for him, though its unbearable blaze in his mind had lessened as the years passed.

The liturgy that the priest was intoning had not changed since he had stood in a similar, though smaller church in Russia, over a century ago. If he closed his eyes and shut out the visible reminders of twenty-first-century Britain—the clothes, the hairstyles, the paraphernalia of modern life—and breathed the incense-filled air deeply, he could almost believe he was there again, two thousand miles and several lifetimes away. It was as if Kostya was standing beside him, his presence felt but not seen.

Dr. Sherman kept his eyes closed for a long time. A tear began to collect in the corner of his eye, but it did not roll down his cheek. He had shed all the tears he was going to shed. It probably went altogether unnoticed by those around him, or perhaps it was mistaken for a sign of piety.

The church had been an important part of his life back then, before Mikhail had found him and his life had changed forever—a place where he and Karina communed with others of the village. The memories he had of that church were untainted by later events—in his own life, and for the Church itself—and he was glad he had left before the end, which had begun in the Revolution and had seen the end of the Brotherhood. It left him afflicted with horrible regrets—regret at his naïveté in joining the Brotherhood, regret he ultimately casued Karina's death, regret for Kostya, regret at the way he had reacted to his pain by betraying the Brothers to a terrible revenge. Their deaths did not play on his conscience, for he knew that justice had been served. But bound inextricably to their deaths was that of Kostya, and he would gladly have given the Brothers their lives back for the return of his son.

The Russian Orthodox Church was a part of the old, tsarist Russia, and it defended the old regime after the Revolution. For the Bolsheviks, it had represented an intolerable enemy, and thousands of clergymen, as well as monks and nuns, had been brutally murdered in a campaign of terror and persecution. A catastrophic crop failure in 1921 had finally given Lenin the pretext for seizing all of the Church's land and wealth, and moving to put an end to this ideological enemy once and for all.

By that time, Edward had been long gone. He was grateful that he didn't have to see all that went on in Russia in the years after he fled; glad that he didn't have to witness the persecution of the Church and glad that he did not have to live through the cruelties of Lenin's and Stalin's regimes. He would rather remember things as they were before the Revolution, before Mikhail and everything that came with and around him.

Smell is an evocative sense, though what we see accounts for 80 percent of the information our brains receive. As he stood there with his eyes closed, breathing in the sweet smell of incense, he could remember that time. He could remember the feel of the hard stone floor under his feet as he stood through the long services. He remembered the words of the liturgy: the same words he heard now, but spoken in a deeper voice, with a different accent. He remembered the priest who spoke them, the priest to whom he had made confession, who had married him to Karina, and who had baptized Kostya. His family was still alive for that moment, content, although so innocent that they were unaware of their contentment.

He knew that when he opened his eyes, they would all be dead again, his recollection no more than a trick that the senses played on his mind. He knew he would not remember how they looked anymore; when he tried to think of their faces his mind would skate over them, unable to fill in the details that came so easily when he was here in the church. The sharp, clear feelings that he was so sure of now would revert to the faraway shadow of an emotion, no more than the memory of a memory he once had.

Edward Sherman, formerly Eduard Chermen, kept his eyes closed for a long time, until the priest had finished and the parishioners filed out, carefully stepping around him so as not to disturb his prayers as they left.

# 54

"I never knew my mother."

They were back at Emily's now, chatting after the dinner that Tom had cooked for them both. Emily was reclining along the length of the settee, her head cradled on a pair of cushions. Tom sat opposite her in one of the two matching armchairs, feet stretched out and resting on the other chair. It was getting late, past Emily's normal bedtime, and she was starting to feel tired. She was not sure whether she would go in to the lab or not the next day. Edward did not expect her to put in a productive day's work as often now. So, in a sense, anything she did was a bonus. The main reason she went to work at the moment was for the human contact, and she was getting her quota of that now. She was getting to know Tom better, and didn't want him to leave just yet.

Despite their growing friendship, Emily sometimes felt like she did not know him at all. At times, she sensed an emotional distance in Tom, a tendency to give nothing away. His behavior had an uncanny resemblance to Edward's faults. She, by contrast, was an open book, the same on the outside as the inside. With her, what you saw was what you got. She figured she just needed to take the time to earn his trust and let him become comfortable with her.

They sat talking about Zoe, drinking decaf coffee made from Emily's filter machine. Tom would not normally drink decaf, finding the taste to be inferior, but for reasons of Emily's health, he obliged her.

"How did it affect your upbringing?" Emily asked. She worried a lot about her daughter suffering for the lack of one parent. In some ways, she'd always thought Edward could fill that gap, though there were things that he could never substitute for.

"I don't know. I guess I became quite an independent child from it." There was that distance in his voice again.

"What about your dad?" Emily could not help but ask, thinking that she would be in the same position in only weeks' time. "Was it hard for him too?"

"It's hard to tell with him. It was just a fact." There was little emotion in Tom's words. "We have something of a love-hate relationship. He doesn't give away much of his feelings."

There was a pause from Emily, as she tried to find something to say. Tom saw he had made her feel awkward, and immediately let her off the hook.

"It's okay. I didn't know her so I can't miss her."

"Still…it must have been hard for you. How did you turn out so…" she paused, searching for the right word, "normal?"

He raised an eyebrow: normal? "Well, being this sorted shade of normal doesn't just happen overnight. It takes years of hard work."

Emily did not know whether he was really joking, or whether there was a kernel of truth behind that statement. Probably he had intentionally meant it to be ambiguous. He did that sometimes; it was his way of bringing a little levity to a serious situation, of making it okay for them to talk about it. She wondered what had happened, and how much it had really affected him. She also knew, from her experience with Edward, not to risk hurting others by asking too many questions. If there was something he wanted to tell her, he would bring it up when he was comfortable. She decided to revert to her favorite subject—Zoe.

"Given the choice, I want Zoe to have a proper family. But sometimes, things don't work out that way. A lot of kids are born into single-parent families nowadays, and mostly they're okay. And it's not like Zoe won't have any male role models around. I'm not completely on my own." It was obvious that she was talking about Sherman.

"Edward's been a good friend to you?" It was more of a statement than a question.

"Yes. I honestly don't know what I would have done without him." She felt like that needed qualifying; Edward *had* been a good friend to her, but he was probably not going to share in the responsibilities of this child as a father would, and she certainly did not want to broadcast that impression to Tom or anyone else.

"I've been very lucky with Edward—luckier than I've any right to be, in my position. There must be hundreds of single mothers who would do anything for that kind of support. Still...it won't be the same for her as having a real dad, someone around every day to be there for her." She cast her eyes around at the piles of baby shopping, distributed around the sitting room everywhere there was space, and several conspicuous places there was not. Her head dropped back to the cushions with a mock groan. "Someone to help with the decorating wouldn't go amiss either."

"Well, I'm glad to know men are still useful for something." He did not offer to help her finish the nursery, and she did not swallow her pride and ask him.

The conversation reached a natural break, and Tom took the empty coffee mugs through to the kitchen, washing them up along with the rest of the dinner things. Emily did not come to help, or stop him from clearing up her kitchen. She remembered being thankful for his studiousness before nodding off on the settee, her blond hair pillowed around the cushions she rested her head on.

The settee was broad and comfortable, and Emily slept soundly. She did not wake when Tom came back through the sitting room, or hear the door when he eventually left, many hours later. When she finally did wake at six the next morning and struggled to relocate to the bedroom, she found that he had spent the rest of the night in the nursery, finishing the wallpapering and painting.

## 55

Eduard Chermen, Edward Sherman—phonetically the shift was almost imperceptible, but it epitomized everything that happened to him when he left Russia. On the surface, he presented himself as an Englishman, the new name and language giving him a fresh start and identity. Underneath, nothing had changed and he was still the man who had lived in Russia all his life, who still thought in Russian, dreamed in Russian, and cried out in his sleep in Russian. His heart was still in those nameless corridors, with Kostya and with his only love, Karina. He had nothing to stay for anymore and, the day after the fire, he had left the country for good with the papers and deeds he had taken from the Brothers. Everything else he left behind, like Mikhail hoping to make a complete break with a life to which he could never return. It was not so simple in practice.

In those first days, he found himself unable to feel any emotion at all. He was empty, hollow and tense, like canvas stretched too taught over a frame. He found himself looking in on how he supposed he should feel, without actually experiencing the emotions themselves. He barely slept, hardly ate, incapable in his state of shock to understand even what his body was telling him. He traveled compulsively, always moving, scarcely aware of whether it was morning or afternoon. The dam finally broke a fortnight later, when he found himself in a cheap hotel room in Lisbon with no recollection of how he had arrived there. Looking in the mirror, he scarcely recognized his own face. He sat against the bed insensible, crying for hours, before finally falling into a sleep that lasted through most of the next day. Later, when he woke, he found himself in his right mind and ready to begin reclaiming his life. In front of the mirror, he shaved off the beard that had obscured his face in the last two weeks: the sign of his retreat from the outside world and withdrawal from reality. Mikhail had worn a thick beard, hiding behind it to conceal his identity. He would not be one of them.

Eduard did not squander the opportunities that money, freedom, and time gave him in the interwar years, though he did not move around as much as Mikhail did. His life was a series of measured and calculated steps, each with a specific design in mind. His first step was to secure the fortune that he had taken from the Brothers in Russia and to put a large part of it into safe, future-proof investments. He changed his name—a subtle anglicization to Edward Sherman—at the same time both a conscious choice to blend in with Western society and an unconscious desire to put at arm's length the Russian past he wanted at once to forget so badly and hold on to so tightly. He obtained papers that claimed he was born in Switzerland in 1875, to English parents. In the future, as he periodically changed his birth certificate and other papers, he kept the same date of birth. August 15 was not his birth date, but that of his dead wife, Karina. She was one memory he wanted to keep alive, and this was one tangible way of doing it.

He hoped that the confusion of nationalities and languages would enable him to claim a variety of tongues as his first language, depending on what circumstances required. This would provide valuable breathing space while he brushed up on his English. He intended to spend time in England and America as soon as possible, so he needed to pass as a native. In the meantime, he did not want to be caught in a mistake. Although competent and extremely intelligent, he lacked the easy talent for languages that Michael had seemed to enjoy. Edward had to work at it. He set about the task of his education with an enduring will.

After the Second World War had provided the impetus for the greatest surge of technological progress that the world had ever seen, Edward kept himself well read, always looking for new products to invest in. In the 1950s, he was captivated by the search to discover the structure of the DNA molecule. As time passed, he watched the story unfold, and realized that the answers to his condition were not unfathomable, but held encoded in every cell of his body. By the mid-

1980s, as genetic fingerprinting was developed and genetic markers were found for more and more diseases, he grasped its implications and opportunities. Edward completed his education and began his own research, preparing for a time when science could unlock all the secrets his DNA had to offer. By the nineties he had been published frequently in scientific journals, and his expertise in genetics brought fame to the university. His stature provided him a proverbial front row seat as the Human Genome Project catalogued the entire DNA molecule.

During this long period of personal renaissance, Edward never considered remarrying, although he had several times had the opportunity if he had so wished. He was intelligent, rich, and attractive, and never lacked company of any kind when he desired it. People found him interesting and thoughtful. He was often the center of attention, but always preferred to direct that attention towards others. Women of all ages had expressed an interest in him in the past. He had never reciprocated, though always remained scrupulously courteous throughout. It was not just that he still remembered his wife of a hundred years ago, and the son that he had lost in the castle fire. He knew—had known since the day the soldiers had held him back from the flames—that everything in this world was transient. Everyone he knew, anyone he could find it in himself to love, could be only a temporary part of his life. When viewed in the context of another century or two centuries, a partnership of thirty or forty years represented a fraction that he did not care to trifle with. Once he had believed that "until death us do part" was a long time, during an age when life expectancy was short and women prone to die in childbirth. Now he realized that the course of a normal human life could never be enough for him. There was so little time to share that he would prefer to forego the blessing altogether, in order to avoid the inevitable end and pain that it would bring. Finally, having provided a focus for his life for the last twenty years, his work gave him an answer to that, too.

# 56

Emily sat stunned in her lab chair. *Edward was going to be furious.* She had emailed him the results of DNA test—on the hair taken from Tom's sweater. *What have I done?*

The test itself had brought back no bad news—far from it. Tom was as clear as he could be. He lacked any genetic faults whatsoever. Even the healthiest of patients usually displayed at least one or two minor problems—but that wasn't all. The report read:

**M-Trait:**          **- + Partial**

Tom was M-Trait partial—*he had one of the Methuselah genes!*

After all the people they had tested, Tom Oldham was the lab's first hit—one in a million—literally as genetically perfect as a human could be! She knew Edward would be so excited. He *had* to know about this. She emailed him the results as an attachment immediately, with the subject line, "LOOK AT THIS!!!" Then she had picked up the phone to call Edward with the news. When his voice mail message came on, the euphoria of her discovery began to wear off, and instead she started to consider the implications of her actions. Tom had not given her permission to carry out the test. She had taken a hair from his fleece to find out what *she* wanted to find out—and what he, clearly, was not yet ready to know. She had betrayed his trust, and she had done so in a way that was not only unethical, it was probably illegal.

Emily now questioned her good intentions as she placed the phone back in its cradle. Had she done the test for Tom's benefit, or to satisfy her own curiosity? She admitted to herself that it was the latter. If he had been normal, she would have thrown away the test data and the prepared sample, and forgotten about the entire episode. Even if the data were significant, she should have let Edward claim credit for the discovery, when Tom eventually came in of his own accord. But it was too late for that. The email she had sent was evidence of her crime.

Emily cursed her need for approval. *What would Edward do?* The project was very important to him, and this kind of misdeed could cause serious problems. She was fairly sure that Tom would not kick up a fuss, but the point nevertheless stood: she overstepped ethical boundaries while working on *his* project. If anyone found out about it, the project could lose funding, and certainly lose respect. There might even be legal action to face. The subject line of her email, instead of drawing attention to her initiative and hard work, now seemed to scream her crime to him: "LOOK AT THIS!!!"

There were two alternatives. She could wait for Monday morning, when Edward would check his email, and then face his displeasure, or, she could get to his email first. She did not like to compound her existing betrayal with another, but she did not like the idea of facing Edward's anger—or, worse still, his disappointment in her. Emily tried not to think too much about her decision, preferring to act while she still had the nerve, and consider the consequences later.

Edward's office was locked. She had never known it to be locked before, but she was very rarely in the lab when Edward was away, so perhaps he often secured it on Saturday nights. She sighed, and found the ring of spare keys that hung in a cabinet in the storeroom. Security by obscurity, she reflected—the keys were out of sight, but not exactly hidden. Because the main door to the lab was locked when everyone was out, Edward clearly did not reckon on any more than the most casual of opportunist thieves.

As she entered his office, the motion detector clicked the lights on. She would have preferred them off, but she had no choice with the automatic lighting system that was installed throughout the Medical Center. Edward's computer hummed gently on the desk in front of her, the fan gently whirring away. The computer never slept. Even when Edward was away, he always had it running some kind of program—a simulation, a gene search routine—something to make the most of every minute of the day. She touched the mouse, and the computer monitor flashed into life. Ignoring the program on top, which she immediately recognized as a DNA comparison program, she opened the email program that lay, minimized, on the taskbar at the bottom of the screen. Every five minutes the inbox refreshed, and any new mail was displayed. She found hers instantly by its subject title, and the large attachment sent with it. Two others had arrived after it. Swallowing her guilt, she deleted her mistake with two clicks of the mouse.

Minimizing the email program, ensuring to leave everything as she had found it, she glanced again at the other application running. *What do we have here?*

It was a gene comparison program, designed to search out similar characteristics between two genetic profiles—finding shared genes and groups of genes. The program could be used to determine whether two given individuals were related, by pinpointing shared genetic material. The nature of the relationship could often be established, too. Another similar purpose was to ascertain which genetic faults or other characteristics a parent had passed on to a child.

The two sets of results lay side by side on the screen, with the computer listing the thousands of entries in its database as it searched through the remaining possibilities. It took Emily several seconds to get her head around what she was looking at. The results lay under two identifiers: *EC and JDOE*. Neither name used the correct protocol of first initial followed by last name and date of birth. What was Edward hiding?

A progress bar at the bottom of the screen showed that the DNA comparison was complete. The full comparison usually took a few hours to run, which was why Edward had left it overnight. Emily clicked on the icon. The comparison of the first set of chromosomes had produced preliminary projections. In the middle of the screen lay the result: "$2^{nd}$ degree relative." A second-degree relative was someone who was two meioses away, someone who shared a quarter of the genes: an uncle, a grandparent, or a half brother. JDOE—probably John Doe—was one of EC's relatives. Okay—but why the secrecy? Was Edward doing a special project for law enforcement? She was sure they had their own DNA staff specialists.

Looking for more clues, she clicked on the EC identifier to the left, bringing up the linked file of his details. EC was "XY", male. He had light brown hair, blue eyes. He was blood type B negative. A brief medical summary underneath provided her with another answer, and it wiped the curious expression right off her face.

**Ancestral Derivation:** Unknown, Slavic, All else <5%
**Genetic Disorders:** High Risk of Angina Pectoris
**M-Trait:** + + Positive

Emily stared at the screen, unable to take it in. For almost a minute her mind reeled, trying to make sense of what she was looking at—what it meant, whether she could trust it, or if she had made a mistake. She sat down heavily in his swivel chair and rubbed her eyes, trying to put the pieces of the puzzle together. EC—whoever he was—*was an Ultra!*

Emily Preston inhaled involuntarily. *What was going on? Who did Edward know that was nearly immortal?* Hoping to become less perplexed, she clicked on the profile for John Doe. If he was related to EC, perhaps that would tell her something. John Doe's profile summary had only one significant item that her eyes found quickly:

**M-Trait:** + + Positive

Trying to contain the dizzy feeling and rising nausea she was feeling, Emily leaned back in the padded chair with her eyes closed. John Doe was positive for the M-Trait too. *Who were these people?*

The new knowledge she gained in a few scattered minutes on Edward's computer devastated Emily. The truth was obvious. *Edward knows that the M-Trait exists.* First she felt betrayed, and then scared—she desperately wanted to leave the lab. As quickly as she could, Emily carefully closed the programs on Edward's computer, locked his office, and replaced the spare keys. Grabbing her purse and coat, she exited the lab.

After a few minutes, the motion detector clicked the lights off behind her, leaving everything in the lab as it once was. But for Emily, her life had irreversibly changed forever.

# 57

Michael had already spent two weeks in Alexandria before he met Hashim. He was taking a month's holiday there, time away from his life of managing assets and overseeing his small financial empire in America. The Middle East was not a place in which he would consider living for any length of time for many reasons, not least the political; it was not stable enough to set up home there. Israel, in particular, was unsafe, and despite his longing, he had not returned there since the Six-Day War in 1967. But much of Egypt was safer; it did not have the same incidence of suicide bombings and other terrorist acts, although he remained as vigilant as ever.

It was a cloudless day, and the sun shone down on his pepper-gray hair and reflected off the white cotton clothes that he wore. He drank frequently from one of the two liter bottles of mineral water that he carried everywhere in his rucksack, the local water being so salty as to be practically undrinkable. Even in spring, it was far hotter here than he was used to. He had spent several months recently in significantly colder climes, and the pale skin visible between the straps of his open sandals was quickly tanning. As ever, he was careful to avoid burning, and carried with him a high-factor sunscreen. Whatever his hopes for the future, melanoma played no part.

Michael had long given up hope of finding Eduard. He knew that his best chance had been in the days immediately after the end of the Brotherhood in 1917, when he had followed the man to Switzerland. He had been too late that time and therefore, he assumed, too late for good. Now after almost ninety years, what chance did he have, finding a man who did not want to be found, when he had the whole world to hide in? He could change his name, find a new identity in a new country, as Michael had done, and go unnoticed for the rest of his long life. The only thing that might work in his favor was that Eduard did not know that Michael was still alive. Later, he would realize how vastly he had underestimated the importance of that piece of information.

Picking his way through the busy streets, he moved past the Terbana Mosque and into the Suq district. It was even busier here as he made his way through the crowds, turning from side to side to weave around the people coming towards him, but always moving forwards. An amazing wealth of goods was available for sale here: food, spices, jewelry, plants, clothing, and anything else he might care to own. Michael was careful to avoid eye contact with any of the shopkeepers on either side of the street, who would otherwise try to convince him to buy something as if their lives depended on it.

After a little way, he turned down one of the narrower side alleys, like a smaller blood vessel branching from an artery, and turned to watch the stream of people rushing past on the street he had just left. A little further down, he ducked into a doorway. Inside it was blissfully cool, air-conditioned to protect the computers from overheating. The Internet café was one of his lifelines to the outside world—the way he kept up with international news, found local information, and organized his transport and his bank accounts. It was a strange contrast, stepping from the antique world of ruins and ancient history outside into this technological haven.

"*Qahwah, min-fadlak.*" He paid for a coffee and sat at one of the little tables to enjoy the air conditioning; his work on the computers would take only ten minutes and he was in need of a break. A waiter brought over a thick black Turkish coffee a couple of minutes later, before disappearing off into the back again.

"*Shukran.*" *Thank you.* Michael had never had much trouble communicating when he came to a new country. His Arabic was still relatively rudimentary but he was learning fast, picking up words and phrases every day as he engaged the locals in conversation.

The coffee had the color and consistency of thin tar, and was heavily sweetened and flavored with cardamom and maybe a hint of something else. At the tables around him, Arab men held similar drinks in tiny cups, playing backgammon and smoking flavored tobacco through water pipes. Michael took a sip of the coffee and closed his eyes, trying to tune out the background noise and listen to a single conversation at a nearby table, picking out the words to practice his Arabic.

"*Injileezee?* English?" The man was leaning across from the next table. He was thinning on top, with a large, hooked nose and an even bigger smile, which displayed the gaps where several teeth were missing.

The truth was more complicated, but Michael spoke English as fluently as a number of other languages. "Yes...*na'am, injileezee.*"

"Ah, you speak Arabic!" He seemed delighted at the idea.

"*Qaleel.* A little. Not much."

"You play?" The Arab indicated the backgammon board in front of him.

Michael was not surprised at the offer; he had found most of the people friendly, eager to please him and very hospitable. He had nothing else pressing to do, and welcomed the opportunity to spend some time in the cool and chat. It would give him an opportunity to practice his Arabic too.

"*Ismee Michael,*" he introduced himself.

"Hashim." Hashim pointed to his chest, eyes bright and smile ever broader, to emphasize the point. Michael wondered whether the pipe contained only tobacco.

He let Hashim win the first game narrowly, allowing him to give some advice on his tactics. He won the second, and bought them each another Turkish coffee afterwards. This time the mystery flavor was stronger, and he realized it was rose water.

They talked in English for some time, Michael about Europe, and Hashim about the political circumstances in his country and the rest of the Middle East. Amidst the violence and the suicide bombers in Israel, his real fear was that chemical and biological weapons might be used. That would start a war that would claim too many lives on both sides.

Hashim sucked at the water pipe, through which he was smoking what turned out to be tobacco cut only with molasses. He offered it to Michael, who accepted solely to avoid offending his new acquaintance. As a rule, he despised the smell of cigarette and cigar smoke and avoided them almost religiously to prevent damage to his lungs. When he tried this, he found to his surprise that it was not unpleasant.

"New diseases, new...strains, man-made, very dangerous—no cure for them." Hashim seemed genuinely worried about the possibility of an attack from which there was no escape. "Yes, very dangerous technology."

He thought for a minute, as if considering whether to let Michael in on a secret. He raised a forefinger, bidding him to wait a minute. Then he pulled a folded magazine from his bag. It was an Arabic language publication, and Michael did not recognize the title when he deciphered it, but it seemed to be some kind of *New Scientist* equivalent. Hashim flicked through and opened it to particular page, turning it so that it was the right way up for Michael. "Good technology."

Hashim began to explain more, but Michael did not hear anything. From the page a face stared up at him that, for almost ninety years, he had seen only in his memories.

"Sharman." Arabic did not have the letters and sounds to properly represent the name, but there was no question about it. Ninety years, and a lifetime later, there was Eduard's picture—he had barely changed. After the brief reflex of surprise was over, Michael's emotions settled and he found that instead of the sense of anger or pain he expected, his enduring feeling was one of hunger. The intervening decades had done nothing to diminish his craving for revenge.

## 58

Back in her flat, it was suddenly safe for Emily to feel all the emotions that she had experienced when sitting in front of the computer screen at Edward's office—disbelief, fear, and anger assaulted her in swift succession and she collapsed onto the sofa to have a good cry. But it was only minutes before her mind naturally began to analyze all the new information she had discovered.

Clumsily rising from the sofa with her ninth-month pregnancy doing its best to hinder her, Emily shuffled into the kitchen to get a long drink of water. It was cooler in there, and she sat at the table with her chin in her hands, with a blank sheet of paper and a pencil. Emotions were a good motivator for some people, but Emily enjoyed her innate ability to use reasoning as a tool to understand the events in her life.

Although she had few facts, and could never ask Edward questions concerning what she learned from his computer, there were assumptions that might allow her to make sense of this new, bizarre data. She first wrote down "Edward" and began to jot down her random thoughts. *The M-Trait is a reality—not a theory. Edward knows that M-Trait is not a theory. For how long? Instead of trumpeting the discovery of M-Trait, Edward hides it. Why hide it?* Emily tapped her pencil on the paper for a few moments before deciding to move on.

Next she wrote down "EC." *Edward knows EC or else he wouldn't have used initials. EC has the M-Trait. EC has Slavic ancestry and a disposition for angina. Is that a coincidence? Does Slavic include Russian ancestry? Edward does speak Russian. And he has the same hair color, same blue eyes. What was his blood type--was it B, or had she remembered that wrong? Could the "E" of "EC" stand for Edward?*

It was circumstantial, she knew. But the series of coincidences would also be highly unlikely. Slowly, but boldly, Emily penciled in "EC = Edward." For reasons she couldn't understand at the moment, it felt right. With it surfaced the feeling of betrayal. *Edward has the M-Trait? How old is he? Why is he a scientist? Why fake research on the M-Trait theory? Why am I part of this charade? Was I chosen or am I an unwitting bystander? What does this phony want?*

What hurt worst, she realized, was that a man she thought she had known for years had stabbed her in the back. Edward, a man she had trusted enough to share part of her life with, had lied to her about who he was and what he had been doing all this time. And she hadn't suspected a thing.

Realizing she was losing focus, Emily switched to another name. She wrote down "John Doe." *John Doe is a close relative of EC. If EC = Edward, then Edward has a relative that's alive? I thought his relatives were all dead.*

Not able to make sense of this particular train of thought, Emily found another spur of logic. *Edward used initials for EC, why not use initials for John Doe? Maybe Edward doesn't know who John Doe is. But then how did he obtain John Doe's DNA sample?*

Confusion began to overcome Emily, so she drew in a deep breath and closed her eyes to steady herself. A name came to mind, but she immediately dismissed it. She then wrote down "Tom." *Partial M-Trait. Connected to John Doe? Connected to EC? How? Partial and positive M-Traits found on the same day? Is this a coincidence? How can there be any connection?*

That line of thought was going nowhere. Emily's mind naturally brought up the other name, and she felt obligated to write it on the paper—"Zoe." Sighing heavily, she let go, ruminating on her daughter-to-be. It was only a moment before the torrent of thoughts burst through. *Zoe is an implanted embryo. The embryo is modified with an unknown male's sperm. Edward helped in modifying the embryo. If Edward = EC and secretly possesses the M-Trait, then—*

Emily gasped when the appalling question occurred to her. *What is Zoe?*

## 59

Tom returned to Sherman's house with mixed feelings. He had to return to finish arranging Edward's death, but he would also have to check the freezer—to see if Edward had found Margaret. He knew Edward would never report the frozen corpse to the authorities—he might prefer to keep a low profile and dispose of it himself. Nevertheless, if there was no body, then his visit was an extreme risk that could ruin all his plans.

Therefore, this had to be his last visit—he was ready for closure on this episode of his life. Once Sherman was dead, he would take Emily and leave the country. He had wasted enough time pandering to his father's wishes. It was time to live his own life, out of his father's shadow. He was ready to take that step now.

The tabby cat, now quite familiar with his visits, meowed a greeting, demanding some attention. She was getting fat, he noticed. A predatory animal by nature, domestication had reduced her to a less active role—perhaps the result of being forced into a lifestyle that she had not been designed for. Unlike Tom, and his father, she had not been able to adapt to her new environment. So many different environments—he was growing tired of adapting, even if his father never had.

Back to the job at hand, he used his copied keys to open the black metal security gate and back door for the very last time. As he stepped into the kitchen, he removed the two AA batteries from his pocket. It was time to implement his plan.

On the wall beside the boiler, the central heating control provided the reassurance he needed. Sherman obviously didn't have the heat on in the late summer, but the nights were starting to cool, and the boiler was still used for the hot water. It came on mostly during heavy use—

in the morning, when he showered, and in the evening for cooking and cleaning. Thinking for a moment, Tom pushed the advance override button and heard the muffled *whumph* as the boiler lit. By the time the doctor returned, the boiler would have been running for hours, heating water and allowing CO to seep into the house. And when Sherman came in that night, it would have reset to the original program and he would expect it to be on for the chilly evening; he would never know the difference. Lastly, it took only a moment to place the dead batteries into the carbon monoxide detector above the boiler.

Now it was time to check Margaret. The memory of that visit, never far from the surface, came to mind again. Unbidden, he remembered the noise that Margaret made as he broke her neck with his hands—just the briefest and quietest of whimpers before it was too late.

Tom wondered whether Sherman had needed anything from the freezer since he had deposited his burden there. Opening the large door and lifting aside the bags of frozen peas and hash browns, he saw that Margaret was stiff as ever, with a half-inch of ice frost now covering her.

Tom made his way back into the house. Absurdly, a term he had heard in an American gangster film came to mind, and he found himself trying to stifle a snicker; he had "iced" her. Under the frozen peas, Margaret slept on, perfectly preserved and undisturbed. He figured she deserved that much.

Out in the back garden, Tom moved the foliage aside so he could see the vent that took the waste gases away from the boiler, and away from the lungs of anyone in danger of inhaling them. It was a horizontal flue, and exited low on the outside wall due to the elevation change on the property. The grate was screwed to the wall with rusted flat-head screws. He had almost brought a screwdriver with him to make things easier, but realized that he could not take the screws out without damaging the covering of rust, and that would be to suggest foul play to anyone who looked closely enough. New screws would not do, either. The rust was his ally. It proved that the ventilation system was old and dilapidated. Negligence and not malice needed to be the verdict.

Tom had heard of some cases in the States where people had died of CO poisoning when snowdrifts had covered their external vents. Even given the British weather, he knew he could not rely on snow in late summer and would have to improvise. Instead, he fed in thin twigs and general garden detritus, some moss and the remains of an old, abandoned bird's nest which he had found at the base of one of the silver birch trees; its inside still downy with the soft feathers the bird had used to line it. Then he carefully pushed the ivy back through the grate, as it had been when he first found it. It had grown several inches in the intervening weeks, encouraged by summer rains mixed with hot days. When he finished, he judged the flue to be thoroughly obstructed, and downright dangerous. The vent itself was now all but invisible to the naked eye, hidden behind the organic exterior of the stone house.

Before he left, Tom noticed the cat flap and wondered whether he should leave it open or jam it closed. He didn't want the cat going the same way as Sherman, but not knowing where she was at the moment, he left it open. Then he locked the back door and security gate, the mechanism shutting in his hand with an air of finality—this job was over. He remembered his first visit, when the lock had given in his hands. The two moments seemed to form neat bookends for the last few months. Maybe it was a little too neat, though. There were parts of the last few months that Tom didn't want to finish.

When Edward was dead, what would happen to Emily? In one sense, it didn't matter: Tom knew that it was out of his hands. If it turned out that he didn't have the M-Trait, then he would have to cut ties with his father anyway. If he did, he would be welcomed into the fold. But then he couldn't be with Emily. It was a Catch-22 situation, all hinging on the presence of those two elusive genes in his body. At the present moment, there was only one man who could answer that question for him. Fortunately, the wait would be over soon.

With a final goodbye to the tabby cat—a tickle under the chin—he glanced at his watch, surprised at the amount of time that had passed in his task and daydreaming. He slipped out of the garden door and jogged down two streets to where his car was parked.

It would not do to be late. He had an appointment to keep.

# 60

Chorionic Villus Sampling (CVS), a prenatal diagnostic procedure to test for fetal abnormalities, is typically carried out ten weeks into a pregnancy. The procedure involves acquiring a sample of the placenta, which is attached to the fetus by the umbilical cord and contains the genetic fingerprint for the baby. The sample can then be subjected to the gamut of DNA analyses. The risk of losing the unborn child from this procedure, by miscarriage, is less than 1%.

Emily never told Dr. Sherman about her CVS test. As far as Sherman was concerned, nothing was wrong with Zoe. He had arranged her genetic profile himself, and for her to check the fact externally would be to call into question both his professional skill, the trust she placed in him, and, moreover, the quality of their friendship. Nevertheless, Emily wanted to be sure about her daughter's safety—and it would put her mind to rest.

CVS was not usually offered without good reason, due to the cost involved. That is, unless there was a chance of the offspring having an inherited condition, there was no point in going to the trouble. She told her doctor about a case of Cystic Fibrosis in a distant part of her family—she just wanted to make absolutely sure about her child. The procedure lasted only twenty minutes, and the results came in nine days later. As she already knew perfectly well, the test confirmed that her child did not possess the rogue gene on the long arm of chromosome 7, the harbinger of Cystic Fibrosis. Neither did she harbor any of the other abnormalities routinely tested for. Still, Emily requested that she be allowed to take away the test samples for further analysis. It was highly irregular, but in view of her work and the facilities afforded to her at the university, her request was honored.

The unmarked white box had been a forgotten keepsake that, almost six months later, still lay hidden at the back of one of the lab freezers awaiting the time when future study was necessary—for whatever reason. Now after stumbling across both Tom's and Edward's genetic secrets, Emily had an unsettling motive for studying the sample from her womb.

The lab freezers operated at much lower temperatures than the commercial kitchen variety, and Emily pulled on a thick pair of gloves before she opened the door. The contents steamed as she pulled out a drawer, sending waves of freezing condensation rolling across the floor like smoke. It was oddly beautiful. Above her head, the illuminated seven-segment displays that showed the temperature within the freezer slowly ticked up towards zero. She found the box undisturbed where she had left it, closed the freezer and brought the sample over to her workspace. At this point, she had two alternatives. She could bag it in one of the lab's containers for biological waste and dispose of it, or she could do what she should have done six months ago but had lacked the nerve and opportunity to carry through.

For a second time in a week, she was about to perform a DNA test using the lab's facilities without Edward's knowledge. Thankfully, her guilt was much weaker now, even though her actions were quite legal this occasion. Emily thawed the sample and went about carrying out the preliminary requirements for the analysis, knowing that once Zoe was born, it would be almost impossible to perform the test. Her presence in the lab would raise eyebrows if she came back too soon, especially just to process one test, and she did not think she could get it processed anonymously. Perhaps in a year or so, when she came back full-time, it would be possible—but that would be too late. She needed to know now.

She did not make a note of the test in their records, so that a casual glance by Sherman would not give her away. A reasonable number of tests went through every day, and the results would come back to her user area on the computer system, not the joint one to which the whole lab had access. She knew that Edward had done the same in the past, and had not questioned it.

# M-Trait

When finished, she sat down in a corner of the lab and shook her head, ashamed at her deception and at the uncertainty of what she might find. The results would be back within a few days, and she would be able to access them remotely from the computer in her flat, ensuring they would remain secret from Sherman. The software she had at home was not as advanced as that in the lab—which required an expensive license and high-performance machines to run—but she would manage. She was looking for the answer to only one question.

*What was Zoe designed to be?*

# 61

*Eduard is alive!* The knowledge had burned behind Michael's eyes as Hashim translated the article from Arabic to English so he could absorb its contents. The man called Dr. Edward Sherman could be found in London, England working on a research project cataloguing genetic diseases.

A brief, almost amusing aside at the end of the article captured Michael's attention even more: Sherman's belief in a "Methuselah" gene, a characteristic that would prevent aging and theoretically even death, when found in conjunction with a clean bill of genetic health. The doctor theorized the possibility of a mortal being with an extended life, an "Ultra-mortal" or "Ultra" for short. Michael didn't think much of the label—his mind was elsewhere. He smiled at the picture of Dr. Edward Sherman, more of a snarl of hunger than an expression of humor.

Eduard didn't know he was alive, and that would be the seed of his undoing. His confidence in his aloneness was his weakness. Now, everything had changed. Michael was the hunter, and he would soon know all he needed to bring him down. He marveled at the irony of it. For so long, Eduard had been within his grasp—had he realized the extent of the man's complacency, he might have found him years earlier. Instead, he had waited nearly a century, and traveled halfway around the world, just to find a man who had no intention of hiding himself. He should have realized, long ago, to have less faith in Eduard—the man possessed a lousy survival instinct.

In less than an hour, Hashim's unsolicited friendship had answered the two questions that had haunted him for the better part of a century: that of his longevity, and what had happened to Eduard. It pleased him that the two were so closely connected, despite the complications it might bring. It brought a feeling of completion, and seemed to make sense of the last several decades. The delay in finding Eduard was extremely provident after all.

Michael did not leave Egypt immediately. If there was one thing that long life had taught him, it was patience. Sherman was not going anywhere, and Michael needed time to think what to do, and how to deal with all the murderous intentions that had suddenly resurfaced, filling his mind with possibilities.

He spent the rest of the day as planned, walking among the ruins of the Greek and Roman civilizations that had settled in Alexandria, centuries and millennia earlier. The sun blazed down on him, but he barely noticed in the intensity of his personal discovery. As he took in the amphitheatre and catacombs of the Roman occupation, that searing revelation of Sherman's existence burned in his mind. From that moment, rather than being the aimless drifter he had been since leaving Russia, he was a man with a purpose. His time of wandering in the wilderness was over.

Two days later, he purchased a ticket for New York City and flew home. He arrived at ten in the evening, went straight through the green channel at customs, and caught a cab to his offices in Manhattan.

It was almost midnight by the time he arrived in his office, after first partaking in a hot meal from an all-night diner a block away. The sleepy security man let him in without raising an eyebrow; Michael's hours were hardly conventional at the best of times. He unlocked the door with one of a dozen keys on the ring that he carried everywhere with him, and took the elevator up to the twelfth floor. He could see the city spread out beneath him from here, pulsing and alive even at night.

The first task was to unearth every bit of information on Dr. Edward Sherman. He could hire a firm, but Michael wanted the type of information that most outfits could not acquire legally. His son, Tanek, was the right choice for this project. He would do anything asked, and most importantly, he was expendable. The boy was aging and would eventually realize his mortal limitations. Each conversation with his son had been difficult since the moment he found out about his father's longevity.

"So, what about me?" Tanek had asked him, after dropping that pile of papers and photos on Michael's desk, upon his return from Salamanca. Michael had noted the tight knot of self-anger in his stomach for allowing this situation to happen. He genuinely hadn't thought that his son would try to contact his mother's family, and had certainly not expected him to follow it up by researching Michael's own movements.

"What about you?" Michael had leafed through the material his son had gathered. His relationship with Tanek was forever changed—his son was now a threat, not just dead weight. He needed time to think. Jakob, the mortal son who had resented his family so much, was immediately uppermost in his mind. Difficult times brought difficult decisions.

"It raises some questions about me—about my life ahead."

"Mmm, imagine so," he answered as his son stared impatiently. "I just don't know—there's no way of telling, other than to wait. Don't you think I would have told you if I already knew?"

"Depends on what you had to say. I assume that mortality isn't a very desirable trait in a son."

"You'll have to trust me. In a few years, it'll show in your face, one way or another."

"So that's it? Sit and wait?"

Michael thought quickly. He needed to keep his son around while he decided what to do—as a loose cannon, he could be dangerous.

"Do you know what your name means, Tanek?"

"You told me it meant 'immortal' in Polish."

"It's what I've always hoped for you. And I have every confidence that it will happen—but you need to be patient. Learn that now because, believe me, you need patience if you are to live as long as I have. In the meantime," Michael stood up and fixed his son with a firm gaze, "we have work to do."

Looking back on that uncomfortable meeting years ago, Michael was glad he had kept his son busy and close. He knew too much to be allowed his freedom—that was all too clear. Michael had seen enough sons grow up to know that Tanek, now almost thirty, was aging like a normal, mortal human. He was well on the way to the grave, and perhaps that process needed to be expedited, for him as well as for the man who betrayed the Brotherhood.

He turned to the newspaper spread out on his desk and opened it to the Obituaries section. Downing the rest of his coffee, he ran a pen down the list of names, stopping at a name that seemed properly English:

**OLDHAM.—THOMAS, in hospital after a short illness, on 4<sup>th</sup> March, aged 8 months. Dearly loved and sorely missed twin brother of Jonathan. Donations, if desired, to the American Cancer Society...**

Thomas, Tom. Michael mouthed the word, then spoke it aloud to himself: "Tom." *Th<sup>e</sup>'oma, twin*, an Aramaic name; he liked it. Thomas Oldham had barely begun his life before it had ended, but where he left off, someone else would begin. Jonathan Oldham would never know it, but somewhere his brother's namesake would live on for a little longer.

Michael folded the newspaper and picked up the phone. The kind of people he needed to contact for this type of work didn't keep conventional hours—he would compensate them well for a few hours of lost sleep.

The rest of the week would be spent in his office preparing—Michael needed to find out all he could about Sherman that had been published in the media. That would be enough to set in motion a plan to topple the house of cards Sherman had built for himself. Everything could be orchestrated from within his communications center in New York, until he was truly needed. There was no point risking his own skin when there were others to do that for him.

# 62

Almost four months to the day after picking the locks to Sherman's house on that spring morning, Tom found himself in the doctor's lab. He originally had the appointment for Wednesday, but the lab had called and rescheduled for late Friday afternoon—the receptionist said it would give him and the doctor more time to discuss the procedure.

Dr. Edward Sherman led him into an expansive lab with a number of workstations—all empty—and then off to a separate office, the doctor's private room with a computer desk.

"Tom Oldham, isn't it? I'm Edward Sherman." That was a lie, of sorts, though one spoken so lightly and fluidly, and so many times before, that it had taken on the appearance of a truth—even to the one who spoke it.

The doctor was genial in his ease, comfortable with first-name terms from the start. "Thank you for offering to help in our research. Emily tells me you've been showing quite an interest in the project."

He motioned to Tom to take a seat in the swivel chair on the other side of the desk. Sherman sat in his own seat and hit a few keys, bringing up a database program on the computer screen to record Tom's particulars.

"I hope my data will help." Tom replied while scrutinizing Sherman's behavior, his words, and his tone for any hint of suspicion. Coming here was a risk, but a calculated and affordable one. Still, he had the feeling of walking into the lion's den, though his rational mind told him he had nothing to fear.

A brief appointment here, a wait of a week, and he would hold in his hands the proof, one way or another, that was so important to him and his father. He simply could not afford to miss this opportunity, since the doctor would not be in a position to provide that information for much longer. It was best to make use of him while he was still alive.

"Emily said that—was it three of your direct relatives?—are known to have reached at least a hundred. Most impressive." Sherman raised an eyebrow appreciatively.

Tom nodded his agreement. That was also a lie, of sorts—touché. It was fun playing Sherman at his own game, knowing so much about him but not letting on.

"Well, I gather you know a bit about what we do here from Emily, so I won't bore you with the usual spiel. But feel free to ask any questions you might have." Sherman's blue eyes sparkled, like pools lit by underwater lamps.

"Thanks. I understand most of it—but maybe you can recap the high points while you extract my vital fluids." With guidance from the doctor, he rose from the chair and crossed to the nearby medical couch where he reclined. Edward motioned for Tom to pull up his left sleeve, exposing the crook of his arm.

Sherman busied himself with the equipment for taking a sample of blood. He pulled on a pair of latex gloves—very similar, Tom noticed, to the type he wore to avoid leaving fingerprints behind when he broke into the doctor's house. Then from a box full of sealed plastic packs on one of the workstations, Sherman pulled a needle and some tubes.

"Just rest your arm here." He tied off the rubber tube and, after a few moments, selected the vein in the crook of Tom's elbow, testing its resilience with his gloved fingertips first. "Good. No problems there."

Tom did not so much as wince as the needle found his mark, even with Sherman's rough thrust. He smiled to himself. *I'm so vulnerable here. But poor Edward really doesn't suspect a thing.*

"So, while we wait a moment, let me tell you what will happen." Edward had grown accustomed to explaining his work to the volunteers who donated their blood to him, and was quite capable of giving an off-the-cuff presentation.

"We use a version of the DyNAmo, developed by a group of researchers from UK Genetix to process raw DNA data. The Human

Genome project was an enormous undertaking that took ten years and three billion U.S. dollars to map the whole of a DNA molecule. Now just a few years later, our machine can do it in less than a day, and for only a few relative shillings. There are approximately three billion 'letters'—amino acids—in the molecule that code for everything in your biological makeup. The different letters are the only variables, and there are only four of them to choose from."

Now that the needle was in, that side of things would take care of itself with minimal supervision. Sherman turned, grabbed a piece of paper off the desk, and began drawing what resembled a ladder with every rung broken in the middle.

"The DNA molecule looks something like this, although in reality it's all coiled up. We have to straighten it out to read the information. On the left side of the DNA ladder, each rung represents a basic compound of life, one of the four possibilities of amino acids: Guanine, Cytosine, Adenine and Thymine—G, C, A and T. On the other side of the ladder is the opposite pair. G is always paired with C, and A is always paired with T."

In between sentences, Sherman exchanged filled tubes with empty ones. He looked up to check that Tom was still following him with his lesson. He was, but it wasn't holding his interest: the information was too basic. Sherman quickly moved on to the more specialized side of his work.

"Anyway, our machine flags these pairs of bases and reads them with a laser, though preparing the sample still takes us a day or two."

"When you've received the information—when you've read the molecule—what can you do with it?"

Tom's question was earnest, made out of genuine interest and the desire to learn. For all his father had told him about the doctor, Edward was an amiable and intelligent man, and was good company. Under other circumstances, it was quite possible that they could have been friends. It was a shame he was going to have to kill him.

# 63

Dr. Edward Sherman focused on breathing normally and talking easily while he prepared for the right moment to slip Tom the sedative. He hoped that his scientific conversation would keep his special guest from noticing anything unusual.

"What we effectively have at the end of the process is the raw material for further study, hundreds of megabytes of data that have to be analyzed. Theoretically, that could tell us everything we need to know about a person's makeup. It's a huge number of data, but only a fraction of it is of any significance for our purposes. One person's DNA molecule differs very little from another. I'm sure you've read that even the genetic difference between man and apes is as little as one percent." Edward kept talking, stuff that came naturally to him and he did not have to think much about.

In the background, his mind was working furiously on many levels. He was worried about Emily. This man, Tom Oldham, was now a part of her life. What did he want with her? Did he know about Zoe? He must have paused in his monologue at some point, because suddenly it was silent and Tom was looking at him expectantly.

Sherman shook his head to dispel the distraction, rubbing his eyes and blinking to focus on the present. He had taken his time and slowly filled ten larger-than-needed tubes with blood, placing them in a separate container for cataloguing and processing. Then he pulled the needle out and applied an absorbent pad. "Just hold this with three fingers. Keep the pressure on."

Tom did so. "That didn't take long. Do you think it will turn up anything interesting?"

"You're an extremely promising volunteer." He turned back to the workbench, holding up an adhesive patch. "You're not allergic to latex bandages, are you?"

"Not so far." Tom let up the pressure on the pad and let Sherman stick the patch over the needle mark, smoothing down the edges to make sure the contact with the skin was sound all over. He watched as the doctor carefully stripped off the gloves, leaving them inside out, and dropped them in a medical waste bin along with the needle and tubing.

At Sherman's suggestion, he lay there quietly for five minutes, as the glass tubes were labeled and sent off for the next stage of the procedure, and the requisite entries were made in the database. When he had finished, Sherman spoke again.

"It probably wouldn't hurt to stay here a little longer to make sure you're all right. It wasn't too much blood but sometimes people feel a little dizzy. You're not planning on doing anything strenuous later, are you?"

Tom shook his head.

Sherman nodded. In reality, he had taken a little more time—and much more blood—than he usually did, and it was quite likely that Tom would feel the effects if he got up suddenly. He continued talking.

"We use the fastest computers available, but it can still take a while, just because of the sheer volume of stuff to search through—it's really like looking for specific needles in a haystack, one straw at a time. We're also still building a comprehensive database of sequences to dial into. By the time that's finished, it should be a relatively simple procedure to scan for genetic diseases and other idiosyncrasies. But given what Emily has told me about your family, it's quite possible that you'll show very few problems."

That brought him back to Emily again. He did not know how much Tom knew. Given the man's relationship with Emily, which Sherman could hardly assume was a coincidence by now, he probably knew a lot. Hidden from Tom behind the screen, Edward bit his lip and tried to think how he should play this scenario out.

The computer in front of him sounded its tone and flashed a "completed" window as it finished collating the data from the test of a previous patient. The doctor scrolled through the results, scanning them quickly with a practiced eye. They did nothing to help his nervousness, but he was pleased to have a reason to change the subject.

"For example, both this subject's aunt and grandmother died of breast cancer, and she came to us to find out whether the condition was hereditary. I was hoping to be able to reassure her that it was just a coincidence, but it seems that we will both be disappointed after all." There was another pause, there being nothing appropriate to say. "Well, at least she will now know about the genetic defect—forewarned is forearmed."

Tom was curious. "You can tell that she will definitely develop cancer?"

"No, it's not that precise. She has a fairly heavy genetic predisposition to it, is all I can say. Her chances of breast cancer are much higher than average, but in absolute terms?" Sherman shrugged. "It's really impossible to say."

Edward was happy that Tom continued to be interested. The longer Tom stayed, the easier it would be to take him down. He scanned the screen again, pausing momentarily to make sense of sets of codes that were just meaningless numbers and letters to Tom. "Among other things...any of her male children will very likely be prematurely bald."

"It hardly seems fair." It was impossible to tell whether Tom's level tone and deadpan look betrayed genuine concern or hid a trace of mockery, and Sherman did not feel much inclined to pursue the point.

"This is what we're up against. The human race has become contaminated by these genetic diseases. In times past, fewer children would have reached an age to have children and pass their faults on, but improvements in medical science have postponed that aspect of natural selection. My work here is a step towards remedying the balance, bringing things back to the way they should be, before medicine messed things up. We are the victims of our own success."

"Lambs to the slaughter." Perhaps, on balance, there was just a hint of irony in Tom's voice. Sherman regarded him with a long, pensive gaze. Tom was looking him in the eye, and he had the uncomfortable sensation that he was looking through his eyes and into the scene playing in his mind. The two of them remained locked in the stare for some seconds, both defiant, but it was Sherman who looked away first.

## 64

"So what about this Methuselah gene? What are the chances I have it?"

Sherman was quite literally stunned for a moment. Hidden behind his computer screen, he stared speechless, and his jaw tightened. *The man's brazen arrogance!* Very well then, he could talk about it for hours—certainly for far longer than Tom had to wait.

"It's not just one gene—it's two. The odds of anyone having the full trait are minute. There seem to be several factors that combine, and the chances of having even one—"

"So how does it affect the aging process? At what point do things stop? What could a Methuselah positive born today expect from life?"

Sherman glared at Tom before finishing his first thought, "There are two entirely separate sequences of DNA, and both have to be present." The scientist in Sherman took over again. "And aging wouldn't stop. It merely slows down." Years of care about his own identity had enabled Sherman to talk about his work in abstract terms, speaking as if it were all hypothesis.

Tom shot him a puzzled look. "What, so—"

"The aging process would be left relatively unaffected in childhood. Development would take place as normal and the children would grow up like any other." Sherman enjoyed teaching, and his enthusiasm for passing on his knowledge won over his current anxiety and anticipation. "It would only really take effect after adolescence, with the onset of adulthood." He paused to pour himself a glass of water from a covered jug on his desk, sipping it slowly before continuing. He did not offer Tom a glass.

"The child would develop to maturity pretty much as normal. But as the growth spurt nears its end and the hormonal changes in the body stabilize, things might start to take a new turn. It doesn't stop you from growing *up*—that's an entirely different process. It stops you growing *old*. Aging should still continue, but at a vastly reduced rate." He sipped from the glass again.

"How reduced—how long could they live? How does it even work?" The eagerness for answers in Tom's voice reminded Sherman of his students' questions. And he decided to be a good teacher, answering each question thoroughly.

"That's unclear. We have yet to have a subject to study, so the exact mechanism itself is rather uncertain. But here's my best guess to date.

"When you burn a fuel—any fuel—it combines with oxygen. Oxygen is highly electronegative which means, in chemical terms, it loves to grab electrons from other materials. That's what happens in a fire: as oxygen takes on electrons from a fuel, some of the energy in their chemical bonds is given up as heat. The heat enables further reactions, so the fire spreads. The trick is getting the reaction to start in the first place—which is just as well, otherwise anything vaguely flammable would spontaneously combust. You have to help it along, with a match or spark or something of that nature." Sherman sipped again, and then continued.

"Oxygen has this halfway state, somewhere between its normal state and being fully combined with the fuel—burnt. In this state, it's called a free radical, and it's an extremely reactive agent. Once oxygen starts reacting, it doesn't like to stop.

"The point of this is that something very similar happens during metabolism—although in a more controlled fashion, via a chain of enzyme complexes. You breathe; your body burns what you eat. But despite careful safeguards, some of the reactive, oxygen-free radicals manage to escape along the way, causing havoc with whatever they touch. Your cells' mitochondria, where the reaction occurs, are damaged by the fallout. The more you metabolize, the more damage occurs, both to the mitochondria and the rest of the cell. The result is a decline in efficiency for the mitochondria, and ever deteriorating tissues. You and I call this process 'aging.'"

"Many of the hallmarks of aging can be traced to this process. Different genes can be taken out of action by the free radicals, resulting in cancer or heart disease or something as simple as wrinkling. That, incidentally, is why animals with faster metabolisms have shorter life spans. There's a built-in play-off between metabolism and life expectancy." Sherman drained the rest of his glass. "You can live fast and die young, like a mouse, or take things easier and last two hundred years, like the giant tortoise—as a rule." He fixed Tom with a glance.

"The body's natural defense is antioxidants, which neutralize the free radicals—some enzymes have that effect, and other substances like beta-carotene and vitamin E. Consuming extra antioxidants in the form of fruit and vegetables, green tea and so on, supposedly prolongs life expectancy. It appears that one of the functions of the two Methuselah genes is to affect the free radicals the body produces as a by-product of metabolism. The process of burning fuel is almost perfect: virtually a one hundred percent efficient metabolism." Sherman smiled, as if his perfect metabolism was causing his body to radiate life and health.

"How does it work—what's so different?" Tom was engrossed in Sherman's lesson in the science of aging. He absentmindedly scratched at the dressing on his arm; the skin underneath was itching, and he could get little relief through the tough plastic patch.

"At this stage, that's unclear—we haven't got that far yet. Possibly, there is some super-efficient form of antioxidant being produced, which jumps on every stray free radical before it does any damage. The other possibility—or more likely an additional possibility—is that the mitochondria work differently. You get that in birds."

"Birds?" Tom sounded skeptical.

"Yes. Compared to mammals of the same size, birds live a disproportionately long time. Over five times longer, in fact. A rat will live an average of three years in captivity. A bird of the same size, like a pigeon, could easily live fifteen or twenty. It seems their mitochondria produce fewer free radicals. It's like having a clean, efficient power source rather than a dirty one—solar panels instead of a leaky fission reactor.

"Something similar might be going on in this case. Whatever the mechanism, the upshot is that aging is slowed down, perhaps to a point where it is effectively arrested. Exactly what that point is would depend on the individual, as well as on a whole range of external factors like diet and general lifestyle. That's the same in any case—people of any given age might look older or younger than they actually are. Someone who happened to have the M-Trait might be a hundred years old, and look forty. Or, in a best-case scenario, they might look no more than twenty." Mikhail had been one such person, Sherman remembered: after a quarter of a millennium, he could have passed for a thirty-five-year-old.

Tom was clearly interested. "So, at what point do things start to slow down? What are the indications that someone might have the full trait?"

Sherman thought for a moment. "Obviously, we don't know much about what happens in practice. But you wouldn't start to age like other people. The point you'd notice, I suppose, would be when you didn't produce the same aging effects as those of the same age around you. The first gray hair, the first wrinkles—the indication that a person might not have the M-Trait would show up easily in a person's mid-twenties."

He took a step over to Tom and made a show of looking him over. "Maybe—it's hard to say—there's the odd line around your eyes, but that could just be too much sun. A few more years and it'll probably be obvious. I'd say you're around twenty-eight. If you had the M-Trait, you'd probably show the same characteristics when you were nearing a hundred years old. Are you a hundred years old, Tom?"

Tom stiffened noticeably without answering.

Sherman talked on, trying to draw the Tom further into his work and the theories and possibilities that it raised, though he didn't seem to be listening now.

Once, only once, he risked a casual glance at Tom's arm. The area under the patch was a slightly darker shade of pink than the surrounding skin, and he realized he should have used a colored or tinted dressing. As he spoke, his mind made furious calculations: surface area, body weight, chemical concentration. It was difficult to know how long it would take.

# 65

They had been in Edward Sherman's office for almost an hour now. Tom seemed to be losing control as he required both hands to hold himself upright on the couch. Sherman, for his part, was tense and alert. Every moment counted; every second he could gain would tip the balance in his favor. Now, he sensed it was time to make his move. He was not comfortable, and wanted to finish this.

"What do you want with Emily, Tom?" He was perfectly composed, and the question was asked as nonchalantly as if he were offering him a glass of water.

Tom looked up uncertainly from the couch. "What do you mean?"

Sherman eyed him coolly from the broad expanse of his desk. "What do you want with her? You've been spending a lot of time with her recently."

Tom was clearly taken aback, and answered defensively. "We're good friends. We get on well. Why do you ask?"

Sherman shook his head. "Let's drop the pretense. You're not in it for the friendship. So what is it?" He was careful here. He needed to know how much Tom knew about Emily's baby, without giving the game away himself.

Tom continued a little longer with the facade. "Look, I don't know what this is about, but I don't see that it's any of your business. She's a friend, that's all there is to it. If you have a problem with that, it doesn't concern me." He moved forward awkwardly to the edge of the couch, hands gripping the frame as he stared across at Sherman.

"The problem is I think you've been in my house when I'm not there." He let that sink in for a moment. Tom's expression did not indicate that he had heard Sherman, except that something in his eyes changed. "So, are you using her to get to me?"

There was a long pause, during which neither man moved. Finally, Tom answered. "Emily was a nice bonus. Originally I was only trying to find out about you. Then I found that your age wasn't the only thing you were hiding." He looked up at Sherman and smiled. It was clear he felt safe with his advantage over Sherman.

Edward remained silent as a sinking feeling gripped his chest and he fought down the lump in his throat. In a voice he was barely able to keep under control, he hissed at Tom, "Leave her alone!"

Tom broke out in laughter. He sat up on the couch and folded his arms theatrically, pretending to be speechless. Finally he addressed Sherman in a confidential tone. "Edward, you don't…fancy this woman, do you?"

Sherman only glowered. If Tom wanted to waste time, let him.

"Come on, Doc. What could she see in a beat-up old academic like you? You didn't seriously think you stood a chance with her, did you?" The friendly tone was gone, replaced by harsh ridicule.

"It doesn't matter what I want with her." Edward did not want to give anything away about Emily's baby that Tom did not already know. "Leave her out of this!"

"I hardly think you're in a position to dictate what I can and can't do. If I want to take Emily away from you, along with her special child, then I will. And I don't see there's a thing you can do to stop me. So get over it."

*Can't do anything? When you're here, in my lab, on my territory?*

He took another look at Tom's arm, the clear patch covering a perfect square of reddish skin underneath. He was walking a fine line, but Sherman knew he held the advantage. As he riled Tom, the man's blood pressure would rise, and the patch's work sped up. Leaning back in his chair, he put his hand back into the pocket of the jacket slung over the back of it, feeling the familiar cold knurled surface of the dart gun inside.

Tom saw where Edward's hand went and reacted immediately, "Are you threatening me?"

Sherman did not answer, only moving back a little further on his wheeled swivel chair, his hand still in the jacket pocket.

"You're serious? You'd actually take me on in here?" Tom was taunting him now, seemingly entirely unaware of the danger he was in.

"You come after me. You threaten me, Emily, and her child," Edward seethed. "You break into my house and snoop around. Do you honestly think I wouldn't be ready when Mikhail, or one of his flunkies, finally had the guts to face me?"

He watched as Tom shook his head, as if to clear it. He blinked twice and looked down at his knuckles, which were white as he tried to grip the frame of the couch through its thin foam mattress.

Suddenly Tom realized his disadvantage. Sherman had known he was coming after all. He wasn't just someone who turned up for a DNA test who happened to know Emily. Something had tipped him off, warned him ahead of time. His whole strategy had relied on his being anonymous, and on his activities in Sherman's house going unnoticed. Now Tom understood something had gone wrong. He needed to think fast, but he couldn't. His head felt full of cotton wool and the room was starting to turn.

Sherman watched him from the safety of his position in the office. Tom drew a deep breath, shook his head again and focused on him.

"How did you know?"

Edward just smiled.

## 66

As soon as Tom stood up, it was clear something was wrong. Trying to gain an advantage, he hurled himself at Sherman, intending to seize him across the broad desk. But Sherman moved back out of reach and Tom brought himself up clumsily, fists resting on the padded surface, scowling at him.

Sherman saw that he was leaning quite heavily on the desk, supporting his weight as if his legs were not strong enough. With the desk between them, he was quite safe. He tilted his head to look at the dressing on Tom's arm. Beneath the clear plastic, the skin was now a bright red. Tom shook his head to clear it.

"Like I said: forewarned is forearmed. I guess you were allergic to plasters after all." It was tempting to gloat, but Sherman knew this was not over yet.

"What did you do to me?" There was real fear in Tom's voice now. His breathing was shallow, quicker than before, his face flushed and sweating.

"Some medicines require ingestion to be effective. Others can be injected—or inhaled. And some, like yours"—he pointed to the patch—"can be absorbed through the skin. Nicotine is a common example, used by smokers who want to give up. Though I doubt you've ever smoked a cigarette in your life, have you?"

"Nicotine?" Tom's hands were shaking, and it took him a moment to get a purchase on the edge of the patch and tear it off. The needle mark underneath had not yet coagulated, and a trickle of blood welled from his arm. He threw the patch across the desk at Sherman.

"No, yours is something a little stronger than nicotine." He grinned at Tom. "But you can probably tell that by now. It just takes a while to get into the system."

"Why you—" He lunged over the desk again, but Sherman was way back, beyond harm's reach.

"Just a little something I put together when I realized Mikhail was back in town." The narcotic patch had been easy enough to make, though Sherman had not been able to tell how well it would work in practice.

Tom just looked at him, perplexed and dazed.

"Your boss left a hair in my house." Sherman's tone was almost cynical. "So I tested it, of course. And found a perfect genetic profile. Now who could that be? I thought to myself. What are you doing around here with Mikhail? Is he still getting everyone else to do his dirty work for him?"

He reached back over his chair and drew the air pistol from his jacket pocket. Standing, he cocked it, and leveled it at Tom.

Tom didn't know whether he was coming or going as he breathed deeply, trying to shake off the effects of the drug, playing for time. He weakly put his arm up to defend himself from the expected bullet.

"It's just an air pistol. It won't kill you. That would be far too good for you."

The little air pistol held a single dart, tipped with a powerful anesthetic, as effective as it was simple. "The worst you'll get from this is a mild infection. I'm afraid I didn't swab the dart, so I can't guarantee its sterility."

"Wait. Wait a minute." Tom staggered back from the desk, breathing hard. He was in real trouble. Sherman paused as Tom rested, head down and leaning with his hands on his knees. He had not planned on wasting any time at this stage, but he was not prepared for what came next.

More in desperation than with a particular plan in mind, Tom launched himself forwards, over the desk and into Sherman. Unnerved, the doctor realized Tom had not been quite as heavily affected by the skin patch as he had first thought. The flat-screen monitor went flying, followed by a hail of stationery and other paraphernalia as the two of them went crashing down onto the floor.

With a *pffft*, the air pistol discharged, landing the dart into Tom's shoulder. Sherman struggled wildly as Tom pummeled him about the stomach and ribs, desperately trying to do as much damage as he could before passing out.

Edward maneuvered a hand under Tom's chin and pushed his face up, away from him. The vicious punching stopped, as Tom tried to claw at Sherman's face instead. His movements were slower now, weaker and lacking intensity, unable to sustain his force under the effect of the drugs. Sherman was tiring fast too, but managed to get his leg up and brace his foot against Tom's chest. As he breathed in and prepared to kick his attacker away, he felt it—the constricting pain in his chest that signaled an angina attack was imminent. Summoning all his strength, he shoved Tom away from him, sending him staggering into the desk, turning it over with the remainder of its papers and computer peripherals.

The pain was spreading across his neck and left shoulder, his breathing labored. He had to take one of his little white pills immediately, and then rest. The bottle was in the desk drawer.

Tom seemed to lie motionless across the desk, which was upside down on the floor of the lab. The tiny dart still stuck out of his shoulder, feathered end red against Tom's white tee shirt. Struggling against the pain now, Sherman hauled the top drawer out of the upturned desk, spilling its contents everywhere. The amber bottle fell at his feet and he knelt to pick it up. He squeezed the sides of the childproof cap to pull it off and shake one of the pills into his hand.

Without warning, a hand was at his throat, fingers and thumb on either side of his windpipe in a clawlike grip, closing off his air supply. He flailed in panic, the pain in his chest growing instantly to an almost unbearable level as he strained to breathe. He felt his wrist twisted over to the side, forcing the hand open with a sharp pain. The bottle flew from his hand, scattering the white pills across the floor.

His vision was failing now, everything going dark as he choked. He knew he did not have much time. He raised his free hand and, with his failing strength, drove it down into Tom's face with all the weight of his body behind it. The grip around his throat loosened and he managed to draw a deep breath. The second punch, harder than the first and delivered with all the strength and resolve he could muster, connected squarely with Tom's jaw. He went limp.

Sherman slumped to the floor, the pain in his chest terrible and immobilizing, convulsing him in agony as his heart failed to receive the oxygen that it needed.

With his constrictions increasing with each shallow breath, Edward knew he must fetch one of the pills. He opened his eyes—there, just inches away from his head, lay one of the little white Nitroglycerin pills. *It seemed so far away.* Pointing his head toward the pill, he could almost reach it, if he could just manage a little further. Perhaps if he just stretched out his tongue—*he was so close—*

Edward felt the dry tablet adhere immediately to the moist surface of his tongue, and he reeled the medicine in. *Finally.* He breathed deeply, trying to calm his heartbeat as he pushed the pill underneath his tongue. What seemed like an age later, the crushing pain in his chest now almost bearable in its intensity, he rolled over and rested on his back amid the debris of his once pristine office.

He was alive. He had won again. The pain of the episode—the worst he could remember—slowly subsided in the following minutes. In his state of mental and physical exhaustion, all he wished for now was sleep. Just before he closed his eyes, a thought occurred to him, though in his condition it seemed only of incidental interest and lacked the importance he knew he should assign to it.

He wondered which of them would wake up first.

# 67

After finding out about Edward's secret, Emily grew more agitated with each passing day. Zoe might be born at any time now, and she needed to know what that would mean for her and her baby. The consequences would spread wider than that—could she really trust Edward? What had all those years of friendship really meant to him—if there had been anything genuine about his feelings at all?

It was strange being home in the middle of the day, but she didn't want to be at the lab anymore. Part of it was a rational decision; she tired easily nowadays, well into the ninth month of her pregnancy, and couldn't work long without a rest. The other part was she simply didn't want to be around Edward when he was being so overprotective. Of course, that was before she knew about his possessing both Methuselah genes. So what was he being protective about exactly? She wondered, and that brought her to test Zoe's DNA. Was there another secret? It was time to find out.

She felt lonely, and a little afraid. The flat was too quiet, and Emily put on some music to fill the vacuum. Deciding that it still wasn't enough, she opened the sitting-room windows, welcoming the sound of traffic and the comings and goings of city life. It grounded her, and somehow made her feel safer. She sat awkwardly on the settee—it was hard to sit upright, but she realized she couldn't lie back and use her laptop on her lap. She would have to open it up on the coffee table.

More recently, she remembered when Tom had sat on this settee with her. He, at least, was a constant in her life. Whatever was going on with Edward, she knew she could trust Tom. It didn't matter that he was an M-Trait partial.

She remembered her surprise when waking up that morning a couple of weeks back to find the nursery decorating finished. The next time she saw him, she tried to thank him. But Tom had played innocent, refusing any credit. He had simply shrugged, with a look of mock confusion on his face: how on earth did that happen? He was a good friend. Maybe, when this was all over...

She shook herself back to the present and opened a new browser window to log into her user area at the lab. It only took a moment to find the right entry. She had not used Zoe's initials. Rather, she had borrowed someone else's name used in earlier test results, one that would never be needed again. That way, there was no chance of Edward finding it unless he was looking carefully. And he had no reason to look carefully unless he had a guilty conscience.

Emily had run the analysis on the lab computer the night before, and only needed to download the results to her laptop. Still, the specialized software required to interpret the test results created a huge file. After fifteen long, agonizing minutes, the summary file finally appeared in the browser window of her laptop, and she printed it out on the laser printer that sat in the corner of the room.

Emily sighed and started the slow process of moving. It was a considerable effort to rise from the settee and collect the sheets from the printer. She grabbed a pen to help her follow the data, and slowly sat back down again. Much of the data were incidental material, garbage from the gene-sequencer program. Wading through it should not take too long—she knew exactly what she was after. Still, she had to steel herself—she did not want to go through with this. Ignorance was bliss and, if her feelings were right, this was going to open the floodgates. She tried not to think about the consequences, scanning quickly down the first sheet and discarding it as she came to the end.

Halfway through the third sheet, she found it. Emily heard her own sharp intake of breath as her eyes read the output code for the trait she and Edward had been searching for all this time. It stood out at her from the page of otherwise useless characters, black and white evidence of everything she had feared:

| M-Trait: | + + Positive |
|---|---|

The room swam around her as she tried to understand what had happened. Zoe had the Methuselah genes! Her child would be an Ultra! *How could this be?*

Emily tried to reason it out despite her heightened state of emotion. Edward must have gone behind her back while he was carrying out his work selecting a sperm donor. Had he selected his own? She relied on his skill and he had betrayed her—working on his own cause with no thought of her or Zoe. Suddenly she was angry, scared, and confused all at once, shaking in her seat and with tears pouring down her face. *Why had he done this?*

Somewhere, she registered more pain in her lower body. *Zoe!* Emily struggled to her feet, trying to breathe deeply. Not yet, she prayed—*not now!* She pushed the printouts into her handbag, frantically trying to clear her head. The new pain centered in her abdomen, and she scrambled in the side pocket of the handbag for her mobile phone. Who should she call? The room spun and she gripped the arm of the chair for support.

The lasting pain of the first contraction finally brought her back to reality. Nothing she could do at this point would make any difference. Edward had made the choice for her, and she couldn't change it—so she focused on their pre-arrangements.

Zoe, the perfect child, was ready to be born.

## 68

Edward Sherman awoke in darkness. He noticed a light that gently blinked from his desk area. He guessed it to be the baby pager, which had long since passed its ringing intervals and now radiated a green light every other second. Emily was having Zoe—he was missing the birth. Knowing he could not afford to delay, he gingerly pushed himself to his feet. The motion sensing lights in the lab immediately came on. Before doing anything else, he cocked and loaded the air pistol with another one of the tipped darts.

Stooping carefully, he manhandled Tom's dead weight back onto the couch. The physical exertion was not wise so soon after his angina attack, but he did not have a choice. Taking a roll of duct tape, he hung Tom's ankles over the sides of the couch and taped them to the metal legs. Then he pulled Tom's hands together and ran the tape round and round his forearms, binding them from the wrists to the elbows. For good measure, he ran the tape around his chest and under the mattress and frame several times. After a moment's thought, he did the same with his thighs and neck. Satisfied that Tom was secure, Sherman turned the desk back up the right way and sat back down to rest, with the air pistol in his lap. Outside, in the warm summer evening, a light rain was falling, brushing the ground with its soft droplets and marking the end of the heat wave with a promise of new life.

Tom groaned as he tried to swim back towards consciousness, trying to force his eyes open. His whole body was still enveloped in lethargy, heavy and unable to move. He struggled feebly, knowing how vital it was that he should wake. He took a deep, faltering breath, willing the exhaustion away. The effort failed, losing to the anesthetic in his system, and he drifted back into sleep.

Sherman wanted nothing more than to go home and crawl into bed. Extremely tired, he sat back, breathing slowly and deeply. When he felt a little better, he rose from the chair, avoiding the broken computer equipment on the floor. His water glass had smashed on the floor when the desk went over, but the big jug was plastic. He refilled it from the tap on the other side of the room, and took a long drink straight from it. He threw the rest in Tom's face and then sat down again.

This time, Tom woke suddenly. His eyes snapped open and he spluttered the water from his nose and mouth. He struggled, trying to move against the tape, but it only choked him. The top section of the couch was inclined slightly upwards, so he was not lying flat. With his body and neck tied down, even when he turned his head he could only see Sherman out of the corner of his eye.

"Awake yet?" Sherman's deep, resonant voice was calm and betrayed little emotion. He had Tom where he wanted him and, for the first time in weeks, felt some control. Tom made no response, save to cough some more water from his throat.

"So, who are you—and where's Mikhail?" Sherman asked pointedly. With Tom reclining on the couch, bound with tape, it was like some bizarre parody of a psychotherapist's office.

Tom managed only to slur an answer, "What are you going to do with me?"

Sherman did not answer immediately, allowing his captive's mind to run through some of the possibilities. "Probably what you had intended for me." That wasn't true; he actually had no idea what to do with Tom. He really wanted Mikhail, and Tom was his only option to meet that objective, so he couldn't just let him go. He held up the blade for Tom to see. When lifting Tom's limp form onto the couch, he had noticed it in his waistband and removed it from the felt sheath.

"Mikhail always did like knives." Sherman's voice was soft. "I thought he might be the one walking in for a blood test today. What are you? A son? A grandson?"

He watched Tom's eyes narrow as he turned the blade to catch the light that filtered through the blinds. Its silver edge gleamed, and he recalled holding a similar one almost a century ago in another darkened room. Edward held the blade to Tom's face, too close to focus on. "So which is it? Son, I bet."

Tom couldn't nod against the restraining tapes, so he gave an answer. "Michael is my father, yes."

"He always did keep things in the family. So what was it going to be? Kill me here, in my own lab, and leave with Emily and Zoe? You never would have gotten away with it, you know."

"Then neither will you." Tom was quietly defiant, and Sherman had to admit he had a point. It was not going to be easy disposing of him. There was no risk-free way he could get a body out of the lab without anyone knowing. Even if he waited until late at night, there still were security cameras mounted throughout the medical center.

"Perhaps. But on the other hand, what alternative have you given me? I'm hardly likely to let you go, am I?" He held the dagger up again, not as a threat but as the evidence of Tom's intentions. "I did think I might take you out a piece at a time. If you're lucky, I'll kill you first." Now he raised the dagger again, holding it to mean business this time. Tom cringed and closed his eyes as Edward plunged the blade down at his face. There was a thud beside his head, and when he opened his eyes again, he could see the knife in his peripheral vision, sunk into the foam padding of the couch, an inch away from his temple.

Killing Tom in the lab was a solution Sherman decided against—no, there was a better way. His captive did not have to be dead when he left. Edward decided to leave him drugged and bound in the lab until the early hours of Sunday morning, when the building and streets were quietest. It should not be too difficult to escort him out in a wheelchair or leaning on his shoulder, before driving him to a secluded spot in his own car. He would then maybe pour a bottle of vodka down the tired, hungry, disheveled man's throat and over his clothes. A drug overdose would complete the picture—just another homeless addict, without family or identification. He would leave the car somewhere on the way back, in one of the worse neighborhoods, with the doors unlocked. Someone else could take care of the rest. The plan was not without its risks, but it was better than killing him in the lab.

It was all a major inconvenience—Mikhail was the one he wanted, but as usual, he had sent someone else to take the risks for him. Sherman cursed Mikhail's selfishness.

Tom was trying to say something. "You don't have to do this."

Sherman snorted. "Mikhail never gave me any choice—not this time or last time—not when he killed Karina. How did you expect me to react when I found out?"

"Karina?" Tom was not fully awake, his voice still slurred.

Sherman responded angrily. "She didn't have to die. She'd done nothing wrong. And I'm not about to let you treat Emily the same way when she's outlasted her usefulness or becomes a liability for you."

"Come on, Edward." Tom's voice was thick from the drug. "Don't pretend you wouldn't do exactly the same if it came to it."

"Why would I hurt Emily?—I never hurt Karina." Edward was shaking violently; he was barely able to keep the pistol trained on Tom. "Besides, if I let you go, there's no question you'd try to kill me."

There was a pause, as his prisoner thought. Then Tom looked up at him. "Who's Karina?"

There was a moment of silence as the doctor stared at his captive and considered his answer. Then finally, he spoke. "She was my wife. Mikhail had her killed, just because she was mortal. Just for fun. Just like he'll teach you to do with Emily once she's outlived her usefulness and becomes a threat."

"No one's going to hurt Emily, or Zoe." There was determination in Tom's eyes now.

This made Edward angry. "Wrong, Tom. As long as Mikhail's alive, Emily is as good as dead. You must know how he works by now. Any mortal is disposable." He stepped over to Tom's prone form and took a long look at his face. He bent close. "So, unless you were born around the time of the Russian Revolution, I suggest you watch your step, because that includes you, too."

He was out there somewhere. Mikhail was still at large while Edward squandered his time on this messenger. Tom would wait. Mikhail might not. Even in his rage, Edward was ruthlessly precise. Pulling the knife out of the couch and dropping it to the floor, he then placed his hands firmly around Tom's neck, feeling for the pulse of the carotid artery on each side with his thumbs.

"Wait—"

Tom's cry was silenced as Sherman pushed hard with his thumbs, cutting off the blood supply to the brain. Tom's eyes opened wide and he thrashed wildly against the tapes, but it was only a couple of seconds before his struggles subsided and his body went limp. Sherman calmed when he saw the still form. He relaxed the pressure on Tom's arteries, now checking the pulse there with the lightest touch of two fingers.

"Good night." He made sure the man's breathing was regular and unobstructed, then ran the tape over his mouth and round the back of his head a couple of times. He pushed the couch into one of the small storerooms, to the side of the lab where they kept spare supplies and tests awaiting processing. He stared at the man he had imprisoned. From the fickle memories of a century ago, he remembered a similar face—the high cheekbones, the cold, intelligent eyes, the widow's peak.

Physically and emotionally drained by Tom and the angina attack, Edward did not trust himself to drive to the hospital to see Emily. As he made his way through the building towards the main entrance, he decided to call for a taxi. While he waited, he stepped out from the doorway into the rain, lifting his face to the sky and allowing the drops to fall on his skin, hoping that it could magically wash away the stress of the day's events. He did not care that his clothes were soon wet, the rain soaking through to his skin and cooling his body.

Edward wondered about Emily and Zoe. Hopefully she had given birth by now and had added a very special baby girl to the world. He knew she would understand why he had not been there for her—he would use the angina attack as an excuse. But he couldn't wait long, not knowing what Mikhail had planned. They would both be safe in hospital for now, he hoped. As he sped to see her in the taxi, he vowed to keep his promise to Emily to protect her. He had fought Mikhail once, years ago, and escaped with only his life. This time, he would protect his new family too.

## 69

Creeping things, creeping around the edges of a plain—he couldn't see them but he could feel them there, many-legged creatures skittering just out of sight at the edges of reality. Tom's dream landscape was gray, formless, and desolate; far away, far from anything else he knew—somewhere completely out there. It was dark, and although there was the knowledge of the vast space stretching away into infinity, he could only feel his immediate vicinity. Behind and above him, there was the feeling of an enormous vacuum sucking at him, producing a chest-squeezing sense of agoraphobia. There was no color, only the lifeless shades of gray before the darkness began.

Moving into consciousness, Tom realized his head hurt, his mouth was dry, and his legs were asleep. He couldn't move any part of his body—he was wrapped tight, probably with tape. When he opened his eyes, he still saw nothing, though he sensed he was alone in the dark—the faint sound of a fan could be heard somewhere in the room. Sherman was obviously gone. He did not know when the doctor planned to return, or what he could expect when he did. Tom knew he could very well die there, wherever he was—a long, slow death in the dark from dehydration, with only his hallucinations for company in those final hours.

It was a horrible irony, one that ate away at him as he lay prone. Sherman had just cast some serious doubts on Tom's hopes for longevity, having told him he looked too old to have the Methuselah genes. As if to add insult to injury, now it looked like the doctor was going to strip away the rest of his mortal life span, too. Having hoped for years that he might live for ages, his present position was unbearable.

Tom was suddenly unable to stop his imagination running away with him again. First the room was tiny, cramped, and claustrophobic, the walls just beyond his bound hands and the ceiling only an inch from his nose. Then it flipped to an enormous, frightening abyss that stretched away for miles on every side, senseless and dizzying. Finally, as his eyes grew used to the darkness, he realized where he might be. There was a faint rim of light from what could be a door and, breathing slowly through his nose, Tom could smell a faint chemical trace. Maybe he was still in Sherman's lab somewhere.

Struggling to put aside his delusions, Tom took stock of his situation. He tried each limb separately, but Sherman had taped his ankles securely to the arms of a gurney or maybe a couch, spreading him out in an awkward position that gave him very little leverage. His forearms were tightly bound together, and he couldn't even bend his arms at the elbow. He could barely move his head, only as far as the strips of tape around his chest and neck would allow. If he arched his body upwards, he might get some leverage on the bonds around his ankles, but Sherman had taken care of that with the tape around his chest and thighs.

As he lay in the dark, it struck him—maybe there wasn't a way out of this. Maybe it was his fate to lie here until Sherman returned to dispense whatever form of justice he saw fit; an ignominious end that his father would criticize for eternity. Knowing Sherman's last attempt at retribution, he held little hope of mercy. He could not feel the hard shape of his dagger digging into his back; Sherman had taken it and, even if he hadn't, he still didn't have a hand free to use it. *Come on now, think outside of the box.*

Angry with his situation, Tom shook his massively taped body, vibrating every muscle to cause some kind of movement. Suddenly, he heard a "click" and the room was flooded with light. Fearing the worst, he closed his eyes and braced for a blow from his captor, but nothing happened. After a few moments, he realized he was still alone. The light—it was activated by a motion detector. *Of course*, he thought, *all the lights in the lab must be set up this way.*

Bathed in light, Tom knew he was still in Sherman's lab—taped to the couch he had used while talking with Sherman. He found it hard to see anything outside his peripheral vision though—his head being taped so securely. He tried turning his arms awkwardly to the side and stretching out his fingertips as far as he was able to the right, glad that his karate practice had taught him to isolate his shoulder movement—but nothing. Stretching to the left, at the limit of his reach, he found a smooth, cold metal surface along the low back of the couch. From his prone position, he could touch no more than a few centimeters of it. It was not enough to hold on to, but enough to give him a reference point. Forcing his head as far to the right as he could, he could barely pick up some of his surroundings. A metal work surface ran around three sides of the small room at about waist height. There were shelves all around, piled high with files, boxes, and lab glassware. Tom drew a deep breath and held it, trying to filter out the sound of the blood thundering in his ears. *Drip.* There it was, by his head—now he knew there was a sink just a few meters behind his head. The new information was not much of a victory, but it gave him confidence.

He now turned his attention to the couch, spreading his fingers along the cool metal frame again. It was a collection of square steel tubes, impossible to break or bend. He lay on the thin, plastic-covered foam padding, with his ankles heavily taped at the arms. The couch did not roll when he pushed his body forwards. Trying again with more enthusiasm, he found he could get it to scrape across the floor a little at a time.

With the strength of a desperate man, Tom threw himself into a violent series of movements, hurling his body and rocking the couch from side to side, knocking against the metal surrounds, sending tremors through the shelves. Throwing his weight to one side, he tried to unbalance the couch, which teetered for a moment and then fell sideways to the right. He braced himself for the pain. Fortunately, the room was smaller than he thought. With a loud *thunk*, the couch slammed into the countertop, shaking everything on it and rewarding him with a shower of beakers and other lab glassware that teetered and crashed to the floor. When the small barrage was over, he lay still, breathing heavily from the effort. After a few minutes, the light clicked off, sensing no movement in the room. Behind his head, the faucet continued to drip.

After chiding himself for taking a rest, Tom threw his body lightly back and forth until the light switch clicked on again. Focusing again on his sense of touch, he followed the metal frame as far along as he could with his bound hands. There—he felt a slight ridge in the bar. He pictured the couch from his interview with Sherman. It was constructed from hollow metal bars that slotted together like tent poles, probably spring-loaded through the middle—thus held together by the tension. He guessed the couch could be folded away for storage. The ridge he found was the join between the two halves of the frame in the middle of the couch. *If he could just push the halves apart...*

The image of the couch's construction gave Tom the answer he needed. His ankles were firmly attached to the far end, his chest and neck to the other. Straining to elongate his body, he pushed away with his feet, shaking his body up and down to take the weight from the frame. He felt the springs move as he convulsed and the bars slid apart a little. Checking the frame again, Tom could feel the gap with his fingertips. With a second effort, he managed to shake the two halves of the couch a little further apart. With a final, intensive effort, the bars came free and the couch folded in two. He promptly dropped to the floor, sandwiched in the middle. He was glad Emily couldn't see him now—how ridiculous he must look. Tom rested again until the motion light clicked off, though it only took a quick shake to turn it back on this time. *Almost there...*

Doubled up on the floor, he could just reach the restraints around his thighs and chest with his fingertips, but was unable to get a purchase or find the end of the tape to pick at. With grim determination, Tom struggled against the tapes that held his torso, kicking with his legs against the shelves and writhing on the cold floor. He felt a sudden pain in his hand, and the familiar warm feeling of blood. He had forgotten about the broken glass. Quickly, but carefully, he felt around with his fingers, selecting the largest piece he could find.

The process was messy, but effective as he sliced away the tape, and bits of his skin. Ten minutes later, he was free of the couch, standing in the center of the room with his forearms still bound and blood dripping from his cuts.

Tom found the storeroom door locked, but after all he had been through, this was hardly an obstacle. Setting his distance correctly, he focused and then delivered his best kick. The door separated from the jamb with ease.

*Free at last!*

# 70

"Ma'am, someone's here to see you."

Lying on her back, half-sitting up against the pillows of the hospital bed with the blanket pulled up to her neck, Emily could feel her heart pounding. She swallowed and breathed deeply through her nose, tilting her head back towards the ceiling as she held back the tears.

"Thank you."

The middle-aged nurse nodded to her and left to do her rounds. The evening was wearing on, and she was surprised and hurt Edward waited so long to visit. Up until now, he had been overzealous and overbearing; she wondered what could have changed.

Footsteps in the hallway announced his presence some time before she could catch a glimpse of him at the door. Despite her anger, she was speechless. Edward appeared shattered, his face drawn, and he looked like he hadn't slept in a week. He also brought flowers, a big bright bouquet from one of the stalls at the tube station nearest the hospital, not one of the poor substitutes from the gift shop down the hallway. It was all oranges and reds and yellows, its warmth almost tangible as well as visible. He had chosen some of her favorites. Normally the flowers would be seen as a genuinely touching gesture with him, something too difficult to fake. Now she wasn't sure what Dr. Edward Sherman really wanted.

Edward walked stiffly over to the bed, lowered himself to kiss her on the cheek, and then up to gaze at the new child. Zoe slept in the cot by the bed, quietly unaware of the stir her birth had caused. Emily coldly accepted his kiss and watched him as he took in her new child.

He turned back and gently took her hand. "Oh Emily, she's beautiful."

"What happened to you?"

"Angina attack. I'm sorry I couldn't see you earlier. It was a bad one—had to get it checked out." He put a hand over his chest. Even that movement seemed tiring for him.

Emily's voice was taut, without concern for him. "And?"

"No lasting damage. I was lucky." He looked at her face, confused at her tone.

Emily reached under her pillow and pulled out a single, folded sheet of paper. Already it was crumpled and folded, with blotchy marks where her tears had fallen. She handed him the sheet and knew Edward would recognize it instantly for what it was: Zoe's DNA profile, a terse document containing a short summary of her genetic makeup. And there, in the middle of the page, the incriminating set of characters:

**M-Trait:**            **++ Positive**

Edward looked up from the sheet. If anything, he looked even wearier than he had when he walked in.

"Why did you do it?" Her accusation was quiet, the anger suppressed in a muted hiss to avoid waking the baby in the cot next to them. Even so, Zoe stirred.

Edward could not answer immediately. He stared at her, unable to formulate his thoughts into words.

"Why did it have to be my baby?" In the midst of her rage, Emily broke down. Instead of anger, tears now welled up in her eyes.

Edward took her hand again. He breathed deeply, speaking in a soft voice. "I'm so sorry, Emily. I didn't mean for this to hurt you. We were so close—when I screened Zoe and made sure she was clear, it was such a little step to do the rest. She was already 95% of the way there. Don't you see—just a tiny, tiny adjustment to the embryo, and she was perfect. I couldn't bring myself to miss the chance."

Emily looked shocked and then answered through her tears, her voice high and uncertain. "What was it? Tired of being the only freak in the world? Why did you have to make her one too?"

*M-Trait*

Edward looked at her for a long moment. There was something utterly alien about his gaze. In the time since she had asked the question, he had become someone else. There was an emotional distance between them that she had never felt before.

"How did you know about me?" he asked.

"I found your profile at the lab, on your computer." If she was incriminating herself, it hardly mattered now. Edward had gone so far outside of the rules that her own petty crime made no difference. "It's ironic that I cared so much about your precious ethics, when you'd already done *this* to her." She indicated Zoe.

Edward paused and then nodded. "Well, you know what I am now. And Zoe's the same. She is the most perfect female on the planet; she might live a thousand years."

He stared wistfully into the cot. Zoe stirred again.

"Believe me, Emily, it gets lonely after a couple of hundred years, knowing that everyone you meet will get old and die, and leave you behind to start again. I was married once, a long time ago. When I realized what would happen to anyone I grew close to, it was like losing a part of myself. My family, my friends—even you will die some day. But not Zoe."

"But why father Zoe if all you really want is a wife?" Emily asked incredulously.

"That's just it, I'm not the father. You were already an M-Trait partial—I just had to switch the donor's missing M-Trait genes within your embryo with mine."

"I'm what?" Edward had never told Emily that she possessed one of the Methuselah genes. For her, it was his last betrayal.

Emily exited the bed, and lifted Zoe from the cot into her arms. "You cannot have her." She seethed, standing over him in his chair. "She wouldn't be safe with you."

Edward stared coolly at her. "She'll be safe only because of me. I'm not the only Ultra, you know. For a long time I thought I was, but now I know it's not true."

Emily instinctively held Zoe even tighter to her chest as she listened.

269

"There's at least one more still alive. His name is Mikhail and he is very, very dangerous. It's just possible that Tom may be one, too."

Emily took a step back, holding Zoe even tighter. "You're wrong about Tom. He's only a partial."

"How do you know that?"

Emily spoke firmly. "I tested Tom myself. He's *not* an Ultra."

For Edward, this new information on Tom confirmed what he already believed—that Tom was mortal. But he was still Mikhail's son.

Edward realized the danger Emily was now in. However angry she was, she needed to hear this. "Please listen to me, Emily. This is important. I knew Mikhail a long, long time ago. There were a group of us then—hiding out, not able to tell anyone what we really were—Mikhail was fanatical about secrecy. If anyone found out about us, he killed them—do you understand? He didn't care about anyone mortal, they were just to be used—like slaves. Once they didn't have any further use, or were perceived a threat—like my wife—they were eliminated."

Emily regarded him uncertainly. She still had one other piece of knowledge to confront him with. "And how are you different from Mikhail? Isn't he family?"

Edward was stunned that Emily knew so much. He knew he couldn't leave anything out now. "My mother was one of Mikhail's cast-offs—he had no use for a daughter. But somehow, she conceived and bore me before dying in adolescence. I was raised outside of Mikhail's reach."

Emily stared at him.

"I am not like him!" Edward added with emphasis before continuing his plea. "Emily, please—I'm trying to help you. I would never hurt you. But Mikhail will kill you to get to Zoe. I thought he was dead, but I was wrong."

Listening with growing discomfort, Emily did not know how to deal with all this new information.

Edward's next words were clearly made with a great effort. "Tom is connected with Mikhail. They both know about Zoe and they are both dangerous."

Emily was not sure if she should believe Edward, but his frankness scared her. In one stroke, Sherman had destroyed almost every level of support she had. She was stuck here in the hospital, with a new baby, and no one she could trust.

"Tom is bad? How do you know?" She looked down at Zoe, not waiting for an answer. "What am I supposed to do now?"

Edward rose quickly from the bed. "I need to take care of Mikhail." He seemed to be saying it to himself more than to her. "I need Tom to tell me where Mikhail is, and I need to end this nightmare."

He now moved away from the bed, as if to leave. "I'm sorry that I've put you in this position, Emily. I promised to look after you and I will. I don't know how, but I will make sure you're okay."

Before Emily could ask more questions, Edward was gone. As he disappeared through the door, she found herself throwing the vase of flowers at him, scattering pottery shards and bright petals as it smashed on the doorframe. Zoe began to cry.

# 71

After escaping from the storeroom, Tom spent the least amount of time possible in Sherman's lab, knowing that the doctor might return at any moment to finish what he started. Using the sharp corner of a filing cabinet, he managed to cut through the tape binding his forearms, finally freeing his hands. He cleaned up the injuries from the glass as well as he could, scrubbing them and his haggard face in the sink, and then using bandages from one of the lab's first-aid kits to cover the worst of the cuts. He would end up with a couple of scars, but he was lucky not to have sustained more harm.

He ran his hands through his uneven hair, trying to smooth it down. It was still sticky from the tape Sherman had used to gag him, and a few clumps of hair had to be cut away from the duct tape with a pair of scissors.

Surprisingly, Tom found his knife on the floor in the debris of the smashed computer equipment in Edward's office. He pushed it back into the felt sheath in his waistband. Next to the sheath was his cell phone, and he saw that he'd missed a call. A text message had been left by Emily, which only said, "Z!" their code for Zoe's birth.

He needed to visit Emily in hospital. Sherman would have rushed to see Emily, so he desperately wanted to find out what he said to her.

Outside the lab, the light rain touched his wounds, making them sting. He held his hands out in front of him, hoping the drops of water would bring more pain—to wash the agony from his now mortal soul. He sighed. Soon, he would have to call his father, and tell him what happened. The thought counteracted the effects of the rain, numbing him. He leaned heavily against a bench, lightheaded, uncertain for a moment whether he was going to pass out or not. He wasn't ready to call his father or go see Emily yet.

Across the street was a coffeehouse—one of the big, corporate numbers that he usually avoided. But he was desperate. On shaky legs, trying to ignore his emptiness and nausea, he slowly made his way across the road. He placed his order—a large filter coffee with an extra shot of espresso for good measure—paid for it, and propped himself up at the counter while the barista busied herself at the machines. When his coffee was ready, he cooled it with a big splash of cream, poured in several teaspoons of sugar—a despicable act that was required under these circumstances—and then fell back into his seat.

He should never have gone to the lab. Sherman had never met him and didn't even know what he looked like. And yet, somehow, he had been alerted to his presence. Tom had been lucky to escape with his life. He knew that his father would have had no sympathy if Sherman had killed him. Incompetence was as unforgivable as mortality, as far as Michael was concerned.

He took a quick gulp of the coffee. *Yechh!* Even without all the cream and sugar, it would have been disgusting. He continued to drink it anyway hoping that the caffeine and sugar would revive him.

There was something else on his mind, as if he didn't have enough already. For years, his father had hedged his bets, telling him it was too early to know whether he would turn out the same, ancient like him. Now, thanks to Sherman, he was almost sure that he did not have centuries of life to look forward to. And, no doubt, Michael had been all too aware of that for some time now. If that was the case, he wasn't about to waste the remainder of it on his father's schemes.

Forget Sherman, forget Michael: he would take Emily and Zoe and leave. He had worked hard for them and, father or not, Michael wasn't reaping the rewards of his efforts this time. He had nearly died doing his bidding. It was time to shed his father's skin. Life has suddenly become even more precious.

He finished the coffee and waited a while for a jolt to his system. *Time to stop messing around, Tom. Time to stop feeling sorry for yourself. It's your life, so fix it!*

In a couple of minutes, he arrived back at the car park. Tom had parked his car in a corner, hidden away behind a large family-sized van. The van had gone now, and there were only a handful of cars left. Sherman's car was one of them.

Looking over his shoulder to make sure there was no one around, Tom peered through the window. The car was empty. He tried the front door handle, and the back —both locked. Surely Edward had not taken a taxi all the way home? But if not, he must not be too far away—probably at the hospital visiting Emily. And presumably, he would be back for the car before he left. Tom frowned.

The footsteps alerted him, and he ducked down behind the car. Crouching by the driver's side door, he risked looking up through the windows. Edward Sherman was walking across the car park. Tom swore under his breath. The car was right in the middle of the car park. What if Sherman still had his air pistol? He would have to make the first move. Tom cursed his luck. Surely he had not escaped only to fall right back into Sherman's hands? At least, this time, he would have the element of surprise.

As quietly as he could, he unsheathed the knife from his belt. The blade flashed orange in the light from the streetlamps as he controlled his breathing and waited for the doctor to step into sight.

# 72

As the taxi sped back to the lab through the evening drizzle, Sherman's mind was racing. He tried to slow himself down, but couldn't; the facts he had gathered from the last few hours were jumbled together in his head, and he was too nervous and edgy to bring them under control. It was a struggle to put things in order.

Emily had told him one of the things he wanted to know about Tom. Tom was mortal—he didn't have both the M-Trait genes. He had been snooping around Sherman's house; that much he had admitted. But he was not the only one. The hair that Edward had found must have belonged to Mikhail.

So perhaps Tom wasn't the person he really wanted here, though he was certainly dangerous. He was Mikhail's weapon; Mikhail did not like to get his hands dirty with mortal blood, and always had others to do his work for him. And Tom had obviously been more than competent. He had insinuated himself into Emily's life, and found out about Zoe too. Sherman assumed that Mikhail would know anything that Tom knew.

So what had been Tom's objective by coming to the lab? He had taken the DNA test, apparently on its own merits—if he had only needed a pretext to get into the lab to confront Sherman, why go through with the test?

Edward Sherman paused for a moment—and then it came to him out of nowhere. *Because he wanted to know something.*

Tom had told him that he had three relatives who had lived to over a hundred. If he really was Mikhail's son, then that was a huge understatement. He had asked Edward what the odds were of having the Methuselah genes. He wanted to know whether he possessed the M-Trait. *He wanted to know if he was an Ultra.*

Despite his anxiety, Edward nearly laughed out loud. Tom didn't know whether he would take after his father or not, and this was the only way he could find out without waiting around another few years to see if he got any older. The reason he came to the lab wasn't to chase Edward. It was to put his mind at rest, one way or the other. It was a bold move, stepping into Sherman's lab and passing himself off as just another member of the public. It was not the kind of tactic Mikhail would favor, walking into the lion's den like that.

Interesting. Perhaps, just perhaps, Mikhail hadn't told Tom to visit him and Mikhail didn't know about it. And if that were the case, Mikhail wouldn't know where Tom was. Edward slowly calmed as he realized his advantage. Tom wouldn't be getting rescued. He was out on his own, all alone and without any hope of Daddy coming to bail him out. Tom had just turned from a threat into a useful pawn that Sherman could use to bring down Mikhail.

The taxi pulled up at the lab and Edward paid the driver. Briskly, trying to appear confident, he walked through the door. Mikhail was still out there and he would find Emily and kill her to get Zoe. Edward did not know whether Emily would ever forgive him, but he could not allow any harm to come to Zoe. He had to stop him. Armed with the knowledge of Tom's situation, he hoped he might squeeze some useful information out of him. Then maybe he could use Tom as bait for Mikhail.

Opening the door to the lab, he wondered whether he had the stomach to do what was necessary. Tom had already proven strong under duress. Now the unpleasant task fell to Edward of torturing the information out of him. He needed to know where Mikhail was, what he planned to do—everything he could find out. Edward had never tortured anyone before, and did not know whether he could bring himself to dish out more than Tom could withstand.

The door was open to the storeroom. Edward immediately had a bad feeling. He walked in and the motion detector clicked on the light.

Tom was gone.

Edward silently cursed himself and thought furiously. What now? His body answered the question for him. He was exhausted. Now that the tension of the day's events was gone, there was nothing left to keep him going. Locking the doors of the office, he decided to go home. He took the air pistol as insurance.

He walked slowly back through the corridors and out into the night. It was still raining, but he was too tired to care. The car park was deserted. Edward hunted in his pocket for the keys. He did not notice the blood on the door handle. It was not until he had unlocked the door that he felt the sharp point of the knife against his lower back.

# 73

"Open the door...slowly." Tom held the knife against Sherman's kidney. He stood close behind the doctor so that the glint of the blade would not be visible to anyone who passed by. He patted Sherman's pockets down, removing the air pistol from his jacket and placing it in his own coat. Then he placed his other hand on the man's shoulder to complete the illusion of friends talking.

Tom took the keys. "Now get in the car." Sherman did so. "Seatbelt on." He closed the door, stepped quickly round to the passenger side. Sherman did not have enough time to get out. In a few seconds, Tom sat beside him, the knife back against his side. "Hands on the wheel. No sudden movements."

Sherman did so. "What are we going to do now, Tom?"

Tom did not know. He had not meant for this to happen. Here they were, in Sherman's car, and he could do nothing but leave again. He desperately wanted to punish this man for what had happened in the lab, but he could not kill him here. The whole thing was a mess. His father was going to be livid. In the silence that followed, Sherman seemed to sense what he was thinking.

"He'll kill you, Tom." He did not look at the man beside him, but kept his eyes on the wheel.

Tom shivered beside him, and not just from his damp clothes. He knew the answer before he asked the question. "Who will?"

Sherman was slow and measured. "Mikhail will kill you, Tom. He will treat you like every other mortal, as a resource to be used for his ends, and when you outlive your usefulness he will kill you."

The panic rose in Tom's chest. "You don't know if I'm mortal, and neither does he. He won't kill me."

"No, you're wrong—Emily checked it out. You're just a regular guy, Tom—genetically impressive, but you're aging like everyone else. Anyway, Mikhail doesn't put his own kind at risk—he knows what you are. Only mortals are expendable to him."

Tom's first defense was denial. He dug the point of the knife a little harder into Sherman's side. "He doesn't like you much, and you're 'his kind.' Can you blame him?"

"What about the hair I found at my house—it wasn't yours. It was Mikhail's." Despite the knife at his neck, Edward was gaining confidence now. "Did you know he'd been there?"

Tom swallowed hard. Maybe Sherman was lying. "How do you know it's not mine?"

Edward was as steady and measured as before, calmly talking Tom around to the inevitable conclusion. "The hair I found was dark. How long ago did you bleach your hair?" Tom was silent. "Besides, it was M-Trait positive. Ask Emily, she saw the results herself."

A long pause this time, as Tom breathed heavily.

"He'll kill you, Tom, like he killed my wife," Edward added.

Tom said nothing.

"He won't let you get away with Emily and Zoe. He'd never give up the opportunity to have them for himself." Each new sentence from Edward was another nail in the coffin, his inexorable logic penetrating Tom's fragile mind.

"This isn't your fight, Tom. It's your father's. And he'll kill us both to get Zoe. We can't let that happen."

Tom withdrew the knife a little. "So what, then? Are we just supposed to go our separate ways? Forget all this and—" Tom was brought up short by the sound of his phone ringing. He pulled it from his pocket, knowing who it would be. Two, three rings. On the fourth, he answered it.

"What?"

*"Where are you?"*

Tom knew that Michael's voice was probably audible to Sherman. Thinking fast, he answered. "I'm at the lab, in the back car park."

"Is all well?"

Tom took a deep breath, trying to still his heart. "Fine--minor hitch. I'll be with you soon. Where are you?"

"*I'm not far away. I'll meet you there in ten minutes.*" The line went dead.

Tom snapped his phone shut and swore quietly.

"Ten minutes, Tom. You don't have much time to decide." Edward was as nervous as Tom. Both their lives were on the line now. "Go. Go and tell Emily about him. Warn her he's after Zoe. You don't have to tell her the rest about you. She already knows about me."

Seconds stretched on for an interminably long time as Tom frantically tried to think.

"Or we can stay here and wait for him." Sherman was getting tenser as the seconds passed, but tried not to show it.

After what must have been only a few moments, Tom sheathed the knife and turned to Sherman. He was feeling the panic, knowing what would happen if Michael saw them together. He would know something was wrong, know Tom had been lying. He could not imagine his father's punishment for betrayal.

He practically fell out of the car onto the tarmac, slamming the door behind him so Sherman could drive away. "Get out of here. Just go—get out of here as fast as you can or we're both dead."

The powerful car accelerated fast, screeching around the corner and onto the road. Tom breathed deeply, standing in the light rain once again, desperately trying to order his thoughts. *I'm safe, for the moment,* Tom thought as he walked to the entrance of the car park, waiting for his father.

Neither he nor Sherman had noticed the figure in a long coat standing in the shadows behind a pillar in the car park, not far from the doctor's car. Michael walked around the back of the building, and Tom saw him approaching from the opposite direction from which Sherman had left.

"Good evening, Tanek."

# 74

Michael's voice was as calm and disinterested as ever, but somewhere deep under the surface he felt a hatred for the boy he had brought up. If he had ever been unsure of what to do with him, seeing Tom in Sherman's car had decided it.

Michael did not know what they had discussed in the car, but that last line, shouted by Tom as Edward drove away, said it all. *"Get out of here. Just go—get out of here as fast as you can or we're both dead."*

Tom had betrayed him for Sherman. Any betrayal by a son was bad enough, but to sell out to Edward Sherman was utterly unforgivable. Behind his pillar, Michael had watched and waited as Sherman's car sped into the distance and Tom began to relax. When his son wandered out of sight, Michael left his hiding place and walked around to meet him.

"What brings you to Sherman's lab?" Michael asked. He took in his son's tired, haggard look, his creased and dirty clothes, and the cuts on his hands. Something had happened here, and it had gone badly for Tom. In the end though, they appeared to have settled their differences—how unfortunate.

Tom could only hope his father hadn't seen him with Sherman, and answered as if he had not, "I'm going to visit Emily later. I wanted to make sure that Sherman wouldn't be there. Figured I'd wait here until he left, and see which way he drove. He went home by the look of it."

Michael nodded, saying nothing. His son changed the subject. "Why are you here?"

*Checking up on the treacherous son who thinks he can ally himself with Sherman, lie to me and get away with it*, thought Michael. *Making sure that the useless mortal I spawned doesn't try to double-cross me and run away with Emily.*

"I was tying up a business deal nearby, as it happened. I thought it would be as well to meet before this evening."

"What for? Everything is set," Tom said, petulantly.

"There's no room for error here, Tom." This was crucial. Michael had to know whether or not he could trust Tom to follow through with the plan they had decided. The conversation he had witnessed a few minutes ago suggested not, and that complicated matters.

"It's all set up. The vent is blocked, and the batteries in the carbon monoxide detector are dead. The boiler should be on—I made sure of that. And with the rainy weather to keep it on—he should easily be dead by midnight," Tom explained.

"Okay. Go ahead and visit Emily first, then return to Dr. Sherman's at 2 a.m. Call me when he's confirmed dead."

Michael had no intention of waiting that long. He would go early to find out what happened to Edward. If Sherman died by gas poisoning, all the better. If Tom had warned Edward about the blocked vent, Michael would take care of it himself. Either way, he would make sure that by the time Tom turned up, Sherman would be finished. Then all he had to do was get rid of Tom—he had thoroughly exhausted his usefulness anyway. That would be easy enough, and Tom could be framed neatly for Sherman's murder. No loose ends. With Tom and Edward out of the picture, he could take Zoe whenever it pleased him.

"Was that everything?" Tom appeared keen to leave. Michael did know what Tom would do next, but he did not want to arouse any suspicion by keeping him back.

"Yes. Don't forget: 2 a.m." The two men stood there, looking at each other. Michael knew he was losing him. As Tom turned to walk toward the hospital and Emily, he caught his son's arm and turned him around. "You've done well, Tanek. I'm proud of you."

His son stared back at him, trying to betray no emotion. Michael felt nothing for his son in return. Tanek was gone from him, and must die for his treasonous choice.

## 75

Emily's eyes were still red and teary when Tom knocked at her door. Zoe had just fallen asleep again, and she wasn't ready for a visitor—especially this one.

"Come in." Her voice was croaky. She sniffed, trying to put on a brighter face. She realized she was pleased to see him, despite Edward's warnings.

Tom came in and wordlessly took a seat on the bed. She kept her head down, watching only Zoe, as he put his hand around her shoulder and drew her close to him in a hug. "I'm sorry I missed Zoe's arrival. Are you okay?"

Emily shook her head, no. They sat quietly for a few minutes, neither of them speaking, until she seemed to feel better. She wiped the tears away with her sleeve and looked up at him, taking in his pale, exhausted face, the cuts on his hands, and his chopped up hair. He looked even worse than Edward had looked. "What happened to you? Are you okay?"

"Not really." For the moment, that seemed like enough explanation for both of them.

"Edward came to see you?"

It felt like more of a statement than a question to Emily. She nodded, yes.

"He did something that wasn't very good for you..."

His voice was so, so weary, it sounded like every word was an effort. Emily nodded again, waiting for him to continue.

Tom held her tighter as he finished his thought, "...and to Zoe."

She looked up at him again. "How did you know?"

Tom sighed deeply. "I saw Edward today. We talked about it."

"What?" Emily was stunned. She had only just found out, and yet Edward had talked to Tom about it? Maybe Edward was right about Tom.

"We talked in the lab, when I went for a DNA test. And then again, after I managed to escape."

Emily looked from his face to his hair and hands, realizing how battered and hurt he must be. She took in the damage. "This happened to you at the lab? Edward did this?"

Tom nodded. He turned his hands over and over, resurveying his injuries in front of her.

Emily mulled over what she knew in her mind—everything Edward had told her and what she observed had happened to Tom. Things were beginning to fit together, and she didn't like it. She was not sure how to start. "He said some really bad things about you, Tom..." She left it open for him to explain.

Tom swallowed. He took only a moment to think before answering awkwardly, but it was enough for Emily to know that Edward had been telling the truth.

"What did he say about me?" Tom hedged—obviously not wanting to give her an answer right away.

"He talked about someone called Mikhail...and you." Emily's tone had cooled. She pulled herself up, so that she was sitting upright, and so that Tom had to remove his arm from her shoulders. He looked at her pensively.

"Tom, tell me everything. Is what Edward said is true, that you and Mikhail will kill me to take Zoe? Is that why you really went to the lab today—to kill Edward?" Emily's stream of thoughts and questions came out in a cascade of words as she correctly analyzed the situation. "He knew you were after him, didn't he? He was ready for you. That's how this happened." She pointed to his cut hands and bruises.

"I would never hurt you, Emily." His voice was hesitant, as if treading carefully as he spoke. Then he moved to face her. She did not meet his gaze, until he reached up and gently nudged her chin around so that she was facing him. When he next spoke, the conflict in his voice had gone. "I would *never* hurt you, Emily. Do you understand?"

She nodded, now confused more than ever.

"I care about you very much." He breathed deeply, using the time to collect his thoughts. "I've always cared about you. Yes, in answer to your question, Mikhail is—is after Edward. But I went to the lab today to find out whether I was like him and Edward. I needed to know whether I had the Methuselah genes."

"You could have saved yourself a trip. You're not like Edward."

Tom looked at Emily deeply and knew she was telling the truth. "So, it's true. Edward told me you'd run the test and found out before he had."

Emily realized her position with Tom, and she decided to use it. "There are some things I need to know, too. Like why are you working with Mikhail, and how can I ever trust you again?"

"You can trust me. I told you, I would never hurt you, and I meant it. I can help you—I can protect you from Michael."

"And I'm just supposed to believe you? How much have you kept from me? What do I really know about you? For all I know, your name's not even Tom."

There was an embarrassing pause as Tom lowered his head and stared at his feet in guilt, "I…"

"It's not, is it?' Emily looked at him in disgust. "Your name's not even Tom? Great."

The pain and anger of betrayal became almost too overwhelming for Emily to stand. After a moment of silence, the words that came out were caustic and overtly sarcastic.

"This is insane! Some lunatic named Mikhail is trying to kill me to take my child, who was designed to live a thousand years because Dr. Edward Frankenstein tampered with her DNA. But me, worry? No problem—I have James Bloody Bond here, who claims he can protect me and my daughter—but whose name, it turns out, I don't even know!"

Tom was silent as it all came out—the hopelessness of her situation, the unfairness of it all, especially for Zoe, who had done nothing to deserve any of this. She suddenly found herself beating his chest with her fists, almost screaming at him. "What else haven't you told me, Tom, or whatever your name—"

"Tanek!" he shouted, and the shock of it stopped her screaming. "My real name's Tanek." She realized that he was holding her wrists, tightly but not painfully, and talking quickly. "It supposedly means 'immortal.' My father gave me the name because he thought I'd be just like him. But now it just sounds like a sick joke. Michael—Mikhail is my father."

Shocked by his confession, Emily tried to physically pull back, but Tom refused to let go of her, the words coming out all at once. "Michael and Edward used to know each other, a long time ago, in Russia. Something happened between them. I'm not sure what, but neither has ever forgiven the other." He fell silent again. Emily waited for more. "Michael's going to kill Edward. Or Edward will kill him first, if he gets a chance."

"And if Mikhail succeeds?" Emily gazed over into the cot where her baby was sleeping. Her throat was sore from the screaming. "He'll come and take Zoe, because she's like him?"

"Yes. That's what he wants, apart from Edward dead. And once he's done that he'll kill me too." Tom was entirely matter-of-fact.

"Why does he want you dead?"

"Because I'm a disappointment to him—because I'm never going to live as long as him—because I'll try to stop him from taking Zoe…" The last words came out almost apologetically, "…and because he knows I love you."

Emily stared at Tom before answering, incensed by his confession. "Well that's just wonderful."

She tried to be both angry and brave, but by the end of her statement she only felt an engulfing desire: *I must think about Zoe first.*

Tom put his arms around her again. "It'll be okay—everything will be okay."

"How? How can it be okay?" Emily demanded.

"I don't know. But I can't do what my father says anymore." He got up and stood by the bed, the weight of the world on his shoulders.

"All my life, I've done what he said, hoping I'd turn out like him. Now that's all changed."

Tom paused a moment to understand his own feelings. "I just want to get rid of him, and be with you, and not worry about any of this."

Emily grabbed Tom, holding him at arm's length, and uttered her words with all the conviction she could muster, "You fix this then. You make it right—make sure Zoe's safe! Then maybe I'll trust you."

Tom nodded—accepting her challenge. He then bent down and kissed her on the forehead. Before she could say anything more, he left.

Emily wondered if she would ever see him again.

# 76

Home seemed different to Edward somehow, as a house seems different when seen after a long vacation. It was as if he had changed, but his surroundings had been left behind by his development. What had he become, since he left these walls this morning? For all the change, it was still home, and its warmth and security were mercifully welcome as he closed and bolted the front door behind him, leaning back on it. The ordeal was far from over, but he felt safe for now.

Edward stripped off his soaking clothes in the hallway, leaving them by the door to be dealt with later, and found a dressing gown from the drying rack in the utility room. Then he went back and dead bolted the back door. He could take Mikhail on here, if he had to, but he doubted his adversary would try anything so open and dangerous—especially without Tom. That was not Mikhail's style.

He went through to the sitting room and poured himself a large measure of amaretto and fell into one of the comfortable armchairs. Perhaps, in time, Emily would forgive him. One day, she might even regard his actions as a gift to her and Zoe. Until that time, he needed to make things right. He had another gift to give her. Reaching into his pocket, he extracted his cell phone and spent a few moments clumsily pressing buttons until he was satisfied.

Finished with his task, Edward Sherman sighed. He was warming up nicely, and the alcohol on his empty stomach was making him very pleasantly drowsy. He should eat something before he fell asleep again, otherwise he would wake feeling even more awful. But the chair was too comfortable, and it was too easy to ignore his stomach and sink into a blissful, peaceful slumber.

When Edward Sherman awoke a few hours later, the euphoria had lifted. He was not sure at which point sleep ended and waking began. He moved slowly back towards consciousness as if he were swimming up from the bottom of a deep pool. It took some time to gain control of his senses and focus on the clock of the video recorder, its green numbers nothing more than a blur in the darkness. He blinked hard, opened his eyes wide, and then blinked again—12:16 a.m. It was still raining outside, more heavily now, and the wind was gusting, banging the shades loudly against the windows. He was still warm—too warm, wrapped in his heavy toweled dressing gown—and the seat had packed down under him as he sat there. He was stiff and sore from the position in which he had fallen asleep, though extremely lethargic and somehow unwilling to move in his discomfort. His head was not clear, and his mouth was dry and tasted strange. A dull headache was growing in the back of his head, and he hoped it was not a migraine coming on. He needed a drink of water and something to eat—probably some toast, marmalade, and a cup of green tea. Then he could swallow a couple of painkillers and retire to bed upstairs. The thought of clean linen and a comfortable, warm bed was very inviting. It would be nice to take a hot bath or shower first, but probably it would be all he could do to fall into bed.

It was a real effort to push himself up from the seat. The carpeted floor was firm and reassuring under his feet, but he was dizzy and needed a hand to steady himself against the furniture as he made his way through to the hall. In the kitchen, Dr. Sherman filled the kettle and sank into one of the wicker chairs at the table, massaging his temples with his forefingers. It was becoming difficult to keep his eyes open: definitely a migraine. Sherman knew the fluorescent strip light would be far too bright for comfort, so he opened the door of the refrigerator and used its light to find what he needed. Even that hurt his eyes and he closed it, allowing his vision to adjust to the darkened room. With his tea and toast, he returned to the table to drink a couple of soluble painkillers in half a glass of cold tap water. He sat there in the dark, only the blue pilot light of the boiler properly visible. The pain in his head was getting worse, and he was beginning to feel nauseated. Already, the memory of his lucky escape seemed as distant as the fear, pain, and triumph had done in the university car park. It had been a very full day. A low groan escaped Edward's lips as he reseated himself. Bed seemed a very attractive idea, but he wasn't sure he could make it there at the moment. He did not quite trust his legs to support him. It did not matter, he could sleep right here. He was so tired, he could probably sleep anywhere. He would just put his head down here on the kitchen table, just for a few moments, until the pain was not so bad and he could go upstairs. So tired.

Outside the kitchen window, in the darkness and the rain, there might have been a figure watching. It could have been a trick of his mind in the darkness and because of the migraine, but it was not important anyway. He was far too tired for it to matter, for anything to matter anymore. The tablecloth was smooth and blissfully cool against his hot cheek and, despite his pounding head and the nausea, he found himself swimming back towards the unconsciousness that promised to relieve his pain and exhaustion. Gratefully, willingly, he embraced it.

# 77

Michael stood by the wall in Eduard's garden, listening to the gentle sound of the rain falling around him. Standing at the edge of the garden, bordered by trees and shrubs, he closed his eyes and listened to the countless splashes of water against the leaves.

He had waited a very long time for this. As soon as he had heard about Eduard, the activity of revenge had moved with breathtaking speed. It had been a busy five months. So much happened in such a short time, so much had changed since the day he had spoken to Hashim in the little Internet café in Alexandria. His life had been turned upside down again, as it was in Russia when Eduard sold them to the soldiers and, before that, when he had left Barak's house—and again, before that, in the little village where he was born. That first life was so long ago now that the memory was like looking into an obscure reflection: a faraway image in a cracked mirror. He gave scant thought now to that young man, fifteen billion heartbeats and over three and a half centuries ago.

He took out his mobile and tried Tom again, but Tom was not answering. After seeing his son talking to Sherman in the car park, Michael had wondered whether he would turn up at all. If his son had any sense, he would run now while he still had the chance.

The trees screened him as he watched the house. Feeling something solid against his foot, he crouched down behind the curtains of leaves. In the corner lay a small granite stone with a plaque, its surface slick and shiny in the rain, despite the cover afforded by the birches. He drew out the little penlight torch he had brought with him, brushed the wet debris from its surface and found a memorial with an inscription.

## *Brandon Franklin Hurst*

> IN MEMORY OF KARINA, GONE BUT NOT FORGOTTEN
> *"YOU HAVE MADE MY DAYS LIKE A HANDBREADTH, AND MY AGE IS AS NOTHING BEFORE YOU. EACH LIFE IS JUST A BREATH."*
> PSALMS 39:5

Karina. He remembered Sherman's wife well. She had been a striking woman, with strong features. Not exactly beautiful, but compelling—there had been something about her, he remembered thinking once: a bright, lively woman—at least to begin with. The sparkle in her eyes had dulled during the years with the Brotherhood, though that was the lot for most mortals anyway. Eduard never did learn to see it like that. Mortal life was only an instant between two eternities, and a single human life barely even touched the span of history. Even a life of centuries was nothing compared to the millennia of civilization that came before and would come afterwards: even Ultras couldn't live forever.

Michael crossed the garden briskly, glancing through the kitchen window before he stepped out of sight. It was almost dark inside, but he could see the shape of the modern day Edward Sherman slumped over the table, ready to die.

Using the extra keys he had made, he quietly unlocked the gate and back door, leaving them open to ventilate the house while he was inside. He had no intention of suffering the same fate as Sherman. With the night wind blowing in to replace the carbon monoxide-laden air of the kitchen, he knew he would be safe for a few minutes—he didn't need any more than that. Besides, he had no angina to contend with. When he was done, he would close the door and let the boiler finish its work.

Softly, with one hand on the hilt of his dagger, he stepped through into the kitchen. The cold night air blew in with him. Edward stirred and groaned at the breeze. Unsheathing his blade, Michael grasped him by the hair and lifted his head from the table.

"Awake, Eduard?"

Sherman groaned, barely able to open his eyes. It took him almost a full minute to focus on what was holding his head up. Finally his eyes cleared to the moment and the face directly in front of him. Still, he was only able to mumble, "Mikhail," which brought with it a ragged breath and a deep cough.

Michael released his head, and Edward slumped back onto the table. "It's been a long time, Eduard." He was as easy and unhurried as if he had been meeting a friend in the park. This was his hour—his chance to put right what had happened almost a century ago. "I guess you didn't see it ending like this." He pulled up a chair and sat at the table, next to Edward.

Helpless, Edward coughed again and retched. He tried to say something, but Michael couldn't understand what. He leaned closer and listened intently.

"Leave Emily and Zoe out of this."

Michael laughed. "You don't have to worry about Zoe. I'll make sure she's taken care of very well. I'm sure I'll do a better job than whatever you were planning." He leaned back on his chair, never taking his eyes of Edward.

Sherman's eyes narrowed, but he did nothing save draw another rattling breath.

"Mmm, Zoe." Michael leaned forwards again, repeating the name to him. "Yes, Zoe—she's going to be very special. You hit on a bright idea there, Eduard. I've got to hand it to you, that was smart. How did you do it?"

Edward tried to pull himself upright. His eyes rolled with the effort. He managed to get his head off the table and resting on his arm before it was too much for him.

"No? The best magicians never reveal their secrets, I suppose. Never mind." Michael sheathed the knife, knowing that Sherman was in no condition to present a danger to him. "I never thought a woman could grow old. All those years, I thought it was the preserve of the men. But now, thanks to you, it's all changed. It's just as well I'll be around to bring her up properly. Make sure she understands what she is and what that means." He sighed. "You never did get it, did you? It's a real shame you didn't stay with us, Eduard. You're a bright man. The sky could have been the limit—you could have had it all.

Edward continued to fight the effects of carbon monoxide, with little success.

"Was she worth it, Eduard? Was Karina worth this? Dying alone here with your past catching up with you. What a waste."

Edward lifted his head with considerable effort. His slurred words could not mask the venom he felt. "You killed Karina—you animal."

Michael's laughter filled the room as he prepared his next words, which he knew would penetrate deeper than any knife. "And Kostya, too. Remember the fire, Eduard? That was just for show—to disguise the killing of your son with my bare hands. How enjoyable the memory still is today."

The emotional pain registered in Edward's eyes, but he was unable to move the rest of his body. He was dying.

"It was only fair, Eduard. How many of our Brothers, my family, did you execute? You bastard!"

Michael grabbed Sherman's hair again, lifting his head to ensure his captive audience heard every word. "Eduard, you've had a long life. I guess it had to end sooner or later. But I'm glad it ended *this way*." The last two words were a snarl. Michael dropped Sherman's head and got up from his chair.

"So long, Eduard. Breathe deeply, and—sweet dreams. Don't worry. I'll close the door on my way out."

It was time to go. Michael turned his back on the expiring man at the table and walked to the kitchen door. He was about to step through, when a noise from the garden alerted him. It was little more than a rustle, almost inaudible over the sound of the rain, but every hair on the back of his neck rose. *Tom was early*. Silently, he took a step backwards into the kitchen, and unhooked the fire extinguisher from beside the door.

# 78

When he left the hospital, Tom swelled with the new sensations within himself. It took a moment to work out what was happening. Tension, confusion, freedom, fear—the realization that his life and everything in it, was suddenly obsolete. Michael, his lifelong mentor, was not calling the shots anymore. Instead, he was out on his own—perhaps without his father's oppressive control, but without his protection either. He felt naked. He wasn't sure what to do next. As he drove out of the city, he forced himself to think.

Tom recognized that Edward Sherman was the only thing keeping him alive. Michael was expecting him to finish off the job by taking down Sherman. After that, he was of no use to his father. Edward had probably saved his life by warning him, albeit to help himself, so there was a reluctant gratitude attached to that involuntary act. He did not really know what had happened between the two men, almost a century ago, but that was their business. However tonight turned out, he was through with both of them. He would take Emily, Zoe, and save all their lives.

If that was to happen, Tom knew he had to undo the damage he was instrumental in causing. Perhaps, if he succeeded, it would offset some of the pain he had unleashed. Perhaps it would be his act of redemption, enough so he could look her in the eye next time he saw her. But to be loyal to Emily, he knew he would have to take on his father. He hoped he was up to such a formidable task. He then realized for the first time the reward for taking such a risk: a better life. *I'm mortal—I'll die anyway—so go for it!*

Sherman's house was dark when he slipped through the garden door and hid in the bushes on the other side of the wall, as he had done that first time. He pulled on his gloves; he should not need them, but if Edward was already dead, he did not want to leave any evidence behind. Tom crossed the garden and knelt at the grate. The ivy was slick with the rain, and it was hard to get a purchase on the thick leaves and twigs that blocked the vent. When he pulled at the stems, they snapped instead of withdrawing from the grating. This was taking too long. He moved to the window and stared in at the scene in Sherman's kitchen, cupping his hands around his face to see past the reflections in the glass. The doctor lay slumped over the table, motionless. For a moment, Tom thought he was too late. Then he saw Edward move, pushing himself up onto his arms and trying to raise his head.

The buzzing of the phone in his pocket made him jump. At their meeting in the car park, Michael had told him to go to Sherman's house at 2 a.m. Tom arrived early on purpose. He could warn Edward, take him to hospital if need be—whatever had to be done. Then he could escape before his father called or turned up to make sure Sherman had died as planned.

There was no need to ask who was calling. It took Tom a few seconds to find the phone through the layers of jacket. He opened the phone and held it to his ear.

"I got here early to make sure everything worked as planned. Sherman's dead—it's over," Tom announced into the phone. He then listened quietly for an answer that didn't come. So he closed the phone, and put it back in his pocket. He was off the hook—now he had the rest of the night to himself. After checking to make sure that Edward was okay, he would return to his flat to pack. He could be a couple of hundred miles away before Michael realized he was gone.

Tom was surprised but relieved to find the back door wide open. Edward must have realized the danger when he felt ill and taken steps to clear the gas. He jogged through to the kitchen and shook the doctor by the shoulder, trying to rouse him.

Edward weakly lifted his head. Tom strained to hear the words, "Watch out."

But it was too late. As Tom turned, Michael stepped from his hiding place behind the door. The first blow from the end of the fire extinguisher caught Tom squarely in the solar plexus, forcing the breath from his lungs and doubling him over. As he cried out, the second blow hit him. This time, Michael wielded it like a club, catching Tom on the side of the head with a terrific crack that knocked him off his feet and left him half-conscious on the floor.

"Good of you to turn up, Tanek—better late than never." He let the extinguisher hang at his side, stepping back so he could see Tom and Sherman at the same time. He looked down at the prostrate form of his son. "If you'd had any sense you'd have run while you had the chance, with Emily or not."

"Dad, please..." Tom's voice was slurred and he was struggling to see straight.

"You didn't really think you were going to get away with Emily and Zoe, did you? Who did you think you were playing with? I'm not about to let ordinary people like you make the decisions for my life." Even now, his speech was calm and measured.

"I'm your son." Tom's voice was barely a whisper.

Michael dismissed the accusation. "You're mortal. You're going to die just like everyone else."

He turned to Sherman. "Except Zoe. Now there is a child I can be proud of."

Tom managed to roll over onto his side, trying to get to his feet, but he was still too dizzy. As he did so, he felt the hard shape in the pocket of his coat. For a moment, his disoriented mind couldn't place it. Then he remembered—Edward's air pistol. He slid a hand into the pocket, as Michael continued.

"For twenty years I hoped you would be the beginning of a new line." Michael shrugged dispassionately. "But I guess you served your purpose."

Tom pulled the pistol out of his pocket and tried to level it at Michael. His father stopped dead and looked down at him on the floor. Then he took a swift step towards Tom to kick the gun out of his hand. Tom pulled the trigger a fraction of a second before Michael's foot connected with his wrist, sending the pistol clattering across the kitchen.

Michael looked down at his chest, and saw the little feathered dart sticking out of him. He looked back to Tom in shock. Then his fear gave way to anger, and he pulled it out and flung it across the room. He raised the fire extinguisher high above his head, ready to bring a final, lethal blow down on Tom's head.

In the stillness of the moment, as Tom realized the end was coming, it registered that his father's face betrayed an odd emotion in this final act—an expression of total pleasure. The look broke Tom's spirit. He closed his eyes and weakly raised a hand up to protect himself, but the blow never came.

Somehow, Edward had found the strength to drag himself up from the table and throw himself at Michael. Tom watched helplessly from the floor as his father struggled in Edward's bear hug, the doctor desperately holding on to pin Michael's arms to his sides. His eyes were closed as he gripped the other man as tightly as he could. The two men fell to the floor, Michael's breathing now almost as labored as Edward's as the drug took effect and he fought to stay conscious and free himself. His struggling grew less violent, and instead he tried to pry Sherman's hands apart. Then Tom saw Edward's eyes glaze over, his body twitch, and his head fall to the side, with his hands still tightly clasped around Michael's waist. Michael's struggling slowed too, and although he at last managed to loosen Edward's iron grip, it was too late.

After a minute of watching for anymore movement, Tom at last struggled to his feet. He pulled the latex gloves off Michael's hands and placed them in his pocket. He checked first his father's, and then Edward's pulse. Michael's was slow and steady. Edward was dead. He somehow had the presence of mind to wipe down the butt of the air pistol and press it into Edward's hand. Then he stood at the doorway, breathing the fresh air from outside, as he decided how he would end this.

Tom had the foresight to empty his father's pockets of anything that might lead back to him—his passport, mobile phone, and wallet. A cut on his father's forehead from where he had fallen dripped blood onto the ceramic tile floor. As an afterthought, Tom smeared some of

Michael's blood from the tile into the middle of the passport. It might come in handy one day, either as evidence against his father, or as a piece of the jigsaw in Emily's research.

Tom knew that, if Michael was allowed to live, he and Emily would never be safe. His father would find them, somehow. On the other hand, he wasn't sure if he could kill is father directly. A distant siren decided the matter for him. Tom did not know whether the police were headed this way, but he realized that he must leave immediately. The carbon monoxide would do the job for him. This way felt easier—he did not have to do anything. Tom left Edward Sherman's house, closing the door behind him and his past.

# 79

*What do I do?*

Still in the hospital, Emily was paralyzed with fear. Beside her, Zoe slept quietly on, unaware of the trouble her birth had created. Outside, scenarios that would affect her and Zoe for the rest of their lives were being played out without her having a say in what happened. Somewhere, there was a man who wanted to take her child, and wanted her dead. She did not know where he was, or even what he looked like. She was helpless. If she waited here, he would find her.

*Run then.* If he couldn't find her, he couldn't hurt her. Before, she might have been tempted to stay, to put herself in the hands of the police, or even Tom, and hope they caught him. Now, she had Zoe to think of, and she wasn't prepared to take any chances.

Emily removed the hospital gown and dressed. She quickly packed everything she needed into one of the two hold-alls she had brought with her. Everything that wasn't essential she left behind; she couldn't carry both and Zoe at the same time without help. She was working on autopilot now, trying not to think about what she was doing in case she tried to reason herself out of it. She did not know where she would go. Wherever it was, it was smart not to stay in any one place too long.

While helping her pack belongings into a knapsack, Emily heard her phone bleep. Picking it up, she noticed that a text message had been sent to her. It was from Edward:

```
EM, SO SORRY
GIFT 4 YOU
BANK OF ZURICH,
#895567834
```

*M-Trait*

```
PWD KARINA
ALL MY LUV
EDW
```

Despite her anger at Edward's betrayal, something about it made her smile. Never having integrated well into the text-messaging generation, he'd written an awkward mixture of abbreviations and longhand. But she knew what his gift probably entailed. Later, when she accessed the accounts, she found that Edward had ensured her financial well-being enough for three lifetimes. Quietly, to herself, she thanked him.

Emily saved the message and as quickly and quietly as she could, she left her room and walked down the corridor. There were few doctors or nurses around; those that she did see were preoccupied, busy with more important patients, and paid her no attention. She ignored the security guard as the sliding doors opened in front of her and Zoe, and she stepped out into the night. She forced herself to keep walking, leaving behind everyone she knew and all the places familiar and safe to her. Outside it was cool and damp, the darkness lit only by the neon lights around the hospital. It was surprisingly quiet. Behind her, the doors slid shut.

# 80

Tom woke, groggy and disoriented, his head against the kitchen table. It was getting light. He had only meant to put his head down for only a few minutes while some coffee brewed.

It took him a while to come fully awake. A long drink of water from a bottle in the refrigerator helped as he started to piece together the events of the last evening in his mind. Before phoning Emily, he began to flick through the local stations on tele, just in case Edward's and his father's death had become news.

It did not take long to find what he was looking for. An early morning news bulletin announced the deaths of two people in a house in the suburbs. One, the owner of the house, was a scientist at a local university. The other body had yet to be identified. Police were appealing to anyone with knowledge of their deaths.

Tom clicked off the TV and gave a long sigh of relief. It was over. The weight of the world seemed to lift from his shoulders. Finally, he was free. After a good breakfast and a long shower, he would visit Emily and tell her the good part of the news. He would also have to break the news about Sherman, if she hadn't already heard.

While toasting a bagel, he phoned Emily's hospital room. There was no answer. He assumed she was visiting with her mother or other family members outside her hospital room, but it still made him nervous. He abandoned the meal and left for the hospital immediately.

On the road, he phoned again, but there was still no answer from Emily's room. He then tried her flat and mobile phones, but they all went to voice mail. When he arrived at the hospital, he started to have an awful feeling in his gut.

Tom all but ran to Emily's room. It was empty. Some of her effects were still there, but it was obvious she left in a hurry and wasn't coming back.

At the front desk, the receptionist studied the computer screen in front of her, unhelpful and unsympathetic. "Sorry, guv. It looks like she left sometime in the night without formally checking out."

"And no one did anything to stop her?"

"Can't stop people leaving if they want to."

"Did she say where she was going? Anything?"

The girl shook his head. "I guess she just left." She paused a moment, now curious about something that was clearly none of her business. "Is she in some kind of trouble?"

Tom answered mostly to himself, "I don't know."

As he sprinted back to his car, Tom felt the first signs of panic rising in his stomach. Behind the wheel, he tried to be calm and focus, but it was difficult to even breathe. *Think!*

After more unanswered phone calls, Tom drove to Emily's flat and then out to her mother's house on the outskirts of London. There was nobody home.

Finally, out of other ideas, he drove to the lab. When he saw the police cars outside the entrance, he drove straight on, continuing for a quarter of a mile before pulling over into a side street. He flipped the radio on and tuned through the channels, looking for a local news broadcast. Coming up on the hour, it did not take long to find one.

Details were sketchy, said the reporter. What they did know was that two bodies had been discovered at a house in the suburbs. "Dr. Edward Sherman, a research scientist, was found dead in his kitchen. A second body was found in his garage, concealed in the freezer."

Tom gasped to himself. *Margaret! The cleaning lady!* The second body wasn't his father's.

"...a man seen leaving the area in the early hours of the morning is sought for questioning. He is approximately forty to sixty years of age, six feet tall with shoulder-length dark or graying hair and a beard."

*He's alive!* An emotional chasm seemed to swallow Tom whole. He stopped the car by the side of the road, too stunned to drive.

The report continued. "Authorities are also searching for Dr. Sherman's assistant, Dr. Emily Preston, who left Mercy General Hospital under mysterious circumstances with her newborn child—and may have been abducted..."

Tom stared at the radio as his living nightmare deepened. *How did they connect Emily so quickly?* Now the real panic began to set in. Tom felt scared, confused, and utterly empty. He had failed. He had nowhere to go, no one to turn to. Tom, for the first time in his life, did not have a clue what to do. And thanks to his own complacency, his father had Emily and Zoe—or at least a head start in finding them.

What were his options? The answer was immediate—*I must stop my father!* Tom didn't know how he would accomplish this feat, but he needed to start now.

Putting the car in gear, Tom drove on toward an unknown future.

# 81

Michael sat in the barber's chair, relaxing into the padded leather seat. He was less than a hundred yards from the university, and in the large mirrors around him he could see the occasional police car zip up and down the boulevard, obviously working the crime scene at Sherman's lab. A few miles away, he knew there was a similar scene unfolding at Sherman's house. By the barbershop door, Rufus slept in the afternoon sunlight.

The barber was of the old school and did not hurry. The shop was expensively furnished and his clients rich—he understood that harried behavior was considered bad form. Michael had removed his sunglasses, and could watch the progress of his transformation as he coaxed details about the progress of the police inquiry from the proprietor.

"A bad business, this death at the university," he suggested.

"The death itself was at Dr. Sherman's home, not at the university—and there were two killed," replied the barber, a man of about sixty with white, thinning hair slicked back over his skull. "They're checking out his office for evidence—some kind of disturbance in there yesterday." He snipped judiciously at Michael's hair, trimming away the longish mane into a close cut with neat short back and sides.

After barely escaping from Sherman's house, Michael had gone straight back to his hotel room and cleared out his possessions, leaving his keys at reception. He was not worried that his departure would raise suspicion; it was an expensive hotel that he had used several times before—and money talked. He immediately went and checked into a private clinic and spent the night under observation. He did not think there would be any lasting damage from his ordeal, but he had not come this far by being complacent. Later that morning, he worked the phones, probing for information from all his contacts. Not surprisingly, he discovered quite quickly that Emily and her newborn daughter had left the hospital sometime in the night.

He did not know where Tom and Emily were—if, indeed, they were together, as he assumed—but there was no good reason to leave London yet. He doubted either of them would go too far, under the circumstances, and he could track the situation better from here. If Tom accessed one of his bank accounts, he would know where from. Best of all, the police might do his job for him and find them. He had helped their cause with an anonymous phone tip about the missing Dr. Preston. After all, he was just doing his civic duty.

Before checking out of the hospital, Michael made an appointment with the barber. It was time to cut his hair and shave off his beard. Overall, it wouldn't seem like much of a change, but a few important alterations would allow him to remain an unknown person.

Sitting in the barber's chair, Michael's whole face now felt smooth and cold, the beard gone for the first time in twenty years. The barber showed him the back of his head with another mirror, and called over his assistant to wash and dye the result. Michael tilted his head back, and allowed the girl to do her work.

"Are there any suspects yet—a motive, even?" he asked.

"Not so far." She did her work with efficient movements, quick but gentle. Her motions reminded him of his second wife, Leba, who liked to work swiftly while washing and spinning wool. "Someone was seen limping away from the area last night—maybe a tramp. Police thought it might have been a disturbed burglary. But then there was the body in the freezer, and the mess in his office, too. They checked in here earlier to ask whether we'd seen anything strange around the lab recently." She shrugged. "Nothing out of the ordinary, we said."

Michael's whole body still felt bruised and sore, and he was still a little lightheaded. It was good to have his scalp massaged. He knew that it would be some days before he was back to normal, and that he was lucky to have escaped so lightly. That had clearly not been his son's intent.

When the girl had finished drying his hair, he rose expectantly from the seat and surveyed his new look in the mirror. Dressed in a smart suit and clean-shaven with short dark hair, Michael exuded the aura of a professional executive—the opposite of the stoic, nomadic man that others might recollect in the coming days of an investigation. Just for a moment, his tired mind played a trick on him, and he thought he saw Tom's face reflecting back. He quickly looked away.

He paid and tipped the barber, collected Rufus, and left the shop, walking back up the street away from the university. He hailed a passing black cab and gave the driver the address of a hotel favored by business travelers, one with excellent digital connections.

Perhaps his son had eluded him, and no doubt Emily with him, but Michael had still escaped with his life. Edward Sherman was dead as planned. Fifty, a hundred years ago, a search for his prey would have been almost futile. In today's world, though, it was very difficult to stay hidden for long. In an age where every transaction is logged, every individual tracked and monitored one way or another, they couldn't stay invisible forever. Michael had almost unlimited resources, and all the time in the world to seek out Emily and her prize child.

As the cabbie drove off, Michael smiled to himself. *This was going to be fun!*

TO BE CONTINUED...